MW00344819

The Curse of House Corbant

Patrick Luther

Published by Patrick Luther, 2021.

THE CURSE OF HOUSE CORBANT

First edition. November 9, 2021.

Written by Patrick Luther.

Prologue: Samuel's Discovery

(1760)

S amuel Corbant chiseled away another brick from the cellar wall. Sweat dripped from his haggard brow, despite the coolness of the small wine room. Simply moving the wine shelf off of the wall had been a taxing endeavor. However, the digging itself was another matter entirely. Samuel had managed to build up a small mound of broken mortar at the base of the wall, but it wasn't enough. In the past hour, he had only managed to loosen two bricks. The rest showed no signs of yielding...yet.

Samuel paused for a moment to wipe his face with a rag from his pants pocket, dabbing along his pale cheeks and his black, swept-back hairline. He was already a thin man, but the flickering lantern that was the only light in the room made him look outright ghastly. His wife Annabel would undoubtedly give him grief for covering his well-tailored clothes in dust and chunks of mortar, but he could not have cared less.

He replaced the rag and hoisted his pickaxe for another strike at the wall. *My father must have made great effort to conceal whatever lies behind this wall.* Samuel's lip curled into a contemptuous sneer as he swung the pickaxe once more.

Each sharp clang produced a shower of mortar and the occasional spark as the metal struck unyielding brick. Samuel's grip tightened on his pickaxe as his labors began to yield results. Another brick fell into the passage beyond the wall, followed swiftly by another. His heart began to race, and his aching limbs found new strength in his excitement. Soon each strike was taking out multiple bricks at a time. "Almost there," Samuel grunted, his teeth clenched tightly as he channeled the last of his strength. Suddenly, a pair of bricks fell from the top of the hole Samuel had been toiling at, and the wall began to buckle. With a grunt of both exhaustion and triumph, he struck the wall one last time and jumped back.

With a thunderous crash and a burst of dust from decades long past, the wall fell at his feet. A single bottle of wine fell from the nearby shelf as the bricks struck it. It shattered on the floor and filled the chamber with the pungent scent of its contents. Samuel coughed and waved the dust from his face but to no avail. The wine cellar had neither windows nor doors save for the one behind him, which he had closed for privacy. Perhaps he could open it to clear the dust from the room?

He started towards the door, setting his pickaxe against the wine shelf. He grabbed the brass handle and turned, but the door remained still: locked. Chuckling at his own forgetfulness, Samuel plunged his hand into his pants pocket for the key, but then he remembered why he had locked the door in the first place.

With his features set in determination, Samuel picked up the lantern and peered through the dust cloud towards the now open passageway. He had expected a brick hallway leading to some secretive chamber. What he saw instead resembled a mining tunnel. The earthen walls were sustained by support beams from some long-abandoned construction project. Perhaps his father had meant to extend the cellar further but abandoned the project for some unknown reason. Samuel smirked. How angry would his father be if he could see him now?

He picked his way through the rubble and entered the mouth of the tunnel, the flickering light of his lantern dancing on the walls. The tunnel sloped gently downwards as he walked, its yawning blackness extending onward. Where on earth did it lead? Samuel guessed that it was nearly ten minutes before he reached the far side of the tunnel. It curved sharply to the right, nearly performing a hairpin turn. Puzzled but undaunted, Samuel followed it as the tunnel continued down ever so slowly.

His heart leapt in his chest as the lantern revealed a crude doorway at the end of the tunnel. He quickened his pace. He nearly ran the remaining length but stopped dead and gasped aloud when the light revealed the contents of the underground chamber.

A great stone sarcophagus was half buried in the center of the chamber. Its edges were carved with runes that Samuel didn't recognize, but it was the statue that lay atop the sarcophagus that arrested his whole attention. It portrayed a robed and hooded figure with its hands clasped across its chest. The fingers were long and spidery, with claw-like nails. The face was leering and skull-like, with the flesh around the nose, mouth, and chin withered away to expose the musculature and needle-like teeth underneath. Thorn-like horns encircled the forehead of the face, with additional pairs on the brow, cheeks, and chin.

As Samuel was awed by the vivid detail of the statue and the esoteric runes carved into its edges, he understood why his father had bricked up the chamber. Darius Corbant had always been an extremely religious man. Perhaps that was why he had chosen to build his mansion in the middle of nowhere, far away from the "impure masses."

Samuel's lip curled as his father's voice chastised him from his memory. Even as he looked upon the unholy relic before him, the scars on his back burned as if his father were flogging him once more. The phantom pains only steeled his resolve, and he dropped to one knee beside the sarcophagus and ran his fingers across the runes on the edges.

To spite his father's memory, Samuel had taken to studying the occult after Darius's death. His private study in the manor overhead held a well-concealed trove of lore, from the Celts and the Pagans of Europe to the Voodoo and Hoodoo of the far south. Samuel had gone through great lengths to support his sinister hobby, but despite his wealth of occult lore, he still did not recognize the runes etched into the stone he now caressed. Unsure of what to do next, he said aloud, "I've heard thine whispers, demon. I went through great toil to find thee and have been successful. Now reveal thyself to me!"

In his eagerness to reach the tunnel's end, Samuel had all but forgotten how chilly the tunnel was. However, now the chill pierced his skin like a thousand needles, and he began to shiver in his sweat-soaked shirt. His breath plumed before his eyes in a thick cloud, then dissipated. He wrapped his arms around himself, vainly trying to conserve warmth as his eyes fell on the face of the statue reposed on the lid of the sarcophagus. Inky blackness seemed to have filled the sockets of the face's eyes, though Samuel dismissed it at first as a trick of the light. What he could not dismiss was the feeling that those hollow sockets were looking at him.

Then Samuel heard a soft, dry voice. Surely it was coming from the sarcophagus, but it seemed to come from all around the chamber at once, as if the speaker were everywhere. It said, "Welcome, Samuel Corbant. You have indeed earned an audience with me."

Samuel shuddered. Until now he had only heard that voice in his dreams. Hearing it now while awake chilled his blood further than the coldness of the room. Swallowing, Samuel stuttered, "Th-thou said that thou kn-knoweth what I d-d-desire. Thou s-s-said that thou could g-g-grant it t-to me."

There was a soft chuckle from the disembodied voice. "I do know what you desire, and I can indeed grant it to you. However, such favors come at a price."

"Name it."

As if amused by Samuel's eagerness, the voice continued lazily, "I would ask that the hands of the innocent, stained with the blood of their protector, be placed upon this sarcophagus. Make this so, and I shall grant you what you seek."

Samuel frowned. "Is this a riddle?"

The voice replied coldly, "I have spoken plainly. Do as I have asked, or you will receive nothing. Now begone."

Samuel shook his head as though he had been slapped. "I demand an explanation! What exactly art thou asking of me?" No answer came, and the silence boiled Samuel's blood. Was the thing mocking him? "TELL ME WHAT I MUST DO!" he roared, overcome with frustration. When his question was once again met with silence, he cried out and pounded his fist on the earthen floor next to the sarcophagus. The air had lost its penetrating chill and returned to the natural coolness of the underground. The deep shadows that had filled the eyes of the statue were now gone.

Samuel glared at the sarcophagus. He should have known better. Demons were fickle beings with their infernal games and maddening riddles. Despite his irritation, he could not turn back. His desire...his hunger for vengeance was too strong. He craved the power his father had always used against him. He burned to heap upon his father all the pain he had endured during his life. Samuel would drag his father's soul back from the afterlife himself if he had to in order to claim his revenge.

His resolve unshaken, Samuel turned his thoughts to what the demon had said. "The hands of the innocent," he said aloud, "stained with the blood of their protector..." He repeated the phrase over and over again, until an answer came to him. His eyes widened and his breath caught in his throat. Surely not...but of course it was. Of course the demon would ask something so terrible as this. He pondered for a moment, then closed his eyes and sighed. His desire for vengeance consumed all else.

Yes, he would pay any price...even *this* price.

"NOT MUCH FARTHER, DEAREST," Samuel cooed as he ushered his wife Annabel and three-year-old daughter Melody into the tunnel.

"What is this place?" Annabel asked, her once-sleepy eyes now darting about nervously.

"All will be revealed in time, trust me," Samuel assured her, hiding his annoyance. At least Melody had the good sense to remain silent, unlike her nearly worthless mother.

"Pray, why couldn't this wait until morning?"

Samuel's eyes nearly bulged from his head. His forehead pounded and his jaw tightened. Perhaps he should just do it now and get it over with. Then there would be only silence. Sweet, sweet silence.

He slid his hand into his pants pocket, tracing his fingers along a closed straight razor. Blinking several times to contain his rage, he turned to face Annabel, ready to draw the razor and silence her incessant whining forever, but then he saw Melody. Her bright blue eyes were astoundingly lustrous, even in the flickering candlelight. Her curly black hair hung about her shoulders, framing her pale face sharply against the gloom. She looked back at him in silence, awaiting his instructions. Such a good little girl she was!

Samuel hesitated and turned away, beckoning his wife and daughter onwards. "Just trust me, my dear." Without further question, the three of them continued down the tunnel.

At last, they arrived in the burial chamber. Annabel stood at the entrance with her wide eyes locked on the sarcophagus. "S-Samuel? Wh-wh-what is that?"

"Come closer, my dear. I will show thee!" Samuel replied, beckoning her to the center of the room. To his delight, Melody entered without hesitation, her dark curls bouncing as she came to her father's side. Nervously, Annabel

followed suit. Samuel took her hand and held the lantern over the sarcophagus, then blew out the candle. Melody screamed, but before Annabel could
utter a word, Samuel placed the lantern on the sarcophagus and pulled his
wife tight against him, covering her mouth with his hand. He then slipped
his other hand from hers and pulled the razor from his pocket as he whispered, "My dearest daughter, no matter what happens, thou must remain
silent and still."

"But...but Papa...I can't see," Melody whimpered.

Samuel hesitated again, her fear making his heart contract. His wife
trembled against him as her tears wetted his hand. Annabel was nothing, but
Melody was his jewel, his sweet song. He closed his eyes and took a deep
breath. When he opened them again, a coldness settled over his soul, driving
away any compassion. No price was too great for his revenge, not even the silence of his sweetest song. "Trust me, my dear. Everything will be well." With
immovable resolve, he flicked the razor open and cut his wife's throat. Her
body thrashed and twitched, and her nails dug into his hand, but the damage
was done. He had pressed the blade as deep as he could, silencing her once
and for all.

When Annabel's twitching finally ceased, he tossed her aside. Even in
death, her uses were minimal.

He kneeled in the blackness and whispered, "Melody, come to Papa."

"Y-y-yes, Papa," Melody whimpered. Slowly, her bare feet shuffled across
the earthen floor until at last her outstretched hands reached Samuel's face.

He savored their softness for a moment and ran a hand through her
raven-black curls. As his fingers moved from her hair to her soft, rounded
cheek, Samuel whispered, "Forgive me, my sweetest song." Then he seized her
hair, gritted his teeth, and opened Melody's throat just as he had her mother's.

Samuel let his daughter's twitching body fall to the floor as his breathing
accelerated. It was done. *It will not be in vain.* The thought repeated in his
head as he drew forth a book of matches and relit the lantern. His wife lay
face-down in her nightdress in a large pool of crimson. Melody lay on her
side, her blue eyes wide and staring. The clothing his wife had dressed her in
made her resemble a China doll. Samuel found the resemblance even more
striking now and couldn't stop himself from laughing hysterically as he set

about the sickening task of removing her hands. His eyes were wild as he sawed the razor through her tiny wrists, the remaining blood in her veins squirting for a moment before slowing to a crimson drip. Through tendon and cartilage he sawed until at last, her hands fell from the stumps of her arms, pale and bloodstained.

Then, Samuel scooped up the severed hands and turned back to his wife. She had not spared him from one final annoyance in death. He kicked her over contemptuously, and she rolled to face the ceiling. Her eyes had already dulled, holding the ghost of the terror she had felt in the end. *At least she knew how weak she was in the end.*

Samuel dragged his daughter's hands across Annabel's gore-soaked throat. Pleased with himself for figuring out the demon's riddle, he then placed the bloodied hands on the chest of the statue on the lid. Smiling grimly, he sat back on his knees and bowed his head. "Oh demon, I have done as thou hast asked. Upon thine altar are the hands of the innocent stained with the blood of their protector. Now grant my wish!"

The cold stabbed through Samuel once again, but it seemed fiercer than he remembered. He looked up at the casket and gasped. Shadowy tendrils sprouted from the lid and waved like withered seaweed in the current. The voice came, but it was not grateful or welcoming. "You bumbling imbecile! This is not what I asked of you!"

Samuel was thunderstruck. "But...but I deciphered thy riddle! Thou asked for the hands of the innocent..."

"None are innocent in the eyes of Death, you miserable fool! Your crimes here are unforgiveable!"

Samuel fell prostrate, pleading, "Demon, please be merciful...I misunderstood..."

The reply was cold and most certainly merciless. "My instructions were clear. I asked for the hands of the innocent, but you bring me the hands of a lifeless husk." The lantern flickered as the shadows both around the chamber and waving gently over the sarcophagus deepened. The voice continued, growing louder as Samuel trembled in fear. "This heinous act is unforgiveable. You will be punished!"

Samuel whimpered, "Please..."

The shadowy tendrils ceased their rhythmic waving and shot towards him, wrapping around his arms and legs, their touch like burning ice. He couldn't stifle his scream as white-hot pain shot through his limbs.

The darkness given material form lifted and pulled him towards the sarcophagus. Desperate, Samuel reached for something to grab onto, but the shadows' grip was unrelenting. He both screamed and wept as he struggled in vain. Then he was lifted over the sarcophagus, limbs spread wide, staring down into the coal-black eyes of the statue. Samuel begged, "Don't do this, demon! I will not fail again!"

The voice growled back, and Samuel swore he saw the jaw of the statue move as it did so, "I am no demon...but I will make certain that you do not fail again!" The tendrils tightened their grip, cutting into Samuel's ankles and wrists. Blood spurted onto the statue, and Samuel screamed in agony. As if summoned by the spray of blood, more tendrils shot out of the folds of the statue's robe and stabbed into Samuel's body like long, thin daggers. Each thrust brought forth another crimson spray until Samuel felt his consciousness begin to wane.

His head hung limp, his strength fading rapidly. His flesh shriveled and clung to his bones as his once form-fitting clothes became several sizes too large. If Samuel had any sanity left, it was gone the moment he saw his flesh splitting and peeling away. He tried to scream one final time, but only managed a dry croak before his vision finally faded to black.

The tendrils continued their grisly work until Samuel collapsed into a pile of ashes upon the lid of the sarcophagus. They then enwrapped the bodies of Annabel and Melody and in turn consumed them as they had Samuel. When all that remained of the family was blood and ashes, there was a deep sigh from the disembodied voice as the tendrils of darkness withdrew into the casket.

In a bedchamber in the mansion overhead, the only son of Samuel Corbant awoke screaming.

1. Nightmare

(Present Day)

Don't cry. Ally Corbant got off the school bus at the bottom of the forest-blanketed hill. Brushing her long, black hair out of her face, she shifted her backpack to a more secure position on her shoulder and set off up the cobblestone driveway. She attempted to force her features into an expressionless mask as she ambled her way beneath the boughs of the trees that concealed the sky overhead. Her father said that the cobbles and canopy of trees added to their home's mystique, but they just made Ally feel cut off from the rest of the modern world.

Ally finally reached the crest of the hill and the front lawn of Corbant Manor, her home. She grabbed the bars of the wrought iron gate, her stomach in knots. The mansion was a Gothic and majestic relic of a bygone age, with a looming tower, high gabled roofing, and potted chimney. As Ally stared at it, tears played at the corners of her pale blue eyes. She slammed a fist against the gate as she blinked the tears away. *Not yet, dammit!* She took a deep, shaky breath, wiped her eyes, and pushed the gate open.

Ally crossed the driveway to the covered front porch that wrapped around the right side of the manor. Making her way to the front door, she opened it and slipped inside. The foyer was as opulent as the outside of the house. A staircase led upwards on both sides of the room, conjoining at a grand balcony over the central hall doorway. A wooden angel hung from the railing of the balcony, its wings outspread and its arms open in welcome.

Ally headed up the right side of the staircase, not even glancing out the window of the landing. Once she reached the top of the stairs, she turned down a hallway like the one on the floor below and went to the first door on the right. *Almost there.* With a trembling hand, she opened the door and slipped inside.

Ally's room was utterly at odds with the rest of the house, with ivory walls instead of dark paint, darker wood, and peeling wallpaper. She tossed

9

her bag on the chair of an antique vanity table, then made for her four-post bed. She threw herself onto the covers and buried her face in her pillow. *Finally*. Alone in her room, Ally let herself break down into tears at last.

After crying for at least a half hour, Ally finally sat up. Tears slid down her cheeks as she stared at the ceiling helplessly. Why did the kids at school bully her? It seemed like they went out of their way to make her miserable. While it was true that her family's history was less than savory, she hadn't done anything remotely close to what the stories talked about. What had she done to deserve this treatment?

As a fresh wave of tears hit her, Ally's thoughts turned bitter. To her, the mansion was a symbol of her family's dark past. How could her father stand to live there? All the stories that were told about the place made her skin crawl.

She looked around at her room. Except for the vanity table that had belonged to her grandmother, it was the only room in the house that seemed normal. Every other room resembled something out of an historical museum or horror movie.

I wish I didn't live here. I hate my house, I hate my family, and I hate this whole town! I wish I could go somewhere...anywhere...else.

Ally threw herself back onto the bed and stared at the ceiling as she thought of the nasty things the other students had said about her. Her mother had always told her she wished she had been as pretty as Ally when she was younger, but Ally didn't believe her. Her classmates loved to poke fun at how pale she was, how her hair was too thin, and how deep the shadows under her eyes were. The only makeup she wore was eyeliner, and even then, only on occasion. Still, everyone always said she was in love with eyeshadow. At first, Ally tried to explain how she had trouble sleeping, but no one listened, so she gave up. It was just another reason to hate the town and just about everyone in it.

Ally found the tears welling in her eyes again but quickly wiped them away. After taking a deep breath, she began practicing her smile. It was the smile she wore every day for her mother and father so they wouldn't ask her what was wrong. She couldn't stand the concern in her mother's eyes, or the way her father would rage about how disrespectful and cruel people were.

She didn't disagree with him, but somehow his saying it aloud only made it worse. Instead, she smiled and said school was good when they asked.

After Ally had gotten her emotions under control, she went over to her vanity table to start on her homework. Despite the derision she faced in school, she was a model student. After all, she didn't have many friends to distract her from her schoolwork.

Not ten minutes into her work, there was a knock on her door. "Ally, are you in there?" came her mother's voice.

"Yeah, Mom," Ally answered, pausing mid-sentence on an English paper.

"Maddy's on the phone. Should I tell her you're busy?"

Ally's heart leapt. "No, I'll take it now, Mom." She got up and opened the door to get the phone from her mom.

"Not too long now, honey. Your dad's expecting an important call from work," her mom warned as she handed the receiver to her. Ally's mother was a tall, pretty woman with red hair and freckles. She wore a royal blue Victorian dress that matched her eyes. Ally would never say so aloud, but her mother's fascination with old-fashioned dresses bothered her almost as much as the house they lived in.

"I won't be, Mom," Ally answered as she took the phone. Without further comment, her mother closed the door.

Ally lifted the receiver to her ear, and the voice of her best friend Maddy Chambers spoke. "Hey, Ally. Are you all right?"

Ally closed the door and sat back in her chair. "Yeah, yeah, I'm fine, Maddy."

Maddy didn't sound convinced. "I know Gary said some nasty shit about you..."

Ally winced. There were no secrets in a small-town high school. "Yeah, but I'm used to it."

"You can't fool me, girl. I know it upset you."

Ally hesitated, biting her lip, then blurted out, "Who calls someone a dirty slut for no reason?"

Maddy sighed. "A worthless dickhead, that's who. Forget about him, Ally. Douchebags like that get theirs eventually anyways."

"Maddy, don't go getting into another fight for me again."

"I wasn't planning on it unless you wanted me to, hun. Say the word, though, and I'll make sure he cries for his mama!"

Ally couldn't help but smile. How she had survived before meeting Maddy in sixth grade was a complete mystery. "I bet you would, but the last thing you need is another suspension."

"Eh, I was thinking of dropping out anyways."

Ally groaned. "Please, for the love of God, do not leave me alone with these people!"

"I'm just kidding, Ally! Jeez!" Ally could hear the smile in Maddy's voice, and it made her smile herself. The two of them passed the next hour on the phone, laughing and talking about how stupid the kids at school were. Then Maddy asked, "Soooo...how about that Derek, eh?"

"You mean the new kid?"

Maddy giggled. "I know you have your eye on him."

Ally's face was suddenly far too warm. "Maybe..."

"Don't bullshit me, girl! He's pretty easy on the eyes!"

"Well...I mean...yeah..."

"Well, then?" Maddy asked expectantly.

"Well...he's prolly got all sorts of cool friends...and they'll tell him about my family..."

"Honestly, girl, I ain't seen him hanging out with anyone."

"No one?" Ally asked, not believing it.

"Nope, not a one. It's like he actually sees through all the uppity bullshit."

"Well...that's good I guess..." Ally replied skeptically.

"Why don't you go talk to him tomorrow?"

"What?!"

"Yeah, just walk up and say, 'Hey, nice butt! Wanna go to prom?'"

"God, Maddy! I'd die!"

"Girl, if you don't break out of that shell of yours, I'm gonna have to fix you up!"

"Maddy, please don't..."

"Give it a try, hun! He might like that pretty face of yours."

"I'm not pretty..." Ally argued.

"Girl, you are gorgeous!"

"Stop it, Maddy..."

"All right, fine." Ally could practically hear Maddy rolling her eyes. Undoubtedly Ally hadn't heard the end of it, but Maddy changed the subject back to the "uppity bullshit." However, it wasn't long until the phone began beeping with another call on the line.

"I'm sorry, Maddy...I gotta go."

"Duty calls?"

"Yeah, for Dad," Ally replied.

"Say no more, girl. Talk to ya tomorrow, all right?"

"Definitely. Bye!" Ally hung up and made her way down the hall to the second door across from hers. With a knock she called out, "Dad, work's calling."

After the squeak of a rolling chair and a few footsteps, the door opened. Her father was a tall man with a bit of a gut and prematurely silver hair. He had a bushy mustache and glasses and was wearing a somewhat disheveled suit and a loose necktie. "Thank you, Ally." His deep voice rumbled as he took the receiver.

Ally barely had time to say, "You're welcome, Dad," before he closed the door and began chatting into the phone. Ally frowned. It must've been an especially important call. If it wasn't about his work as a college economics professor, then it had to be about the stocks he traded as a side job. Heaving a sigh, she turned back to her room to continue her homework. So much for the one highlight of another miserable day.

"Ally!" a high-pitched voice squeaked. Ally turned to see her three-year-old sister Cassie running towards her. The moment Ally saw Cassie's pale, chubby cheeks, her brilliant smile making her crystal blue eyes shine, Ally's heart melted. Cassie latched onto Ally's legs and squeezed before looking up at her. "Welcome home!"

Ally couldn't help but smile as she ruffled Cassie's long black hair. "Thanks, Cassie."

Cassie stepped back and jumped up and down excitedly, her little pink dress bobbing as she did so. "Wanna know what I did today?"

Ally knelt down at Cassie's level. "What?"

Cassie giggled. "I gotta whisper. It's a secret!" With a chuckle and a shrug, Ally leaned her ear towards Cassie. With another giggle, Cassie cupped her mouth towards Ally's ear and whispered, "Matt and me caught a butterfly!"

Ally gasped dramatically. Matt was the gardener, a college student not much older than Ally. "Was it pretty?"

Cassie nodded excitedly. "Just like Mommy and you!"

You are too sweet, Cassie. "What did you do with it?"

Cassie's face fell. "Well...Matt said we had to let it go, or it would be sad."

"Did you?"

Cassie nodded. "Yep! No sad butterflies!"

Ally heaved a sigh and ruffled her sister's hair again. *If only, Cassie. If only.*

ALLY WANDERED DOWN one of the mansion's long hallways in the dead of night. The sconces on the walls were unlit, leaving only a pale light shining through the window at the end of the hallway for illumination. She walked towards it, wanting to get away from the oppressing darkness. At first, the only sound was Ally's heart pounding in her ears, but then the silence gave way to soft whispers coming from all around. Her pulse quickened and she broke into a run. Something was behind her, but she dared not look. She urged her legs to work faster, but no matter how hard she ran, the window came no closer.

As the whispering grew louder in her ears, Ally snuck a glance over her shoulder. The hallway behind her was filled with shadowy figures, their outlines barely visible in the gloom. She imagined hands reaching out of the darkness for her, and she tried to run faster still.

A cold breath drifted across the back of her neck, and Ally's legs suddenly turned to jelly. She staggered against the wall, whimpering in terror as she willed her legs to continue forward, but they felt far too heavy beneath her. A scream rose in her chest, but Ally barely managed to utter a weak croak. Any second, the shadow things would be upon her, their cold hands latching onto her and dragging her off into...

Ally awoke, trembling and drenched with sweat. It was not her first nightmare, but it had easily been among the worst. She sat upright and looked around frantically, as if expecting the shrouded forms to be standing around her bed. After several minutes of panicked breathing and nervous darting eyes, she reminded herself that it had only been a dream. However, believing herself was easier said than done while alone in her room in the dark.

Ally laid her head back down on the pillow, afraid to close her eyes. The hallway had looked like the very one outside her bedroom. What if those shadowy figures were outside her door at that very moment? She shook that dark notion from her head and sighed, glancing at the alarm clock on her nightstand. 3:33 a.m. *Go figure.* Her breathing finally calm, she had just closed her eyes when a door suddenly slammed somewhere in the house.

Ally sat bolt upright, her breath catching in her chest. Had someone broken in? Carol the maid and Chad the cook had gone home for the night, and her mother and father had gone to bed before her. The only other culprit could be Cassie and, as far as Ally knew, she was afraid of the dark.

Heart hammering in her chest, Ally slid off her bed as silently as she could and looked through the curtains over the one window in her room. The grounds were pitch black, no light from either the moon outside nor from inside the house shining out.

Puzzled and still very frightened, Ally considered investigating, but the dream was too fresh in her mind. Again, the feeling that cold hands would reach out from the darkness and grab her overcame her. Shuddering to try to shake off the feeling, she instead crawled back into bed and spent the few remaining hours of the night trying to convince herself that she had imagined the sound. Even as the sun rose, however, she still could not forget how sharp and real the sound had been in the dead of night.

"LOOK, IT'S THE CORBANT girl!"

"She looks like a vampire wannabe."

"Has she heard of sunlight? Ugh!"

"I'd die before I'd leave the house with that much eyeshadow. So trashy!"

"Don't stare, she'll stick a knife in you!"

"She's a twig! Eat something once in a while, goddamn!"

Ally had heard it all a hundred times and more, but it never got any easier. Worse still, her lack of sleep the night before made it harder for her to control her emotions. As tears began to fill her eyes, she quickened her pace from the cafeteria to her locker.

"She always walks so fast. She needs to just chill the fuck out."

"Was she about to start crying?"

"Maybe she realized how ugly she is."

"Does she know everyone hates her?"

"She should just kill herself like her grandma."

"Yeah, before she snaps like the rest of her family."

Ally couldn't make it to her locker quickly enough. Finally, she reached it. Entering the combination, she yanked it open. Safely at her locker, she let herself zone out. The whispers of the other students fell into an indeterminate hum, and Ally closed her eyes. *Peace at last.*

Her arms worked of their own accord as they pulled her books from her locker, but soon even they slowed as her exhaustion caught up with her. It was so comfortable with her eyes closed. So relaxing.

"Don't let them fool you. School is hell," Maddy groaned as she practically fell against her locker beside Ally's. Ally squeaked in dismay. Maddy's sudden appearance had startled her awake. Unfortunately, she had also thrown her arms up in surprise. Her books fell from her locker, scattering papers and writing utensils on the floor.

Maddy immediately kneeled and started trying to scoop things up. "Oh God, I'm so sorry Ally! I didn't mean to scare you..."

"It's fine. I was just kinda dozing off..." Ally began before a group of students walking down the hall interrupted her.

"Look! She's as big a mess as her whole family!" a girl taunted. Though Ally refused to look up, she recognized the voice: Gladys Lauderdale, captain of the cheerleading squad and what Maddy would describe as a "mega-bitch."

A guy snorted. "I heard she's a Satanist and tries to talk to her psychotic grandparents."

Someone picked up one of her books and laughed as he looked through it. At last, Ally looked up and recognized him as Gary Maudlin, a big, muscular teenager with short blond hair and a pronounced chin. Along with his letterman jacket, he usually sported a cocky grin. Today was no different as his dull brown eyes pretended to scrutinize the book. It was merely a math book, but he dramatically declared, "Of course she's a Satanist! Look, she's written pentagrams on every page, circled every 13 and 666 she can find. Hell, she's even drawn a picture of a goat's head!"

Maddy stood up and squared her shoulders with Gary, who was nearly twice her size, her green eyes flashing angrily. She was small, only five foot two inches tall with shoulder-length hair dyed black. Still, she tried to be intimidating by dressing in all black with studded pants and matching bracelets. "Why don't you shut your fucking face, asshole!"

The rest of the group stopped walking and turned to watch. Gary was on the football team, but Maddy didn't care. Ally may have admired her guts, but her admiration was dulled by fear for her friend's safety. "Maddy...please don't..."

Gary laughed again. "Yeah Maddy, Corbants don't need anyone to fight their battles for them. God knows they're all lunatics."

Before Ally could stop her, Maddy rushed him and rammed him back against the opposite wall, the math book flying from his hands to the floor. The other students gasped. Maddy hissed in his face, "Say one more thing about her in front of me, and I'll cut your dick off in your sleep."

Gary was in complete shock. The rest of the students watched with bated breath, wondering what he would do next. He wriggled away from Maddy, brushing off his jacket and glaring down his nose at her. Ally didn't breathe.

Then, to her surprise, Gary just shrugged. "I guess psychos travel in packs. Later, witches!" He and his friends laughed as they continued on their way.

Maddy trembled with barely controlled rage while Ally got to her feet. She nervously watched them go, catching a side-eyed glare from the pretty blonde that was Gladys. "You shouldn't have done that Maddy..." Ally whispered.

Maddy narrowed her eyes at their backs, her face contorted with hate. "Someday they will regret the shit they've said about you. I promise you that, Ally."

Ally sighed. "Please...no more fighting for me. You'll never change their minds. It's a lost cause..."

With a disgruntled "Hmph!", Maddy went back to picking up the scattered books. Ally heaved a sigh and returned to the task as well. Once the last of the books were either in Ally's arms or back in her locker, Maddy gave Ally a quick hug around her shoulders. "See you at lunch, girl."

"Bye," Ally mumbled, giving Maddy a squeeze with her free arm before she headed off for class. As her best friend turned the corner, Ally was racked with guilt. Maddy had a rough home life living alone with her drunk father. She pretended not to care and to be tough and confident, but Ally knew better. Maddy was fiercely loyal because Ally was her only real friend. In truth, they really only had each other.

Ally sighed and turned around, nearly bumping into another student named Bart Rogan. "Oh God!" she exclaimed.

Bart jumped and stammered an apology. "S-s-sorry Ally. I sh-sh-should watch where I'm g-g-going..." He looked at the floor, his expression contrite.

Ally couldn't help but pity him. Bart was an awkward boy with a bad stutter. He always wore khakis and polo shirts to school and had these dorky wire-framed glasses. He wasn't a bad looking teenage boy, with his honey-brown eyes and wavy, short brown hair, but he was often mocked for his lack of social skills and shyness about his stutter. In Ally's own attempts to avoid people as much as possible, she had never spoken to him until now. "Don't worry about it, Bart. It's okay."

Bart glanced up at her for a moment, then back at the floor. "I'm s-s-sorry for what h-h-happened this m-m-morning with those k-k-kids..."

Ally waved his apology away. "I'm used to it." Of course it was a lie, but she couldn't bear the idea of him feeling sorry for her. In fact, she wasn't sure which of the two of them got bullied worse.

Bart glanced up at her again and then quickly down once more as if in shame. "Oh...okay...w-w-well, s-s-see you..." He sped past her.

Ally's heart ached. Bart was always so polite, but no one made any effort to get to know him. Perhaps the two of them weren't so different? Suddenly, an idea struck her. She turned and called, "Hey Bart!"

Bart turned back and looked at her without looking away this time. "Yeah...?"

Ally walked up to him, offering a friendly smile. "Why don't you sit with Maddy and me at lunch today?"

Bart's face lit up. "R-r-really?"

Ally nodded encouragingly. "Definitely."

He nodded excitedly. "Okay, I'll b-b-be there!"

She started to turn but made sure he saw her grin once more. "All right, see you then!" It felt good to reach out to him. *At least he would have a friend rather than face it all alone.*

When lunchtime came, Ally took her seat at their lunch table as usual. The cafeteria was one of her favorite places. With students embroiled in their own conversations and determined to shut out outsiders, she could usually slip by unnoticed, provided she entered via the hallway that didn't cross with the lunch line.

She was lighthearted as she set her lunchbox on the table. Her mother insisted she bring her own lunch rather than stand in the line, and Ally didn't mind in the least. She sipped a can of soda and waited for Maddy to show up.

Sure enough, Maddy came about two minutes later, her tray laden with as much as the lunch ladies would allow. Maddy may have been a small girl, but Ally was astonished by her appetite. Before Maddy could even say a word, though, Bart came over with his own tray and sat down nervously. Maddy narrowed her eyes suspiciously. "Not here to start something, are you?"

Ally cut in quickly before Maddy could scare him off. "This is Bart. I invited him to sit with us today."

Maddy's expression immediately brightened. "Well then, welcome to our own private circle of hell! I'm Maddy, and my sin is not giving a shit!" she declared while stabbing her fork into a slab of Salisbury steak.

Ally chuckled, and Bart managed a nervous but genuine smile. The remainder of the lunch hour passed with Maddy lamenting how boring her classes were as usual, then poking questionably malicious fun at Ally's tormentors. Bart even laughed once or twice, though he always cut it short and resumed his nervous silence. At first, Ally had feared that Maddy's exuberance would overwhelm him, but he didn't seem to mind. In fact, he seemed to enjoy listening to her rantings and ravings.

At the end of the hour as they stood up to leave, Maddy turned to Bart. "Listen, if you need people to hang out with, or want someone roughed up a bit..."

"Maddy!" Ally warned.

Maddy grinned. "Just saying. Anyways, you're cool with us, so don't be a stranger, all right?"

Bart looked down and murmured, "Th-th-thank you..."

Maddy smiled brightly. "Don't mention it, man."

Ally had never been happier.

The rest of the day passed mostly without incident, until Ally was making her way to the bus for the ride home. Just as she was about to exit the cafeteria doors, she found a group of students blocking her path. To her horror, it was the group from that morning. Maddy had already left for her walk home, leaving Ally alone and defenseless.

"You didn't think you'd gotten away with that little stunt this morning, did you?" Gary sneered, his thick arms folded across his chest.

Ally took a step back, her throat tightening. "I...I didn't do anything."

"But your friend did," Gladys jeered in her snide voice.

"Pity we couldn't catch her, so you'll have to give her a message from us," Gary said as he cracked his knuckles.

Ally's eyes widened. She was used to the taunts and name calling, but this was something else entirely. Maddy was the fighter, but Ally had always gotten by without getting into a fight until now. She trembled in fear. What could she do? There were five of them with no teacher in sight, not that they would have been much help.

Ally tightened her grip on her backpack with sweaty hands and pleaded, "Please...just leave me alone."

Gladys cackled. "Not so tough without your bitch of a friend to stick up for you, are you?"

"What are we waiting for then? It's about time a Corbant got a good beating anyways. Might set the family straight!" Gary declared, getting a cruel chuckle from Gladys and the others. They began to close in.

Somebody help me, Ally prayed as she prepared to turn and run, but suddenly there was someone between her and her tormentors. He was a tall boy with short, dark hair in black jeans and a black t-shirt. She couldn't see his face as he kept his back to her. Her rescuer scolded the other students, "Five against one? How brave of you."

"Who the fuck are you?" Gary grunted as he took a step forward and squared his shoulders to the newcomer. Gladys was uncharacteristically silent, her eyes wide as she sized up the stranger.

The mysterious boy replied, "Someone who won't stand by and watch, unlike the rest of you around here. Enough is enough. Leave her alone or this gets ugly."

"Two against five still isn't good odds for you is it, Mr. Tough Shit?"

The stranger chuckled. "Wanna bet?"

Ally was stunned. Who was this guy? Whoever he was, he was radiating both calmness and confidence, leaving the gang hesitant.

After a couple tense minutes, Gary snorted and turned, leaving without a comment. The others followed suit soon after. Gladys shot Ally a murderous glare before turning her nose up and storming off.

Ally stared at her savior in shock. "Thank you...so much..."

The newcomer turned to reveal his identity, and Ally's breath caught in her chest. It was none other than the new kid, Derek Meers. He was pale but not unusually so, and his eyes were a dark brown that reminded Ally of a warm blanket she kept at home for colder nights. He flashed a subtle but charming smile. "Don't mention it."

"Why did you step in like that?"

Derek glanced at the doors the group had exited from. "There's no telling what they might have done. Kids are cruel, but especially kids who think they're big shots."

"But they would have pummeled you—"

Derek laughed. "All I had to do was bluff. For all they knew, I was some kung fu master trained in dark dungeons from an early age."

Ally blinked, furrowing her brow. "Are you really?"

Derek laughed again. "Not even. I just know how to get to people. My name's Derek, by the way."

"Ally...Ally Corbant," she replied, then braced herself for the stunned recognition of her family name that usually led to the early death of any potential friendships.

It never came. "Nice to meet you, Ally. Better hurry, though, or you'll miss the bus. I'll watch your back from here." Derek smiled again, leaving Ally feeling oddly lightheaded. She mumbled a quick "thank you" to him and hurried out the doors.

"HOW WAS SCHOOL TODAY, Ally?" her mother asked as they ate in the dining room together.

Ally was prepared for the question, as always. "Nothing new really."

Her father snorted. "No surprise there. Fairly sure you have all the same teachers I did!"

Cassie giggled and Ally smiled, but her dad's joke tugged at her thoughts. Her agitation must have shown because her mother asked, "Something wrong?"

Oops. Ally weighed her options before throwing caution to the wind. "Why do we still live here?"

"Excuse me?" her father asked, frowning.

"I mean..." Ally began, eyeing Cassie. Her eyes were alight with curiosity. *Be careful.* "I mean...with all the stuff...that people say."

"You're asking this again?" her father grumbled with a sigh.

"Well, I mean..." Ally stammered. *Now you've done it.*

"Come on, Cassie! It's movie night!" Ally's mother said abruptly before scooping Cassie up from the dining room chair and heading towards the door.

"But Wednesdays are movie nights..." Cassie protested, looking to Ally for help.

"Well I think it's time we changed it up!" her mother said, carrying her out the door into the hallway. Ally stood up to follow them. *Maybe...*

"Sit."

Trying to hide her nerves, Ally slowly slid back into her chair. Her father took his glasses off and set them on the table before rubbing his temples. "I thought we had been through this, Ally."

Ally bit her lip. "Yeah, but..."

"This house has been in this family for more than two hundred years. It's our home."

"But..."

"You know how lucky we are? Some families have to pay for where they live. This is *our* house. No one else's." Her father jabbed a finger into the table for emphasis. Ally couldn't think of a reply before her father continued. "Try to understand, Ally. I know the things people say about us, but running away won't make them stop. The only way to fix our family's reputation is to take some pride in what we have and what we've done. The town is named after our family, for God's sake!"

Ally hung her head. "I know."

"Then why do you act like you're ashamed to be a Corbant?"

Because I am. It took all of Ally's will not to say the words aloud, but instead she mumbled dejectedly, "I'm sorry, Dad."

Her father sighed and put his glasses back on. "Someday when you're older, you'll understand." At a silent nod from Ally, he added, "Now let's go join your mother and sister, and act like a family should, all right? None of this moping, am I clear?"

Fat chance. "Yes, Dad."

THAT NIGHT, ALLY NEARLY flew out of bed as she woke from another nightmare. It had been a particularly horrible dream about a woman wandering around in the art room of the house with a noose around her neck. Even as she looked around her room, Ally could still clearly picture the woman's hollowed cheeks, bloodshot eyes, and purple tongue hanging from between shriveled lips as the moldy rope trailed behind her moth-eaten gown.

Ally brushed her hair out of her face with a trembling hand, then closed it into a fist against her chest as if to still her pounding heart. She then turned and sat on the edge of the bed, trying to regain control of herself. The details of that horrible woman were still vivid in her mind's eye.

Ally looked around nervously again to bring herself back to reality. No dead woman rolled her blue-green head back and forth as she roamed about aimlessly. The image reminded Ally of her Cassie's own beloved stuffed bear. She held onto it so frequently that all the stuffing had been pushed out of the neck so that its head flopped around. Ally had always found it amusing, but now it made her shudder.

She sighed and buried her face in her hands. "Only a dream," she said to herself quietly, hoping hearing it aloud would help reassure her. She repeated it over and over until the idea began to finally settle in. Then she heard a noise that caused her breath to catch in her chest.

There were footsteps coming up the foyer stairs. They were soft and slow, with the steps groaning beneath the weight in a way that raised the hairs on the back of Ally's neck. She scrambled into bed and slid under the covers. The sound continued until the footsteps reached the top of the stairs and then paused. Ally lay quietly, drenched in fresh sweat and trying desperately to control her breathing as she peeked out at her door. She clung to the covers of the bed as a blanket of protection and prayed for it to be over. Then, someone slowly knocked on her door.

Ally covered her mouth to prevent a scream. The knocking was slow and deliberate, but relentless. It continued like the beat of a metronome.

Knock. Knock. Knock. Knock.

Ally threw the covers up over her head and tried to block out the sound as tears filled her eyes.

Knock. Knock. Knock. Knock.

Terror constricted her throat. How was no one else hearing this?

Knock. Knock. Knock. Knock.

Please, God, make it stop! Ally pressed the bunched-up covers against her ears.

Then the knocking stopped. Ally lay still for a moment. She considered peeking from under the covers, but then a cold chill enveloped her. It was as though the room had suddenly been completely drained of heat. Soaked in sweat as she was, Ally shivered and clenched her teeth to keep them from chattering.

There came a whisper from beside Ally's bed. The voice was not one she recognized, but it would be one she would never forget. It was dry, soft, and muffled, as though it were coming from beneath some thick material. "The walls...remember." Ally couldn't stifle a whimper at the sound. Then, as suddenly as the chill had descended, it was gone.

Ally lay still for several minutes, listening carefully, but there was nothing else. She peeked out from under the covers nervously, praying that all she would see would be her empty room with the door shut. She was not disappointed.

Ally let out a long sigh. Was she losing her mind? Was the pressure of everyone being so nasty to her at school finally causing her to lose her grip? She wished she could say yes. The alternative...that what had just happened was real...was almost too much to take.

She tried to relax again, but sleep was a far-off dream. She spent the rest of the night staring at her door, too afraid to close her eyes. She only looked away when her alarm sounded, telling her to get ready for school.

Ally groaned as she rolled out of bed. It seemed that whether she was at school, asleep, or wide awake in her own bed, her life was a constant nightmare.

2. Friends

"You'd think they'd lay off if they really believed you'd go batshit and kill everyone," Maddy grumbled at lunch as she glared at a group of students at a distant table. They were staring at Ally and company, laughing amongst themselves.

Ally sighed as she stifled a yawn. "They can't really believe it, otherwise they probably would."

Bart looked at her. "Have you b-b-been getting enough s-s-sleep lately?"

Ally shrugged. "Not really."

Maddy stabbed her chicken breast with her fork. "It's so fucking stupid!"

"Maddy!" Ally exclaimed.

"I'm sorry, Ally, but it is! Why can't people just leave you alone? I mean, come on!" Maddy took a deep breath as she was about to launch into one of her famous "People Suck" speeches. Suddenly, she stopped and stared wide-eyed behind Ally.

"What is it?" Ally asked, bewildered.

"Am I interrupting?" came Derek's reply from behind her.

Ally nearly jumped and turned in her seat to face him. "Oh! Hi, Derek. Not at all. What's up?" The words spilled from her mouth in a rapid cascade, making her blush immediately.

Derek shrugged with his lunch tray in hand. "Thought I might come sit with you, if you don't mind." Ally couldn't believe that he took her word vomit in stride.

Maddy grinned. "Not at all! Come join the local freaks!"

Bart laughed, but Ally was mortified. "Maddy!"

"What? He might as well get used to it if he hangs with us. So, where are you on the fringes of small-town high school bullshit?" Maddy asked, watching Derek but glancing at Ally with a triumphant smile that made Ally roll her eyes.

Derek sat down. "Just new kid jitters, I guess. First time starting at a new school."

Bart sipped some orange juice while nervously eyeing the newcomer. Maddy glanced at him, then back at Derek. "Oh, this is Bart, by the way. He's really shy."

Bart flushed a little, but replied, "H-h-hello."

Derek smiled at him. "Nice to meet you, Bart."

Ally sat in stunned silence. Had Derek not heard the gossip? Did he not have any idea that she was made fun of so relentlessly? Did he even care? Her stomach was in knots, and her mind was awhirl. Thankfully, Maddy did most of the talking for her. "Where did you move from anyways?"

"South of Indy, so not that far, I guess," he said, shrugging.

"Nope. So, you're not completely new to Indiana life. Sweet!" Maddy glanced at Ally again, and Ally had to look away to fight her blush. Derek was sitting beside her, and she was more than aware of how close he was. She snuck a glance at him out of the corner of her eye while he listened intently to Maddy's rambling. His handsome features seemed only more so up close.

Her eyes traced every inch of his profile, amazed at how his face looked both soft and strong at the same time. *If only he would look this way.* Ally wanted to look into his warm brown eyes again. Then she remembered herself and quickly turned away as her cheeks burned. She had been gawking at him, open-mouthed, like a creep. Thankfully, no one seemed to notice.

"So," Maddy began, shifting in her seat to face Derek fully, "do you live here in town?"

Derek chuckled a little before answering. "My parents bought a little farmhouse just outside of town."

"Farmhouse, eh?" Maddy observed with narrowed eyes and a smug smile.

Ally blinked and stared at Maddy. "Are you...interrogating him?"

Maddy grinned in return. "The freaks of Corbanton High have an application process, if you please!"

Bart snorted into his orange juice, and Derek chuckled again. Ally's stomach fluttered.

Maddy continued, "Any animals?"

"Not yet. Mom wants horses again. She grew up around them. Dad wants chickens for our own eggs."

"What about you?"

"I want a quiet place to get away from people."

Maddy blinked in surprise, then grinned at him. "I don't know about quiet, but this lunch table is a good place to get away from people!"

"If only," Ally grumbled. The kids from the nearby table were staring again, but their smiles and whispered conversations were absent.

"They got a problem?" Derek asked with an annoyed tone that delighted Ally. *God, he's too amazing.*

Maddy turned and gave them a little wave with a cheesy grin. "Yep, they sure do."

Oh no, here it comes. Ally braced herself.

"Why do they have..." Derek began, but then the bell rang. Ally gasped, not realizing that she had been holding her breath. "Well, I guess I'll see you guys around," Derek said as he got up to leave. Maddy looked disappointed, but Ally was relieved. *Saved by the bell.*

The rest of the school day passed with Ally suffering the usual taunting and teasing. It felt like there was a spotlight on her as she walked down the hallways, turning heads in her direction no matter how inconspicuous she tried to make herself. The teachers did nothing to help. Most of them pretended not to notice or just avoided her altogether. Her family's reputation seemed to make her unworthy of their protection.

As usual, Ally was only mildly relieved by the time she got off the bus to make the walk up the cobblestone driveway to the mansion. The late September air was beginning to turn crisp, and a gentle breeze rustled the trees. She closed her eyes as she walked, letting the sounds and smells of autumn's approach soothe her. She kept them closed until she crested the hill, her feet following the familiar path of their own accord. She stopped just outside the front gate and gazed up at the mansion. More than two centuries of history looked back at her, and almost all of it stained with blood, as her classmates liked to remind her. Ally sighed as her eyes traced their way from the top of the tower to the third-floor balcony, and from there to the hanged woman leering out at her from the art room window...

Ally's heart nearly stopped. She did a double take at the art room window to see if her mind had played tricks on her. Unsurprisingly, the window was dark and empty. Ally took a moment to breathe. *Must've imagined it.* She then pushed the gate open and made her way inside, though she was unable to stop a chill running down her spine as she crossed the threshold.

Soon enough, Maddy's nightly phone call drove the hanged woman from her mind. Maddy was all gloat that night. "What did I tell you, girl?"

Ally sighed as she rolled her eyes. "He just sat with us for one lunch period."

"And he got all protective when the nosy shits wouldn't stop staring. I tell you, he's the one!"

"Maddy, don't be stupid. We just met."

"And he decided to come see you again! If you ever had a chance for a dreamy high school romance, this is it!" Maddy said with dramatic flair.

Ally was glad Maddy couldn't see how red her face was. "I've never thought about any kind of high school romance…"

"Yet here's this pretty hot guy who has decided the high school freaks aren't so bad, not to mention who he chose to sit next to."

"I noticed that…"

"See!? Quit being the humble sweetheart for once and admit it. He likes you!"

"So what if he does? Once everyone tells him about my family, he'll turn out just like the rest," Ally blurted out, exasperated. She wanted to believe that Derek truly was different, but he was not the first new kid that had taken a shine to her in his early days at the school. Three times a new face in the class had come forward to try to strike up a conversation with her. Then he would learn who Ally was descended from, and soon the friendly words would turn into cruel jeers or just avoiding her altogether.

Maddy didn't reply right away. Ally hadn't meant to let her thoughts come spilling out of her mouth like that, but her exhaustion had loosened her lips. She wondered if she might have said too much, but then Maddy said, "Look, sooner or later, someone with a brain is gonna show up, notice how gorgeous you are, flip everyone else off, and you both will cruise off into the sunset in some badass car."

Ally sighed. "Stop getting my hopes up…"

"I know, I know, but don't worry. If he fucks up, I'll put the fear of God in him myself."

"Maddy…"

"I'm dead serious, Ally." Suddenly, Maddy's usually sarcastic and playful tone vanished. "The only way you're gonna get out from under your family's shadow is if you start thinking you deserve to be, and girl, *you deserve to be.* You're a sweetheart. You're beautiful. You're smart. Any guy who's not a sheep would be lucky to have you!"

Ally sighed again. "Then why don't they come and get me?"

"Cause there's nothing but sheep at that hellhole, but Derek...he ain't no sheep. He's a wolf, and he's looking for a mate. That's you, girl."

Ally rolled her eyes. "I don't think that's quite how he's looking at it."

"Close enough." Ally suddenly heard a door slam followed by yelling on Maddy's end, and her friend hurriedly said, "I gotta go...stay strong, girl." She hung up.

Ally's heart sank. Whenever Maddy's father came home and immediately started yelling, it wasn't good. Ally set the receiver down on the bed and sat in silence, wrestling with her guilt. There she was, bitter and depressed about being teased and bullied at school while Maddy stuck by her side through it all, even sticking up for Ally when she could. Then Maddy would go home and deal with her abusive father, while Ally came home to a family who loved and supported her. It wasn't fair.

Ally made up her mind. It was selfish of her to drown in self-pity while her best friend did all she could to pull her back up, despite her own problems. Ally needed to pull herself together. Maybe Maddy was right and Derek was different. She had proven time and again that she only had Ally's best interests at heart. Maybe it was time for Ally to take a chance on her best friend's advice. If nothing else, it would remind Maddy that Ally trusted her implicitly. That couldn't hurt, could it? Plus, if Maddy was right, then she'd have something to gloat about. Ally chuckled to herself. If nothing else would make Maddy happy, that certainly would.

Emboldened by her newfound resolution, Ally was surprised to find how easily she was able to smile with her family through dinner that evening. She even laughed as Cassie mispronounced the word "responsibility," which she had apparently learned that morning from their mother. Finally, Ally was back in her room and ready for bed. Exhaustion got the better of her that night, and she fell asleep the moment her head hit the pillow.

FINALLY WAKING UP RESTED, Ally went about her morning routine and got to the end of her driveway a little earlier than usual. It was chillier than it had been the day before. A light fog blanketed the hill around her house. Ally heaved a sigh as she leaned against a tree. *I shouldn't have left so early.* The morning dreariness threatened her good mood. Why did her family have to live somewhere so creepy?

A twig snapped somewhere in the woods, and Ally's breath caught for a moment. *Just a squirrel, or a deer...maybe.* She strained her eyes to see through the gloom in the direction of the sound. Then, there was the telltale growl of the school bus engine. Ally turned back to see its headlights coming towards where she stood. Relieved, she walked out from under the tree and stood in her usual spot just off the side of the road. As she got onto the bus, she chanced a glance back into the woods. For a moment, she thought there was a vaguely human shadow somewhere in the trees. *Stop it, you're just freaking yourself out.*

Ally spent the bus ride focusing on how to behave around Derek. She couldn't pull off an air of confidence or suavity without making a joke of herself, and she had no idea how to flirt. The very thought made her cheeks burn. Still, she couldn't help but imagine his face. His warm, brown eyes were so comforting, and his cheeks looked so soft, and his lips...

Ally had to cut her thoughts off there. She couldn't be staring at him all the time imagining what kissing him would be like. Still, the image danced in her mind, making her stomach do backflips and her cheeks hot.

Calm down. Coming on too strong would probably scare him away, whether or not he cared about her family history. Maybe she needed to think of him as just a friend for now? Maybe if she could learn to relax around him instead of letting her nerves get the better of her, then they could go from there. Treat him no differently than she had Bart or even Maddy when they had first met. Yeah, that seemed doable. *Just a friend...for now.*

Ally's resolve only hardened when she saw Maddy. Maddy never overdid her makeup, preferring eyeliner on its own. However, she had gone heavy with foundation that morning. Ally's heart ached for her best friend; her dad had hit her. Maddy said nothing about it and behaved as she always did, but Ally wasn't fooled. Her friend's tough girl attitude was shaken, and any mention of it might bring her to tears. The last thing she needed was to be caught crying in school, so Ally reluctantly said nothing.

"So, given any thought to what I told you last night?" Maddy asked offhandedly.

Ally shrugged as she closed her locker. "Maybe. Honestly, I passed right out the moment I laid down."

Maddy laughed. "No wonder there's some pep in your step today! A night's sleep can be an ass saver, girl."

Ally smiled in response but didn't get a chance to reply before a familiar voice said from behind her, "Morning, ladies."

Ally turned and found herself less than a foot from Derek. He was leaning against a neighboring locker and smiling his subtle half-smile. She liked that smile more and more every time she saw it. "Hey, Derek," she said with more firmness than she thought herself capable of in his presence.

"Everything all right?" he asked casually.

Ally nodded. "Not bad at all, for once."

Derek raised an eyebrow. "Your mornings usually rough?"

Ally shrugged. "Unfortunately, that incident two days ago wasn't an isolated event." *Here we go.*

"What do they have against you, anyways?" he asked, and Ally adored hearing the annoyance in his voice.

Ally bit her lip as her nerves shifted into overdrive. Should she tell him now? She glanced at a clock on the opposite wall. *Not enough time.* "I'll tell you at lunch," she assured him.

Derek nodded, his expression unreadable. "See you then." He then ducked past them and headed off to his first class. Ally turned and looked at Maddy, whose mouth was hanging open in stunned silence.

Ally felt her ears go red. "What's that look for?"

"Girl, you're gonna tell him?"

Ally nodded. "He'll find out sooner or later. Best he hears it from me first," she explained, half to herself and half to Maddy.

Maddy's face lit up with a brilliant smile. "My little girl is all grown up!" They high fived each other, and Ally couldn't help but laugh. Despite the looming dread of telling Derek about why she was hated at school, she felt good.

Ally's resolve held for most of the morning until her math class. She must have been staring off into space as she pondered the approaching lunch hour, because the teacher's voice cut through her thoughts like a hot knife. "Miss Corbant?"

Ally nearly jumped in her seat as the teacher, a short, plump, middle-aged woman in a turquoise turtleneck and black skirt, turned to face her. "Mrs. Holstrower?"

Mrs. Holstrower narrowed her beady brown eyes at Ally. "Might I ask what is so interesting about that empty space on my wall?"

A few of the other students snickered, and Ally's cheeks burned. "N-nothing."

"Then why, pray tell, were you staring at it so intently?"

"I...I..." Ally's heart hammered. *Please, don't do this now.*

"Need I remind you that there is a test at the end of this week?" Mrs. Holstrower warned as she approached Ally's desk with her hands on her hips.

"I know," Ally said simply, trying not tremble in fear.

"You know, do you? Then tell me what the process is for multiplying matrices."

Ally's eyes widened. "In...in front of...the whole class?"

"Did I stutter, Miss Corbant?"

Ally gulped. "Well..." Even as she shakily explained how to multiply matrices, Ally couldn't block out the giggling of the other students at her expense. Mrs. Holstrower seemed completely unaware, however.

When she finished her explanation, Mrs. Holstrower gave a curt nod. "At least you have been paying attention...for the most part. I suggest you keep your attention on the lesson in its entirety, where it belongs."

Ally was a mess. Immediately after the bell rang, she left the math classroom and went straight to study hall. When the study hall teacher asked if any students wanted to go to the library to study, Ally volunteered immediately. She spent most of the hour in a relatively secluded chair in a corner of the library, crying silently. As though her nerves weren't strained enough from facing the daunting task of sharing her morbid family history with

Derek, math class had been a total nightmare. It wasn't uncommon for the teachers to be cold to her, but Mrs. Holstrower had been outright cruel.

Finally, the bell tolled for lunch. Ally took several deep breaths, left the library at her usual pace, grabbed her lunch, and took the less-used hallway to the cafeteria. Relieved to be the first to arrive at the table, Ally took her alone time to figure out how to explain things. Much to her surprise, when Maddy sat down, she didn't interrupt Ally's inner monologue. She merely gave Ally an encouraging smile and started to eat. Bart sat down next to Maddy, and soon she was talking his ears off as usual. Shortly after, Derek sat down beside Ally.

Not wanting to give herself time to chicken out, Ally dove into her explanation. "So...I told you I'd explain why they treat me like crap..." Derek said nothing but looked at her attentively. She swallowed, and then continued. "My family...the Corbants...have an ugly reputation here. I don't know how it started, but many of them have ended up being horrible people...murderers, thieves, and worse, but the very worst was my great-grandfather Aros. He was the director at Corbant Sanitarium just outside of town."

Ally paused, waiting for the light of recognition or shock at her words to cross Derek's face. His expression betrayed neither reaction. Instead, he merely nodded slowly, encouraging her to continue. She took another deep breath and obliged. "There had been rumors of mistreatment and abuse at the asylum for a couple months before the riot. When it happened, not many escaped...but those who did told the cops horrible things. I won't go into details..."

Her voice trailed off. Come to think of it, she had always been too terrified to investigate the details for herself.

It took a moment for her to suppress a wave of nausea at the thought of stories she had been told about the asylum before she could continue. Still, Derek did not interrupt her. "There was an investigation. They uncovered a lot of...strange...things at the asylum. Naturally, it was shut down. Aros was killed in the riot. It was a miracle that the rest of my family wasn't lynched..." The last sentence spilled out of her mouth before she could stop it. Ally blushed as her resolve finally broke.

Maddy thankfully stepped in to save the day. "Everything for the Corbants went quiet after that. Not since the asylum has there been any kind of psycho bullshit from her family, but still, people treat her like she's a scalpel-waving lunatic with a thirst for piss and blood, not necessarily in that order."

Ally couldn't help but flush at Maddy's bluntness, but every word was true. She waited for Derek's reaction, but not long. "So, they hold all of that against the entire family still?" he asked. Ally nodded, not sure what to say. Then her heart leapt at Derek's assessment. "Their loss. I haven't seen you waving any scalpels or sipping from cups of mysterious red or yellow liquid."

Maddy smiled triumphantly, but Ally shrugged. "I guess they think the apple never falls far from the tree."

Derek looked her fully in the eyes and said, "I know one apple that couldn't have fallen farther from that tree." Ally grinned wider than she ever had, her heart feeling like it might explode. He then added, "You should smile more."

"Why?" she asked, still grinning despite herself.

Derek shrugged before getting up to dispose of his tray. "I guess I just like seeing you happy."

As he walked away, Maddy smacked the table and pointed at Ally. "Bitch, I told you so!"

Ally couldn't stop grinning, even though she couldn't believe what had just happened. "I...I don't know what to say..."

Bart observed, "He l-l-likes you."

Ally didn't know how red she could turn until that moment, but Maddy filled in for her, "And she likes him! Girl, you've hit the jackpot!"

Ally shrugged, still blushing, then looked at Bart. He looked up at her and smiled meekly. "He s-s-seems like a r-r-really nice guy."

"You are, too!" Maddy interjected, and Bart immediately flushed as red as Ally felt. As Maddy watched Derek come back, she grinned in a way that Ally had seen a hundred times before. However, this time was different. The smile was subtle, but Maddy's green eyes were alight with a sparkle that Ally somehow understood. Maddy looked at each of the three of them. "Us four...we don't need anybody else. We're the freaks of Corbanton High, and all we need is each other. Nobody else matters. Friends 'til the end, right?"

Bart smiled and nodded. "'Til the e-e-end."

Derek sat down and nodded as well. "You guys are cool. I'm in."

Maddy looked at Ally. "Friends 'til the end?"

Ally looked at all three of them, their eyes on her. Finally, she nodded, repeating the phrase. Maddy had never looked happier.

Ally got home that day feeling more lighthearted than she ever had after school. The usual taunts and jeers had followed her through the hallways, but she was suddenly oblivious to them. With Maddy's triumph and Derek's continued interest in her, Ally was on top of the world. There was a spring in her step as she made her way up the driveway. Even as she crested the hill and the mansion loomed into view, she couldn't stop herself from smiling.

As Ally entered the foyer, she found Carol the maid dusting the angel. "Hi, Carol!" Ally called cheerfully.

Carol blinked in surprise, her brown eyes puzzled, but she smiled in return. "Welcome home, Ally. How was your day?"

Ally grinned. "Never better."

"Glad to hear it, dear," Carol observed, nodding her head before brushing a strand of red, curly hair from her face and returning to her dusting. Ally climbed the stairs and skipped past her, ignoring Carol's puzzled glance. However, when Ally got up to her bedroom door, she heard her little sister Cassie talking from her own room next door. Cassie was usually napping when Ally got home. Puzzled, Ally walked up to her sister's door and listened.

"No, I don't know that game," Cassie said as if carrying on a conversation. A few seconds later, she added, "Oh, Ally's outside?"

Ally froze. *How did she know I was here?* Before she could move, Cassie opened the door and looked up at her, smiling brightly. She waved excitedly at her and squeaked, "Hi, Ally!"

"Hey, Cassie," Ally replied nervously. "What are you up to?"

"Talking to Sam. Wanna come meet him?" Cassie tittered.

It wasn't uncommon for children Cassie's age to have an imaginary friend, so why did Ally find this sudden development so disturbing? She decided to play along, however. "Sure!"

Cassie then grabbed Ally's hand and pulled her into the room. "Sam meet...oh wait, he's gone." Cassie looked around wildly, then frowned as she pointed to a chair that had been turned away from the matching desk to face Cassie's bed. "He was there a minute ago."

Ally shrugged despite the rising hairs on the back of her neck. "Maybe he's shy." Cassie looked crestfallen, and Ally felt horrible immediately. "I'm sorry, Cass. Want me to go look for him? He can't have gone far."

Cassie shook her head. "No, when he wants to, he'll come see you."

Ally furrowed her brow. "What makes you say that?"

Cassie hopped up onto the bed and kicked her legs back and forth as she looked up at the ceiling. "He told me."

"Oh. All right then." Ally didn't know what else to say. *Creepy.*

"Ally..." Cassie began shyly.

"What's up?"

"Don't make Sam angry. He seems nice but unhappy. You should never make unhappy people angry."

Ally's skin crawled. She tried to hide her trepidation as she replied, "I won't, Cass. Promise."

Cassie grinned brightly, hopped off the bed, and threw her arms around Ally's legs. "You're the best sister ever."

Ally rested her hands on her little sister's back and stared out the window, considering the irony of the situation. When she had come home, she was overjoyed about forming her own group of friends at school. Now she was slightly terrified by the idea of her little sister making a new friend of her own, imaginary...or otherwise.

3. A Matter of Faith

"So, what's on the topic list for today?" Maddy asked as she sat down with her tray at the lunch table.

Derek scratched his chin. "Here's one for you. What do you guys believe in?"

"H-h-how do you m-m-mean?" Bart asked with a frown.

Derek shrugged. "Religion. Life after death. That sort of thing."

Ally thought about her answer. She had never outright believed in the supernatural until recently, but it was probably best not to mention the creepy happenings at home. Still, she did have an answer for at least part of his question. "Well, my parents raised me as a Christian. They're not super strict about it or anything, though."

"Do you still follow the Bible, though?" Derek asked as he looked at her.

Even though he had been sitting next to her for almost a week now, Ally still had to fight a blush every time those warm eyes turned her way. "I mean...I guess so. I believe in God but...I'm probably not as dedicated as I should be."

Derek frowned. "What makes you say that?"

"Well, I don't go to church or anything..."

Maddy interjected, "They're prolly just as uppity towards your family as the other shitheads in town."

Ally shrugged. "I wish I could say you were wrong."

Derek heaved a sigh. "So, even in church, they can't let your family's history go?"

"Actually, they're really nice...in church. When we see any of them on the streets, it's a different matter. I guess Dad got fed up with the hypocrisy."

Maddy speared a chicken tender with her fork. "Fuck 'em, I say."

Derek then turned to face her. "I take it you're not a Christian then?"

Maddy took a bite and swallowed before answering. "Not for a long time now. If there is or ever was a god, he stopped giving a shit centuries ago."

"So then what do you believe in?"

Maddy threw her hands behind her head and leaned back in her chair. "What I see and what I hear. I've looked into loads of other religions. Hinduism, Paganism, Satanism..."

Ally sighed with a rueful smile. "That was just one of your suspensions, though."

Maddy shrugged. "I dabbled a bit, but anything real is hard to come by. I guess that makes me an atheist at this point."

"Not much for the concept of faith, are you?"

"Like I said, I believe in what I see and what I hear. From everything I've seen, there's not much evidence of anything divine about this world or the next."

"Still, that's what faith is: believing in something with or without evidence."

Silence hung in the air for a moment after Derek's words. Then to everyone's surprise, Bart said, "V-v-very wise, D-D-Derek." Silently, Ally agreed.

Maddy frowned. "Why you gotta go and be all profound and shit?"

Derek shrugged. "I like to think about the bigger picture. What about you, Bart?"

"W-w-well, my p-p-parents are a-a-agonistic. They w-w-want me to d-d-decide for m-m-myself e-e-eventually."

Maddy nodded sagely. "Very wise, Bart."

Bart blushed furiously and Ally frowned, but Maddy held up her hands in surrender. "I'm just teasing! Somebody around here's gotta have a sense of humor!"

Derek laughed. "Stop me if you've heard this one. So, a philosopher, an atheist, an agnostic, and a non-denominational Christian are having lunch together. Who's the first to speak, and what do they say?"

Maddy grinned. "It's the atheist, and she asks, 'So, what's on the topic list for today?'" All four of them laughed. "I guess I'm not the only one, then. Thank God!" Then, the bell rang and they hurried off to class.

Later that evening, Ally was lost in thought as she ate dinner with her family. Maddy had always been there for her, but adding Derek and Bart to the mix had suddenly turned school from a survival test into something she actually looked forward to. She loved how they talked every day and how they all made each other feel included. There was no outsider among them, and each was encouraged to contribute by the others. Ally even caught herself smiling as she recalled the laughs they'd shared. At last, she was starting to feel like a normal teenager.

"Ally, I got a question."

Ally blinked as Cassie's words snapped her back to reality. "Yes, Cassie?"

"Do you believe in the devil?"

Ally blinked. "Ummm..." *What do I say? She's only three!*

"There's a God, so there's a devil. There can't be good without evil," their father chimed in. *Thanks, Dad.*

"What made you want to ask a question like that, Cassie?" their mother asked.

Cassie poked her food with her child's fork. "Sam."

A chill ran down Ally's spine, but no one else noticed.

"Why is Sam talking about the devil?" Their mother's brow furrowed with worry. *So, they know about Sam, too.*

"No reason," Cassie replied without looking at anyone.

"Maybe I should ask Sam that myself," their father joked.

"But he only talks to me," Cassie stated with a pouty frown.

"Does he go to the chapel with you on Sundays?" At their mother's question, Ally glanced at the door off the dining room that led to the small but ornate chapel of the house. Ever since the family had withdrawn from the local church, it had served as their new church on Sundays, though Ally no longer had to go if she didn't want to, unlike Cassie.

Cassie shook her head. "No. He knows that that's special time."

"Good on him, then," their father declared.

A few minutes of silence passed as they continued eating. Ally had tensed when Sam had come up, but her tension had begun to slip away again until Cassie asked, "Daddy, what's a scourge?"

Their father coughed, but then his eyes bulged. He tried to cough again but seemed unable. "Honey?" their mother asked as she stood up. Their father waved his hand over his throat as he kept trying to cough with no results. "Hang on, dear!" their mother said as she pulled him off of his chair and gave him the Heimlich maneuver. After only three quick thrusts, a glob of steak flew out of his mouth onto the table.

Their father coughed as he slid back into his chair. "Pretty sure you just saved my life."

Cassie clapped. "Mommy's a hero!" With all the commotion, her question must have been forgotten. However, Ally did not forget.

Later that night, Ally passed Cassie in the hallway on her way to the bathroom. Cassie always stood outside her door to wait for their mother to tuck her in. Recalling the question at dinner, Ally stopped and turned to Cassie. "Hey Cassie, why'd you ask Dad what a scourge is?"

Cassie shrugged. "Sam said his dad used it on him when he was little. Wanted to know what it was."

For the second time that night, a shiver ran down Ally's spine. "Why is Sam telling you these things?"

"Cause he's lonely. He needs a friend. Friends tell each other stuff, don't they?"

"What else has he told you?" *Please be nothing.*

Cassie looked at the floor and shuffled her bare feet under her pink pajamas. "He says his dad believed in God and that's why he used the scourge on him. Why would someone who believes in God do that, Ally?"

Ally wanted to tell Cassie not to worry about such things. *She's only three years old!* Still, if Sam was more than just an imaginary friend, Ally didn't want to risk making him angry. Choosing her words carefully, Ally said, "Just believing in God doesn't make somebody good. They still have to do good things, too."

"Oh. Okay, Ally."

Ally paused for a moment to consider asking if Cassie was afraid of Sam but thought better of it. Talking about Sam creeped her out to no end. Not knowing what else to say, Ally turned to head back down the hallway.

ALLY CAME HOME THE Friday of that week beside herself with excitement. Maddy's dad would be gone for the weekend, so she had invited all three of them over for a sleepover. Ally wasn't sure how Bart or Derek would convince their parents to let them come, but Ally already knew she would be there. Her parents seemed to value her friendship with Maddy almost as much as she did. However, when she came in the front door, she found Cassie sitting on the floor staring up at the angel on the balcony. "Cassie, what are you doing?" Ally asked, perplexed.

Cassie replied innocently, "Wondering why Sam don't like the angel."

Ally's eyes widened. This situation with Sam was becoming increasingly alarming. "Do you not like the angel?"

Cassie shrugged. "I think it's pretty. Daddy says it keeps us safe from bad people."

Ally sat down beside her cross-legged. "Do you believe him?"

Cassie didn't answer at first. She stared intently at the angel, then replied, "Mostly."

Ally examined her sister. Cassie's questioning eyes and solemn expression betrayed an internal struggle that shouldn't have been taking place in a three-year-old's mind. Ally asked, "Why mostly?"

Cassie shrugged again. "Sam says there are bad people here. I don't think he'd lie."

Ally shivered, hoping that Cassie wouldn't notice. "Where are these bad people?"

Cassie looked around the room, then whispered, "In the walls."

If there was any color in Ally's face, it had certainly drained at those words. She recalled the disembodied voice that had come into her room last week. The soft, weak whisper echoed through her head: *the walls remember.* It was an odd coincidence...or at least she hoped. Once again, Ally wondered if her house was haunted.

Cassie's words interrupted Ally's internal debate. "Ally...you'll keep me safe from the bad people, right?" There was genuine fear in Cassie's brilliant blue eyes.

Ally threw her arms around her little sister and whispered, "No bad people are ever gonna hurt you."

Cassie hugged her back, nuzzling her head into Ally's chest. "Thank you, Ally."

As Ally pulled away, she said, "I'm not gonna be staying here tonight, though. Will you be all right?"

"Mommy and Daddy will be here, right?"

"Right."

Cassie grinned brightly. "Okay, then I'll be fine!" She got up and went up the stairs to her room. Ally was not far behind, though she didn't go to her own room. Instead, she knocked on the door opposite of Cassie's room. Her father's voice answered from within with a gruff, "Yes?"

"It's me, Dad. Can I talk to you for a sec?" Ally asked.

"Come on in," was her father's response.

Ally let herself into her dad's office. It was pristine, with a desk and two bookshelves opposite the door Ally walked through. Hanging on the wall to the left were several charts and graphs tracking stock prices, profits, and estimations of buying and selling trends. Though her father loved his work for the college, he was moderately obsessed with the trade. He was seated behind his desk, typing on a computer that took up half the desk, when she came in.

"Hey, Dad," she said, making sure he was paying attention.

Without breaking stride in his typing, he replied, "Hey, Ally. What's on your mind?" Ally tried to read his expression, but the reflection of the computer screen on his glasses hid his eyes from view. Throwing caution to the wind, she said, "Maddy's invited me to a sleepover at her place tonight."

Her dad stopped typing and glanced up at her. "How will you be getting there?"

"Maddy's dad is gonna pick me up," Ally lied as she had several times before.

"What about getting home?"

"I'll be back around noon tomorrow the same way."

"Will there be any boys there?" he asked with a raised eyebrow.

Ally had prepared herself for the question but couldn't stop her stomach from clenching when it was asked. Hoping that her nerves didn't show, she lied again. "Nope."

Her father scrutinized her for a moment, as if looking for a sign that she was lying. Ally was used to it and did her best to hide her nerves. After nearly a minute, he looked back down at his computer and resumed typing. "I don't see why not."

Ally suppressed a sigh of relief. "Thanks, Dad!"

"Have fun, and call when you get there."

"I will, Dad. Promise." After she left the office, she couldn't help but punch the air in excitement. That night was going to be one of the best nights of her life.

Shortly after, Ally left the house with a backpack stuffed with overnight things. As she left the front door, she found Matt the gardener trimming the hedge bushes around the front porch with a pair of shears. He paused and waved as sweat glistened at his brown hairline. "Off to Maddy's, I assume?"

Ally rolled her eyes but grinned all the same. "Duh?"

"Tell her I said hi, all right?"

"Sure thing," Ally said with a giggle. Perhaps she needed to warn Maddy about Matt before the next time she came over? He wasn't much older than them, but she was certain that Matt wasn't Maddy's type.

As he went back to his work and started to whistle, Ally set off down the driveway. The mansion was just outside of town, and Maddy lived near downtown, but Ally didn't mind the long walk. Besides, it would be easier to not have to explain to either of her parents why there was no car in Maddy's driveway. It was far from the first time Ally had made the walk, and she enjoyed the quiet solitude it offered. The streets of town were empty, as most students were still in afterschool activities, and most adults were still at work.

Soon enough, Ally was at Maddy's door. Her house was tiny compared to the mansion. It was a single story with dingy, white aluminum siding. Unsurprisingly, Maddy didn't leave Ally waiting at the front door for long. Before she even knocked, Maddy opened the door, grinning broadly, and ushered her in. "Welcome home, girl!"

Ally giggled. "Well, home for tonight, anyways." She could no longer contain her excitement. Maddy's house was small, but that was part of its charm. "Before we get too crazy, though..." Ally began.

Suddenly, there was a phone flying at her from across the living room. Ally yelped and fumbled it before finally getting ahold of it and dialing her home number. Maddy giggled. "Come on, girl. We've been through this a thousand times. Like I don't know the drill."

Ally stuck her tongue out at Maddy as the phone began to ring. Soon, Carol's voice answered, "Corbant residence."

"Hi, Carol. Let Dad know I'm at Maddy's now, please?"

"Oh, of course, Ally! Anything else?"

"Nope, that's it. Bye."

"Have fun!"

You have no idea. Ally hung up and tossed the phone back to Maddy. She then sat down on the loveseat opposite the TV, exaggerating a prim and proper air as she crossed her legs. "So, when are the other guests arriving?"

Maddy hung the phone up in the kitchen and came back laughing. "Bart said around six-ish, and Derek about seven."

"So just us for a couple hours?"

"Yep, just like old times!" Maddy answered with a grin.

Ally giggled and spread out on the loveseat, letting her feet hang over the side. Maddy sat down in a recliner in the corner next to the loveseat. After a minute or so of silence, she said, "So, when he goes to kiss you..." Ally groaned, and Maddy giggled. "You know he will!"

Ally sighed and twirled a strand of her hair around her finger. "I dunno if I want him to or not..."

"Why wouldn't you?"

"Well...I guess..." Ally had never been good at expressing her feelings without embarrassment. She thought over carefully how to phrase her response, then said, "I guess I just...don't want us rushing into anything, you know?" Her response hadn't been as firm as she had hoped it would sound.

Maddy laughed. "Come on, girl, live a little! Hell, I'll leave you both alone in my room all night if you ask nicely!"

Ally sat upright and turned to look at her, her mouth hanging open in mock offense even as she blushed furiously. "You wouldn't!"

Maddy winked mischievously. "Don't tell me you haven't thought about it."

Ally laid back down without answering. In truth, she hadn't thought about it. She had been so caught up in her own euphoria at having Derek's attention at all that she hadn't even considered what it would be like to be intimate with him.

Maddy gasped in disbelief. "Seriously?"

"What?"

"You seriously haven't thought about kissing him or anything like that?"

Ally's cheeks burned. "Well...no. Yes. Maybe? I don't know." Maddy took a deep breath, no doubt preparing another motivational speech, but Ally added quickly, "I've just been...I dunno...enjoying the fact that he hasn't turned asshole on me."

"I don't think he'll be turning asshole on you anytime soon."

"What makes you say that?" Ally asked, both nervous and eager.

"He barely takes his eyes off you, girl. I watch. I know," Maddy said conspiratorially, pointing to her temple and nodding.

Ally rolled her eyes. "So what do we do till they get here?"

Maddy shrugged. "Watch TV? Dance party? Naked pillow fight?"

Ally blinked and shook her head. "Keep your fantasies to yourself."

"Seemed like a fun idea."

"Ever done it?"

"Have we ever done it?"

"No."

Maddy threw her hands up. "There ya go! If I haven't done it with you, I haven't done it."

Ally thought about what Maddy had just said, frowning. Nervously, she asked, "Do you...do you think people wouldn't be so cruel to you if you didn't hang out with me?"

"I dunno, maybe."

"Don't you care?"

Maddy scoffed. "Hell no. I've got you, girl, plus Derek and Bart now. Who else do I need really? Not a bunch of fake bitches and stuck-up assholes."

Ally sighed, smiling. "What would I do without you?"

"Die of boredom, most likely," Maddy said with a shrug as she twirled a strand of her hair.

Ally nodded, and the pair of them started laughing for no obvious reason. Perhaps it was the easiness between them or the excitement for the night yet to come. For whatever reason, they laughed well and long before they finally resumed their banter. Within an hour, there was a knock at the door. Maddy got up to answer while Ally resumed her position on the loveseat.

"Hi M-M-Maddy," came Bart's voice from the front door.

"Hey Bart, come in!" Maddy said excitedly.

"I b-b-brought some chips and s-s-soda," he said as he came in with a case of pop in one hand and a bag of nacho cheese chips in the other.

Maddy grinned. "Why hadn't I invited you over sooner? Just put them in the kitchen, this way!" Bart had brought both Maddy's favorite pop and chips. *Interesting.* Perhaps Ally wasn't the only one staying with her crush tonight.

When Maddy and Bart came back from the kitchen, Maddy offered him the recliner, which he took with his usual politeness. Then Maddy flopped herself down beside Ally, and the two of them started giggling wildly. Ally said, "I think there's only room for one laying down here."

Maddy winked again. "We'll put that to the test tonight."

Ally blushed and then pushed Maddy onto the floor. "Nope!"

Maddy hit the floor with a thud and then rolled back and forth for a while, laughing. It was infectious. Soon Ally and even Bart were laughing with her. The night was off to a great start. Hopefully it would only get better.

Another hour of banter passed, and then Derek arrived. Thanks to the lightheartedness of the time leading up to his arrival, Ally was perfectly at ease when he came in with his own case of soda and bag of chips. Once he arrived, Maddy made a pair of frozen pizzas for them all. Then they ended up back in the living room, Maddy cross-legged on the floor with her back to the TV, Bart in the recliner, and Derek and Ally sitting on the loveseat. Conversation flowed as usual, but as time passed, Ally caught herself sliding closer to Derek unconsciously as she talked. By the time she realized she had been doing it, there was less than an inch of space between them. She blushed and fell silent, but Maddy saved the day by taking total control of the conversation.

Then, much to Ally's surprise, Derek slid his arm around her shoulders. She let out a gentle sigh and let herself slide that last inch towards him, fully giving herself over to his embrace. It felt calming and protective, like a warm, thick cloak draped about her shoulders. She didn't rejoin in the conversation, but instead let herself just enjoy being close to him like this. It was a feeling she had never felt before and would not soon forget.

Eventually, the conversation came around to villains in books they had read. On this subject, Bart was particularly vocal. It surprised no one that since he didn't have many friends besides them, he spent a lot of time reading.

He said, "I th-th-think the b-b-best villains are the ones th-th-that aren't c-c-completely bad."

Maddy looked at him curiously. "How so?"

"Well, w-w-when their m-m-motivations make s-s-sense from their p-p-point of view, you k-k-kinda feel s-s-sorry for them."

Derek nodded in agreement. "They're a lot more realistic that way, too. Depending on how they became the way they are, you can see how a person might develop their world view."

Maddy shrugged. "Personally, I prefer a bad guy with no redeeming qualities whatsoever. They're easier to hate that way."

Bart thought a moment before replying, "Th-th-that's true, b-b-but I still th-th-think that a s-s-sympathetic villain is m-m-more realistic."

Derek chimed in again. "I agree. Most people who do bad things in the real world aren't one hundred percent bad themselves, are they?"

Bart then added, "L-l-like Ally's family."

There was a stunned silence in the room following Bart's words. Maddy's eyes were wide with shock and Derek tensed a little. Though the comment did stir up a lot of bad memories of accusations and jeers that had been tossed Ally's way over the years, Derek's presence beside her seemed to ease the pain they brought with them. Quietly, she asked him, "Do you really think my family wasn't all bad?"

Bart looked at her fully when he replied, "Y-y-yes, I do."

Ally felt a surge of affection for him. In that moment, she was very glad that she had invited him to sit with them at lunch that first time.

Derek relaxed and added, "You know, it's possible that some of the stories about your family's history are exaggerated."

Ally admitted, "I mean...the thought had never occurred to me. I know the asylum story is one hundred percent true, but some of the others..."

Maddy finally spoke up, "To be honest, a lot of them just seem too ridiculous to be true. Maybe he's right, Ally."

Ally's heart felt like it might explode. Why had she never considered that before? She had always believed everything that everyone said about her family, never really questioning it for herself. The one or two times she had asked her parents about the rumors they had avoided the subject, which was pretty damning in its own right. Still, maybe in her blind acceptance, she had al-

lowed the stories to make her hate her family unfairly. "Maybe you guys are."
She could not put her joy into words. Maybe, just maybe, her family history
wasn't as bad as everyone said. Maybe.

Maddy added, "Well, let's look at what we know. The asylum business
was pretty fucked up, but that was fifty years ago. Your dad wasn't even born
yet, was he?"

Ally shook her head. "Nope. He was born in '48. Still...the asylum closed
the year before."

Maddy threw her hands up. "That just proves my point! He was born
just around the same time it was going on, and he turned out all right all the
same, didn't he?"

Ally nodded. "More or less. He does have a small obsession with the
stock market, but...well, he seems to know how to work it, doesn't he?"

"What does your dad do anyways?" Derek asked, looking at her fully for
the first time since he'd slid his arm around her.

Ally couldn't look back at him. Their faces were too close. She replied,
"He's an econ professor at a local college. He trades stocks on the side."

Derek nodded, impressed. "I suppose he would know how to work the
market then."

Maddy snorted. "Understatement! Ally's house has servants and everything!"

Bart and Derek both looked at her, and Ally blushed again. She hadn't
talked about her life at home with them. "I mean...it's just the maid, the gardener, and the cook, and...well...they're more like family friends...that Dad
pays...and stuff..."

Derek, Bart, and Maddy all laughed at that. Ally was stunned. Her family's fortune was usually more ammunition for the bullies. No few times had
she been accused of thinking she was better than everyone else because of her
family's money, but neither Derek nor Bart seemed to care. It made her feel
even more at ease with them. Then Derek said, "I'd like to see your house
sometime."

Ally managed to keep from blushing when she replied, "You probably
will." She finally decided to look at him then. His expression was soft and
easy. For a moment her eyes traced his lips, wondering what it would be like.
Her breathing accelerated slightly as her eyes shifted back up to his. He was

smiling that adorable half-smile at her, and for a moment the desire almost overcame her. Instead, she lowered her head and laid it on his chest. Though she wasn't looking at Maddy, she knew that her best friend was grinning triumphantly. In fact, Ally couldn't help but smile herself.

The night passed with the four of them sitting around talking about whatever came to mind. It wasn't until 1 a.m. that exhaustion finally caught up to them. Maddy had an extra mattress stuffed into her closet that she pulled out for Bart, so the pair of them stayed in Maddy's room, leaving Derek and Ally alone in the living room. Ally had an inkling that Maddy had purposefully ensured that the two of them would be alone for the night. As Maddy bade them goodnight, Ally watched her with narrowed eyes. As if to confirm her suspicions, Maddy gave her a fluttery wave before closing the door.

The pair of them sat on the loveseat in silence for a while. Then Derek asked, "Did you have fun tonight?"

Ally heaved a gentle sigh. "Yes, I really did."

Derek's hand reached up and stroked her cheek softly. "I'm glad." Ally shuddered a little at his touch. It was an odd sensation to be conjured by such a simple gesture, but the gentleness of it said what words could not. In that simple stroke of her cheek was an affection that she had craved for a long time. Rumors of her family's villainy had dogged her for so long that she had thought she would never know it until now.

As the thought crossed Ally's mind, Bart's words from earlier replayed in her head. She said, "It was especially nice to finally be able to believe that my family wasn't always as horrible as I've always thought."

"You thought they were all bad?"

Ally nodded slowly. "Everything everyone says to me...the stories they tell...it's as if every single member of my family has gone off the deep end at one point or another."

"But now you know better."

"Not quite," Ally admitted, "but I believe it now."

"What's the difference?"

Ally didn't respond right away. She mulled the thought over for a minute or two, then recalled what Derek had said earlier that week during their conversation about faith. *That's what faith is: believing in something with or with-*

out evidence. The truth of those words was something she had felt at the time but didn't fully understand until now. It was far simpler than the idea of who or what had created the universe or what happened after death. It was simply the belief that despite every terrifying claim that was flung at her, that there was some good in her family history. If Ally had faith in nothing else, she had faith in that.

She finally replied, "Faith."

They looked at each other then. Ally gazed into Derek's warm brown eyes. She could lose herself in his eyes with no shame or regret. She let herself smile a little. *So, this is what it's like to be in love.* Her heart fluttered, but she didn't mind. Again, his thumb stroked her cheek gently, and she placed her hand over his as she closed her eyes to savor the feeling. When she opened them again, he was looking at her with a hint of hesitation. "What?" she whispered softly.

His eyes darted to her lips, then back to hers, "Would you mind if I...?"

Ally's stomach did a backflip, but she nodded slowly. She wasn't sure she had ever wanted anything so badly in her life. He hesitated, taking a deep breath as he leaned closer to her. Ally's heart accelerated, pounding in her ears as she closed her eyes once again. Then his lips touched hers. It was soft and gentle, but Ally felt like her heart would explode. She kissed him back, letting her hand slide around the back of his neck. How long the kiss lasted, Ally couldn't tell. It could have been a few seconds, maybe several minutes, or perhaps several blissful hours. Either way, when they finally broke apart, she was breathless.

Derek blinked, his breathing rapid. "Wow."

"Yeah..." Ally gasped as her heart thumped in triple time.

"Not too much...?" he asked nervously.

Ally took a moment to steady her breathing before answering, "No." It had been everything she had imagined her first kiss would be and so much more. The feeling had been so spectacular that she couldn't help herself. She pulled him back to her and kissed him again, savoring every second. Her lips parted slightly as she breathed him in, losing herself to the moment. Desire surged through her, setting her every nerve alight. Still, just a kiss was enough for now. *Slow down,* she thought to herself, even as she leaned into him further.

When they broke apart again, she laid her head on his chest and closed her eyes. To her surprise, his heart was racing just as much as her own. He ran his hand through her hair gently. With a breathless chuckle he said, "I guess you liked it."

"I loved it," she whispered, smiling to herself. The night had gone far beyond anything she had ever hoped for. She nuzzled his chest, sighing contentedly, and both of them were fast asleep within minutes.

4. Need to Know

When Ally got home the next day, the first thing she did was dig out a marker board from her closet. It had been a gift for Christmas a few years prior, but she had never found a use for it until now. She propped it up on her vanity table, covering the mirror completely. Then she dug through one of the vanity drawers for the unopened package of markers that went with it. She ripped open the package and laid the red, green, blue, and black markers out in front of the board. She then picked up each color and created a key at the upper-right corner of the board. Black was for known facts, red for townsfolk speculation, blue for more plausible stories, and green for her own theories. Satisfied, she then picked up the black marker and looked at the board. Ally took a deep breath. *Time to get to work.*

There came a knock on her door. "Ally?" her mother's voice called.

Ally froze. "Yeah, Mom?"

"Just wanted to ask how the sleepover was!"

Ally let out a slow breath of relief before replying, "It was great, Mom!"

"Are you busy?"

Uh-oh. How should she answer? What would her mother think of her sudden interest in the family's history? Then, Cassie's voice interrupted her thoughts from out in the hallway. "Come on, Mommy! It's almost teatime!"

"Oh right, Cassie!" their mother replied, followed by the clunk of Cassie's door closing. *I love you so much, Cassie.*

After a moment to recollect her thoughts, Ally began writing with the year the asylum was shut down: 1947. She then summarized and abbreviated everything she knew from that date onward to fit on the marker board. Her grandfather Wayne Corbant was the son of Aros's brother Phillip, a veteran of World War II, and had lost a leg to a grenade. Oddly, she had no idea how or why he had died, only that it had been before she was born. As she wrote, she felt a pang of sadness. What kind of stories might she had heard if he had lived a little longer?

Brushing the thought away, Ally then listed the children Wayne Corbant had had. Her father had been the eldest of three children, with the twins Crysania and Christopher born just two years later. Though her father didn't like to mention the twins, Ally's mother had told her how Chris had died in an accident, and Crysania had died while playing in the stable when it caught fire. The ashen ruins still stood at the far western edge of their property. Her father had made no attempt to rebuild over them or even acknowledge that they were still there. Ally didn't really blame him.

Then, Ally noted the year of Wayne and Chris's deaths in 1958. She frowned. Crysania had died in 1959, the year after Wayne and Chris. No wonder her father was so quiet about the family's past. He had only been ten or eleven years old when he'd lost his father and both younger siblings. *Poor Dad.* She hesitated for a moment, wondering at how much more tragedy and heartbreak she might find in her family's history. Was she ready for it? Could she even be ready for it?

Ally sighed and brushed the thought aside. She needed to know the truth about her family. The real story was undoubtedly twisted and contorted by the combination of years and hearsay. It was her responsibility to separate the fact from the fantasy and maybe find some faith in the blood that ran through her veins. Her determination renewed, she capped and put down the black marker and picked up the blue marker.

Ally then summarized the stories about what had happened to Aros's wife Arabella and daughter Constance. Arabella died not long after the asylum closed. Many suspected it was suicide, so Ally wrote "suicide" in blue. As for the fate of Constance, she switched to the red marker. With the stories of the horrors that had been committed at the asylum, some said that Constance had been used in some kind of sick experiment. Others claimed that Constance had died at the same time as Arabella. A third story theorized that Constance had run away from home out of shame over her father's crimes.

Ally paused again, capping the red marker and frowning at the board. If Constance ran away, did that mean that she had relatives out there somewhere? Ally reached for the green marker but changed her mind. *Not important.*

Instead, Ally once again picked up the blue marker and wrote down keywords for the various stories about atrocities her family had committed, marking out a square exclusively for those connected to the asylum. Outside the square, she wrote about a black widow who killed her husbands less than a month into the marriage and claimed their fortunes to add to the Corbants' wealth. She also wrote about a butcher who kidnapped males—ranging in age from teenagers to middle-aged men—then tortured and molested them in hidden rooms all over the house. That story in particular made her skin crawl, but she pressed on with her work. With any luck, that particularly gruesome story would end up being grossly exaggerated or, better yet, an outright lie.

Ally continued writing the various tales of her family's misdeeds: a brother and sister who slept together out of some sense of family purity, an old man who strangled a little boy for no reason other than looking at him, an adulterer who left one of his pregnant mistresses homeless, and numerous lost minds and suicides. She poured all the information she had heard onto the board, filling almost an entire half with the stories the townsfolk and students had told over the years. Only then did she realize that she had heard no stories about what had really happened in the asylum. For that, she needed the red marker.

Students frequently accused Aros Corbant of extremely twisted experiments. Still, Ally doubted if any such obvious horrors could have been committed without arousing suspicion from the townsfolk. She racked her brain for some time trying to remember detailed stories about what went on there, but all she could think about were the jeers and taunts, none of which had any real evidence or shred of fact to solidify them.

She then looked at the clock. It was almost 6 p.m. *Any second...* As though responding to her thoughts, her mother's voice called from the foyer, "Dinner!" Ally made sure all of her markers were capped and headed down. The rest would have to wait until later.

THOUGH ALLY SPENT THE rest of the evening going over every detail she had ever heard about her family, she had little to add after dinner. Cassie had been particularly chatty all through the meal, leaving Ally little chance to think. Once she was back in her room and staring at the board, however, she found there wasn't much left to think about. She spent the remaining hours of the night making sure she had covered everything she could think of before she was satisfied.

Ally went to the bathroom to brush her teeth, all the while thinking over all the information she had written on her board. *It all really begins at the asylum.* That was where she needed to start. She had avoided looking into it all her life out of fear. Now, however, her fear was tempered by a determination that had never been there before. Her thoughts carried her through the bathroom door, directly across from her parents' bedroom near the end of the second-floor hallway. Much like the rest of the house, the bathroom did little to assuage Ally's anxiety, with its purple wallpaper, black tile floor, black cabinets, and clawfoot tub. Undaunted, Ally looked at herself in the bathroom mirror as she brushed her teeth. *No matter what I might find, I have to at least look.* Then she froze.

For a moment, Ally swore she saw someone standing in the bathroom doorway through the mirror. She hadn't gotten a good look, but there had been a vague figure dressed in black with a pale face. She whirled around, but there was only the empty hallway. A chill ran down her spine.

"THE WEEKEND TOO ROUGH for ya?" Maddy remarked playfully.

Ally yawned. "Just had a lot to think about last night."

Maddy whispered conspiratorially, "Like how those lips of his taste?"

Ally's eyes went wide and she blushed furiously. "N-no..."

Maddy giggled. "You still gotta tell me what happened after we left you two alone! Come on, I *need* details, girl!"

Ally brushed her hair in front of her face to hide her blush as she dug through her locker, taking much longer than necessary to find her first hour book. By the time she finally closed the locker door, she had regained her composure enough to answer, "Actually, I was thinking of all the research I gotta do."

Maddy frowned. "Research? Into what? Lap dances?"

Ally surprised herself by laughing. "No! Just...about my family. What you all said that night...it made me want to find out for myself."

Maddy furrowed her brow in concern. "Ally...you shouldn't feel obligated to try and prove your family's innocence to us. It's really not that big of a deal..."

"It is to me. All my life everyone has told me what horrible people we are just because of our last name. I'd like to prove them wrong if I can."

Maddy looked at Ally in stunned silence for a moment, then flashed her a sly grin. "Sounds like my girl is growin' up!"

Ally giggled, still blushing. "Maybe I am."

Ally spent that morning waiting for study hall. When it finally came, she asked to go to the library as usual. Normally she did it to get away from the secretive whispers and dark looks, but that day she had something else in mind. Once she was in the library, instead of going to her usual secluded seat in the corner, she went up to the librarian sitting behind the counter. "Excuse me?" she asked.

The librarian, a small woman with short curly hair, round and wrinkly cheeks, and astoundingly thin lips looked up at Ally and her normally warm smile shriveled away. "Can I help you?"

So that's how it's gonna be? Holding her ground, Ally asked, "Does the school keep copies of old town newspapers?"

The librarian raised an eyebrow. "This is not some sort of historical archive, Miss Corbant. The materials in this library are strictly educational."

Ally bit her lip. "Well, I was...I mean...I was hoping to learn more about the town's history."

The librarian's nose wrinkled with disgust. "There's only one newspaper kept here, and it is strictly for research purposes."

"Well, that's why—"

"For what class?" the librarian snapped.

Ally blinked in shock. "Well...I...more because...well, it's not for a class."

The librarian stared at her with narrowed eyes before heaving a sigh and looking down at her desk. "If it were anyone else, I'd say no. Since it's obviously personal for you, I'll allow it this time. The pages are kept in a binder on the shelf in the far corner. They are delicate, so don't take them out of their protectors."

"Th-thanks," Ally mumbled as she hurried off to the corner. *Just let it go. There's work to do.*

The black binder was unmarked, sitting on top of a short bookshelf filled with texts on state history. Taking a deep breath, Ally opened the binder to the first laminated page of a copy of the *Corbanton Herald* from 1947. Ally's hand trembled. *Of course, the only newspaper they have is when* that *happened.* She read the terrifying headline:

Horror at Corbant Asylum

Corbant Asylum has been a staple of Corbanton since 1857. Founded by Leonardo Corbant, who broke ground on the project in the spring of 1856, Corbant Asylum was believed to use state-of-the-art science and medicine to treat both the physically and mentally ill in the most humanitarian and hospitable manner possible...or so we thought. For the first time in the asylum's history, a riot broke out in the maximum security ward at the beginning of this month. As can be expected, the asylum immediately went into lockdown to ensure that the more dangerous inmates presented no threat to the public. Unfortunately, with almost all on-site staff left dead or otherwise incapacitated by the riot's conclusion, the mechanism was not reversed until a mere week ago. What was discovered once the switch was thrown shook the entire town.

Aros Corbant, son of Augustus and Lillian Corbant, had long presented a face of kindness and trust to the community, but from what the handful of survivors of the asylum riot can attest, the truth was well-hidden behind a friendly demeanor. Of nearly 1200 inmates and staff, only six survived long enough for extraction. The stories they told spoke of a head doctor who oversaw horrific experiments with little to no explanation or logic. One former patient spoke of... (cont'd Page 4)

Ally hesitated. Obviously, the article had cut off to avoid going into gory details on the front page. Until then, all of the supposed horrors of the asylum had been left to her imagination. The moment she went to page four, all of that blissful ignorance would be dispelled. After steeling her courage, she finally turned the page with a trembling hand and continued reading.

...witnessing a man being vivisected without the use of anesthesia and his internal organs being removed one by one. Another spoke of a restrained patient being force-fed pieces of his own flesh. These and other atrocities too horrible to mention took place on Aros's watch. It was poetic justice that Aros's staff met their end by being subjected to a handful of the "treatments" they had employed. The community is still reeling from the horror that took place right in our own back-

yard, but none are more stunned than Aros's wife Arabella and daughter Con-
stance, who have professed complete ignorance to Aros's misdeeds.

Arabella stated, "He had taken to spending the night at the asylum. I should
have known something was wrong then. I just could never have imagined him
capable of something like this. He had always been a gentle man. When I visited,
they always seemed happy under his care, but everything changed when he was
forced to renovate due to the overcrowding from the War. He became more irri-
table, but I never would have imagined anything like this. I feel like I don't even
know who I was married to." His daughter Constance, 26, refused comment.

As the matter is under further investigation by local authorities, there is lit-
tle doubt that yet greater atrocities will be uncovered. The chief of police would
like to warn the public from pursuing information on the matter for themselves,
as such investigations are most assuredly not for the faint of heart.

Ally was baffled. She wanted to believe that Arabella's account of Aros's
character was genuine but based on the patients' statements concerning the
antics of the staff, she just couldn't. What kind of "gentle man" would oversee
the dissection of a still-living being, or even consider making someone canni-
balize himself? Even more disturbing was the news that he had taken to staying at the asylum overnight. Was he so obsessed with the misery and pain he
was inflicting that he couldn't be away from it for even a minute?

Still, despite Ally's revulsion at Aros's incrimination, something seemed
off. She could not look past the line when Arabella referred to the over-
crowding and renovations. Did the strain of having to care for more patients
than he could house get to him and cause him to crack? Ally shook her head.
Even that couldn't have been enough to turn a kind-hearted doctor into a
murderous madman. The two could not coexist in a single being, could they?

Ally sighed in frustration. Instead of finding answers, she had only found
more questions. With nowhere else to go, she turned to the obituary page
and read:

Aros Michael Corbant, M. D.

Director at Corbant Sanitarium, Aros, aged forty-eight, died in a riot. Body
never found. He is survived by his wife Arabella Jean Corbant, daughter Con-
stance Rain Corbant, and nephew Wayne Edward Corbant. Aros was preced-
ed in death by his brother Phillip Angus Corbant, sister-in-law Gwendolyn

Stephanie Corbant, father Augustus Darian Corbant, and mother Lillian Angelique Corbant. Funeral services will not be taking place.

Ally stared at the tiny obituary for a moment. Almost all of the family who had died before Aros she had never even heard of. *What happened to them all?* She closed the binder and buried her face in her hands. She had already exhausted the school library's only resource on the matter, and only gotten more questions in return. Now, she had no idea where else to go. The enormity of her task was overwhelming. *There's no way...*

The ringing of the lunch bell interrupted her multiple rereading's of the lone newspaper. Ally closed the binder gently before leaving the library. Her thoughts on what she had learned carried her to the lunch table. There, she remained silent until finally she decided to let her friends in on her research project. Her findings left all three puzzled, but none more so than Derek. When Ally gave voice to her thoughts on the article, he concurred, "I think you might have something there on Aros."

Maddy's usual playful attitude was nowhere in sight. "I mean, there are always signs, aren't there?"

Ally nodded gravely. "Always. The interview with Arabella made her seem completely oblivious."

Bart stared at his plate, frowning, "A-a-and it all st-t-tarted with the r-r-renovations?"

Ally nodded again in reply.

Derek scratched his chin as he stared at his half-eaten lunch. "It really doesn't make any sense for him to lose it like that out of the blue. I've heard of people snapping under strain, but this seems just too..."

"Over the top?" Maddy offered.

Derek sighed and nodded. "Exactly. Ridiculous, even."

"H-h-how so?" Bart asked.

Derek frowned. "Force feeding someone to themselves? Vivisection? What was the point? What did they hope to gain from it? It honestly seems like pure senselessness."

"Maybe it was," Ally said with a shrug.

They all sat in silence for a while, poring over both facts and speculation. Then, Derek said, "Well, it looks like if you want answers, you're gonna need some help."

Ally looked at him. "What do you mean?"

Maddy caught on. "Yeah! We can dig with you!"

Bart nodded. "F-f-four are b-b-better than one."

Ally looked at each of them in turn. "Guys...you don't have to do this."

"We know," Maddy interjected, "but we want to help. Right?" Derek and Bart both nodded. She then gave Ally an encouraging smile. "Then this is *how* we help. I'll help you dig through the library during my own study hall!"

"I'll hit up the town library. I bet they have more than just one copy of the town newspaper," Derek offered.

Bart nodded. "My m-m-mom is in the l-l-local historical s-s-society."

Maddy stared open-mouthed at Bart momentarily before shrugging back at Ally. "See? She'll probably have loads of connections we can use!"

Ally sighed. *No point arguing.* "All right then. We'll compare notes tomorrow and every day after until we find what we're looking for."

"W-w-what exactly are w-w-we looking f-f-for?"

Ally bit her lip, trying to find the words. Then, Maddy answered for her. "Proof that Ally and her immediate family aren't the only good people named Corbant." Fortunately, the bell rang seconds later. Ally wiped the mist from her eyes as they all stood up and headed off to their next classes.

Ally didn't get another chance to research before school was out for the day. The whole trip home she contemplated all that she knew and all that she had learned, already picturing key words from the article on the whiteboard in her room. Soon enough she was looking the information over in the asylum box, written in black. *Terrifying...but true.* Then, her excitement ebbed. *Now what?* She had done all she could at home, and now she was at a loss. Frustrated, Ally went downstairs to kill time with her sister and mother until bed.

THAT NIGHT, ALLY CAME back to her bedroom wrapped in a towel after a shower. Despite her growing unease about the house and what may or may not be living (in a way) in it with them, she'd whiled away hours with Cassie and her mother before and after dinner. Even her father had joined in for a game of jacks on the coffee table in the parlor, leaving the whole family in good spirits. Ally even wore a smile as she stepped into her room, always loving the transition from cold, wood flooring to soft, fluffy carpet beneath her bare feet.

Suddenly, the door slammed shut behind her. Ally's body seized as though she had touched a live wire, and she dashed for the safety of her bed. How she kept from screaming was beyond her, but the moment Ally hit the mattress, she rolled around and sat up to stare at the door. There was nothing to see. Nervously, Ally's eyes traced the white panels of the door to the crack beneath it, expecting to see a shadow on the other side, but something else drew her attention instead. The indent of her bare feet on the carpet had already faded, but that was expected. What caused Ally's throat to contract was the impression of two shoes indented in her carpet immediately in front of her door.

Ally gasped for breath as her chest seemed to shrink. She couldn't tell if she was imagining the eyes upon her or if something was actually staring at her. Then, one of the impressions lifted, only to reappear a pace towards the bed. *Oh God, no!* Ally slid back against the wall, pulling the blanket up to her chin with bloodless hands.

One step led to another until the invisible intruder was standing directly beside the bed. Ally's eyes glistened with tears of horror. *Go away. Go away. Please go away.*

The presence of the thing was oppressive, not unlike standing in the spotlight on a stage before an entire audience. The intensity of the thing's stare bore through her, rattling Ally to her core.

Then all it once, it was gone. Ally couldn't say how she knew, but her visitor had left her. The spotlight was off. *What the fuck was that?*

Ally ran a trembling hand across her chin before pressing it to her still-racing heart. Was her digging attracting attention? All she was doing was writing her findings on the whiteboard, but maybe that was enough. Maybe the more she learned, the more these supernatural events would happen to her. Would it be worth it? *Only one way to find out.*

Ally took a deep breath. She had to know.

SLEEP DID NOT COME soon enough for Ally that night, and when she was finally in the library again, her exhaustion dogged her research. She had taken to the shelf beneath the binder looking for local history, but Ally had to fight drifting off while she worked. Admittedly, she felt safer in the well-lit library than she had that night in her own bedroom, but she couldn't afford to waste time catching up on sleep when she had answers to find. However, her aimless floundering through book after book and exhaustion left her efforts fruitless, and it was a very disheartened Ally that took her seat in the lunchroom that Tuesday.

"Son of a *bitch*!" Maddy grumbled as she slammed her tray down.

Ally jumped, blinking the sleepiness from her eyes. "What?"

Maddy speared a baby carrot with her fork and glared at it. "Our school library is a fucking joke! Beyond the asylum article, I couldn't find shit!"

"Me neither," Ally lamented. This was not starting off as well as she'd hoped.

"Plus, the librarian hovered over me like an overgrown bat."

Ally sighed. "At least she didn't snap at you."

Maddy snorted. "She prolly wanted to! Bitch couldn't find a reason...this time."

Derek set his tray down next to Ally's, followed soon by Bart beside Maddy. "Any luck?"

Ally shook her head, and Maddy huffed, "Hell no!"

Derek shrugged. "Well, I got something." Ally perked up immediately. "I managed to find out who built your house. Apparently, it was a guy named Darius in 1732. It seems that he claimed the land by the authority of the king of Britain, but it was almost all Indian territory at the time."

Ally frowned. "How did he manage to claim the land, then?"

Maddy shrugged. "Maybe he was a lord or something and had his own army?"

Derek frowned and scratched his chin. "Maybe. I looked into native lore to see if they had anything to say about it, but apparently all they did was try to warn him away from the site where he was building. Something about it being sacred to them, but there wasn't much detail."

Ally sighed. "So, I live on an Indian burial ground?" *Great.*

Derek shook his head. "If it was anything like that, they'd have mentioned it."

Maddy interjected, "So this Darius...Corbant, I'm assuming?" Derek nodded, so Maddy continued, "So this Darius Corbant shows up, claims the land in the name of the king, the natives warn him not to build his mansion on a sacred hill, and so that's exactly what he does?"

"Sounds about right," Derek said, nodding.

"Maybe he thought his faith would protect him," Ally said. "Dad always said that the angels and stuff all over the woodwork at home were part of the original house back in the 1700s. I bet Darius was very religious."

"Makes sense," Derek agreed.

Maddy laughed. "I wonder if his faith did protect him in the end."

Derek shrugged. "Records are sketchy from back then. If he'd lived closer to a settlement rather than in the middle of nowhere..."

"You mean Bumfuck, Egypt?" Maddy blurted out.

All four of them laughed, then Derek continued, "Yes, that. If not BFE, then maybe there'd be some record of what happened to him."

"Which raises another question," Maddy added, all humor gone. "Why did he move so far away from everyone else at the time?"

Derek shrugged again. "Your guess is as good as mine."

Ally stared at the center of the table, frowning. "Still more questions..."

"I g-g-got something, t-t-too."

All eyes turned to Bart. He flushed for a moment, and Ally blinked. He looked more nervous than usual. He stammered, "I a-a-asked my mom a-a-about the f-f-family. Sh-sh-she told me..." He took a deep breath. "M-m-my grandpa was a p-p-patient at the a-a-asylum when the r-r-riot h-h-happened."

Ally's eyes widened. "He...he was actually...*there*?"

Bart nodded gravely. "He s-s-survived by h-h-hiding in a b-b-broom closet. Th-th-there's s-s-something else, t-t-too." Before Ally could ask what, Bart ducked below the lunch table. Maddy leaned back to watch him, frowning. Ally waited with bated breath until Bart resurfaced with an old notebook. He set it on the table and slid it towards Ally.

Nervously, she took it and turned the blank cover towards her. "What is this?"

Bart bit his lip before whispering. "My g-g-grandpa made a s-s-scrapbook."

Ally's heart hammered in her chest. Maddy asked, wide-eyed, "A scrapbook of what?"

Before anyone could say anything else, Ally opened to the first page to a hand-written forward and read aloud:

"'What follows is my attempt to make sense of what happened at Corbant Sanitarium. I had known Dr. Aros Corbant for nearly two years before everything went wrong, and I say with the utmost conviction that there was not a kinder soul on this earth. I was happy there, but then the expansion began, and everything changed. I saw Aros commit grisly acts that not even the most heinous mind could have imagined. He was neither reluctant nor uninterested in his work. Rather, he seemed to take an obscene pleasure in the horrors unfolding around him. Whatever happened there was something unnatural. The man I knew as Dr. Aros Corbant was not capable of such horror. I was determined to find out what led him to this, and so I began a record of the Corbant family history, so that perhaps I might discover whatever evil drove Aros, my friend, to madness. This endeavor has been neither easy nor pleasant. The family history is littered with tragedy, misfortune, and evil. To my dying day I will swear before all of God's creation: the Corbant family is cursed. I weep for them and pray that one day that curse will be lifted.'"

Ally looked up at her friends. Everyone was wearing the same shocked expression. "Bart...this is...amazing."

Bart bit his lip again, his eyes fixed on the table, "I-I-I wasn't s-s-sure how you'd f-f-feel..."

Excitement rose within Ally. "This is everything we need! No more digging through old history books!"

Maddy took a deep breath. "But...Ally...what if you don't like what you find?"

Ally heaved a sigh. "Based on what I just read...I probably won't. Still, if Bart's grandpa thinks that the family itself isn't at fault, that's gotta count for something, right?"

Derek finally spoke, "He did say that Aros was a friend. He basically confirmed everything we'd already guessed about him."

"Exactly!" Ally exclaimed.

Bart glanced up at Ally at last. "I d-d-didn't r-r-read it m-m-myself. I th-th-thought you sh-sh-should be the f-f-first."

Then, Maddy planted a long, hard kiss on Bart's cheek. His face turned brick red as she grinned. "You have literally saved our asses."

Ally smiled before looking back down at the book. *All the answers. Right here.*

THAT NIGHT, ALLY WENT through page after page of Bart's grandpa's scrapbook. Each was loaded with newspaper clippings, copies of public records, and other documents that slowly pieced together the Corbant family history. The red, blue, and green on the markerboard gradually gave way to black as conjecture and hearsay was replaced by solidified fact. To Ally's triumph, many of the articles spoke highly of the Corbants. Their contributions to the town's development were unquestionable, from Gertrude Corbant's procuring a printing press in 1817 to start the newspaper that would become the *Corbanton Herald*, to the official founding of the town of Corbanton by Oliver Corbant in June of 1825. With every contribution to the town she read about, Ally felt a surge of pride in her family.

Unfortunately, the philanthropy was always punctuated by tragedy or scandal. Gertrude had married twice, both husbands dying shortly after the wedding. *She must be the black widow.* Gertrude's brother Lamuel was lynched by an angry mob for killing their sister Genevieve. Gertrude died later of tuberculosis. Oliver, too, met his end in tragedy as he suffered a heart attack in the manor study.

Ally's sense of victory was quelled with every grim revelation. Then, a newspaper clipping caught her eye. It described a group of Union soldiers who had gone missing while staying in town. Bart's grandfather wrote above it, "Connected?" Then, he had drawn a line to a court document concerning Madeline Corbant accusing those same soldiers of raping her. Was this where the kidnapping story had come from? If so, was the motive purely malicious, or was it revenge? Ally began looking over the case evidence, but her concentration was shattered by a scream from the hallway.

Ally jumped in fright, bumping her whiteboard and sending it and the markers spilling onto the floor. "Shit!" she cried before she could stop herself. She stood still for a moment, her heart pounding. The scream had sounded like a man's voice, and not one she recognized. Nervously, Ally crept to her door. With a shaky hand, she pulled the door open and stuck her head out.

Her eyes swept the length of the hallway again and again. *Maybe I imagined it?* The house seemed undisturbed. Her mother and Cassie's voices drifted up from the floor below, though Ally couldn't make out what they were saying. Then, movement caught her eye from the foyer doorway. Ally turned towards it, but there was nothing. *No. There is something.*

Ally stepped out of her room to get a closer look, and the blood chilled in her veins. At the top of the stairs was a single bloody handprint. It glistened in the soft hallway lighting, alarmingly fresh. Ally pressed a trembling hand to her chest as if to slow her racing heart. Then, in a single blink, the handprint was gone. Ally blinked again and reexamined where the handprint had been, but there was nothing. The wood was pristine.

Swallowing hard, Ally backed to her door and returned to her room.

THE FOLLOWING SCHOOL day came and went, with Ally pouring over the scrapbook's contents through study hall and relating all she had learned to her friends during lunch. By the time she came home that Wednesday afternoon, she was certain she had the scrapbook thus far memorized. However, as she stood outside her bedroom door, her sister's voice drifted down the hallway from her own room. Ally snapped out of her trance-like state and listened. Cassie asked, "What does that mean?" *Don't get an answer. Please don't get an answer.* To Ally's relief, Cassie came out and looked up and down the hallway before seeing her and smiling. "Oh, hi, Ally!"

Ally managed a smile, hoping to hide her fear. "Hey, Cassie!"

Cassie looked up at her, her eyes questioning. "What does immortal mean?"

Ally was taken aback. "Where did you hear that from?"

"Sam told me about an immortal princess that lived here, but he didn't say what immortal was before he left. Why does he leave whenever you come home?"

Why do I really not want to know? Once again, Ally had to hide her unease from her sister. "I don't know why. Maybe he's still just shy."

"Maybe," Cassie said, her little face puzzled, "but I hope it's not 'cause he doesn't like you."

Ally gulped. "Me too, Cass. Anyways, immortal means it can never die."

Cassie gasped. "So, it means living forever and ever?" she said with childish wonder.

Ally nodded. "Yep, forever and ever."

Cassie looked back to her room, her eyes distant. "So, a princess who would never die lived here...I wonder where she lives now? Maybe I can meet her!"

Ally forced a soft chuckle. "Maybe." She then slipped into her room and closed the door a little too quickly behind her. The Sam situation was getting out of hand. Still, if her theory about Sam was right, maybe he knew more than what three-year-old Cassie's mind could comprehend. What if there was an immortal princess in the house at one point? Maybe by some definitions, she had never left. Before Ally even began to jot her notes on the whiteboard, she decided to investigate the possibility of a so-called immortal princess the next day.

That night, Ally dreamed she was walking down what looked like a mineshaft. The wooden supports were rotten and encrusted with filth. Ally's only light source was a lantern she held aloft, but its light was too dim to illuminate further than a yard ahead. Somewhere in that yawning blackness there was the soft, chiming melody of a music box. The music box grew louder as she continued, its tune a mournful lament with a haunting beauty. The lantern began to flicker and weaken, the candle inside nearly spent. Ally's heart accelerated. She didn't have a replacement. Finally, it died completely, and the darkness enveloped her utterly.

Ally shrank against the wall, cowering in the dark as the music box continued to play. The beauty of the melody was lost in the dark, leaving only the haunting resonance of every somber note. As she sat hugging her knees, the music continued to grow louder, even though she had stopped moving towards it. *It's coming here.*

Ally trembled and hugged herself tighter as a voice began to sing along with the music box. It was the voice of a woman, though not one Ally recognized. It sang each note in a single breath, matching its pitch perfectly but unable to sustain the notes for their entirety. Whoever it was, Ally guessed that they were having difficulty breathing.

Call out to it? Something about its weak gasping made her pity the source, but her fear choked the words before they could emerge from her lips. Then the music faded and the voice with it. For a moment, the only sound was Ally's shaky breathing. Then, she suddenly noticed how deathly cold it was, not realizing what it meant until a different voice beside her whispered, "At night...the walls...remember..."

Ally awoke with her face buried in her pillow. She squirmed and writhed to untangle herself from the sweat-soaked bedclothes, then curled up on the edge of her bed against the wall. She trembled with tears in her eyes. The whispering voice at the end of the dream was the same voice she had heard that night beside her bed after the dream of the hanged woman. It had sounded stronger in the dream, but otherwise entirely the same. The words still rang in her head. *At night, the walls remember.* She tried to stifle her terror enough to think, but every shadow in her room felt like it might move to engulf her, with or without a chilling voice to announce its intent.

Ally sat against the wall, hugging her knees. Once an hour had gone by, she was finally able to convince herself that she was safe and alone for now. With her fears calmed, she began to ponder the dream she had just had. There had been the singing voice as well this time. That voice was distinctly different than the one that had whispered to her, nor was it the same as the hanged woman. *Can't forget* that *nightmare soon enough.* Still, the distinctness of the singing woman gave her pause. *Was it some kind of clue?* Was the voice from the cold trying to guide her somehow? Considering her little sister's possibly un-imaginary friend, she couldn't rule out the possibility.

Ally looked at her door, imagining something that she couldn't describe waiting on the other side. The idea chilled her blood, but her determination was growing stronger. She whispered to whatever it might be, "What are you trying to tell me?" No answer came. Ally couldn't be sure if her reaction was relief or disappointment. The more she thought about her circumstances, the less they frightened her. Perhaps she was starting to get used to the idea of living in a haunted house, so long as the more permanent residents wished neither her nor her family harm.

That brought Ally's thoughts back to Cassie and Sam. Why was Sam singling Cassie out and wary of Ally's approach? Also, why did Sam dislike the angels that decorated the woodwork of the house? Didn't ghosts usually prefer the house as they knew it? According to Ally's father, the woodwork was all from the mansion's original construction. It was one piece of the puzzle that didn't quite fit. She considered talking to her parents about Sam, but quickly stifled the idea. They thought of Sam as no more than an imaginary friend and would probably dismiss her.

It seemed that the only people Ally could turn to were her friends. The thought of their help in her endeavor was comforting.

She smiled a little and slipped back under the covers. Her quest for answers would continue in the morning. In just a couple of hours she would talk to Maddy.

5. The Immortal Princess

Ally was far less tired that morning than she had thought she would be. All she could think about was the pursuit of answers. Her single-minded focus left her deaf to the usual taunts in the hallway. Only Maddy managed to break her concentration. "Hey, girl! Earth to Ally!"

Ally's head snapped around to face her. She blinked her eyes back into focus. "Oh? Sorry, I zoned out."

"I could tell. You didn't even bat an eyelash at the creeps this morning. I'm impressed!"

Ally shrugged. "I guess I was just too far away to notice."

Maddy laughed. "Well, wherever it was, you'd be better off going back. God knows it's better than here."

Ally laughed in response. In spite of everything, she was in high spirits. Her family might still be the most hated in town, and her sister might be friends with someone long dead, but she was making progress in dealing with both problems. She wasn't sure how her journey would end, but for the first time in years, Ally felt like she was taking charge of her circumstances. She would see things through and hopefully come out better than ever afterwards.

The morning classes came and went, and soon Ally was in study hall once again. *Immortal princess.* The Corbants were the closest thing to royalty Corbanton had ever known, so it had to be a family member. *Immortal means you can never die.* Ally absently thumbed through the pages of the scrapbook.

She would not die!

Startled, Ally flipped back two pages to the newspaper clipping concerning Gertrude Corbant's brother Lamuel. At first, she hadn't paid any mind to what the clipping said he had been raving about as he was hanged. Ally had dismissed it as the ramblings of a madman, but then she read what he had been saying over again. *To his last breath, Lamuel Corbant insisted that Genevieve would not die.*

Ally sat back in her chair. If there was any shred of truth to the story Sam had shared with Cassie, then Genevieve had to be the immortal princess. Ally looked over the information concerning Lamuel's death again. Did he simply believe she couldn't be killed, or was there something else at work? The article also mentioned that Genevieve was never found.

She's still there. That's why Sam mentioned her. She never left. She's still in the mansion.

Ally froze. *Sam.* In all of her research, she had yet to come across any mention of him. Ally flipped through the scrapbook from start to finish, poring over every deed and misdeed, but the name Sam or any variant thereof was never mentioned. She went over every article and document with growing intensity right up until the bell rang. Frustrated, Ally left the library with one still puzzling question left unanswered. Who was Sam, and where did he fit into all of this?

Once everyone sat down at lunch, Ally immediately recounted all that she had learned from her research, though she stopped short of her discovery about Genevieve. Her voice trailed off, and Maddy raised an eyebrow. "Anything else?"

Ally bit her lip as she debated on whether to let her friends in on what was going on at home. Eventually, she threw caution to the wind and told them about her little sister and Sam. All three looked horrified. Maddy stammered, "Ally...that...that's creepy..."

Ally bit her lip again before answering, "I know..."

"A little cliché, isn't it?" Derek observed.

Ally looked at him. "How do you mean?"

"It always starts with the kids, doesn't it?" he said gravely.

She shuddered involuntarily. "I know...that's exactly what I thought when it all started..."

"H-h-has anything else s-s-strange happened?" Bart asked.

"Well..." Ally began nervously. How much should she tell them? Would they think she was crazy? *Oh well, they're in this deep already.* "There've been some things...and I've been having these creepy dreams..." She then launched into an explanation of the dreams she'd had over the past week or so and the eerie occurrences at night, as well as the disembodied voice that had followed

the dream of the hanged woman. Ally was surprised to find them less horrified by the dreams than the story of her little sister...or the voice.

Derek said, "You're sure it wasn't part of the dream?"

Ally nodded, the voice ringing through her mind afresh. "I couldn't have
imagined it if I'd wanted to."

Maddy's eyes were wide. "And again, in the mine shaft thing..."

Ally nodded. "Same voice...well, except for the one singing." Silence hung
in the air around them for a moment until she bowed her head and blurted
out, "You all think I'm crazy."

Each immediately spoke up to reassure her, but Maddy's voice eventually
came through. "Ally, I know you, girl. If you say these things happened, then
they happened."

Bart nodded, and Derek said, "I mean...with the house being as old as it
is, and with all the weird stories about it..."

"Do you believe in ghosts?" Ally asked.

Maddy spoke first. "I didn't, but I do now."

Bart nodded again, and Derek said, "Always have."

Ally looked at him in surprise. "Always?"

Derek shrugged. "Maybe I'll tell you about it sometime. For now, let's focus on your situation."

"What about this so-called 'immortal princess' of yours?" Maddy asked.

Ally sighed. "Lamuel never said where he buried her."

"At night, the walls remember," Bart said. All three looked at him, and
Ally went pale. It was the first time someone else had spoken the words
aloud, and she hadn't been prepared to hear it. Bart flushed a little but didn't
look away from them as he explained, "M-m-maybe it's literal. Maybe she was
b-b-bricked up."

"Like in a Poe story?" Maddy asked excitedly.

Bart nodded. "E-e-exactly."

Ally frowned and sighed again. "That narrows the search a little, but not
by much. You do know how big my house is, right?" She was surprised at the
frustration in her voice, and her expression softened. "I'm sorry...that sounded worse than I meant it to..."

Bart gave her a warm smile. "No w-w-worries."

"Maybe you should ask Sam," Derek suggested.

"He's always gone whenever I'm around," Ally countered, shaking her head.

"What about the voice from the dream?" Maddy asked.

Ally raised an eyebrow. "Which one, the singing one or the creepy one?"

"Why not both?" Derek replied.

Ally didn't get a chance to reply before the bell rang, but she now had a great deal to think about.

BEFORE BED, ALLY SAT in the chair at her vanity table, looking over everything she had added to the board. Pieces of the puzzle were coming together for certain. She had found out what she had initially been looking for, and more, but her search and her sister's situation had led to different questions—questions that it seemed no other source could answer.

Ally's heart pounded in her chest, but she found her courage and looked up at the ceiling. "If you can hear me, tell me where to find the immortal princess." No reply came, and Ally was once again uncertain whether to be relieved or disappointed. With no other idea of how to proceed, she crawled into bed and rolled about restlessly for an hour or so before finally falling asleep...and dreaming once again.

This time, Ally was dancing in the manor's ballroom with a stranger dressed in all black and wearing a black Venetian mask. Ally was dressed in a red gown that looked at least a century out of date, but she didn't feel the least bit uncomfortable or out of place. Something about her dance partner felt familiar, and her feet seemed to know the dance without her having to think about it. Candles in wall sconces lit the ballroom, which was filled with the same tune from the music box, this time on the grand piano, though no one was playing it. The song ended, and she and the stranger bowed to each other. He then took her by the hand and led her over to the middle of three wardrobes next between the doors to the music room and storage room. The wardrobes always seemed out of place to her, but her dad said they were there for guests to hang their coats up.

The stranger opened the doors on the middle wardrobe, and Ally looked inside. At first, she noticed nothing amiss, but then she heard soft breathing coming from within the wardrobe. Puzzled, she leaned closer. The breathing grew louder and then turned into the breathless singing Ally remembered from last night's dream. In a moment of clarity, she said, "I found you." Immediately, Ally woke up. She was again entangled in the bed sheets but didn't seem to notice. Instead, she noted the deathly chill in the room. Her breath rose before her eyes in a fine mist, and she shivered.

Within a moment, however, the chill passed. Ally sat up and looked at her door, her eyes narrowed. That chill only seemed to come around with the mysterious, disembodied voice. Had whatever it was been in there watching her sleep?

Then a strange thought occurred to her: what if that had been the stranger she was dancing with in the dream? His face had been completely covered by the mask, and his hands had been gloved. In the dream it had seemed appropriate, but awake she wondered if there was a purpose to it. Maybe it was that thing's way of giving her what she had asked for—a man she couldn't see guiding her to what she needed to know. Calmly, she whispered, "Thank you."

Ally thought of nothing but the dream from the moment she got up for school to the moment she was at her locker. Like clockwork, Maddy was there mere seconds later. Her usual morning banter was cut off when Ally said, "Maddy, I think I'm losing it."

Maddy laughed. "Girl, you're friends with me. I'm pretty sure you already lost it."

"Maddy, I'm serious. I think I'm losing my mind."

The smile died on Maddy's face. "Why you say that?"

"Last night I had another dream. I was dancing with this guy, all dressed in black, in the ballroom to the song from the last dream. When we stopped, he took me to one of the wardrobes, and I heard the singing again. Then when I woke up, I felt that chill again, but then it disappeared. I told it, 'thank you.'"

Maddy frowned. "So...that means you've lost it?"

Ally grunted in frustration. "I feel like I have."

Maddy didn't reply. *Odd.* Then there was a voice from behind Ally. "Hey you!" Ally froze. It was the voice of Gladys Lauderdale. "Look at me when I'm talking to you!"

Ally turned around nervously. Gladys stood surrounded by at least half of her cheer squad. Maddy snapped, "What the hell do you bitches want?"

"Shut up!" Gladys retorted. She then locked her eyes on Ally. "I'm only gonna say this once, so listen up. Stay the hell away from Derek. He's too good for you."

"Oh yeah?" Maddy countered, then gave a sarcastic laugh. "If he's too good for her, then he's way too good for your skanky ass!"

"I said shut up, bitch!" Gladys barked. She then took a step towards Ally and hissed, "Stay away from him, or you'll regret it. Got it?"

Ally looked back at her. For as long as she could remember, Gladys had been one of her chief tormentors. She constantly reminded Ally that her family was subhuman monsters, and that Ally was no better. Almost every horrible thing Ally had heard about both herself and her family had come from Gladys at one point or another. *She's wrong, though.* Emboldened, Ally took a deep breath and turned away from her dismissively. "You don't have a say in it, so get lost."

A few seconds of silence followed Ally's words. Gladys's eyes flashed. "Is that how it's gonna be then?"

Maddy stepped in. "You're damn right that's how it's gonna be!"

Gladys looked at her with an upturned nose for a moment, then glared back at Ally. "Watch your back," she warned with a sneer. She then turned and walked away with an overdone flip of her hair.

Ally glared at her as she left, then turned to grin at Maddy, only to find her looking dumbfounded. Maddy asked, "Girl, what has gotten into you?"

Ally shrugged, blushing slightly. "I dunno. I guess I'm just tired of being pushed around. Why did she walk away, though? I thought she might try to hit me."

Maddy tipped her a sly wink. "I made sure she saw me stick my hand in my pocket. With my rep, I figured she'd think I had a knife."

Ally's eyes widened. "No, you didn't! What if she tells a teacher?"

Maddy laughed dismissively. "They can search me! I ain't got nothing to hide!"

Ally rolled her eyes but grinned. "Thanks."

Maddy shrugged as she began walking away to go to class, giving Ally another wink. "I've got your back, girl."

At lunch, Maddy immediately informed Bart and Derek of the morning's confrontation. Bart seemed worried, but Derek laughed. "Typical. She must think she can have any guy she wants."

Maddy agreed. "Prolly only 'cause she spreads her legs for every one of 'em."

Bart was the only one not laughing. "C-c-careful Ally. She m-m-may try to c-c-corner you."

Ally rolled her eyes. "Let her."

Bart furrowed his brow. "Why so c-c-confront-t-tational?"

"All the research and stuff. You were right; my family wasn't all bad. As a matter of fact, they did a lot for this town," Ally explained.

Maddy grinned. "Translation: she finally feels like she doesn't deserve their bullshit."

Ally shrugged, though she agreed. "I guess so."

Then Derek did something completely unexpected. He slid a hand up to Ally's cheek, turned her head to face him, and kissed her fully on the lips. The suddenness of the kiss only added to the electricity Ally swore was racing across her skin. She wanted more, but quickly broke away. "What...was that...?" she gasped.

Derek flashed his half-smile. "Proof that we're on the same side."

Ally's heart hammered in her chest as she flashed a smile of her own back at him. Undoubtedly people had seen what just happened but, for once in her life, she didn't care. *Let them look.*

The remainder of the day passed as it usually did, though Ally once again had a spring in her step. Derek's affection as well as her newfound pride in her family seemed to have become a shield against the usual ridicule. Ignoring it all now came easily to her. She was deaf to every jeer, insult, or taunt. Her newfound immunity to the nonstop pestering gave her a sense of triumph. Let them say what they wanted, but she knew the truth. Yeah, some of her family had been bad apples, but what they had done for the town and the people in it more than made up for it. For the first time in her life, Ally was proud to be a Corbant.

As she headed out to the buses at the end of the day, Ally heard someone call her name. She looked over her shoulder to find Gladys coming towards her, flanked by two of her friends. Ally's heart sank. Of course, it was too good to last. She turned back around, but found the door blocked by a third friend of Gladys's named Rhonda Scriver. She was a little taller than Ally, but much more muscular. Her hair was also black, but short and always in a ponytail. She was well known for her skill at track and gymnastics and for being Gladys's personal bodyguard.

Ally groaned and started towards another door when a hand seized her by her hair. Before she could even cry out in pain, Ally found her face planted hard against the glass door. Her head throbbed, but even that couldn't keep her from recognizing the voice that whispered in her ear, "I told you to stay away from him!"

Without hesitation, Ally threw her elbow back, driving it into Gladys's diaphragm. Whether out of pain or surprise, her grip on Ally's hair slacked as she coughed and gasped for breath. Seizing the opportunity, Ally then grabbed for the door. However, another hand was already there. She looked up at the owner. It was Rhonda. Ally tried to keep the tremor out of her voice as she pleaded, "Please, just let me go."

Rhonda shook her head, grabbed Ally by the shoulder, and turned her to face Gladys. Ally couldn't believe the strength in Rhonda's grip. Gladys was massaging just below her chest, and she looked murderous. "You fucking bitch! Hold her!"

Rhonda grabbed both of Ally's arms and held her tight as Gladys rounded on her. Ally tried to struggle, but Rhonda's grip was like iron. Then Gladys punched Ally in the face. Stars exploded in her eyes, and the left side of her face tightened up immediately. This was followed by another punch to her stomach. Ally doubled over, Rhonda still holding her up. Ally coughed and gasped as Gladys spat, "Suck it up, bitch! I'm not done with you yet."

Ally finally caught her breath and looked up at her, gasping, "You're...the bitch."

Gladys's eyes widened in disbelief, but the look was quickly replaced by a scream of rage as she raised a clenched fist to strike another blow.

"GLADYS LAUDERDALE!"

Gladys stopped dead and spun on her heel. Despite the pounding headache she had, Ally recognized the voice as Mr. Harving, her chemistry teacher. He was a middle-aged man with glasses and a prematurely thinning hairline. He walked up to them, his arms folded and his expression severe. "Explain yourselves!"

Rhonda released Ally, and she struggled to stand up straight as Gladys stumbled over her words to try and find a way out of the situation. Ally could almost laugh at how pathetic she seemed, but Mr. Harving was not amused. "All of you, to the office, now!"

Ally's heart sank as the five of them walked to the office in silence. Mr. Harving left Rhonda at the principal's office before taking Ally to the nurse, Miss Prout, a short woman with curly blonde hair and a kindly but careworn face. She took one look at Ally and sighed. "That's gonna be a black eye. What happened?"

Ally recounted everything that had happened from the moment Gladys called her name. She had little doubt that Gladys's story would differ, but it didn't really matter. Ally had thrown her elbow instinctively, but the school policy would not be so understanding. That she had struck back at all was a guarantee for suspension.

When she finished her tale, Miss Prout sighed again. "You Corbants tend to bring out the worst in people, don't you?" Ally stared in shock as Miss Prout left to get an ice pack. *Still can't let it go without a comment, can they?*

Miss Prout returned and tossed the ice pack at Ally before telling her to wait while she spoke with Principal Marr. Soon enough, Miss Prout returned, instructing, "Mr. Marr will see you now. Keep that on your face."

Ally said nothing as she left, feeling like a prisoner walking to the gallows. It wasn't far to Mr. Marr's office. Once inside, she found herself facing Mr. Marr, who was seated behind his large, cluttered desk. Behind him, the walls were adorned with numerous shelves of books. He was an exceptionally large man with short blond hair and a booming voice. Three chairs sat against the wall opposite from him, two of which were occupied by Rhonda and Gladys. Neither looked up when Ally walked in.

Mr. Marr said, "Good afternoon, Ally. Please sit down." Ally did as she was told in silence. "Would you please tell me what happened between you, Miss Lauderdale, and Miss Scriver?"

Ally felt like a broken record as she repeated word for word exactly what she had told Miss Prout. When she finished, Ally fell silent and waited. Mr. Marr's expression was unreadable. He leaned back in his chair and heaved a sigh. "I would really expect better from the captain of the cheerleading squad, Miss Lauderdale. In a position of leadership such as that, you should hold yourself to a higher standard of behavior than this sort of blatant attack on another student. You will both be suspended from school tomorrow."

Gladys and Rhonda both hung their heads, and despite Ally's own anxiety, she felt a sense of savage glee in their dejected behavior. Then, Mr. Marr's phone rang. He picked it up, listened for a moment, then said, "I'll send them out. Thank you." He hung up before turning to Gladys and Rhonda. "Your parents are waiting for you out front. You may go. I expect that this incident will not be repeated, ladies."

Gladys and Rhonda both stood and shuffled out, looking like prisoners. Once the door closed behind them, Mr. Marr turned to face Ally, his expression sympathetic. "Unfortunately, since you did strike Miss Lauderdale, we can't call you one-hundred-percent innocent in this situation. If you hadn't done that, perhaps the situation wouldn't have escalated as it did. Therefore, I will have to suspend you as well. You will return to class on Monday at the regular time."

Ally teared up, but she nodded. It was her first suspension. While true that she would miss only Friday, it was a black mark on her otherwise spotless record. She tried with all her might not to break into sobs as Mr. Marr phoned her parents. Worse still, her punishment was no lighter than what Gladys and Rhonda had received, despite them being the attackers in the first place. After he got off the phone, Mr. Marr said, "You can wait for your parents just inside the front door."

Ally nodded and got up to leave as Mr. Marr opened a drawer and began rifling through it. She made her way to the couches that sat in the main entrance hall and sat down. It didn't take long for her to bury her face in her hands and begin sobbing. How was any of this fair? Who knew what Gladys and Rhonda would have done to her if she hadn't tried to defend herself? Ally had a black eye, but she had no doubt that Gladys would have rather broken her nose instead. Was it more of the Corbants "bringing out the worst in people," as Miss Prout had put it? Ally's feelings catapulted from shame to rage but quickly gave way to fear. What would her parents say about her getting suspended?

It only took five minutes for her dad to pull up in his car, but to Ally, it was an eternity. Wiping the tears from her eyes and holding the ice pack to her face, she went out the front door and got into the car. She couldn't look at her father and winced when he said, "Tell me what happened."

Ally hesitated. His tone was unreadable. Then she took a deep breath and recounted the tale for the third time. When she finished, her father didn't respond right away. She still refused to look at him, thankful that the ice pack obscured her vision of him entirely. Finally, he said, "You shouldn't have gotten suspended. You had every right to defend yourself."

Ally finally turned to face him, thunderstruck. "So...you're not mad?"

He chuckled. "Would you like me to be?"

Ally laughed nervously in return. "I...I guess not."

"I'll be damned if any daughter of mine is just going to let some girl beat the hell out of her. No Corbant will ever play the victim."

Ally smiled with relief but then looked out the window. Her dad's words reminded her of all that she had learned about the family...including the location of the so-called immortal princess. Perhaps she would be seeing her for herself sooner than she had planned.

"YOU WHAT?!"

"Yeah, I got suspended."

"Girl, I'm so proud of you!"

Ally laughed. "How did I know you'd say that?"

"'Cause we're best friends, duh!"

Ally was lying on her bed, her feet against the wall and her hair hanging off the side as she chatted with Maddy on the telephone. After both her parents' and Maddy's reactions, the idea of being suspended wasn't as frightening as it had been at first. "Maybe I'm turning into you," she said with a smile.

"Well, better see a doctor about that."

"Symptoms include bad attitude and a lot of swearing."

"Sounds about fucking right." They both laughed "So...Derek's gonna want to call."

Ally's heart fluttered, but then she imagined her mother or Carol answering the phone and hearing a boy's voice. "I...I don't think that's a good idea. My family still doesn't know about him."

"Why don't you tell them?"

"Well...it'd be harder to have our sleepovers and...stuff," Ally stammered, leaving out her own mortification at the thought of her mother gushing over her having a boyfriend. Then, there was a knock at Ally's door.

"Who is it?" she called. There was no answer. Ally frowned as she flipped her legs over the edge of the bed and sat up. "Cassie, is that you?" Still, there was no answer.

"What's going on, Ally?" Maddy asked, puzzled.

"I dunno. Someone just knocked on my door, but they aren't..." Before Ally could finish, the door flew open, slamming against the wall. Ally screamed and jumped back onto the bed.

"Oh my God! Ally!" Maddy yelled from the phone.

Ally didn't answer but instead stared at the empty doorway. The door was wide open, but there was nothing there. "I...I'm okay, Maddy," she said shakily.

"What happened?" Maddy asked, her voice panicked.

"The door...flew open. There was...no one," Ally stammered. Her eyes were still fixed on the empty doorway, scanning for any sign of movement.

"What...?" Maddy asked nervously.

"Let me call you back tomorrow, okay?"

"Ummm...all right. Be careful, Ally." Then Maddy hung up. She had never sounded so nervous.

Ally slid off the bed and went to the doorway. After a second's hesitation, she poked her head out into the hallway and scanned from one end to the other. There was no trace of her phantom visitor. The temperature was also unchanged, ruling out the presence of her mysterious guide, which did little to comfort her. Then, she had an idea.

Ally set off down the foyer stairs and headed down the first-floor hallway to the first door on the left. It opened into a short hallway with painted portraits of past family members on either side. Even with the sconces lit, knowing that Ally was looking at the likenesses of spirits that might still be lingering in the house chilled her to her core. She rushed through the hallway to another door that led into the parlor, an opulent sitting room with an empty fireplace. From there, she turned to a set of double-doors and entered the ballroom.

The massive ball room dominated the east wing of the house on both the first and second floors. The parlor doors opened up under a balcony with a wrought-iron spiral staircase leading up to it on the left. The grand piano lay a few feet from where she now stood, and there were ornate wooden chairs placed between the large windows on the north and west walls, but the room was otherwise empty. The curtains over the windows were open, flooding the room with light. There was an ornate stage on the west wall, its framework carved with numerous angelic figures, but its curtain was down. Ally couldn't recall if she had ever actually seen the stage in use. A gorgeous, unlit, crystal chandelier hung from the cloud-painted ceiling. For a moment, Ally could almost see her dance with the masked man once again, even in the brightly lit room.

Remembering why she had come in the first place, Ally turned to the right and passed the grand piano to the first wardrobe. As she reached for the handle, she stopped. *Nope, next one.* Heaving a sigh, she moved to the second wardrobe. Even in the ball room flooded with daylight, the memory of the whispers gave her pause. Still, she needed to confirm what her dream had told her. She pulled the wardrobe doors open, but there was nothing unusual inside. A bar hung across the top with several wire hangers, but much like the stage, it hadn't been used in recent memory. Underwhelmed, Ally knocked on the back of the wardrobe and whispered, "Hello?" There was no answer.

"Hello?" Ally repeated, a little more loudly this time. Several minutes of silence passed before Ally shut the doors in frustration. Had it all been merely a dream after all? Everything the cold voice had told her had led to this, but there was nothing here. Two dreams had guided her to this. Ally racked her brain to recall the first dream with the mineshaft and the music box. It had ended with the voice whispering, "At night...the walls...remember."

Ally froze. She had forgotten about that little detail. *At night, the walls remember.* She stared at the wardrobe, understanding filling her with dread. She would have to come back at night. *Of course.* The idea of creeping through the house in the dark was terrifying, but if that was the only way to get her answers... Ally took a deep breath as she left the ball room. *If that's what it takes, then so be it.*

Ally spent the rest of the night staring at her marker board, her eyes tracing each story word for word. By now she had them all completely memorized. Finally, she heard her parents close their bedroom door. After that, she went to her window and watched the lawn. Once the lights downstairs were out, she could be certain that both Chad the cook and Carol had left.

Several minutes passed before the lawn finally fell into darkness. Then, Ally opened a drawer at her vanity table and pulled out a flashlight, clicked it on, and then turned off her bedroom light. Once her eyes adjusted to the darkness, she slowly opened her door and crept out into the hallway.

It was as though Ally had stepped right into one of her nightmares. The hallway was silent and deserted. She tried to block the memory of the dreams from her head as she made her way to the foyer. She descended the right side of the staircase on her tiptoes. Already, the shadows in the house had taken on an air of menace. Ally wanted to run down the stairs, but she needed to not be caught. She might be able to explain her late-night wandering as wanting a snack or simply being restless, but her nerves would most likely betray her and lead to uncomfortable questions. Relief washed over her when her feet touched the hardwood of the foyer floor, but as she rounded the banister to face the ground floor hallway, her relief was replaced by the feeling of being watched.

The hair stood up on her neck, but Ally swallowed her nerves and entered the hallway. She crept to the first door on the left and placed a hand on the knob before freezing. She was about to enter the portrait hallway again. She shuddered as she imagined the eyes of her dead family members staring at her from their paintings on the walls. *Hell no.* Instead, she made for the second door on the left, which led to the music room.

She turned the handle slowly, then slid the door open as lightly as she could. Once it presented a crack large enough for her to fit through, she slipped inside. The room was filled with chairs, a variety of instrument cases, and a baby grand piano, a small cousin for the grand piano in the ballroom. Thankfully, a path had been kept clear through the clutter.

After creeping across the room, Ally came to a door directly opposite the one she had just entered through. As she grabbed the handle, she shone the flashlight around the room behind her, still feeling as though she was being watched. She tried not to imagine a shadowy figure peeking at her through the narrow opening she had left in the hallway door. She kept her eyes on it nonetheless as she slowly turned the handle and opened the door into the ballroom. Once again, as soon as the opening was wide enough, she slid inside.

The ballroom had never been so threatening. The curtains over the windows had been drawn for the night, plunging the massive room into a darkness that made it feel cavernous. She panned her flashlight across the still-empty room. The angelic faces carved into the framing around the stage were far less welcoming than Ally had ever imagined them. When the dot of her flashlight beam gleamed off their eyes, it gave the impression that they were looking at her. Swallowing, Ally turned to the right. Immediately in front of her was the first wardrobe. Her heart in her throat, she crept past it towards the second wardrobe.

When she was halfway to it, she thought there was a noise from the balcony behind her. She turned around and shone her flashlight up to it. If there had been a sound, there was nothing there to have caused it. However, as she scanned the balcony, there was something out of place. The door that led from the balcony and into the drawing room was slightly ajar.

Ally didn't know what to make of it. Carol made a point of leaving no doors in the house open when she left at night in case of fire. Trying not to think of who or what might have opened it, Ally resumed her creeping towards the wardrobe. After what seemed like a lifetime, she made it. Swallowing hard, she reached out a trembling hand and pulled the wardrobe open. Just as she had earlier, all she found was the back of the wardrobe. Nervously, she whispered, "H-hello...?"

Ally waited, not knowing what to expect. A minute passed, maybe even several. The hair on the back of her neck continued to bristle. The feeling that she was being watched was overwhelming. Once again, she panned the flashlight around the room to confirm its emptiness, but the feeling persisted. Thoroughly creeped out, Ally whispered again, "Hello?"

Again, there was no answer. Perhaps it had all been just a dream after all. Then, to both Ally's amazement and horror, a voice whispered back from within wardrobe, "Hel...lo...?"

6. Forbidden Secrets

Ally recognized the voice instantly as the one that had sung in her dream. She leaned forward and whispered, "Are you...the immortal princess? Are you Genevieve?"

Another long pause met her question at first, but eventually the voice replied, "Yes..."

Ally sat inside the wardrobe, facing outward. Once more she panned the flashlight around the room, not wanting to expose her back while she listened to the princess. Once she was satisfied with her scan of the ballroom, Ally whispered, "I...I need to know some things."

"I...know...too much..."

"Is that why Lamuel buried you?" Ally asked nervously.

"No."

Ally frowned. "Then why?"

"Be...cause...I could...not...die."

"Are you...still alive...then?"

The pause before the reply was longer this time, but still the reply came. "Yes."

"How?" Ally asked, her curiosity getting the better of her.

The pause before that answer was the longest yet. For a moment, Ally thought she might get no answer at all, but eventually Genevieve whispered, "Because...of...the One...Below."

"One Below?"

"The One...was here...before...everything."

"Who is the One Below?" Ally asked, fearful of the answer.

"It does...not...give...a name."

"Does it have a name?"

"Yes."

"But it doesn't give it?"

"No."

Ally inhaled slowly, considering her next question. She had more than she could count buzzing through her head, but one stood out from the others. "Is it...a demon?"

A long pause preceded the answer once again, but Ally was relieved to hear, "No."

"Then what is it?"

"I do...not...know."

Ally frowned, disappointed. Still, she did have many more questions. The next was the most important to her. "Who is Sam?" This time, no answer came. Ally asked again, "Genevieve, who is Sam?" Again, there was no answer. Ally pleaded, "Genevieve, please. Whoever Sam is, he's talking to my little sister. Is he dangerous?"

Once again, Ally thought no reply would come, but when it did come, Ally's blood turned to ice. "Yes."

Not good. Ally took a moment to steady her nerves before asking her next question, "Is he going to hurt her?"

"No."

Ally sighed with relief, but then asked, "Then what will he do?"

The reply was delayed, but the most chilling yet. "Hurt...you."

Even better. Ally swallowed. "Why will he hurt me?"

"He...hurts...them...all."

Ally looked around the ballroom again, more frightened than ever. "What does that have to do with my sister?"

"He...will...use...her."

"Use her for what?" Once again, Genevieve didn't answer. Ally asked again, "What will he use her for?"

Finally, the princess replied, "Tired...must...sleep."

"You're tired? Will you be awake tomorrow?"

"Tomorrow...night."

"I'll come back then."

"Who?"

Ally blinked, confused. "Who what?"

"Who...are...you?"

"I'm Allison, but everyone calls me Ally."

"Ally...be...careful."

Ally swallowed, but answered, "I will be. Sleep well, Genevieve."

A soft sigh issued from the back of the wardrobe, and then there was silence. With the conversation over, Ally replayed it in her mind. She was both frightened by and fascinated with the immortal princess. How was Genevieve still alive? Why couldn't Lamuel kill her? Whatever the truth was, Ally doubted that Genevieve was still human. The thought made Ally shudder. Still, if she was going to protect her sister, and possibly the rest of her family, she needed answers first. Hopefully tomorrow night the princess would be willing to give her more.

Ally began to make her way back to her room. She moved as slowly and quietly as she had coming to the ballroom, but with a greater sense of urgency. The feeling of being watched had grown so oppressive that her eyes were never still, and every shadow set her nerves on edge. She made it through the music room and ground floor hallway without incident. After entering the foyer, she climbed the staircase two steps at a time. However, when she turned at the landing to face down the second-floor hallway, she saw something that made her freeze in horror.

The moonlight was just bright enough to illuminate the outline of someone standing in front of the window at the end of the hallway. Ally immediately shone her flashlight down the hall, but when the beam reached the window, there was nothing standing in front of it. *Go figure.* In that instant, however, the feeling of being watched was stronger than ever. Somehow, she could also tell where she was being watched from, but she was terrified to look.

Slowly and reluctantly, she lifted her gaze to the foyer ceiling over her head. The shadow of a figure sat huddled where the wall met the ceiling directly above her, its arms outstretched. Before Ally could shine the flashlight up at it, it lunged at her with a feral hiss.

Fuck! In a blind panic, Ally ran to her bedroom and slammed the door shut, not caring how much noise she had made. She had never experienced anything so terrifying in her life. Slowly, she stepped back from her closed door until she felt her legs touch the edge of her bed. With her wide eyes still fixed on the door, she sat back onto the bed, trembling in fear.

Knock. Knock. Knock.

Not again. Ally slid back onto the bed as far from the door as she could get and hugged her knees to her chest. The knocking continued slowly and deliberately for nearly a full minute, then turned into furious pounding.

Bang! Bang! Bang!

Ally pulled the covers up around her like a protective shield. The door rattled in its frame as the pounding grew louder.

BANG! BANG! BANG!

Whimpering in terror, Ally covered her ears and prayed for it to stop.

BANG! BANG! BANG!

When she was certain that the door would give out against the onslaught, the pounding finally stopped. Ally didn't dare breathe. She stared at the door with wide eyes, and her ears strained for the slightest sound. There were a few seconds silence, but then someone...or something...uttered a malicious chuckle from behind the door.

Ally shivered, keeping her eyes locked on the door still. Clearly what had just happened was meant to scare her. Was it Sam? Was he trying to dissuade her from talking to the princess? Without more information, Ally couldn't think of a more logical conclusion. She shivered again. Clearly the princess knew things that Ally wasn't supposed to find out.

Ally had no idea how long she watched the door, but no further disturbances occurred. As her fear began to wane, it was replaced by determination. Ally wasn't about to sit idle while someone, living or dead, tried to hurt her or her family. She whispered, "You'll have to try harder than that to stop me." The firmness of her words surprised her, but she found strength in saying it aloud.

Sleep would be out of the question, so instead she grabbed her flashlight and turned her attention to the marker board to detail what she had learned. She would have quite a story for Maddy next time she called!

ALLY WOKE UP WITH HER face down on the vanity table. What time she had finally passed out, she couldn't say. Judging by the angle of the light from her window, it was nearly midday.

She set the marker board aside to look in the mirror. The right side of her face was red, but the swelling on the left side had subsided. All that remained was a dark bruise under her eye that looked almost black on her pale skin. She ran her fingers along the bruise and winced. It was tender. She then ran a brush through her disheveled black hair to make herself more presentable before heading downstairs to get something to eat.

The mansion was much less frightening in the daylight, but Ally was wary nonetheless. Every angelic face in the woodwork seemed to mock her fear. Any trace of comfort she had found outside of her room had vanished after the previous night's incident.

She went into the kitchen to find Chad the cook preparing a small lunch. She asked with a yawn, "What's on the menu, Chad?"

Chad looked up from his work at her. He was a portly man of almost thirty with a clean-shaven face, sharp blue eyes, and dark, bushy eyebrows. Ally couldn't remember ever seeing him without his hat or apron on. He observed, "A little late for breakfast, isn't it?"

Ally yawned. "I'll take whatever is served." When Chad raised an eyebrow with a hint of a smile, she added, "Within reason." The cook's sense of humor was not to be underestimated.

Chad smiled. "I'll make you a sandwich then. That work?"

Ally smiled. "Thanks, Chad." She then went into the dining room but stopped as soon as she passed through the door. Cassie was sitting at one of the two long tables in the room, gripping the edge of the chair and kicking her legs back and forth while staring at the table.

Cassie turned to look at her with fearful eyes. "Did Sam do that?"

"Do what, Cass?" Ally asked nervously.

"Hurt your eye."

Ally walked over and sat down beside her sister. "No, it happened at school. That's why I'm home now, so I can get better."

"Oh. Sam said he met you last night. He said you were doing something bad."

That asshole. Ally shivered. "I wasn't doing anything wrong, Cass."

"That's not what Sam said," Cassie chided, but then she whispered earnestly, "I think you made him angry. Please don't make him angry, Ally."

Ally took a deep breath, considering her next words carefully. Finally, she asked in a soft whisper, "Does he scare you?"

Cassie didn't answer right away but looked back at the table. "Only when he's angry," she mumbled, kicking her legs nervously.

"Has he gotten angry at you?"

Cassie shook her head. "No, only you."

Ally shuddered again but then smiled at Cassie. "Let me worry about that then. As long as he's not angry at you, everything will be fine."

Cassie cocked her head, her pretty blue eyes echoing Ally's own fears. "Are you sure?"

Ally nodded and patted Cassie's shoulder reassuringly. "I'll take care of everything, Cassie. Just you wait and see."

It was not even 3:30 yet by the time the phone rang. *Maddy must have called the moment she got home.* "I got it!" Ally called as she raced for the dining room, where the phone hung on the wall next to the door. She picked it up and said, "Hey, Maddy."

"Hey, girl! How you holding up in jail?"

Ally giggled. "The food's good, but I'm not getting along with my cell mate."

Maddy sighed. "Well, just hit 'em like you did Gladys and it should be all right."

"Did I miss anything important?"

"Other than Derek and Bart asking about you, the former looking like a lost puppy and the latter all concerned and stuff, no."

Ally blushed a little. "Why would Derek look like a lost puppy?"

"Prolly 'cause his girl isn't around."

Ally's blush intensified. "Well...nothing's official yet..."

"Girl, he planted one on you in the middle of the cafeteria. You might as well be wearing a sign that says, 'Derek's Girl.'"

Ally huffed indignantly, but if she was honest with herself, the idea didn't sound all that unappealing. Then she remembered what she had to tell Maddy. "Well, as it turns out, something happened last night."

"What do you mean?" Maddy asked. Ally then explained everything, from meeting Genevieve to the threatening shadow and her sister's reaction.

When she finished, Maddy didn't reply right away. After the long pause, she asked, "Why are you still living there?"

"'Cause I'm not old enough to be out on my own yet."

"Ally, this shit is getting scary."

Ally sighed. "I know, but it's *been* scary for me for a while now."

"Are you gonna try to talk to her again tonight?"

"I have to. I need to know more."

"What more do you need to know? Sam's got it out for you now that you talked to this princess chick."

Ally thought for a moment. In all honesty, she wanted to know everything. If Genevieve had been locked up for as long as Ally thought she had, then she knew more about the family's history than any other source, even Bart's grandfather. Still, Ally had to prioritize her questions. Finally, she said, "Maybe she knows how to stop him."

"If she did, why wouldn't she have done it already? Oh...wait, never mind. Forgot about the whole 'buried alive' bit."

"So, I have to talk to her again."

"Ally, you shouldn't."

Ally was shocked. She had never heard Maddy sound so scared before. It wasn't like her. "Why not?"

Maddy took a deep breath before saying, "Sam is dangerous, and talking to Genevieve stirs him up. He'll either try harder to scare you or do something much worse if you don't stay away from her."

Ally bit her lip, considering her counterargument. Not often did she and Maddy not agree on something. Still, Ally couldn't give up the chance to learn more. She said, "I'm going back tonight, like I told her I would."

Maddy sighed. "Then you'd best not go alone."

Ally's eyes widened. "I am NOT taking Cassie along!"

"Whoa, hold up! I meant me, girl."

"Oh," Ally said, surprised. She hadn't expected that.

"Ask your parents. I'm pretty sure they won't mind. Dad's out of town again, so as soon as you say the word, I'll head out that way."

Ally was hesitant. "I dunno, Maddy. You said it yourself; Sam is dangerous. You'd be putting yourself in his crosshairs."

"If it means I can watch your back this time, then it's worth it."

Ally was shocked at the pain in Maddy's voice. Did she blame herself for Ally getting jumped at school? She said quietly, "Maddy...it wasn't your fault."

"I know, but I still should've been there. Doesn't matter now. You gonna ask?"

"I...I guess."

"Then get to it!"

"Okay, okay!" Ally assured her as she made for her bedroom door. "Mom?" she called, but there was no answer. Then, Ally remembered Friday was art day. Her mother and Cassie would be in the art room on the third floor, painting. Instead, Ally went to her dad's office. She knocked, then covered the receiver with her hand. "Dad?"

Seconds later, he poked his head out of the door. "What is it?"

"Can Maddy stay over tonight?"

Her dad raised an eyebrow. "That her on the line?"

Ally tensed a little. "Yes."

Her dad narrowed his eyes at her. "Her idea or yours?"

Ally was struck by the oddness of the question, but answered, "Well, we kinda decided together..."

Then her dad grinned at her to let her know he was joking. "Of course she can come! Does she need a ride?"

Ally relaxed and grinned back. "Nope, her dad's bringing her." The lie came just as easily as ever.

Satisfied, her dad said, "You know the rules. Don't wake your sister, and don't make a mess."

Ally rolled her eyes, still grinning. "Of course, Dad. Thanks!"

He smiled at her before disappearing back into his office. Ally went back to her room and uncovered the receiver. "Well, you better start walking."

Ally swore she heard Maddy jump to her feet. "On it. See you soon, girl!" She hung up.

Ally set the phone down on her bed and sat down beside it. She could barely contain her excitement. For the first time since everything started, someone else was finally going to face it with her. It was the most comforting thought she'd had since Derek's kiss in the cafeteria. Still, her excitement was dulled by worry. Was she endangering her best friend by getting her directly involved? Maddy wouldn't have it any other way, but would Sam feel more threatened with the pair of them? Would he resort to something drastic? *He should have thought of that before he started messing with my little sister.*

Ally's lip curled. If he wanted to play dirty, she could, too.

7. Sam's Warning

Soon enough, the doorbell rang. Ally sprang from her bed and raced down the stairs yelling, "I'll get it!"

Ally barely got the door open before Maddy burst in and threw her arms around her yelling, "Oh, I've missed you so much!"

Ally giggled. "Stop, you're making a scene!"

Maddy threw her head back and laughed. "Have I ever not?"

Ally wriggled free, still giggling. "It's what you do. Come on!" The pair of them headed upstairs to Ally's bedroom.

Once the door was closed, Maddy said, "Have they seen this?"

Ally turned from the door to find Maddy staring at the marker board. "Nope. Carol stopped cleaning my room years ago. Parents thought I should do it myself."

Maddy looked it over, frowning. "Are you sure you're not becoming a little obsessed?"

Ally threw herself onto the bed with a sigh. "I dunno. Since I started finding answers, it's just gotten hard to stop."

Maddy raised an eyebrow. "I noticed," she observed with a hint of concern.

Ally sat up. "It's fine, Maddy. Once we figure out how to deal with Sam, I won't need it anymore."

"I bet you already have most of it memorized anyways."

Ally blushed, thankful that Maddy was still looking at the board. "Only the more well-known bits."

Maddy turned to look at her, her face grave. "Are you sure you want to do this if it makes Sam mad?"

Ally nodded without hesitation. "She'll tell us how to stop him. I'm sure of it."

"All right then," Maddy said before throwing herself on the bed beside Ally and kicking off her shoes. "So how do we kill time 'til the audience with her royal highness?"

"That's just a nickname, but I dunno. Naked pillow fight?"

Maddy blinked and frowned at Ally. "That's my line!"

Ally shrugged, blushing. "Just a suggestion."

Maddy grinned mischievously. "Sorry, but if you want to see all of this," she said as she ran her hands down the length of her body sensually, "you're gonna have to work for it."

Ally rolled her eyes. "I really don't get you sometimes."

"Bet you'd like to."

Ally pushed her away. "You wish!"

Maddy threw her arms wide on the bed. "Only for you, baby."

"If you say it any louder, my parents will suspect that we are actually lovers."

"Haven't you heard? If we don't make people question our sexuality when we're together, how can we even be called best friends?"

"I thought you weren't into popular opinion."

"Only if it's not any fun. Speaking of 'love,' how old is your gardener?"

Ally's eyes widened. "I was gonna warn you about him, but I forgot..."

Maddy raised an eyebrow. "You forgot to mention that the gardener likes to undress me with his eyes?"

"I...I didn't think it was *that* bad."

Maddy grinned. "It's not, he's just really friendly. The kind of 'You're really cute and we should hang out' friendly."

Ally sighed in relief. "Well, he's only seventeen. His dad is in Dad's class, and he needed a part-time job for some after-school program he's in, so Dad hooked him up."

"Cool. He's kinda cute, too, but not my type. By the way, you wouldn't happen to have any paper, would you?"

Ally got up and went to her vanity table, where she kept a stack of notebook paper in a drawer. She took out a handful of pages, grabbed a pencil, and brought them over to Maddy. "Anything else?" she asked.

"Nope," Maddy answered as she scooted to the floor, took the pencil, and began to draw.

For the next hour, Ally watched in silence as Maddy drew a picture. Though she wasn't in any art classes, Maddy was fantastic with a pencil and paper. Before Ally's eyes she did caricatures of herself, Ally, Derek, and Bart. Then she added in the middle a heart with the words, "friends 'til the end" in fancy, looping letters. Ally hadn't realized just how much their little circle had come to mean to Maddy until that moment. Her affection for her best friend soared.

When Maddy finished, she picked it up and offered it to Ally. "For you, my dear. A gift on behalf of the Vice President of the Freak Squad."

Ally took the picture and set it beside her. "Who does that make the president then?"

"That's you, of course!"

"What makes me so special?"

Maddy rolled onto her back and spread her arms again. "The fact that this circle wouldn't exist if not for you."

Ally wondered if it were possible to love her best friend any more than she already did.

Time passed with the pair of them chatting, drawing, and bantering about whatever came to mind. Ally thought she was horrible at drawing, but Maddy continuously encouraged her. They passed a cheerful enough meal with the family as well before returning to their drawings in Ally's room. Eventually, however, the time came. After Ally had changed into her night-gown and Maddy into her sweatpants, they each grabbed a flashlight. Puzzled, Maddy asked, "Why do you have two flashlights in your bedroom?"

"Remember that time we made the pillow fort and told scary stories?"

"Duh!"

"I just kept both flashlights," Ally explained. Then, she turned on her flashlight and switched off the bedroom light. Maddy's flashlight clicked on not long after. "Ready?" Ally asked as much to herself as to Maddy.

"Let's do this," Maddy said resolutely, giving Ally heart. She opened the door, and they slipped out into the hallway. The moment they were outside her bedroom, Ally felt eyes upon her again. At least the feeling was not as oppressive as it had been before. Perhaps the presence of someone else made Sam cautious? She then noticed Maddy slide a little closer to her. Undoubtedly, she could feel it as well. In nervous silence, they set off down the dark hall.

They made it to the ballroom without incident. It seemed that Ally's guess that Sam was keeping his distance wasn't far off. Soon enough, Ally was opening the wardrobe once again. She whispered, "Genevieve, are you there?"

They waited for a moment, but soon the answer came. "Yes...Ally."

Maddy inhaled sharply, her eyes wide. Ally looked at her and held a finger to her lips. "I brought a friend. Her name is Maddy. Is that all right?"

"Yes...best...you not...come...alone."

"That's what I said," Maddy added quietly.

Ally shot Maddy a glare to silence her, then asked, "Do you know how to stop Sam?"

Genevieve didn't answer at first. Ally wondered if she was considering her answer, but then she said, "Only...the One...Below."

Ally shivered but asked urgently, "What about the One Below?"

"Sam...fears...the One."

"How do we get to the One Below?" Ally asked eagerly, ignoring the uneasy look that Maddy shot in her direction.

"In...the tower."

"What about the tower?" Ally leaned forward. Again, she ignored the look Maddy gave her or her friend's outstretched hand.

"The tower...where...he...kept...me."

"Where who kept you?"

"My...brother."

"What does that have to do with the One Below?" Ally was nearly pressing her face to the back of the wardrobe.

Maddy whispered, "Ally...calm down."

"No!" Ally said, her voice rising, "Genevieve, what does the tower have to do with the One Below? How can it help me stop Sam?"

Maddy didn't speak again. The only voice that answered Ally came from the wardrobe. "He's...here."

Maddy grabbed Ally by the arm and pulled her out of the wardrobe. Ally tried to throw her off, demanding, "Genevieve, answer me!"

Maddy pleaded, "Ally, be quiet! Can't you hear it?"

"Hear what?" Then she did.

"Heh...heh...heh..."

It was a low, soft chuckle. Ally's head whipped around for the source, but there was none.

"Heh...heh...heh..."

Where are you, you bastard? Was he mocking her? Ally's temper rose as she stepped away from the wardrobe, her flashlight panning wildly.

"Heh, heh, heh."

He is *mocking me.* Through gritted teeth, Ally hissed, "Where the fuck are you?"

"Ally...up there!" Maddy whispered. Ally didn't need to ask where Maddy meant. Ally turned her flashlight towards the balcony, finally catching sight of the shadowy figure.

"Heh, heh, heh."

Stop fucking laughing at me! Ally stepped forward, glaring at the shadow. "What do you want?" There was no reply. "What do you want with my sister?" Ally demanded.

"Heh, heh, heh," and then silence. The shadow man had simply vanished. Before Ally had time to wonder where he had gone, Cassie's scream tore through her ears.

Panic-stricken, Ally bolted out of the ballroom with Maddy hot on her heels. Her sister's piercing shrieks rang through the entire house. When they finally burst into Cassie's room, however, they found her sleeping peacefully, her breathing soft and slow. Ally's hands clenched into fists. *That was a warning.*

Maddy whispered, "Ally...let's get back to your room."

"I won't let you hurt her," Ally growled, tears welling up in her eyes, her fists clenching and unclenching. She then started towards Cassie, her arms outstretched to scoop her up.

"Ally, come on! You'll just scare her!" Maddy insisted, grabbing Ally by the hand and trying to drag her out the door. *I don't want her out of my sight!* Ally tried to shake Maddy off at first, but Maddy insisted, "Come on, don't wake her over this!" At last, Ally let Maddy pull her back into the hallway and through her own bedroom door. Once inside, Maddy pushed the door closed. "That...was fucked up."

"I won't let him hurt her," Ally repeated, standing in the middle of the room, her eyes still wide and misty.

Maddy turned and grabbed her by the shoulders. Her green eyes locked on Ally's as she added, "We won't let him hurt her. Come on girl, snap out of it!"

Ally blinked, then threw off Maddy's hands to go sit on the bed. Before she could stop herself, she burst into tears. Maddy sat down beside her and pulled her close. Ally sobbed, "I...I've never been...so scared..."

"Me either," Maddy admitted. Ally shook uncontrollably. The screams had sounded completely real. The moment she had heard them, her heart felt as though it had been ripped out of her chest, only to be forced back in when they found Cassie unharmed. Every time she thought she was getting control of herself, her sister's screams would echo through her thoughts again, and she would begin sobbing anew.

Maddy finally said, "You'd better ask your parents if I can stay tomorrow night, too."

Ally looked up at her, trying to blink away her still-flowing tears. "W-what...?"

"Genevieve said the tower, so that's where we've got to go."

Ally wiped her eyes with her blanket. "But...but he'll try...to stop us."

Maddy nodded gravely. "That's why you'll need me."

Ally could not put her gratitude into words. Despite everything that had just happened, Maddy was staying with her. She whispered, "Thank you."

Maddy gave her a comforting smile. "I'd never abandon you, girl."

Ally smiled wanly but then sighed. "We'll have to go at night again. The tower room is off limits, according to Dad. If anyone catches us there, it'll be trouble." The trip from her room to the art room at the base of the tower would also leave plenty of opportunities for Sam to harass them some more, but Ally kept that thought to herself.

Maddy shrugged. "Can't make things too easy, can we?"

"I guess not. Think we'll get any sleep tonight?"

Maddy rolled her eyes. "Hell no."

Maddy was as good as her word. Neither of them slept a wink that night, despite climbing into bed together. Ally figured that they'd need to be rested for whatever was going to happen the next night, but her sister's screams were still too fresh in her mind. She also assumed that Maddy would not soon forget the shadow man. Not even the rays of dawn offered any comfort. Ally simply sat up and said with a yawn and a stretch, "Now to act like everything is normal."

Maddy yawned in turn before adding, "And not sneak glances over shoulders or into dark corners."

"Don't even bother," Ally warned. "You'll end up seeing something you'll wish you hadn't."

"Too late," Maddy admitted with an uncharacteristic shudder. Then she added, "Food might help."

Ally nodded but didn't reply as she got up and led the way down to the dining room for breakfast. For the first time, the house was no less menacing during the day than it had been at night. Hearing her sister's screams, real or fake, had forever changed how she felt about the place. Even Maddy seemed tense despite her exhaustion.

As they entered the empty dining hall, Ally asked, "So what'll it be?"

Maddy answered, "Just some toast and orange juice."

Ally nodded, then headed to the kitchen. Chad hadn't arrived yet, so she poured two glasses of orange juice and made two pieces of toast for each of them. She took them out to Maddy and sat to eat. Neither said anything until both plates and glasses were empty. Then, Ally said, "I won't be talking to Genevieve anymore."

"Promise?" came a voice from the door into the hall. Maddy let out a small squeak of fright and Ally nearly jumped out of her seat as she whirled around. Cassie was standing there, the door slightly ajar behind her. Ally wasn't sure if she was imagining it, but Cassie looked as frightened as them.

Ally nodded slowly, wondering how she could explain her fright to Cassie. "Promise."

Cassie came up and sat on the chair beside her. "Sam woke me up. He was very angry," she said with a shudder.

Ally's blood ran cold. What had she done? "What did he do?" she asked, almost afraid to know the answer.

"He said bad things would happen if you talked to her again," Cassie whispered, her eyes full of fear.

"Well, no bad things are gonna happen. I'm done talking to her."

Cassie looked at her imploringly, tears in her pretty blue eyes. "Ally, I'm scared."

Ally's heart broke. Whatever façade Sam had put on for Cassie was starting to crack, frightening her. *I have to stop him. I have to.* As she draped an arm around Cassie's shoulders, Ally said, "Maddy and I will protect you. Don't worry."

Cassie looked at them both in turn. "Promise?"

Both Ally and Maddy nodded, and Maddy added, "I'll beat up anything bad that comes your way. No worries."

Cassie managed a smile at her. "You're so tough. I wanna be like you."

Maddy blushed slightly but answered, "Well, let us look out for you, and you'll be able to grow up and be just as tough as I am."

Cassie's smile brightened. "Then I'll beat up all the bad people!"

Ally hugged her again. "Not if we do it first."

When they returned to Ally's bedroom after breakfast, Maddy turned to face Ally. "Why don't we go now?"

Ally frowned. "But Carol..."

"...isn't here yet, and your dad left first thing. All we have to worry about is Cassie and your mom. Neither should be a problem."

Ally blinked in surprise. Why hadn't she thought of that? "You're right. Let's go!" They left her bedroom once more. This time, they turned right instead of left and headed down the hallway towards the back of the house. At the end of the hallway, they turned right and ascended a staircase to the third floor. A flight of steps, a landing, and another flight brought them to a door. Ally opened it and entered the third-floor hallway, which was identical to the two directly below it. She led the way to the last door on the right of the hallway, which opened to a long room with three telephones in the middle.

Maddy had never seen the telephone room before. As she frowned in confusion, Ally explained, "Each phone is for a different floor. The third is for the basement."

Maddy's eyes darted around nervously. "Let's go before he figures out what we're up to."

Ally nodded in agreement and led them to a door on the far left of the telephone room. She opened it to the game room. Inside were numerous toys from Ally's childhood as well as antiques that had been in the family for a generation or more. The older the toys were, the more they gave Ally the creeps. Among them were several porcelain dolls, a wide-eyed and grinning jack-in-the-box, and an antique mechanical monkey with a pair of cymbals.

They rushed across the game room to another door leading to the art room. As soon as Ally opened the door, the memory of the hanged woman flashed through her mind. *She had been in the art room.* Ally shuddered as the bloodshot eyes and rolling head reappeared vividly in her mind.

Maddy asked, "What's wrong?"

"Just a chill," Ally said dismissively before finally opening the door. The art room had four easels in it. Three were empty, but the fourth held an unfinished painting of a vase with flowers in it and another sketched beside it. *Mom's getting pretty good.*

Ally turned to the left, where a wrought iron spiral staircase led up to the tower room. She had never tried to climb it, even when she was younger. Before she could begin to doubt herself, she took the first step up.

Immediately the staircase rattled. Ally gulped but took another step. Maddy wasn't far behind. After Maddy crossed the fifth step, the staircase began to creak ominously. Ally's stomach lurched. She felt extremely vulnerable, even though they were less than halfway up the staircase. Her pace quickened a little. As she climbed, Ally couldn't tell if the staircase was moving or she was getting dizzy. Then, the art room door burst open.

Ally looked down and immediately regretted it. The floor seemed so far away, making her legs turn to jelly. Maddy said, "Ally, there's no one there. Keep going!" Ally tried to move her legs, but they were so wobbly that she had to grab the railing for support. She had never known that she was afraid of heights. *What a time to find out.*

Maddy groaned, "Ally...it's him."

The stairs rattled and adrenaline finally pumped strength back into Ally's legs. She took the stairs two at a time, reaching the top in only a few seconds. The stairs led to a trapdoor. She groaned; the trapdoor was padlocked.

"I got it, hang on," Maddy said as she squeezed past, pulling a pin out of her hair.

The staircase rattled again. Ally dared not look, but she had no doubt that the shadow man was coming. A gruff, stern voice barked, "Don't you dare!"

Maddy exclaimed, "Yes!" and pulled the padlock off. Ally threw her weight against the trapdoor and pushed it open. As she and Maddy climbed into the tower room, the gruff voice screamed in rage below them. Triumphant, she closed the trapdoor and took stock of where they had ended up. The octagonal tower room was deathly cold. The round windows on all eight walls were heavily cobwebbed and coated with thick dust. The mid-morning sun provided no more than dim lighting, and there was no other light source.

After her eyes had adjusted to the gloom, Ally examined the room's contents. Beneath one window were two ragged blankets spread out on top of each other and a moth-eaten pillow. A pair of tall, narrow bookshelves stood between two windows each, filled sparsely with books too covered in dust to even make out the titles, while a brass telescope sat at another window. Between the bookshelves was a large antique desk with a spindly chair under it. *How on earth did they even get that monster up here?* Ally could have laid across the desk with her arms spread and left no part of her hanging over the edge.

"How..." Maddy said, aghast.

Ally shook her head and walked up to the desk. Its surface was bare except for a thick layer of dust. She turned her attention to the drawers on either side of it while Maddy looked at the books on the shelves. The first drawer Ally opened contained only a withered quill and dried up inkwell. The contents of the second were far more sinister. There were several small bones, including three rodent skulls and a short, rusted dagger. Ally called to Maddy, "Come across anything like this in your dabbling?"

Maddy looked up from the book she was leafing through and peeked in the drawer. "Looks like a few dead pets."

"What about the dagger?"

Maddy shrugged. "Could mean anything, really."

Sighing, Ally opened the next drawer and gasped. Inside was a silver chalice engraved with the images of hundreds of screaming faces. The inside of the chalice was stained an odd, rusty hue. Opening the drawer wider, Ally discovered a skull marked with several astrological symbols, a small effigy of a goat-headed woman with angel wings and hooves for feet, and a jar containing what appeared to be a shrunken head. "What about this?" Ally asked quietly, her eyes wide.

Maddy once again peered over a fresh book and her eyes went wide as well. "Well...that's an alchemy skull. The head is...a head...but the statue is Baphomet."

"What's Baphomet?"

"A demon," Maddy whispered, and Ally shuddered. "From what I've gathered here, this is a collection of all sorts of things to do with black magic, from demon summoning to Voodoo. Whoever made this really got around."

"Were they looking for something specific though, or just collecting?" Ally wondered aloud.

Maddy shrugged. "Maybe both?"

Ally then opened another drawer to find several candles of various shapes and sizes.

Maddy returned the book and examined the drawer's contents with Ally. "I'm betting whoever it was was performing a ritual of some kind."

"That's comforting," Ally observed sarcastically.

"Sorry, just trying to help," Maddy said with an apologetic smile.

"Don't be, it just...it kinda freaks me out to think that somebody was doing black magic here."

"I get it, hun. Anyways, what's in the last drawer?"

With a hint of foreboding, Ally opened the final drawer to find a leather-bound book, its pages composed of parchment in mismatched sizes. Ally pulled the book out and blew the dust off. The cover was blank. Undeterred, Ally opened it to the title page, but what she saw made her freeze. Inside was written *Memoirs of Samuel Corbant.*

Ally turned to look at Maddy, whispering, "It's his journal."

"Well then, let's read it!"

Ally looked down at it for a moment, hesitant. She had no idea what she would find in that little leather book. If Maddy's assessment of the desk's contents was accurate, it would certainly be unpleasant. "I...I'm not sure I want to."

"If there's any idea on how to stop him, it'll be in there."

Ally sighed. *She's got a point.* It also might tell them what he had been doing with all these occult books in the first place. Against her better judgment, she began to read Sam's journal.

8. The Source

The first page contained only one sentence, and it was a dedication. "To Darius Corbant: if thine angels exist, then may they weep when I rip thee from them and pull thee into a special Hell of my own creation, just for thee."

Ally shuddered as she read the words aloud, shaken by the raw hatred in them. She then turned the page and read, "September 29, 1753. At last, I am free. Let these pages be the only confession that I leave that it was I who ended my father's life just last night. His illness had rendered him too weak to rise from his bed, and it was all too easy to still his breath with his own pillow. Never have I felt such exhilaration, even when I watched my mother fall to her death by my hand from the attic window.

"Still, taking his life was not enough. If his piousness is to be believed, then he has gone to some place beyond my reach. My victory is soured by the idea of him knowing an eternity of peace! By all that defies his wretched god, I will find a way to bring him back to this earth and leave him a hollow shell of a man if it takes my very last breath. Death is too good for him!"

Ally paused, again revolted by the degree of hatred in what she was reading.

"Seems he had some daddy issues," Maddy said, trying to lighten the mood with a half-smile, but her eyes were fearful.

Hesitantly, Ally turned the page and continued. "January 4, 1754. Annabel Morgan and I were finally wed today. The timing was convenient since Annabel had not bled since before last month. Best if we are married before anyone suspects as I do and ridicules my child as a bastard. It had best be a son. Loathe as I am to admit it, the family name must endure, but not because of my father. Rather, in spite of him. The family will become what I shape it to be, not what he had planned. I wonder how many more children Annabel will produce before she becomes useless. Perhaps a large family will serve me well.

"March 3, 1754. My suspicions have been confirmed. Annabel has become quite voracious, and her belly has begun to swell. I must admit I am more excited than I had thought I would be, though her symptoms are quite troublesome. I hope whatever she produces is more willful and less of an intemperate slave to its whims than its mother. It is fortunate that my father's wealth was vast indeed, possibly the only intelligent act he performed in the entirety of his pathetic life. If not for his actions, Annabel would eat me out of house and home.

"Of further annoyance is her insatiable lust. Before she was with child, she had been far more willing to do whatever I desired, but now she simply craves her own pleasure. I may be forced to deprive her to remind her of her place.

"August 31, 1754. At last, Annabel has given me a son, and his name shall be Edward. I foresee that his contribution to this family's greatness will be remarkable indeed. I must admit I am more partial to him than I had anticipated, but though he will want for nothing, he will receive no tenderness from me. Undoubtedly his idiot mother will supply that enough for the entire countryside. I must endeavor to teach him the truths of this world: tenderness is merely a tool. Use it sparingly lest it lose its power, or thy heart become as thou doth behave. This world will prey upon a tender heart without mercy. The only way to endure is to show less mercy still."

"What the fuck is wrong with this guy?" Maddy asked, flabbergasted.

Ally shook her head. "A lot of men thought like him back then." Even so, there was a coldness to Sam's words that went beyond the common practice of his time. Maddy shot her a skeptical look.

Ally took a deep breath and read on. "January 20, 1755. I leave for England tomorrow. Though Annabel made every attempt to force me to bear her and Edward's company, I convinced her that I must go alone. Perhaps it is in the Old World where I can find some manner of clue as to how to pull my father's soul back to this world and torture it. I do not plan to return until I have what I seek. Annabel insists on constant correspondence. If it will silence her, then I will oblige. Not for her sake, but for Edward's. If he is to value my council, he cannot be allowed to think ill of me. Hopefully when I have returned, Annabel will no longer be quite so tedious. I will need to take steps to ensure that this journal remains hidden until my return.

"April 4, 1756. At last, I have returned! The Old World did not disappoint, though avoiding suspicion was more tedious than my wife had ever been. Perhaps my tolerance for her foolish antics will have increased, but I am doubtful. However, I digress. I managed to locate numerous grimoires and treatises on the Black Arts, as well as documentation of the names and roles of various demons. Once I have sorted through this mess, perhaps I will begin to piece together a way to properly punish my father's soul."

Ally looked up at Maddy. "Does he even care about his son?"

Maddy shrugged, shaking her head. "Prolly only as far as he can use him."

Ally shuddered but continued. "October 9, 1756. Annabel is with child again. Her usefulness continues to surprise me despite how irksome she has become since my return. After this child is born, I might consider arranging an accident for her. Two should be enough, unless I can find another wife, though I may forego that course simply because of how dreadfully tedious they can be. My research continues, and I believe I have at the very least a way to entrap my father's soul once I have called it forth. Soothsayers used such a spell for Divination, but I believe with the proper alterations, it will turn this house into a cage. I will perform the ritual tonight.

"The ritual is complete! Lo, as I reached the zenith of my chant, the house did shutter at my power! T'was wondrous to behold! However, I am now fairly exhausted. Come the morrow, I must discover if I was truly successful."

"October 10, 1756. The stable boy will not be missed. His young spirit was a suitable sacrifice to test my spell..."

Ally stopped, her stomach turning over. Sam had murdered the stable boy—of that she had no doubt. Maddy's face had gone pale. Still, whether out of morbid curiosity or desperation for the answers she was after, Ally read on. "Not long after the boy's demise, I could feel his presence within the house. I am confident that my entrapment ritual was successful. I wonder if there is a way to control him..."

"Oh my God..." Maddy gasped.

"What?" Ally asked, perplexed.

"His spell...it has to be the reason the house is haunted. It's been trapping their souls here," Maddy whispered.

Ally's eyes widened in horror. Sam had cursed the house. "Is there any way to undo it?"

"Read on, maybe there's something in there," Maddy suggested.

Nervously, Ally continued. "October 11, 1756. I have begun to hear a Voice in the night, accompanied by a Deathly chill. At first I suspected the soul of the stable boy come to torment me, but the voice I hear is quite unlike his. It seems to call to me, though I know not from where. Perhaps further research will explain this queer phenomenon?"

"Sound familiar?" Maddy asked.

Ally shuddered and nodded before reading on, "March 21, 1757. My daughter Melody came into this world this morning. Never in this vile world have I ever seen such a beautiful thing. To my last breath, I will ensure that she knows her value and will settle for no man less than worthy."

"Wow, I didn't think he had it in him," Maddy said, surprised.

Ally nodded. "I guess he did have a heart after all."

"I wonder what happened to her."

Ally didn't answer. Instead, she returned to the journal. "April 22, 1757. The Voice came to me in a dream! I asked who or what it was, and it identified itself as the One That Dwells Below. Most intriguing! I entreated it for further information, but it was elusive in its answers. Perhaps my experiments in attempting to reach out for my father's soul drew its attention to me. As of yet, I have been unsuccessful in my original goals, but there is still yet time for my labors to bear fruit.

"January 1, 1758. The One Below calls to me every night now. Nary a wink may I gain without hearing that Voice and feeling the chill that accompanies it. It whispers of knowledge on how to achieve my desires. Perhaps it is a demon of some sort? I wonder what it will ask for in return. I must seek an audience with it directly.

"April 30, 1759. A thousand devil's curses upon these infernal grimoires! I have labored for more than a year, but not one of these tomes has yielded any information concerning who or what the One Below might be. Still, it calls to me every night. I fear I might lose my wits if an answer is not found soon. Perhaps a summoning is in order? Yes, that must be the answer! If I can call the One Below into my presence, all shall be revealed! I must begin in earnest.

"May 3, 1759. The summoning ritual was a disaster. Though I performed every facet of the ritual to a fault, there seem to be forces at work against me. Upon completion of the incantation, the mansion did shudder, but nothing else occurred. I heard the One Below cry out in anguish. I am loathe to admit it, but I fear I may have inadvertently destroyed it.

"June 2, 1759. The One Below still lives! Last eve in my dreams I walked through a tunnel. At the end, I heard its voice as clear as a knell. It is bound somewhere beneath the house. That must be why the summoning ritual failed. I must find the entrance to the tunnel from my dream if I am to meet the One Below at last."

Ally paused, trembling. The parallels between Samuel's experiences and her own were too obvious to overlook. She looked at Maddy, who nodded encouragingly, then continued. "December 21, 1759. I am fairly certain that the entrance to the tunnel in my dreams lies in the cellar. I have exhausted all other possibilities of the house and grounds. The greatest challenge will be finding time to investigate when the servants or my children will not be underfoot to interrupt.

"March 1, 1760. At last! Behind one of the wine shelves in the cellar, I discovered a bricked-up doorway. To think I had searched every nook of the house but that very spot. I shall need a pickaxe to break down the wall. I may have to travel afield to find one.

"April 4, 1760. I have returned from New England with the pickaxe. Tomorrow night, I will begin." That was the final entry.

Ally set the book back down on the desk. "So that's it then," she declared simply.

Maddy looked worried. "That still doesn't tell us how to stop him."

Ally scratched her chin. "It must have something to do with the One That Dwells Below. That's our next..."

"ALLISON DENISE CORBANT!" Ally's heart skipped a beat. *Mom.* She considered not answering, but then her mother yelled, "I know you're up there! That trapdoor was padlocked this morning!"

Shit. Ally yelled back, "C-coming Mom!" She and Maddy exchanged guilty looks, then began the descent down the spiral staircase.

Once they reached the bottom, Ally's mother rounded on them. "You *know* that that room is off limits! Don't you realize how dangerous those stairs are, not to mention the flooring up there! Who knows what kind of shape it's in!"

"But Mom, we found..."

"I don't care if you found El Dorado up there. This is unacceptable. Carol is going to take Maddy home, and you are not to leave your room until you return to school on Monday except to wash or use the bathroom, is that clear?"

Ally hung her head in defeat. "Yes, Mom."

Her mother pointed to the door. "Go to your room. Now."

Ally did as she was told, unable to hold back tears. She had never seen her mother react so strongly, but Ally usually didn't make trouble in the first place. Her mom followed her to her room with Maddy close behind. Once they reached her bedroom, Ally said, "Well, goodbye, Maddy."

Maddy managed a meek smile. "See you Monday, girl!"

Ally smiled as best she could before going into her room and shutting the door. She threw herself on the bed and pounded her fists on the mattress repeatedly. Whether Sam was responsible for her mom's reaction to them being in the tower room or not, Ally couldn't help but feel like he was somewhere in the house laughing at her. Being confined to her room was one thing, but having Maddy sent home was something else altogether. Without her best friend, she knew she was more vulnerable. Worse, Sam knew it, too.

After Ally heard the front door open and close, her mom came up to her room and knocked. *Here it comes.* "Come in."

Her mom stepped in, closing the door behind her. She looked at Ally for a moment, her expression puzzled. Then, she said, "Ally, I want you to tell me if Maddy is talking you into doing anything bad."

Ally was shocked. Her mom had never seemed to think of Maddy as a bad influence before. "No, it was my idea to go up there."

"What on earth were you looking for...oh my God, Ally, what is all this?"

Fuck. Her mom had seen the marker board. Ally quickly tried to recover the situation. "Just some research. I wanted to know more about the family..." Her voice trailed off as she waited for her mother to read the parts about the immortal princess.

However, when her mom turned to look at her, she was smiling. "Now it all makes sense. Why didn't you just ask your father in the first place?"

"Well...I know he doesn't like to talk about his side of the family..."

Her mom nodded. "So thoughtful...I really am proud of the young woman you've become, Ally. Just do me a favor and don't go anywhere else that's off limits, all right?"

Ally nodded obediently. "Okay, Mom."

"Your punishment stands, but you can talk to Maddy when she calls as long as I have your word that she's not talking you into anything."

"I promise, Mom."

"All right then," her mother said before turning to leave, but then she stopped and added, "Also, thanks for making Cassie feel better. She told me that you and Maddy said you'd beat up any bad people that came around. That made her really happy, so thank you."

Ally offered a smile. "No problem!" Then her mother left, and Ally sighed with relief. If her mom had read the notes concerning the immortal princess, she would probably have sent Ally to therapy. She almost thought that her mom was going to ban her from hanging out with Maddy on top of it all, but thankfully that didn't happen. All things considered, she couldn't complain too much about being confined to her room. It seemed to be the only place that Sam didn't mind her being.

Ally let her thoughts go over all that she had read from Sam's journal. He had truly been a vile man. His intense hatred for his father and his complete disregard of his wife's needs or wants made Ally's skin crawl. Worse, his selfish hunger for vengeance had condemned the souls of the house to be trapped there. Perhaps it was even his fault that the One That Dwells Below had gotten involved. Ally had heard numerous stories about black magic drawing the attention of dark forces from beyond, but she had never taken them seriously until now.

Furthermore, the journal had provided no insight into what Sam's intent was with Cassie, which made Ally nervous. She reconsidered her relief at being confined to her room. With her trapped there, Cassie had no escape from Sam. Only her presence seemed to keep him at bay. Then again, Ally didn't even know how to keep Cassie away from Sam without being around her every second, which of course was impossible.

Ally pounded her fist into the bed again in frustration. She needed Maddy. Ally's nerves couldn't hold without her best friend. Sam undoubtedly was aware of that. Ally punched the mattress again before standing up and pacing the floor. The morning's events had made one thing clear: Sam was in control of the house and almost everyone in it. Without Maddy, Ally was alone against them all.

Ally threw herself back on the bed and groaned. She closed her eyes. *Calm down. Breathe.* Letting her frustration and anger grow only led to her losing concentration. She needed to keep her mind sharp if she was going to do anything about Sam.

After a few minutes of controlled breathing, she gathered her thoughts and started by looking at what she knew. Sam obviously didn't want her learning anything. Every time she found a source of information in the house, he intervened.

Still, there was one source that Ally had not yet tapped. She whispered to herself, "The One That Dwells Below..." *What could it be?* Both Sam and Genevieve had only referred to it as that, and Sam had not recorded his meeting with it in his journal. Perhaps he had died soon after. On that note, Ally considered going to face the One Below a bad idea.

Then Ally remembered the whispers that had led her to Genevieve in the first place. Since finding the immortal princess, that voice had been strangely silent. Had that been the voice of the One Below? Would it try to help her, though? Sam's thoughts had made it seem as though the One Below wanted to make a deal. Why then would Sam stop her from finding it?

Ally looked up to the ceiling, considering her next course of action. She had tried calling out to that voice before, and it had answered in her dreams. Perhaps she could try again tonight.

9. The Darkest Revelation

The phone rang. Ally jumped out of bed and made for the door, only to stop when she remembered her punishment. Ally resumed pacing the moment the phone stopped ringing, hoping that it was Maddy. Her heart leapt as soon as the knock on her door came. She asked who it was, and her mother's voice answered, "It's me, Ally. Maddy's on the phone."

Ally rushed to the door and threw it open eagerly. Her mother took a step back. "Whoa, a little excited, are we?"

Ally flushed. "Well...you know...not much to do in here."

Her mother chuckled. "It wouldn't be much punishment if there were, but here's your one phone call."

Ally caught her mother's joke and wasn't sure whether to smile or act contrite. Instead, she smiled in the most apologetic way she could think of as she took the phone. She then closed the door and threw herself back down on the bed. "Maddy, oh my God..."

"Did anything happen after I left?" Maddy asked immediately, her voice earnest.

"Mom asked if you were a bad influence, but I told her that it was my idea in the first place. Then she got distracted by the marker board." Maddy inhaled sharply and Ally quickly added, "It's all right, she didn't see anything too weird. I managed to pass it off as just some family history research. Then she lightened up a bit. That's why we can talk now."

Maddy breathed a sigh of relief. "Well, there's that at least. Are you confined to quarters then?"

"Yep."

"Well, at least then I can be sure you're not doing anything stupid."

Ally scoffed. "As if you should judge."

"Well, anything stupid *I've* ever done has never had anything to do with creepy dead people or demons or girls who can't die."

"You've been thinking about it all, too, huh?" Ally asked.

"Duh! It's scary shit!" Maddy exclaimed.

"You're telling me..."

"Still, I was hoping we'd get to go into the cellar tonight..."

Ally's eyes widened. "You were seriously hoping for that?"

"Well, yeah! I mean, don't you remember?"

"Remember what?" Ally asked, confused.

"Genevieve said that Sam fears the One Below."

Ally was thunderstruck. How did she forget that part? Now that Maddy mentioned it, she recalled the moment with perfect clarity. "Of course..."

"So, if we're gonna stop Sam, we need to talk to that thing."

"I...I..." Ally stuttered.

"What's up, girl?"

"Well...Sam has tried to stop us at every turn. If he thinks I'm going down there..."

There was a long pause, then Maddy said dejectedly, "I see..."

"I wish you were here..." Ally admitted, the words paining her with the depth of their truth.

"Me too, girl...I don't want you trying anything like that alone."

"Once I'm back at school, though..."

"Yeah...then Cassie's on her own." The concern in Maddy's voice deepened Ally's affection for her best friend.

"Well, we still don't know what Sam is planning yet."

"Whatever it is, it's all about her."

"Yeah..." Ally's voice trailed off as she tried to think of what Sam might want with her little sister. She then decided to confess her own plan to Maddy. "So...you remember how I called to that voice that led me to Genevieve?"

"Yeah?"

"Well...I'm gonna do it again tonight."

Ally waited. She couldn't be sure, but she hoped that Maddy was carefully considering what Ally was going to do. Finally, Maddy said, "That might actually be a good idea."

"Really?"

"Yeah, why wouldn't it be?" Maddy asked.

"I...well...you said I shouldn't try anything stupid..."

"What would be stupid is marching down to the cellar and trying to summon demons," Maddy lectured. "From what we've seen so far, Sam can't get inside your head. So, maybe trying to get that voice to tell you more might be your only bet at this point."

Ally was surprised that Maddy was so on board with her plan. Still, it was heartening. "Thanks."

"For what?"

"I dunno...I guess I just needed to hear that it wasn't a terrible idea."

"Look," Maddy said, her voice serious, "I want to protect your sister as much as you do. She's adorable and doesn't deserve to get mixed up with a creep like Sam before she even gets into all the high school bullshit. If I have my way, she's gonna grow up to be a smoking hot badass bitch that doesn't take anybody's shit and owns the world."

Ally couldn't help but giggle. "That would be pretty cool to have a badass sister."

"In a way, you do already," Maddy said softly.

Ally didn't quite understand at first, but when it came to her, a tear rolled down her cheek. Ally had once again forgotten just how much she meant to Maddy. She had never known a family like what Ally had, and it was then that Ally realized that Maddy thought of her more as family than her own father. She smiled despite her tears and said, "Yeah. Yeah I do."

"So, what are you going to ask it?" Maddy asked, her voice choking a little.

Ally had never heard Maddy cry before. The sound was strange to her but no less moving. She sniffed and answered, "I'm gonna see if it can tell me Sam's plan."

"'Cause once we know the plan, we can figure out how to stop it, right?"

"Exactly," Ally said, the strength returning to her voice.

"Well..." Maddy said just before a door slammed on her end of the phone. "Good luck, girl," she said hastily and hung up.

Ally's heart sank. She had hoped to spend the rest of the day talking to Maddy, but it sounded like her father had returned early. Ally set the receiver down, buried her face in her hands, and cried freely. She was overwhelmed by all the emotions that spun around in her head. First was fear for her sister and herself. Second was her ever-growing affection for her best friend. Not far behind that was her sorrow at what Maddy suffered through with her deadbeat father. Soon after that came a longing to see Derek again, followed swiftly by missing Bart.

Ally had no idea how long she cried, but by the time she was done, a new sense of determination had washed over her. Her hesitation seemed to have left with her tears. In its place was the knowledge that she alone could protect Cassie from Sam. If she had to call out to disembodied voices or even try to brave her way into the cellar to do it, then so be it.

Chad brought Ally's dinner up to her room but didn't stay to chat. She ate a little but ended up leaving most of it on the plate, which she set outside her door. Her stomach grew more restless the later it got. Ally had never had a problem with waiting before, but the longer she sat around, the more she could feel the weight of the stakes on her shoulders. It was only eight o'clock when she decided to get ready for bed. She poked her head out of her door to see if anyone was around and found Carol passing by in the hall.

Carol raised an eyebrow. "Aren't you supposed to be staying in your room?"

"I need to brush my teeth. Doesn't that count as washing?" Ally countered, though she kept her voice low.

Carol nodded, her expression still accusatory. "Very well then."

Carol's taking this punishment more seriously than Mom did. "Then if you'll excuse me," Ally murmured as she squeezed past Carol and made for the bathroom. Ordinarily she did her nightly routine with the door closed, but she was suspicious of how closely Sam would watch her while she was outside her room. All the while, she kept her eyes on the doorway through the mirror. A part of her wanted to let him know that she was watching for him, too.

When Ally finished, she peeked out of the doorway and glanced down both ends of the hallway. Nothing was out of place. She rolled her eyes. Undoubtedly Sam was mocking her paranoia.

She indignantly made her way back to her room, pausing only for a moment to press her ear against her sister's door. Cassie had been put to bed mere minutes before, leaving a perfect chance for Sam to talk to her. Rewarded by nothing but silence, Ally continued to her room. After she closed the door, she turned out the light and sat on the edge of her bed, going over what she was going to say. After a while, she glanced outside her window at the gently swaying trees just beyond the lawn. It was now or never.

Ally looked up at the ceiling and whispered, "If you can hear me, I need your help again. I need to know what Sam plans to do with my sister." As before, there was no answer. Ally hadn't really expected one. Silently, she slid under the covers and closed her eyes. Much to her surprise, she fell asleep quickly...and dreamed once again.

Ally was back in the tower, but she wasn't alone. There was a woman curled up in the pile of rags, her black hair splayed out over the now-clean pillow. Moonlight streaming through the windows provided the only illumination. The room was no different than how Ally had found it that morning, minus the dust. Then the trap door opened, and a figure holding a taper stepped into the room.

It was a tall, pale man with dark brown hair in a ponytail. He was wearing a button-down shirt with the top button undone and a black vest over black pants, and on his feet were woolen socks but no shoes. At the creak of the floor beneath his weight, the woman in the ragged bed stirred. She turned over to face the newcomer, and Ally gasped. She had expected a ragged crone, not the face of the most beautiful woman she had ever laid eyes on. Her pale skin almost seemed to glow in the moonlight, and her brilliant blue eyes were dazzling. The woman rolled around to sit up with difficulty, then crossed her legs in front of her, her bulging stomach resting on her heels. She was heavily pregnant.

The man asked, "Are you well, Genevieve?" *Holy shit.*

Genevieve nodded. "It hasn't been too cold since you replaced the locks on the windows. Thank you, my brother."

The man who must have been Lamuel smiled. "It was the least I could do. I know this is even more difficult for you than it is for me..."

"For the good of the family, though, it has to be this way," Genevieve reassured him, then grimaced in pain. Her hand caressed her stomach gently. "It's nearly time."

"You know I will have to deliver the baby myself," Lamuel said, his eyes grim.

Genevieve nodded. "I know, and I trust you. You can say it was left on the doorstep by a stranger."

Lamuel looked down ashamedly. "You do not deserve this, my dear sister..."

"That does not matter, brother. The child does not deserve to be labeled as a product of adultery, let alone the truth of its origins..."

Lamuel winced. "Must you bring it up? Isn't it enough that the filth that did it paid with his life?"

Genevieve closed her eyes for a moment, winced again, then said softly, "Yes...and no. I cannot forget what our brother did, nor that it was he who left me with child."

Lamuel's tension left him at the statement. "I...I'm sorry, Genevieve...I forget that you bear that reminder with you every moment..." His tear-filled eyes fell to her bulbous stomach.

Genevieve smiled, and Ally swore the room lightened with the beauty of it. "Think naught of it, brother. You have spared me the ridicule of the village, and I know that it will be in good hands with you."

Lamuel kneeled next to her. "Do you mean to treat it as your own?"

Genevieve winced again, then replied, "I...cannot be sure. Despite everything...I can't hate it. It may be half of him, but the other half is still part of me. I am reminded of that every time..." She winced again, her voice rising an octave as the pain caught her mid-sentence. After a few seconds of slow breathing, she continued, "...every time I feel it."

Lamuel reached out and caressed her cheek. "Someday, it will know who its mother was and be grateful."

Genevieve's eyes saddened. "I hope it can forgive me when it finds out..."

Lamuel didn't answer as he stood up and headed back to the trapdoor. "Will you ring the bell when it is time?" Genevieve nodded, and Lamuel said, "Very good. Sleep well, my dearest sister."

Genevieve winced again, then said, "I love you, brother."

Lamuel smiled at her, then paused halfway down the trapdoor. Slowly, he turned his head to look at Ally. She felt her blood freeze in her veins when his blue eyes locked on hers and he whispered, "Your resemblance is striking." Then suddenly, the room and all within it dissolved. Suddenly, Ally felt the strangest sensation, as though she were floating through empty space.

Then, she was back in the tower again. It was sunset now, and Genevieve was sitting on the edge of one of the windows, sobbing. Her stomach no longer bulged; she had had the baby. She said over and over, "Why, brother? Why?"

"Why what?" Ally asked, though Genevieve didn't seem to hear her. Then, Ally felt that familiar chill. Genevieve must have felt it, too. She stopped crying and looked around, confused.

Then, the voice spoke, "It...was not...your brother."

"What?" Genevieve asked fearfully.

"It...was not...your brother," the voice repeated.

Genevieve stood up. *She's even my exact height.* "What do you mean? Who are you?"

"Another...made him...take...your child," replied the disembodied voice.

"Who? How do you know this?" Genevieve demanded. She had begun to shiver, clothed in nothing but her thin nightgown.

"I have...been here...a long time."

"Who...what are you?" Genevieve asked as she huddled into her makeshift bed, pulling the ragged blanket tight around her shapely, shivering body.

"I am...the One...That Dwells...Below," came the answer.

Ally's eyes widened. It *had* been the One Below the whole time! It had been trying to reach her from the cellar just as she was seeing it reach out to Genevieve now.

Genevieve said, "I know nothing of any 'One That Dwells Below'..." Her voice trembled, and she pulled the blanket tighter around herself.

"The one...responsible...for your brothers' madness...is Samuel."

"Samuel? Our grandfather? He's been missing for years."

"He...met his end...in the mansion. Now...he endures...beyond death."

"He...he haunts...the house?" Genevieve whispered.

"Yes...and drives his family...to heinous acts...out of hatred."

"But why? Why does he hate us?"

"You...are alive." With those words, the scene dissolved again, only to re-form the tower once more. This time, Genevieve was pacing back and forth much as Ally herself had done mere moments ago while awake. Genevieve looked up and said, "One That Dwells Below...I believe my brother means to kill me. I am defenseless against him. What should I do?"

Soon enough the cold filled the air again. "I...can help," it said cryptically.

"How?" Genevieve asked, still pacing.

"You...could live...forever."

Genevieve froze. "What?"

"Your brother...could never...kill you...because...you...would not...be able...to die."

Genevieve's eyes widened. "I...I..."

"Consider...carefully," the voice warned.

Genevieve's eyes darted around nervously. "I...I don't...want to live...forever." Then the scene dissolved once more, only to reform once again in the tower. Genevieve sat in the chair at the desk, staring out the window blankly.

Then came the cold, and the voice whispered, "You know...it is...nearly time."

"I know," Genevieve answered. Her voice was firm and resolute. "If he comes to kill me tonight, I do not have the strength to fight him off. The only way I will survive is if I accept your offer."

"Then...do you...accept?"

"Not yet," Genevieve replied, rising from the chair and turning to face the center of the room. She looked thinner than before, but her determination and firmness gave her an air of authority that Ally couldn't help but admire. It even seemed to enhance her gorgeous features, withering though they might be. "If you are powerful enough to grant me everlasting life, then why not turn your power on my brother to prevent his actions yourself?"

"My...power...has...limitations."

"What do you ask in return?" Genevieve demanded, unwavering. She received no reply, then shook her head. "I know how this works. You would grant me immortality, but there must be a price. What is your price?"

After what felt like an eternity, the voice spoke once more. "Once...you are free...bring to me...the hands of innocence...stained...by the blood...of their...protector."

Genevieve narrowed her eyes. "Why?"

"So that...I too...may be free," the voice whispered.

Genevieve thought aloud, "So once I am free to do as you wish, I bring you this?"

"Yes..."

Genevieve bit her lip. "I don't know…" Then, her head cocked as if she were listening. At first, Ally heard nothing, but then there it was: the rattling of the staircase beneath their feet.

Genevieve moved to the center of the room, her eyes upturned as she asked, "He is coming, isn't he?"

"Yes…"

Genevieve threw her arms up in defeat. "Then I am out of time. I will do as you ask, just spare me from murder at my brother's hands!" The staircase rattled again. Ally's breathing accelerated. *Whatever you're going to do, just do it already!* Then Genevieve doubled over. She clutched at her chest, breathing heavily, then buried her face in her hands and screamed. She fell over into the fetal position, writhing and shrieking.

Ally watched in silent horror, her hand over her mouth. Genevieve's writhing body rose into the air. She grasped and clawed at the air around her, but to no avail. Her agonized shrieks only grew in volume until it seemed she would rip her hair out with the intensity of her pain. Then she fell to the floor with a dull thud and fell silent.

Ally nervously crept closer as Genevieve began to stir. Suddenly, the trapdoor burst open and the room was once again flooded by flickering light. Before the scene dissolved into darkness once again, Genevieve turned her head towards the trapdoor. Her brilliant blue eyes had turned to a deep shade of red, and her flesh seemed to have lost any color that remained. She whispered, "Lamuel…"

Ally sat bolt upright in bed, breathing heavily. She was sweating profusely, but only noticed due to the deathly chill that hung in the room. She turned to the side of her bed and demanded, "What did you do to her?"

The voice whispered from nowhere, and yet everywhere at once, "I…helped her…survive."

"By turning her into some kind of monster?" Ally accused.

The voice sighed in reply. "I…can save…your sister."

"By turning her into a vampire?" Ally wasn't certain that that was what Genevieve had become, but she couldn't rule it out. The notion seemed entirely ridiculous. First ghosts, then demons, and now vampires? If Ally hadn't been so terrified, she might have laughed aloud. Now, however, she was determined despite her fear. *Just like Genevieve.*

The voice replied, "Come...to me..."

"Why?"

"So...we can...speak."

"We're speaking now," Ally retorted.

"Come...to me," the voice repeated, and then the chill was gone.

Ally slapped the bed in frustration. "No! Come back!" The air was silent, still, and warm. She banged her fists on the bed repeatedly, wanting to scream out of frustration. So, two different forces of evil were at work in her house. One was trying to use her sister, and the other was trying to use her. Sam was manipulating Cassie out of spite towards the family, but the One That Dwells Below...what did it hope to gain?

All she had heard was the hands of innocence stained with the blood of their protector. Then, it became clear to her. Sam didn't want the One That Dwells Below to have what it wanted, so it was trying to destroy the only innocent hands in the house: Cassie's.

Ally rose to her feet, slid on a pair of slippers, and went to her vanity table. After throwing open the drawer, she pulled out her flashlight. When she grabbed hold of her doorknob, she hesitated. Was there another way to stop Sam without playing into the hands of this thing in the basement? She racked her brain but could see no alternative. She had no idea how to fight a ghost. She also had no idea how she would be able to keep Sam away from Cassie...except for this.

Determination rising, Ally glared at the door. "Fine. I'll come to you." She clicked her flashlight on, opened her door, and, despite Maddy's warning, stepped out into the dark hall.

10. The One That Dwells Below

Ally's heart pounded in her chest. Sam would undoubtedly try to stop her the moment he realized what she was up to. Still, for the sake of her sister, she couldn't let him. However, she felt Sam's presence the moment her bedroom door clicked shut behind her. *Asshole must have been waiting for it.*

From the corner of her eye, she saw the shadow man standing at the end of the hallway, his silhouette outlined by the moonlight streaming through the window behind it. Despite the chill it sent down her back, she turned towards the foyer and began her trek.

Keeping her eye on the shadow man, Ally crept down the hall to the foyer. She then made her way down the stairs as cautiously as she could. After the events of this morning, if she were caught outside of her room, especially this late at night, it would be disastrous. Thankfully, the stairs did nothing to betray her presence. As she neared the bottom, she hesitated for a moment. Would Sam go so far as to wake her mother? It was a chance she had to take. Every second Sam was allowed to influence Cassie was dangerous.

As she reached the floor, Ally glanced around and saw the shadow man again, this time standing on the opposite landing of the stairs she had come down. Once again, the moonlight through the window brought his shape into sharp relief. *Bastard wants me to know he's there.* Undaunted, Ally entered the hallway beneath the stairs. Just as she was reaching the music room door, it burst open.

Ally threw a hand up to stifle a scream as a little blonde girl ran out, giggling. Her flesh was blackened and charred, and she was accompanied by the nauseating scent of burnt flesh. The little girl ignored Ally, opened the door to the dining hall, and slipped inside with another giggle, leaving nothing but her smell behind. Ally had never smelled anything so horrific in her life. *That was my aunt. Crysania. She burned to death.* Ally pictured the story on her whiteboard, having read and reread it countless times over the past week.

Trying not to retch, Ally passed the music room to the next door on the left: the storage room. Inside she would find the entrance to the cellar. She tried the knob but found it locked. "Dammit!" she whispered. *Forgot about that.* Thankfully, one of the keys was in the laundry room nearby. Ally turned around but paused at the sight of the kitchen door hanging slightly ajar. *An invitation—or a distraction?* Either way, she wanted no part of it.

Ignoring the door, Ally made her way further down the hallway to the last door on the right. The laundry room was possibly the plainest room in the house. It was the same as any other laundry room except perhaps for the laundry chute, which extended to all three levels, from the unused servants' quarters on the third floor and past her parents' room on the second. The key Ally was after hung on a hook at the far end of the room next to the only window.

Ally crept across the room, keeping an eye on as many objects as she could. She half-expected a bottle of detergent to go flying at her at any moment. Oddly, she reached the other side of the room without incident. However, as she pulled the key ring from its hook, the door to the laundry room slammed shut. Ally jumped in surprise, nearly dropping the key; she crossed the room back to the door. The knob turned, but the door wouldn't swing open, as though someone was holding it shut. Ally had little doubt who it was. She pushed with all her strength, but the door wouldn't give. Defeated, she stepped back and looked the door up and down for a solution.

Then, Ally got an idea. She turned back and headed towards the window. Opening the latch, she slid the window up and hoisted herself up to climb out. However, the sound of the laundry chute opening made her stop and look back into the room. At first, she couldn't believe her eyes. Thousands of spiders were streaming out of the laundry chute, swarming over the walls in all directions. Then, as if the stream of skittering legs weren't enough, a pale hand with long, filth-encrusted fingernails reached out of the chute. A second hand joined it, and they pulled into view a figure that Ally's darkest nightmares wouldn't touch.

It was a tall and grotesquely thin woman, dressed in a black mourning gown. Her ebony hair flowed around her head as though in water, and her pale lips and neck were smeared with blood. The woman's breath hissed through her stained teeth, hoarse and labored but louder than the pounding of Ally's blood in her ears. Worst of all was the woman's glazed, staring eyes, which locked on Ally unblinkingly. The nightmarish apparition reached out with its claw-like hands and lurched forward, its head rolling to the side with each step. *Gertrude, the so-called black widow. She died of tuberculosis.*

Snapping out of her terrified paralysis, Ally scrambled out the window. She didn't have the leverage she needed to swing her weight over the sill, however. Gertrude's raspy breath was growing louder. Panic fogged Ally's sense. Any second either the hellish woman would reach her, or the spiders that had preceded her would begin crawling up her legs. Overwhelmed with terror, Ally flailed and kicked desperately until an icy claw closed around her ankle.

It took all of Ally's willpower not to scream. She kicked and kicked, but its grip was firm and unyielding. The hoarse breathing was louder than ever as Gertrude tried to pull Ally back into the room. As Ally's fingers began to slip, she finally regained her senses. Adrenaline surged through her veins, and she tucked both her legs beneath her before lashing out with a kick from her free foot. It connected with something hard and bony, but it was enough to loosen the grip on her ankle. With a grunt of exertion, Ally heaved herself over the sill and tumbled out the window.

Ally landed on her side, facing away from the house. As she climbed to her feet, she glanced back up at the window. The room appeared to be empty once again, though a few small spiders skittered along the sill. *Fucking spiders.* Ally shuddered and then reached for her fallen flashlight, clicking it off. The moonlight was bright enough outside for her to see, and the flashlight beam being seen from an upstairs window was a risk she couldn't afford. She slunk around the corner of the house, considering her next move. All doors out of the house would have been locked by now. She examined the key ring. Could one of the keys work on the back door? It'd be easier than trying to get back in through another window.

Ally slid along the back of the house, ducking under the hallway window to hide from prying eyes. She reached the back door. Still keeping herself tucked beneath the windows, she tried different keys on the lock. It took several attempts, but eventually she found the right one and pushed the door open. It creaked alarmingly loud, making Ally freeze. If she had had any advantage of stealth before, it had been blown. *Great.* Still, she couldn't risk waking her parents—if Sam hadn't already.

Ally slid into the doorway, widening the opening only enough for her to slip by. She winced at each creak of the door, hoping against hope that it wouldn't carry to the second floor. When at last she was finally inside, she pushed the door closed slowly. Thankfully, it shut without a sound. Knowing that time wasn't on her side, Ally crept as quickly as she could to the storage room door, unlit flashlight tucked under her arm, and began trying keys. As she fumbled with the ring, however, all of the doors in the hallway unlatched and slowly opened. Despite her urgency, Ally couldn't help looking up from the keyring.

Standing in each doorway were what Ally guessed to be people from the mansion's sordid past. The burnt girl that was her aunt Crysania stood outside the music room. The hanged woman stood outside the portrait hall door. *Her name was Marie, Oliver's wife. She hanged herself after he died.* At one of the dining hall doors across from the portrait hall was a little black-haired girl with a slice across her throat and blood dripping from the stumps of her wrists where her hands should be. She wore a frilly white nightgown that would have been pretty if the front weren't matted with gore. *Who is she?*

At the second dining hall door across from the music room stood a tall man with dark hair in a ponytail: Lamuel. He looked almost exactly as he had in Ally's dream earlier, but his cheeks were hollowed, his eyes bulging and bloodshot, and his skin had turned a stomach-clenching shade of bluish purple. Finally, at the kitchen door directly behind her stood a thin woman in a simple blue dress and apron. Her hair was stark white and stood on end, and her eyes were wide white orbs peering out from deep, dark sockets that looked eerily skull-like in the dark. Her mouth hung open in what looked like a scream of terror, but there was no sound. *That's Gwendilyn, Phillip's wife and Aros's sister-in-law. She died of a heart attack.*

Her hands shaking violently, Ally turned her attention back to the lock, trying frantically to find the right key. As she attempted another key, she chanced a glance back down the hallway. The specters simply stared, unblinking and silent. A chill ran down Ally's spine. Were they going to try to stop her? Once again, she glanced down to try yet another key. As she did, a cold hand descended on her shoulder. Ally's gaze lifted to the owner: it was the white-haired woman, Gwendolyn. Ally's own panic-stricken face was reflected back at her in the woman's dead eyes.

"You have made a grave mistake," a high-pitched, female voice said, though Gwendolyn's lips didn't move.

Ally slipped out of her grip and slid along the wall back towards the back door. "You won't stop me."

"But I will," a gruff voice with a slight English accent whispered immediately beside Ally. She turned to find herself face to face with a man in a blood-stained white shirt and black suspenders. He was ghastly pale, with a pointed face that reminded Ally of a vulture. His wide, pale eyes sat beneath a brow drawn in anger, and his shoulder-length black hair was swept back off of his high forehead.

"Sam," Ally whispered, her blood running cold.

"Allison Corbant, you have been a very naughty girl," Sam teased, his mouth widening in a toothy, murderous grin.

Ally opened her mouth to reply. She fumbled with the keys as she did so. Things were not looking good. How many seconds would she have if she lunged for the door? Either Gwendolyn or Sam would be on her before she could find the right key. She needed more time. Her eyes fell to the floor, and she heaved a sigh, murmuring, "You win."

Sam's grin faltered. He cocked his head to the side, furrowing his brow in confusion. "What was that?"

"I can't beat you," Ally whispered, stepping back from Sam as she did so.

"Of course you cannot, silly little girl," Sam said with a raised eyebrow as he kept pace with her.

"This is your house, after all. It always has been," Ally continued, turning her back to the door handle. She glanced down the hallway; the other spirits were gone. They must have believed her surrender. Behind her back, she slowly began trying keys once again. It was painstaking work to keep Sam from hearing the jingle of the keys, but everything depended on it. "I was wrong to think I could stand in your way."

Sam sneered. "Like so many others before you, child. I must admit I am impressed, however. None before were wise enough to realize that I couldn't be..."

"Too bad the One Below can," Ally interrupted him, her eyes blazing triumphantly as a key slid home and turned.

Sam blinked as though he had been slapped. "What did you just say to me?"

With a victorious grin, Ally opened the storage room door and dashed through. Sam roared, "You little BITCH!" but Ally had already closed the door in his face. Once inside, she jammed the key back into the door and locked it. Her heart racing, Ally clicked her flashlight back on. The storage room itself was unremarkable. It had no windows, and the only illumination was provided by a single lightbulb with a chain in the middle of the room. Chairs, crates, and tables were stacked neatly throughout the room. With Sam furious at her escape, she wasted no time, turning towards the cellar stairs immediately to her right.

Ally descended the open staircase into what her father called the jar room. The room was filled with shelves that held (naturally enough) hundreds upon hundreds of jars. Not stopping to wonder over the various contents of the room's namesakes, she went to the door across from the stairway landing. As she slid between the shelves, Ally couldn't shake a sense of dread. Then, one of the shelves began to teeter. *Saw that coming.* Her breath catching in her throat, Ally bolted.

Jars rained down around her as the shelves rocked dangerously and then fell with a tremendous crash. Fortunately, Ally made it out from between the shelves before they fell. By some miracle, she had also escaped without stepping on broken glass. Taking a moment to look across the ruins of the shelves and their contents, Ally then turned and opened the door to the wine cellar. Unlike the jar room, the contents of the wine cellar were all stacked neatly against the walls. *Which shelf is it behind?* The root cellar door on her right at least ruled those shelves out, leaving only the shelves on her left and dead ahead.

Ally decided to try the far wall, but not before a wine bottle slid out of its slot in a nearby shelf and flew towards her face. With her adrenaline kicking into overdrive, Ally managed to duck under the flying bottle and darted towards the middle of the three wine shelves. From the corner of her eye, she caught a glimpse of the shadow man pulling another bottle from the shelf. She ducked again, and it shattered against the wall behind her. Its contents filled the room with a pungently sweet smell that made Ally's eyes water. Before another bottle could be hurled in her direction, Ally grabbed onto the edge of the wine shelf and pulled. To her surprise, it shifted an inch or two outwards.

As Ally marveled over her success, a wine bottle struck her hip. Ally gasped in pain as her leg buckled. She grabbed the shelf to hold herself up as another bottle flew over her head. Had she been fully upright still, it would have struck her full-on in the face. Once again, Ally heaved with all of her might, pulling the shelf outward. It slid a few more inches, and Ally chanced a glance behind it with her flashlight. *Yes!* There was an opening in the masonry.

With no more than a second to assess her discovery before she was pelted with another wine bottle, Ally turned her attention back to the problem at hand. She propped her forearm in between the shelf and the wall and pushed, widening the gap until she could fit through. Then, the shadow man was upon her. His icy hands closed around her throat and squeezed. Ally grabbed at his wrists and tried to wrench herself free, but to no avail. Her flashlight fell at her side, rolling until it bumped into the neighboring wine shelf.

Ally kicked at her assailant, but she might as well have kicked at the air. Sam's malevolent voice snarled, "Now I've got you, little bitch!"

Ally's head began to swim. His grip was crushing her windpipe. Out of desperation, she grabbed for the flashlight, its plastic handle a mere inch from her fingertips. *Reach, dammit!* The world around her seemed to be fading away. *Fucking* grab *it!* Ally's arm strained from its socket as she reached as far as she could until, at last, her flailing fingers pulled the flashlight into their grip. Out of desperation, she swung it towards the shadow man's head. As the light fell on his face, the shadows that had obscured him were suddenly blasted away by the flashlight's beam. His eyes flew wide, and he released Ally. He screamed and backed away, holding his hands over his eyes. Seizing the moment, Ally collapsed into the passageway, pushing herself the rest of the way through with her legs while Sam screamed furiously in the wine room.

Ally lay on the dirt floor for a moment, coughing. Sam had nearly crushed her throat with his grip. Gasping for breath, Ally sat up slowly. She was still quite dizzy, but at least Sam hadn't followed her.

Ally looked around with an eerie sense of déjà vu. The passage had been in her first dream about the immortal princess. Every support beam seemed strangely familiar to her as she got to her feet and began her trek down the tunnel. It sloped steadily downward as she went, becoming colder with every step. Ally hugged herself, shivering. *Should've put on a robe or something before heading out.* She continued to limp down the passage, her hip still very sore from the wine bottle hitting it.

Eventually the tunnel curved sharply to the right, nearly performing a U-turn. Undaunted, Ally continued to follow its progress. It felt like an eternity, but eventually she came upon a doorway. She poked her head in and peeked around the corners. Satisfied that no spider ladies, scared-to-death women, or shadow men would jump out at her, she turned her attention to the center of the room as she entered the chamber.

Half-buried in the middle of the chamber was a stone sarcophagus. Ally couldn't help but marvel at the elaborate carving and rune work along its edges. She was particularly awe-struck by the statue carved into the lid of the sarcophagus. *No wonder Sam thought it was a demon.* Then, Ally said, "Well...I made it." *Please be listening.*

The temperature in the room plummeted, and Ally once again hugged herself, shivering against the cold. The shadows around the eyes of the statue deepened until the sockets were twin pools of darkness. Then, the voice spoke loudly and clearly for the first time, "Well done, my child."

"Why did you need me to come down here?"

"The sarcophagus limits my reach. Here, we can speak more freely."

"All right, then. What do we need to talk about?"

"You wish to save your sister from Samuel."

Ally nodded slowly, but then realized that she had no idea if the thing could even see her or not, so she hastily added, "Yes."

"I can help you."

"How?" she asked. "I don't want to be immortal, and I'm sure she won't either."

"Immortality will not help either of you, my child."

"But what if Sam tries to kill one of us?" Ally protested. *Like he just did with me.* Then, her eyes widened. "What...what if he tries to kill us all?"

"He will not try to kill your entire family. As much as he hates all of them, if there are none left, then there is no one left to punish. To him, there is no greater pleasure."

Ally shuddered. "Why...why does he hate us all so much?"

"You are alive. He is not," the voice said simply.

"Is that really all there is to it?"

The thing paused a moment, then answered, "The true meaning of his hatred is his nature. He was, is, and always will be a hateful being. That hate has fueled his spirit in death."

"Fueled? How?" she asked.

"Spirits that linger beyond death cling to their strongest emotions in life. The more potent the emotion, the more powerful the spirit that clings to it. What flame burns hotter than hatred?"

"So...what can we do about him?"

"You know what I require."

Ally frowned. "Yes, but I don't like it."

A deathly silence hung in the air. Then the thing said, "Perhaps there is something else you could do for me instead."

"I prolly won't like that either," Ally grumbled.

"Most assuredly not, but I surmise that you will find it less appalling than my original demand."

"Okay," Ally said, "what is it then?"

"Somewhere in Corbant Sanitarium is Aros Corbant's journal. It contains information that I require. You must retrieve it."

Ally's heart skipped a beat. *Did it just say what I thought it said?* Her eyes widened in horror. She hadn't misheard it, but she didn't want to believe it. "M-me...go...there?"

"I can assure you that whatever Sam has planned for your little sister will easily overshadow any horror that might be found at the sanitarium."

Ally's stomach contracted. Maybe the One Below was right. If destroying Cassie's innocence was Sam's goal, then who knew what horrific acts he might perform to achieve it? The risk was too great. "If I bring this journal to you...you can stop Sam?"

"The information held within the journal will be enough to drive Sam from this house forever."

"What about his curse?" Ally asked. Maybe there was a way to set the other spirits free as well?

"Alas, the damage Samuel inflicted with his dabbling is irreversible."

Ally's heart sank. "Is there anything that can be done to lay the rest of my family's spirits to rest?"

"It all begins with Samuel's demise. Once the journal is within my grasp, his time will be at an end."

Ally couldn't help but get a little excited. If Sam truly were the root of all her family's miseries, perhaps she could be the one to break their curse at last. "Okay, I'll bring you the journal."

"Very good, child. In the meantime, I suggest you avoid visiting any other...questionable...sources of information within the mansion."

"Why?" Ally asked, her brow furrowing.

"Sam has lost patience with you. One last infraction could lead to dire consequences." Ally recalled Sam attempting to squeeze the life from her. Had she used up her chances already? As if it could read her thoughts, the One Below added, "He would not have let you die."

"What?"

"Once you had fallen unconscious, he would have released you. When you awoke next, you would have been in your bedroom."

"But...why not just kill me?" Ally asked, baffled.

"The crux of Sam's vengeance hinges on the misery of your family appearing to be self-inflicted. He would need a vessel to conceal the unnatural nature of your demise."

"A vessel...?" Ally asked, but then she considered what the One Below had said. It made sense. Every misdeed in the history of the Corbant family was invariably pinned on the family's own fallacies. No one suspected any sort of outside force at work. Ally narrowed her eyes at the ceiling, imagining Sam in one of the rooms overhead with growing hatred. "I understand."

"Return now to your bedroom. Speak to no one within these walls of this conversation."

Ally nodded. "All right." As she turned to leave, she paused. She glanced back at the sarcophagus. "How am I gonna get into the asylum, though? It's probably locked up."

At first there was no reply. *Are you still there?* Then, "Your father has the keys. You will find them in his desk."

"That's it?" Ally asked, surprised.

"Things are never so simple," the One Below warned.

Ally took a deep breath. "I...I understand."

"Until we meet again, Allison..." In an instant, the unnatural chill was gone, leaving only the earthen cold of the underground. Without hesitation, Ally began to make her way back up the passageway. *What have I gotten myself into?* Who knew where the journal was? Worse, what else would be in the asylum besides the journal?

Ally reached the wine cellar and peeked out into the room. Once she was certain that the coast was clear, she slid out of the passageway. Then, she had an idea.

"Sam?" Ally called.

The door of the wine room burst open, and the shadow man walked in. Ally kept her light downturned to not frighten him away. *Gotta be more convincing this time.*

Sam growled, "What do you want?"

"I've given up," Ally said firmly.

"Not this time, pathetic child. I will not be made a fool of again."

"Not a trick this time," Ally said as she pressed her foot against the wine shelf behind her and pushed it back up against the wall with a final clunk. "I can't do what the One Below wants."

Silence hung in the air for a moment, and then Sam laughed. Ally's skin crawled at the sound. "So pathetic!"

"Whatever," Ally huffed, not bothering to hide her disgust. With another mocking laugh, Sam vanished into thin air. *Idiot.*

With a hint of satisfaction, Ally left the cellar. Once she was outside the storage room and had relocked both it and the back door, she turned to face the laundry room door. The idea of what she had seen in there earlier made her shudder, but she had to return the keys. Gulping, she pulled the door open.

The laundry room looked exactly as it had when Ally had first entered it earlier that night. She ran as quietly as she could to the opposite wall, closed and latched the window, hung up the keys, then darted out. Once the door was shut behind her, she made her way out of the hallway and into the foyer. She chanced a glance up at the angel that hung above the doorway and scowled. "Thanks for nothing." She managed to get back to her room without incident.

After locking her door, Ally threw herself on the bed and pulled the covers tight around her. She had thought that what she had seen that night would keep her awake for hours, but she must have been more exhausted than she realized. Within minutes, Ally was fast asleep.

Ally dreamt that she was in the tower room once again. It was as if she was reliving when she and Maddy had entered it that morning. Ally was picking up Sam's journal when suddenly Maddy grabbed her arm. "Maddy, let go!" Ally grunted, trying to pull away.

"A-A-Ally..." Maddy stammered, her voice choked.

Ally glanced at her to see Maddy transfixed by something in the center of the room. Her tear-filled eyes nearly bulged from their sockets. Ally turned and felt as though a hundred daggers had pierced her chest. Hanging in the center of the room nearly five feet off the floor with a rope around her tiny neck was Cassie. Her skin had turned a sickening shade of purple, and the collar of her white dress was bloody. Chunks of her fingernails were broken off, and her tongue hung limp from the side of her mouth.

Ally screamed. She screamed as she had never screamed before. She screamed until her mother came in and shook her awake.

11. Safe at Home

"A lly, are you okay!?" Ally's mother shouted, shaking her repeatedly. Realizing she had been dreaming, Ally latched onto her mother, sobbing hysterically. Even though her mother had turned the light on, Ally could still see Cassie's lifeless eyes in her mind, vivid and horrible. Ally clutched at her mother's sky-blue nightgown, trembling as tears streamed from her wide eyes.

"Honey, it's okay. Whatever it was, it was only a dream."

Ally tried to speak, but her throat wouldn't cooperate, and the words came out in another choked sob. It may have been a dream, but it brought Ally's deepest fears to the fore. Nothing could be worse than losing her little sister. Ally trembled and buried her face in her mother's chest as a fresh wave of tears spilled from her eyes.

"Shh," her mother whispered, stroking her hair. It had been a long time since she'd held Ally like that. Still, after a few minutes of hysterical sobbing, Ally finally began to feel its calming effect. Her trembling began to ease, and her sobs softened until, at last, she was quiet. Then, her mother pulled back and looked at her, still stroking her hair. "Now, tell me what happened."

Ally sniffed and said, "It was...Cassie. She...she d-d-d..." She choked and began sobbing afresh, unable to say it aloud.

Ally's mother took her back into her arms and continued stroking her hair. "Honey...nothing is gonna happen to Cassie. She's all right, I promise!" she said consolingly.

Ally sniffed again. "Are...are you sure?"

"Of course, Ally! Why do you think I stay home all the time?"

Ally blinked, puzzled by the question. She pulled back from her mother to look at her. "W-what do you mean?"

Her mother smiled apologetically. "That sounded worse than I meant it to."

"But Mom...why did you say it like that?"

Her mother sighed, and her hands fell into her lap. "I...well..." she began hesitantly. Then, she glanced at Ally's marker board. "I suppose...you're old enough to understand." She took a deep breath, then explained, "When I first started dating your father, I researched his family history and found out much of what you have. At first, everyone told me he was bad news, but he was so charming...so handsome...

"Anyways, after we got married and I moved in, I must admit...the mystique of this house got the better of me." Her eyes grew distant for a moment, and she added gravely, "So much tragedy...all too often to the children...I told myself I'd make sure that it wouldn't happen again. So, when we had you, I asked your father if I could give up work indefinitely. He didn't seem to mind, so I quit my job and have stayed at home ever since, looking after my daughters."

Ally stared in shock. "Did you think...something...might actually happen to us?"

Her mother shook her head. "I always felt safe here, but it was a chance I didn't want to take."

Ally frowned. "You've never been superstitious, though."

"Having children makes you do weird things."

"So, you've always watched..."

"Just in case. Don't think for a second that we would still be here if I believed there was any real danger."

"Oh," Ally said simply, a dark realization striking her. It explained why Sam was so discreet with his actions. Their mother had been watching out for anything out of the ordinary, leaving Sam little opportunity to get to Ally until Cassie was born. Now, with Cassie still too young to understand what Sam was, and their mother lured into a false sense of security by Ally's incident-free childhood, Sam was free to move in on Cassie. Ally's stomach lurched. *Clever bastard.*

Her mother's words got Ally thinking, though. Maybe she should tell her mother. Perhaps the best thing for them all would be to abandon the house altogether, leaving Sam, the One Below, Genevieve, and all other fragments of the mansion's past behind.

Ally closed her eyes, considering her options. What if her mother didn't believe her? Where would they go if she did? Would her father go along with it? These questions and more raced through her mind before she realized how long they had been silent. Startled by the heaviness of the silence, Ally blurted out a question she hoped sounded natural. "But what was your job?"

"I was just an RN."

Ally's mouth hung open. "Really?"

"Why are you so surprised?"

"Well...all the school you went through...and internships...you just walked away...because of us?"

Her mother smiled. "Like I said, having children makes you do weird things. We had more than enough money, and I became an RN when I thought I'd have to support my hobbies on my own money. It was no major loss, really."

"How come you never told me?"

Her mom laughed. "Oh, Ally! How would it look if I told you that I went through all the trouble to become a nurse only to quit as soon as I had a family? That wouldn't be very encouraging for your schoolwork, would it?"

"I suppose not..." Once again, Ally considered telling her mother all she knew, but before she could think on where to start, her mother's voice jarred her thoughts. "You see? Cassie will be fine. That's what I'm here for."

Ally tried to find comfort in her mother's words. However, after seeing what she had seen and knowing what she knew about Sam, she couldn't. Still, she put on her best reassuring smile and said, "All right, Mom."

Her mother stood up and turned to leave. Just before she closed the door behind her, she turned and said, "I love you, Ally."

Ally replied, "I love you too, Mom." Once again, she wrestled with herself over how to explain what she knew to her mother. Then, her mother stepped out of view, and standing directly behind where she had been only a moment ago was a pale and gaunt little boy in black pajamas. In the dim light of the hallway, his face bore a striking resemblance to a skull. His eyes and hair were both entirely black, the latter matted and disheveled. As the door closed, he pressed a finger to his lips.

Ally sat on her bed, frozen. It had been one of the least gruesome apparitions she had seen, but somehow that only made it more chilling. At the very least, its message was clear. Ally was now certain beyond any doubt that if she warned her mother about Sam, things would get ugly. Who knew what Sam would do if they tried to leave? Dejectedly, Ally whispered, "Don't worry...I won't tell anyone." Then she laid back down, wide awake until the comforting rays of dawn crept into the room. *Well, that's not completely true.*

A faint smile passed her lips before she fell into a deep, dreamless sleep.

SUNDAY EVENING, ALLY sat on the edge of her bed, feeling very ashamed of herself. Maddy had called earlier, asking if she had found out anything else. In order to convince anything in the house that she was as good as her word, Ally had lied to her best friend. It was the most difficult thing she had done in her life so far. Maddy didn't seem to buy it, but she didn't press the matter. Whether Maddy was fooled or not, Ally couldn't shake the sheer wrongness of her words. With a promise to see her at school the following morning, Ally had ended the conversation before her guilt could get the better of her.

Now Ally was left alone again, wondering what to do to take her mind off what she had just done. Of course, she'd confess everything to Maddy in the morning, but the thought did nothing to wash the taste of the lies from her mouth.

Speaking of washing... With all the excitement, Ally had forgotten to shower over the last few days. Perhaps some hot water might help to ease her mind?

Ally stepped out into the hallway. Instinctively, she scanned for anyone (or anything), but the hall was mercifully empty. Ally heaved a sigh as she made her way to the bathroom and closed the door behind her. For a moment, she leaned her back against the door and looked the bathroom over. Nothing seemed out of place. It was the same porcelain fixtures with purple wallpaper and black accents that she had known for seventeen years. Heaving another sigh, Ally started undressing.

As she stepped out of her pants, she caught sight of the bruise on her hip. Ally touched it gently, wincing. It was still tender. She then looked in the mirror to examine her neck. To her surprise, it was unmarked. She ran a hand along her throat where Sam's hands had been the night before, but there was no soreness whatsoever. Shrugging her puzzlement away, Ally turned on the shower. Once it was hot enough for her tastes, she climbed into the tub. As always, the water running down her body was soothing. For a couple minutes, she simply stood and enjoyed the feeling before washing herself.

As Ally was rinsing her hair, she closed her eyes. This was always her favorite part. She ran her hands through her long, black hair slowly, hoping that the familiar cleansing sensation would prepare her for the task ahead. Her nerves were strained to their limit, but with the water running across her hair and skin, the tension was melting away. Ally smiled, savoring the fresh feeling as she never had before. *Might stay in here for a while.*

"Ally..." a voice whispered.

Ally froze, hesitating for a moment before opening her eyes. She had no idea how long she'd been in the shower, but the air around her was coated with a thick cloud of steam. She glanced around, but no one was in the shower with her. Nervously, she reached out to pull open the shower curtain.

Suddenly, a hand slapped the curtain. It lingered for a moment, its shape oddly sharp and dark. Ally covered her mouth with a hand to suppress a scream. Slowly, the hand slid down the curtain until it fell away and vanished. Her heart pounding in her chest, Ally turned the water off. All comfort that the shower had offered was gone. Thinking only of retreating to her room, she anxiously pulled the shower curtain open.

A gathering of people stood in the bathroom, crowded over each other. There was Marie, Gwendolyn, Lamuel, Crysania, and the little girl with the slit throat, but they were joined by more, their forms overlapping to fit more people than physically possible in the confined space of the bathroom. With fresh adrenaline pouring into her veins, Ally couldn't help but notice every gruesome detail of the apparitions arrayed before her.

One of them was a bearded man in a wheelchair, his bottom jaw blown away, and the tattered flesh of his cheeks singed and torn as his tongue dangled like a fish on a line from his ruined mouth. Another was a short but gaunt man, his blackened eyes fixated in a wide-eyed scowl as he clawed at his throat, his head rolling side to side. Yet another was a little boy with his head hanging limply to the side, his mouth agape and eyes rolled back and bloodshot. He stood hand-in-hand with Crysania as they stared at Ally. Then, all at once, the entire grisly entourage raised their arms and extended their hands towards her, crying as one, "Free us, Ally!"

Ally screamed and jumped back, only to have her feet slip out from under her. Panicking, she grabbed at the shower curtain as she fell forward, nearly ripping it from its brass rod. Thankfully, the rings held, saving her face from meeting the tile. Instead, she struck the edge of the tub with her knee. Ally slowly crumbled as her leg began to tingle. Then, the bathroom door flew open, and she heard her mother's voice exclaim, "Ally! Are you okay?"

Ally breathed through gritted teeth. "I...I slipped." The pain in her knee was sharp, and her leg was numb. Her mother grabbed a towel and helped Ally climb gingerly out of the tub. She sat on the toilet, wrapping the towel around herself while her mother examined her knee. There was no bruise, and the pain was already receding. Feeling returned to her leg as though it had only been asleep.

Her mother asked, "How does it feel now?"

"Tingly," Ally replied.

"Does it hurt?"

"Not so much anymore."

"Good." Her mother nodded. "Nothing serious. You just hit the nerve. Want me to help you to your room?"

Ally nodded, so her mother helped her to her feet. She draped an arm over her mother's shoulder, and together they hobbled back to Ally's bedroom. Once inside, she sat at the vanity table. Her mother looked her over again, then shook her head. "You are seriously lucky."

Ally nodded. She avoided looking at her mother and instead looked in the mirror. Despite herself, she imagined seeing the apparitions from the bathroom gathered around her in the mirror and shuddered. "I know."

"Thank God those rings held..." said her mother before hugging Ally from behind. "I'm glad you're all right."

"Me too, Mom. Thanks," Ally said, her hands caught in her mother's embrace.

When her mother finally left, Ally climbed to her feet and got herself fresh undergarments and a nightgown. She then sat on the edge of her bed, wiggling her toes to try and shake the last remnants of the tingling sensation. Once the feeling in her leg had returned entirely to normal, she heaved a miserable sigh. *Can't catch a fucking break.* Not even her bedroom was left untainted by some ghostly presence, though it was quiet by comparison. She ran a hand through her sopping hair in frustration.

Ally turned her mind to the task that the One Below had asked of her. Naturally, she'd tell Maddy in the morning, but would she risk enlightening Bart or Derek as well? *Derek...* Her heart fluttered at the thought of seeing him again but sank when she considered leaving him in the dark. Perhaps she should tell all of them? They were her friends, and they'd stuck with her thus far. They knew everything that had happened leading up to the suspension. Maybe it was unfair for her not to trust them with everything else she had learned.

Ally sighed and glared at her door. Beyond that threshold was open season, and she was the game. In a surge of indignant rage, Ally grabbed one of her pillows and hurled it at the door. *This is* my *home, dammit! I want it back!*

12. Prepare for Hell

Ally didn't sleep well that night. A million thoughts raced through her mind the moment her head hit the pillow. Would Maddy forgive her for lying? Could she make it to the asylum in time to save her sister? What awaited her there? Surely it couldn't be any worse than what she was dealing with at home...could it?

Her imagination offered no comfort. Much to her surprise, however, she was wide awake when Maddy appeared beside her locker. Before she could say a word, Ally turned and threw her arms around her. "Maddy, I'm so sorry!"

Maddy stood flabbergasted. "Uh...for what?"

Ally couldn't stop the tears as she confessed, "I lied to you, Maddy."

Maddy sighed and threw her arms around her in return. "I know, girl."

Ally sniffed and pulled back to stare. "Wh-what?"

Maddy smiled comfortingly. "D'you think I'd know you for as long as I have and not be able to tell when you're hiding something?"

Ally blushed. "I...I guess...I didn't think..."

Maddy pulled her back into a hug, reassuring her. "Don't sweat it, girl."

Ally could not love her best friend any more than she did in that moment. She whispered, "I...I'm still sorry."

"Hey, I figured you had a reason for not telling me right then."

Ally nodded as she pulled back again. "Anyone listening couldn't know..."

Maddy's smile faded. "Living or not?"

"Either," Ally answered with a sigh. Then she released Maddy and related what her mother had said after her nightmare.

Maddy frowned. "She's completely oblivious?"

"Doesn't have a clue."

"That's a problem." Maddy then glanced over Ally's shoulder, and her face lit up into a brilliant smile. "Speaking of problems, someone's coming to see you."

Ally turned as Derek scooped her into his embrace while Bart smiled his usual nervous but friendly smile. Derek said, "You had me worried sick!"

Ally hugged him tightly. "I'm sorry about not letting you call..."

Derek kissed her forehead. "Forget it, Maddy told us everything. Are you okay?"

Ally blushed and kissed his cheek. "I'm fine for the time being." As Derek released her, she said to all three of them, "We'd better get to class, but I'll tell you guys everything at lunch."

Derek kissed her forehead before heading off. "See you then."

Bart waved and said, "S-s-see you."

Maddy grinned. "The Freak Squad is together again and ready to fuck shit up!"

Ally rolled her eyes but smiled in return. However, as they headed off to class, she caught Gladys glaring at her from the far end of the hallway. *Just ignore it.* Still, the venom in her eyes told Ally all she needed to know. Gladys wasn't done with her yet.

Ally counted the minutes until lunch time. When the bell finally rang, she rushed from the library to her locker and then the lunchroom faster than she ever had before. She was seated well before the rest of her friends and took the extra time to consider how she was going to go over everything she had experienced since she had been suspended. As usual, she settled on the unadulterated truth and was ready to tell her tale by the time Bart, Derek, and Maddy had all taken their seats. Their food untouched, each of them listened with rapt attention as Ally told the entire story, skipping no details that Maddy may or may not have already heard.

When Ally finished, all three of her friends sat in silence, letting her words sink in. Then, Maddy said, "So that makes our next move pretty clear. We're going to the loony bin."

Ally stared. "What?"

Maddy looked back at her defiantly, raising an eyebrow. "You didn't think that we wouldn't join you on this adventure, did you?"

"I...I had hoped you wouldn't..." Ally stammered.

"Why?" Derek asked.

Ally sighed. "Because it could be pretty dangerous. If the asylum is any-thing like the mansion..." *Or worse.* She shuddered, unable to speak the words aloud.

"Then you shouldn't be going alone," Derek said firmly.

Bart nodded. "M-M-Maddy's helped a l-l-little at your h-h-house. We w-w-want to h-h-help, t-t-too."

Ally looked at them all at a loss. "Why can't you guys just be normal and run away from scary things?"

Maddy laughed. "Girl, normal's no fun!"

They all laughed, and then Derek said, "But if we're gonna do this, we have to plan it right. Does your family still own the place?"

Ally nodded. "Dad says he holds onto it for tax reasons."

"More like he knows no one would buy it," Maddy added.

Probably true, Ally thought.

"Well, thankfully that takes care of any legal issues if we're caught there. Is it locked up?" Derek asked.

"Yeah, I'm gonna have to get the keys. They're in Dad's office."

"That'll make breaking in easy peasy," Maddy said.

Ally nodded, then turned to Bart. "We're gonna need a map."

Bart thought a moment, then said, "I c-c-can g-g-get one."

"Dare I ask how?" Maddy asked with a dramatic flair, fluttering her eye-lashes and resting her chin on the palm of her hand as she looked at Bart.

Bart looked back at her, a smile playing at the edges of his lips as his cheeks flushed. "I h-h-have my w-w-ways."

Then, the bell rang, and all four of them groaned. Maddy said, "Looks like this meeting of the Freak Squad is adjourned. We'll pick up preparations for Operation: Loony Bin tomorrow then?"

Derek and Bart chuckled. Ally smiled and nodded. The discussion left her anxious, but with an odd excitement. Maybe having her friends along might be the best idea yet.

The rest of the day passed so quickly that Ally was taken by surprise when the final bell rang. She had been so deep in thought concerning the planned asylum escapade that her classes had passed her by. However, when she got to her locker, Derek was waiting there for her. He leaned against the locker next to her casually, his arm propped up. *He should pose like that more often.* She asked, "Hey, what's up?"

"Just playing bodyguard," he said casually with a glance around them.

"What?" Ally asked, frowning.

Derek dropped his voice to a serious whisper. "From what I've seen from Gladys, she's not one to let go of a grudge. The last thing we need is you getting jumped again, especially with everything that's going on right now."

Ally tried to act offended, but she was melting inside. She was accustomed to Maddy's protectiveness, but Derek's was different. *It's just...sexy.* Ally blushed furiously at the thought. She said in the toughest voice she could manage, "Thank you, sir, but I can look after myself."

Derek caught on and smiled his half-smile that made Ally's heart flutter. "I know you can. It's everyone else I'm worried about."

Ally laughed, and they walked to the buses together. Plenty of heads turned and whispers passed as they went, but Ally couldn't have cared less. She felt like she was floating rather than walking. Surely this was a dream of a better life than the one she had always known. *If it is a dream, don't wake me up.*

When they got to the buses, Derek said, "So far so good. See you tomorrow?"

Ally looked at him and smiled. "Of course." She stood up on her toes and kissed him fully. She caught him by surprise, but his lips immediately reacted to hers, moving against them in a way that felt right and natural. Ally wanted to kiss him more, perhaps for hours on end if she could, but she instead pulled away and climbed aboard the bus. She grabbed a window seat near the front and sat watching him as he headed back into the school. As he disappeared from view, she remembered every kiss they had shared. They seemed to only keep getting better. With any luck, there would be many, many more to come.

The bus ride home was uneventful. If the other students talked about her at all, Ally didn't notice. She happily relived all the time she had spent with Derek until finally the bus pulled up to her driveway. She got off and headed up the cobblestone path, still content to remain adrift in her happy thoughts. Those thoughts carried her all the way to her bedroom, but she paused as she grabbed the handle. The door to her dad's office was slightly ajar, and someone inside was muttering softly. Curious, she crept to the door and heard her father murmuring to himself, "No, go away. Everything is fine. Nothing is wrong. You have to go away."

It seemed like he was talking to someone, but Ally didn't hear a response. She peeked in, and her eyes widened. The telephone was on its charger, and his chair's back was turned towards the door. Before she could duck back, her dad turned around. His expression shifted from worry to surprise when he noticed her. "Ally! Something I can help you with?"

"No, just..." Ally fumbled for the right words. She was deeply disturbed by what she had just heard. "Just...wondering who you were talking to."

"Hmm? I wasn't talking to anyone," her dad said, acting completely oblivious.

"But I heard..." Ally began, then changed her mind. "Never mind, I must have imagined it."

Her dad shrugged. "If you say so," he said before leaning down to begin typing on his computer.

Ally took that as her cue to leave. She slipped into her bedroom and set her book bag down at the foot of her bed. *Might have to keep an eye on* him *now, too. Great.*

THE NEXT MORNING, ALLY met Maddy at her locker as usual. Maddy asked, "Anything new?" Ally shook her head, deciding to keep her dad's odd behavior to herself for now. Maddy sighed. "Well, that's good, I guess."

"You seem disappointed," Ally observed as she pulled her books out of her locker for her first classes.

"Not really...more like relieved," Maddy said.

Ally looked at her then. She did seem a little more relaxed now than she had been when Ally first arrived. If she hadn't known Maddy for so long, she might not have noticed at all. "You and me both."

Maddy didn't reply. Instead, her eyes shifted to over Ally's shoulder and then narrowed. "Uh-oh..."

Ally turned and saw Gladys and Rhonda walking towards her. Rhonda's expression was unreadable, but Gladys's face was contorted with disgust. She sneered, "So, back to your whoring ways?"

Ally shrank away from her. She was in no mood for another confrontation, and with the plans in the works, the last thing she needed was another suspension. However, Maddy stepped in with a reply of her own. "Funny question. Are you?"

Gladys glared at her. "Say one more word and you'll be picking your teeth up off the floor."

Maddy grinned, her green eyes flashing. "Try me, bitch."

"Excuse me, ladies, is there a problem?" came Derek's voice from behind Gladys.

Gladys's eyes widened and she stepped aside, flipping her hair and putting on a dazzling smile. "Nope. Just setting something straight, is all."

Derek eyed her with obvious disdain. "All finished?"

Gladys looked as though she had been slapped. "Well...yeah," she said simply, at a loss for words.

"Good," Derek said as he slipped by her and slid an arm around Ally's waist, pulling her against him. "Good morning, Ally," he said casually as if nothing untoward had happened.

Ally blushed but couldn't help but smile as she answered, "Morning."

Gladys looked as though Christmas had been cancelled. Without another word, she stormed off.

Ally turned towards Derek, grinning. "Great timing."

Derek gave her a peck on the cheek. "I smelled blood and figured the sharks were on the hunt."

"Yep, and Queen Shark Bitch loves stirring the water," Maddy added with an eye roll.

"Good thing I'm around, then," Derek said matter-of-factly.

Ally whispered, "You...you know she wants you...right?"

Derek laughed aloud, startling her. "A blind rabbit could have figured that out. Said rabbit could also tell that she's used to getting what she wants."

Ally nodded, but Maddy answered, "If I had a dollar for every time that she spread her legs, I could retire right now."

Ally would have chastised her normally, but the combination of relief that trouble with Gladys was avoided and her joy at Derek being so open about their being together left her so elated that she just laughed.

Derek smiled and said, "Planning for Operation: Loony Bin at lunch?"

Ally giggled and nodded. "It sounds kinda cute when you say it." She blushed instantly. *Did I just say that?*

Maddy huffed in mock offense, and Derek flushed slightly as he smiled. "I'll see you then." He kissed Ally's forehead and walked off.

Maddy scoffed, "Why wasn't it cute when *I* said it?"

Ally laughed. "Because as much as I love you, I don't swing that way."

Maddy threw a hand to her forehead dramatically and tilted her head back as if she were swooning. "You wound me!"

Ally rolled her eyes, still grinning. "We better get going."

"You only don't like girls 'cause you've never had one," Maddy said with a sly wink before heading off. Ally rolled her eyes again.

As she had the day before, Ally counted the minutes to lunch with a combination of excitement and anxiety. When the lunch bell finally rang, she rushed to the cafeteria. As she sat waiting for her friends, she mentally went over their plan so far. It wasn't long before Bart and Maddy sat down, soon followed by Derek. Once he was seated, Maddy said, "Freak Squad meeting for Operation: Loony Bin is now in session!"

They all leaned forward so they could keep their voices low. Derek asked, "Bart, any luck on that map?"

"St-t-till working on i-i-it."

"Well, we'll need it by Friday."

"Don't worry. If he said he'll get it, he'll get it," Maddy said defensively.

Ally raised an eyebrow ever so slightly, noting how quick Maddy was to come to Bart's defense.

Bart jerked his head toward Maddy. "W-w-what she s-s-said."

"Still," Ally said, "that's only one part of it, though. How are we gonna get there?"

"I can drive," Derek offered.

"We'd still need to meet somewhere, though," Ally thought aloud, then turned to Maddy. "Will your dad be going out of town again?"

Maddy laughed. "Duh! He does every weekend now."

"Sounds like we have a meeting place then," Derek confirmed.

Ally wasn't convinced yet. "Are you certain he's going out this weekend, though?"

"Damn sure."

"Good. Now, what about times?" Ally asked.

"W-w-will we w-w-want daylight?" Bart inquired.

They all thought about the question for a moment. Ally would prefer to go in during the day, but she imagined the four of them wouldn't easily get away with breaking into the property in broad daylight. She was the first to admit aloud, albeit grudgingly, "It'll have to be at night. If we get caught before we find the journal, it's all for nothing."

"Who's gonna catch us, though? The place is abandoned, and everybody avoids it as it is, don't they?" Derek asked.

Maddy shook her head. "People will see us heading out that way during the day. It's a small town. People talk."

"S-s-so, there's n-n-no chance of going d-d-during the d-d-day?" Bart asked, his face drained of color. *He already knows the answer.*

Ally took a deep breath. "No, there isn't."

A deathly hush fell over the four of them. The seriousness of what they were going to face was suddenly very real. Maddy was the first to break the silence. "We should still get together early though."

"Why?" Derek asked, frowning.

"So we have time to prepare and stuff," Maddy said, her voice uncharacteristically earnest. *She's really scared now, too.*

"S-s-so let's sh-sh-show up as early as p-p-possible then," Bart said softly, looking at Maddy.

"Yeah, we'll just show up as soon as we're able, and leave after full dark," Derek agreed.

Ally nodded. "Sounds fair enough."

"Then all we need to do is survive the remainder of the week," Maddy said. As the end of lunch bell rang, Ally was troubled by Maddy's phrasing.

The rest of the day passed with Ally trying to figure out how she would steal the key and get permission to stay at Maddy's on Friday. It was all that was on her mind until she got to her locker at the end of the day and found Derek there once again. She asked, "Is this gonna be a regular thing now?"

Derek shrugged. "Judging by the fact that I keep passing her on my way here, yes."

Ally giggled slightly, then blushed. "She's the least of my problems."

"Maybe in your eyes, but the more rational among your friends would rather you stay in one piece."

"Do you really think she's that dangerous?"

Derek slid his hand into hers and gave it a gentle but earnest squeeze. "Last time you two had a run-in, she gave you a black eye."

"I guess so." Ally leaned against him as they headed to the buses. His presence was so comforting that she wished they could stop walking and just cuddle up somewhere. All too soon, they came to the buses. She turned to him and said, "See you tomorrow." She kissed him as she had before. This time, he was ready for her, and the response was even more intense. Ally felt as though her breath had been pulled from her lungs as her lips moved against his. She slid a hand around the back of his neck, but then he pulled back and looked at her.

Smiling and blushing, Derek said, "Careful now."

Ally answered breathlessly, "Why?"

"People are watching," Derek said with a glance around.

Ally groaned. "All right." She honestly didn't care. She loved kissing him. Let other people stare; she just didn't want to stop.

Reluctantly, she climbed aboard the bus and took a window seat to watch him once more. This time, he stood outside and watched her until the bus pulled away. Her eyes never left his until he was entirely lost to view.

Ally closed her eyes on the ride home, trying to imprint the feeling of his lips against hers in her memory. It was the most wonderful sensation she had ever known. She wanted to lose herself to that feeling a little more every time she felt it.

Finally, the bus pulled up to her house, and she got off, trying to focus instead on the task at hand. She made her way to her dad's office, finding the door closed this time. She pressed her ear to the door to see if her father was in there, but what she heard made her heart skip a beat.

"It's not true. It's not her fault!" her father murmured, barely audible through the door. *Whose fault? Who is he talking to?* Then, her father's chair squeaked, and his heavy footfalls came towards the door. Panicked, Ally backed away towards her own room, but before she could open it, her dad threw open the office door. He looked down at her, his eyes wide in fear. "Were you just listening at the door?"

Ally's heart caught in her throat. His usually eccentric charm was gone, and instead he was accusatory, even threatening. Ally stammered, "I...I heard you talking..."

A vein pulsed in her father's temple. "Haven't I told you not to listen in on adult conversations? It's rude!"

"Dad...I..." Ally cowered against her door.

Then his expression softened. "I...I'm sorry, Ally." The tension in his stance relaxed. "You see, if I'm talking to one of my students and the university finds out someone is eavesdropping, I could lose my job. They take students' confidentiality very seriously."

"Oh." Ally frowned. Her father had never struck her as a liar, but somehow, she knew he was hiding the true nature of his conversation. Still, she would never be able to force the truth out of him. *Might as well ask now about Maddy's.* "Actually, I needed to talk to you anyways."

"What about?" her father asked, raising a suspicious eyebrow.

Ally couldn't help but stiffen apprehensively. "I just wanted to see if I could stay at Maddy's on Friday."

Immediately, her dad's expression relaxed, and he smiled. "Oh! Of course!"

Ally blurted out, "Really?" before she could stop herself. He had never given her permission so easily without asking questions.

Her dad nodded earnestly. "Yeah, have fun! I'll call you when it's time to come home!" he said before backing into his office and shutting the door.

Ally went back to her room and sat down on the bed. Her dad was not acting like himself, and it worried her. Then she got an idea. She went to Cassie's room and found her playing happily on the floor with a pair of baby dolls. Ally said, "Hey, Cassie! How are you?"

"Hi, Ally! I'm good!" she said with a brilliant smile that warmed Ally's heart.

Still, Ally had come on a mission. She asked, "How's Sam?"

Cassie shrugged. "Dunno. Haven't seen him a while."

Uh-oh. Ally frowned. "Oh, okay. Well, tell him I said hello if you see him."

Cassie looked at her with questioning eyes. Had she noticed the color drain from Ally's face? "You okay, Ally?"

"Yeah, I'm fine."

"Okay," Cassie said and went back to playing with her dolls.

Ally returned to her room and sat down on the bed, trying not to think the worst. *There's no proof yet. Don't jump to conclusions.* Still, Ally couldn't help but worry that Sam was now talking to her dad.

The rest of the week, Ally couldn't help but feel like a prisoner on death row. The trip to the asylum loomed like the jaws of some monstrous creature, waiting to swallow both Ally and her friends whole. The combination of Gladys's ominous presence and Ally's dad's increasingly strange behavior made matters worse. He was locking himself in his office now, and if the hall were quiet enough, Ally could almost hear him muttering from inside as she walked by. She hoped that retrieving the journal would help him just as much as her little sister, but she couldn't even confirm if Sam was the cause of his sudden oddness or not. Still, she kept his condition to herself. *They've all got enough to deal with as it is.*

Even so, every day that Ally came home, she told herself she was going to find a way to get into his office and get the asylum keys, but this proved to be easier said than done. The only times her father left the office were during dinner and at bedtime, and Ally's nerves were stretched too thin to try venturing through the mansion again at night, even if it was only just across from Cassie's room. However, when she came home Thursday evening, her father's car wasn't in the driveway.

Puzzled, Ally went to find her mother but bumped into Carol on her way up the foyer steps. "Sorry, Carol," she mumbled, but then asked, "Hey, do you know where Dad is?"

Carol scratched her cheek. "I'm pretty sure he had a conference to attend today. He said he wouldn't be home at the normal time, so I came earlier this morning."

Ally's heart leapt. Now was her chance to finally get those keys! "Oh, okay! Was just wondering."

Carol raised an eyebrow. "You seem oddly excited about that."

Shit. "Well, he..." *Tread carefully.* "He seemed kinda stretched thin lately. I thought it might be good for him to spend some time out of the house."

"You know, I have noticed that myself. It's not really my place to comment, but perhaps you're right," Carol said with a shrug.

"Thanks, Carol!" Ally replied with a smile before continuing up the stairs. Her heart was hammering with excitement. *Now or never.* After she unloaded her school things, Ally poked her head out into the hallway. Once she was sure the coast was clear, she crept over to the office door. Miraculously, it was unlocked. *Must be for Carol.* After casting another glance down either end of the hallway, Ally slipped inside.

Gotta be quick. Ally flicked the light on and tiptoed behind the desk to look through the drawers. Most were stuffed to nearly overflowing with paperwork, but there was no sign of any keys. She tried the long drawer beneath the computer. It was nearly empty except for a single large keyring with a series of antiquated keys. *That's it!*

Triumphantly, Ally snatched the key ring and slid the drawer closed, but as she stood up, she caught sight of two child-like figures standing behind her in the black computer screen. Ally whirled around, but there was no one there. *Get out. Now.*

Clutching the keys to her chest, Ally crept back to the door. However, when she tried to open it, the door wouldn't move. Then, the light went out.

Ally's heart pounded in her ears as she twisted and pulled at the doorknob. A little girl's voice spoke from the darkness, accompanied by the stench of burnt flesh. "Eli is not gonna be happy about this!" *Crysania.* Eli must have been a nickname for her father Elliot.

A little boy's voice added, "Sam won't be either."

Ally whispered back as she continued to fight with the doorknob, "I'm not doing anything wrong!"

"Then why so sneaky?" Crysania chastised as her hideous smell grew stronger.

Ally's stomach did cartwheels. "Just let me go!"

"Why?" the boy asked.

Ally fumbled for an answer. What could she say that might convince them? Instead, she tried flicking on the light, but to no avail. Like the doorknob, the switch was stuck.

A sudden chill descended on the room. Both Crysania and the boy gasped in fear as a familiar voice whispered in Ally's ear, "Go."

Suddenly, the doorknob turned in her hand, and Ally threw herself out into the hallway. She took a cleansing breath of fresh air before opening the door to her own room and slipping inside. Apparently, Sam wasn't the only ghost in the house afraid of the One Below. She stuffed the keys into a pouch on her backpack and sat down on the bed.

An unnerving thought occurred to her. What if one of the children told her dad about the incident? Worse, what if they told Sam? *Too late to do anything about it now.*

Ally spent that evening on edge, especially once her dad came home. However, nothing seemed amiss. He sat with them for dinner and then went to his office while her mother and Cassie went up to the art room. The house was quiet, but her unease could not be put to rest.

Ally locked the door to her room and sat alone. Over and over her mind turned, dreading her father coming to confront her about the missing keys, but the knock never came. Ally listened as first her mother put Cassie to bed, and then her father left the office to start his own nighttime routine, joined by her mother soon after.

Maybe they didn't tell him anything. Maybe the One Below had frightened them enough to keep them quiet, or maybe they had no love for Sam in the first place? Either way, Ally was grateful.

With that fear assuaged, Ally turned to look over her marker board. *The asylum.* The anxiety of her home situation suddenly shifted to overwhelming dread. Would the asylum be better than what was in the manor...or worse? Her eyes retraced every horrific story. Still, if the manor were cursed, then perhaps the asylum wouldn't be haunted at all. She wanted to believe it, but her gut wouldn't let her. For every person that had died at the manor, at least five more had died at the asylum, including in the riot.

No, the asylum isn't going to be anything like the manor. It's going to be worse. Much, much worse.

Ally barely slept that night. Her thoughts about what awaited at the asylum ran wild, conjuring one horrific image after another. Worse still, the manor was as silent as the grave, leaving Ally's senses on high alert. Exhaustion finally caught up with her, but not soon enough. When her alarm sounded, Ally felt more tired than she had before she'd fallen asleep. All that kept her going was the determination to end her family's torment once and for all. Maybe then she might finally be able to sleep through the night.

13. No Turning Back

The next morning, Maddy waited at her locker as usual but didn't break the silence. Ally got her books and looked at Maddy. They both stood for a moment in silence before Ally said softly, "Are you ready?"

Maddy whispered back, "No." There were shadows around her eyes that had nothing to do with makeup. *She didn't sleep well either.*

Ally sighed, admitting, "Me neither."

Soon enough, Derek and Bart both joined them. No further words were spoken as they all exchanged meaningful looks. There was nothing left to discuss. Each of them felt the same trepidation. Ally was grateful though. Without them, she would have been crushed by the weight of everything on her mind. She was stretched thin enough as it was, but with their added support, she felt that she could still pull through.

She huddled up next to Derek, who slid his arm around her and held her tight. Every kiss at the end of the day had brought them closer, and Ally found no greater comfort than in his arms.

It was strange for all four of them to be so silent, but there was nothing more to be said. The plans were in place, and all that remained was to wait. Before long, they had to hurry off to class. Despite the silence, none of them wanted to leave the others' company. Ally understood why the moment they separated. With what lay before them, it was easy to feel overwhelmed without the others around. Ally felt as though all the progress she had made towards overcoming her self-consciousness was nearly lost in her anxiety.

Still, class went on as it usually did. It was hard to believe that the world could continue to function as though nothing was amiss. With how important her friends had made her feel, she had forgotten how little the rest of the world cared. As the teachers droned on about quadratic equations or the difference between speed and velocity, Ally thought only of her friends. They not only made her matter, but they mattered the most to her. She loved all three of them with all her heart, romance with Derek aside. The thought almost made tears spill from her eyes as she made her way to the library as usual. *I've got to tell them.*

After what felt like an eternity in the oppressive silence of the library, the lunch bell rang. Ally didn't sprint to her locker this time. Instead, she wanted to be the last to arrive and see all three of them sitting there waiting for her. For some reason, the idea comforted her. When she arrived in the cafeteria, she wasn't disappointed. All three of their heads turned to face her the moment she entered the room. Derek looked relieved. Maddy smiled as brightly as she could manage. Bart's lips turned upwards slightly before he looked back at his plate shyly.

Ally sat down and opened her lunch box, then paused. If ever there was a moment that she needed to say it, this was it. She looked at all three of them as they ate and said, "I love you guys. You know that, right?"

All three paused and looked at her. Maddy said, "We've all got you, girl." Bart nodded quietly.

Derek slid his arm around her. "We're all in this together now."

Ally couldn't help but smile. If not for them, she never could have found the strength to make it this far. *I owe them everything.* She laid her head on Derek's shoulder and closed her eyes. His arm tightened around her, and neither of them ate for the rest of the lunch period. When she finally opened her eyes, her heart leapt in her chest. Maddy had scooted closer to Bart, and both of them had a hand beneath the table. She hoped that they were holding hands. Bart was so quiet and sweet, and Maddy was strong and supportive. *They're perfect for each other.*

Then the bell rang, and they all got up without a word. Ally felt much better than she had this morning. Though not much had been said, she had heard everything she'd needed to hear. The silence no longer felt tense and oppressive but warm and firm with unified resolution. Only a few more hours remained. Ally both longed for them to pass quickly and dreaded when the end of the school day would come. Each class felt like an eternity until, at last, the bell rang for the day.

In complete silence, Ally made her way to her locker but stopped dead as soon as she rounded the corner of the hallway. Gladys, Rhonda, and Gary were waiting there already. Ally backed away slowly as they turned to face her. Suddenly, Derek, Maddy, and Bart were at her side. Gladys snorted in laughter. "Well, look at the bunch of freaks, all gathered together under one slut's skirt!"

"Yeah, so what's your point?" Maddy snapped angrily.

"My point is you little fucks need to be put in your places," Gladys said dismissively.

"It seems to me the only person who needs put in their place is you," Derek replied firmly. He then stepped forward, putting himself between Gladys and Ally but not blocking Ally's view.

Gary stepped forward and put himself between Derek and Gladys. "You wanna go, punk?" he scoffed.

Derek looked up at him. Gary had a fair few inches of height on Derek, but he didn't shrink from Gary's dark gaze. "Yes, all four of us would like to go home, so if you'd please get out of here, we'll get going."

Gladys laughed disdainfully. "What makes you think I want to let you go?"

"What makes you think we care what you want?" Ally snapped, stepping up beside Derek.

"What did you say, you little tramp?" Gladys said, her eyes wide and menacing as she turned to face Ally.

Ally didn't know what came over her, but she had finally had enough. She rounded on Gladys, "We don't give a fuck what you want. You're a stuck-up bitch who thinks her shit doesn't stink, and you're not used to anyone telling you how it is. Well, now I'm telling you exactly how it is. You can go to hell. Now, get out of my way, or I'll send you there myself."

Everyone was shocked. Gladys looked like Ally had slapped her across the face. Ally shouldered her way past her without giving her a second glance and got her things from her locker. Maddy, Derek, and Bart fell in behind her, ignoring the dumbstruck faces of all three bullies. Once Ally had her things, they started heading for the buses.

Gladys called, "You're gonna get it Monday, bitch!"

Ally didn't even turn around. She held up her hand and gave Gladys the finger. It was one of the most liberating moments of her life.

Once they were outside the cafeteria, Maddy turned to Ally and said, "That...was the most...badass thing I've ever seen!"

Ally shrugged, blushing. "I guess I'd just had enough."

"We all get there sooner or later," Derek said with a smile.

Bart chimed in, "J-j-just kick her a-a-ass next time."

Everyone looked at him. He seemed shocked by his own words but shrugged. "What? She d-d-deserves it." Maybe Ally's little stunt had emboldened him as well.

"She'll get hers eventually. We have a more important issue to deal with first," Derek said, turning to Ally. "I'll see you in a few hours," he said before kissing her forehead and heading back inside.

Bart nodded. "M-m-me too. S-s-see you guys." He then headed off towards another bus.

Ally and Maddy looked at each other. Maddy said, "Girl, let's do this." She grinned, and they set off for Maddy's house. For the entire walk the girls laughed and poked fun at Gladys's expense. Ally had never known that sticking up for herself would feel so good. She hoped that Gladys would fume over it all weekend—small penance for all the misery Ally had felt for years. When they reached Maddy's house, it looked exactly as it had the last time all four of them had stayed over. Ally found the familiarity comforting and went to set her bag down in Maddy's room.

However, Maddy entered the bedroom and closed the door behind her. "So, Ally..." she began.

Ally stared with a raised eyebrow. "What's this all about?"

"You know that suggestion we keep throwing around for what to do while we kill time?" Maddy asked coyly.

Ally frowned. "What about it?"

Maddy grinned and pulled her shirt up and off. "Why not now?"

Ally's jaw dropped. "You can't be serious."

Maddy giggled as she continued undressing. "Come on, you know it's on your bucket list!"

Ally sighed as she grabbed a pillow from Maddy's bed. "Do we have to do the 'naked' part?"

Maddy paused, about to unclip her bra, and looked at Ally. "Does it make you that uncomfortable?"

"Only a little bit," Ally admitted.

Maddy looked crestfallen as her arms fell to her sides. "We don't have to if you don't want to."

Maddy's expression stung Ally. In the end, she conceded. "Actually, I kinda do want to." *Not entirely true, but what the hell? Could be fun.*

Maddy perked right up and said, "Fuck yeah!" as Ally started to undress.

Ally had never had so much fun in her life. Once she got over being shy about her body (not helped by Maddy constantly stating how hot she was), the pillows began to fly, and both were laughing too hard to feel awkward. They traded blow after blow until they were lying on the floor, gasping for breath from laughter. Ally breathed, "The guys...will be...here...any minute."

Maddy giggled. "Are you sure...you don't want Derek...to see you...like this?"

Ally looked at her, blushing furiously and at a loss for words. If she was honest with herself, now that she thought about it, the idea didn't seem entirely unappealing. Still, she was very self-conscious about her body. Heaving a sigh, she said, "What if...he didn't like my body...?" It was such an awkward question spoken out loud, but Ally had to ask.

Maddy rolled over and looked at her. "Girl, you are easily the hottest chick in school. If he didn't like your body, he'd have to be gay."

Ally looked at the floor. "I don't know..."

"No rush, girl," Maddy said as she rolled back onto her back and spread her arms. "When it feels right, it'll happen. Don't let it happen a moment sooner, okay?"

Ally sighed softly and looked back up at the ceiling. "I guess you're right," she said finally, trying not to think too much about whether she would like for Derek to be there with her as she was in that moment. They laid there for nearly a half hour before Maddy finally got up and started to put her clothes back on.

"Bart should be here any minute," Maddy stated.

My turn. "What if *he* wants to see you like this?"

Maddy paused halfway through pulling her shirt back on. She then slipped all the way into it, revealing the last remnants of a blush that had been hidden by the shirt. "I'm not sure he'd know what to do with himself..." she said before her voice trailed off.

Ally sat up and grabbed her own pile of clothes. "I'm sure he'd have no problem letting you take the lead."

Maddy sat down on the floor with a sigh. "I know." There was a longing in her voice that Ally recognized. Maddy had fallen hard for Bart. How could she not? The two of them balanced each other perfectly. Still, Ally didn't press the matter any further as she got dressed. Once they were both fully clothed again, they went into the living room and sat to wait for the guys. Maddy said, "Bart really is the sweetest, isn't he?"

Ally nodded. "I don't think you could find anyone more thoughtful or considerate."

Maddy sat in the recliner, twirling her hair around her finger, and mused aloud, "I wonder how he would feel if I made a move."

Ally thought for a moment about how to reply. Honestly, knowing how shy Bart was made her believe that anxiety might get the better of him, and he'd back away. Still, she didn't want to discourage Maddy. Finally, Ally said, "Only one way to find out."

Maddy looked at her in surprise. "Do you think I should?"

Ally looked Maddy in the eyes. "If it feels right, but definitely take it slow. He's so shy...you don't want to overwhelm him by coming on too strong."

"Yeah...I guess you're right," Maddy admitted, looking a little crestfallen. She usually dove into things headfirst and hoped for the best. Still, if she was willing to admit she needed to take it slow with Bart, he must really mean a lot to her. The idea made Ally happier than she had been all week. Having Derek was amazing, but Maddy having someone too was perfection.

There was a knock at the door. Maddy's face lit up and she got up to open it. Sure enough, it was Bart. She said excitedly, "Hey! Come on in!"

"Th-th-thank you," Bart said with a smile as he entered, a book bag over his shoulder.

Maddy looked at his book bag with a furrowed brow. "Thinking of doing homework or something?"

Bart shook his head. "J-j-just some things w-w-we might n-n-need."

"Like what?" Ally asked, genuinely curious.

Bart sat down on the floor and started emptying his backpack. He set out four flashlights, a few water bottles, a notebook and pen, and a single paper that unfolded to reveal a floor plan of the asylum's west wing. Maddy grinned with delight at how prepared he was, but Ally was puzzled. She asked, "Why only the west wing?"

"It's the m-m-main building. The e-e-east wing is the actual m-m-medical f-f-facility, and the other b-b-buildings are s-s-small."

"The riot took place in the west wing, didn't it?" Maddy added.

Bart nodded. "All p-p-patient wards, st-t-taff offices, and t-t-treatment rooms are th-th-there."

"What's the medical wing for, then?" Ally asked, unfamiliar with the layout of the asylum.

"Injury and d-d-disease for i-i-inmates," Bart said simply.

"Wait. Wasn't anyone there when the riot happened? Wouldn't they have not been caught in the lockdown?" Maddy asked, frowning.

Bart shook his head. "Apparently th-th-they stopped u-u-using it c-c-completely days before the r-r-riot."

"Odd," Ally said, more to herself than to her friends.

Bart shrugged. "A l-l-lot of odd th-th-things happened there."

Ally was about to ask for details, but then there was another knock at the front door. This time, she got up and let Derek in. The moment the door closed behind him she threw her arms around him. He slid his around her with his half-smile and asked, "Miss me?"

Ally blushed but grinned, admitting, "Only a little."

The pair of them sat down on the loveseat and scooted close together with Derek's arm around Ally. Derek said simply, "So now we wait."

Ally nodded. They had agreed to leave no earlier than 10 p.m. It was only half-past 7, so there was time to kill.

Bart put his things away and then sat on the floor. Maddy said, "You know...there is the recliner over there, unoccupied."

Bart looked at her, then looked at the floor. "I th-th-thought you'd w-w-want it."

Maddy sighed. "No, I left it empty for you, dummy." She gave him a playful push.

"Oh," Bart said simply and got up to take his seat in the recliner. "Th-th-thank you."

Maddy then got up and sat beside him on the arm of the recliner. "No worries."

Bart looked bewildered, but neither Ally nor Derek could stop smiling. What Maddy wanted was painfully obvious, but Bart was too polite to even consider it. Ally decided to spur things along a little. "You know, Bart, Maddy likes you."

Both Maddy and Bart blushed furiously. He mumbled, "Oh."

"Do you like her?" Derek asked.

Bart looked at the floor, his face beet red. Maddy said protectively, "Guys...don't put him on the spot like that. You know he's shy."

"N-n-no, it's okay," Bart interrupted her. He then chewed on his lip for a minute before admitting, "Y-y-yes, I d-d-do."

"Then why not let her share the recliner with you?" Ally said, her heart soaring in triumph.

Maddy glared at Ally, then looked at Bart. His eyes met hers, and she asked gently, "Would you mind?"

"N-n-not at all," he said with a shy smile as he scooted over for her.

Maddy smiled brilliantly and slid down next to him. At first, he simply sat beside her, unsure of what to do with himself. Then Maddy grabbed the arm closest to her and slid it around her back. Bart blushed a little but didn't fight her. She leaned close against him just as Ally was doing to Derek that very moment. Both girls exchanged looks and grinned. Derek laughed, and Bart smiled. No one said a word.

Ally closed her eyes, smiling to herself. Despite everything, she felt perfectly at peace. They talked about school, about different careers, and about their life goals. They joked and laughed. Maddy made another pizza for them all, and for a moment, they forgot about the asylum and whatever might lie within it. For a moment, they were just four teenagers hanging out together. For a moment, things seemed normal.

Then, Maddy said, "Hey Bart, I got something to show you."

Bart turned to look at her. "W-w-what?"

Maddy looked up at the ceiling innocently as she said, "Oh, just something in my room." Her eyes met Ally's, and Ally understood what was going on. This was payback for putting them on the spot like she had. Ally narrowed her eyes, but Maddy's only response was a mischievous wink as she got up, grabbed Bart's hand, and said, "Come on, it's really cool!" Ally shook her head as Maddy led him to her bedroom. Before she closed the door behind them, Maddy stuck her tongue out at Ally.

Derek asked, "Does she really have something to show him?"

Ally shrugged. "If she took my advice, no."

Derek looked down at her, frowning. "What do you mean?"

Ally looked up at him. Their faces were incredibly close. Her breathing accelerated a little, but she said, "I told her to take it slow with him since he's so shy."

Derek's eyes didn't move from hers. "I can understand that." His breathing had picked up as well.

"This was prolly revenge for..." Ally began, but then Derek was kissing her. She hadn't been prepared, but her reaction was immediate. She slid her arms around him and pressed her hand to the back of his neck, moving her lips with his. Maddy's scheming was completely forgotten. All Ally could think about was his lips on hers.

She shuddered as his hands moved up and down on her back. She kissed him hungrily, letting loose all the desire that had built up with every kiss over the past week. She wanted more of him. She wanted to lose herself in him.

Then, Derek pulled back, gasping for breath. All he managed to say was, "Wow."

Ally was breathing heavily. She had never felt this way before. She gasped, "I...I know."

"Was that a first for you?"

Ally nodded. It had been everything she had ever hoped it would be and so much more. She said, "We should do it again...sometime."

Derek gave her his half-smile, "When we get back, we can make out all you want."

Ally smiled back. "I'd like that," she said, but inwardly she hoped for more. She wanted to give herself to him completely but was afraid it would push their relationship too far. She could not be happier with what they had, but she couldn't deny that she craved the next step. She wrestled with her desires, trying to keep her thoughts rational. *Not yet. Soon, but not yet.*

Then, Bart and Maddy came out. Maddy was giggling, and Bart had a smile on his face. Derek looked at them both suspiciously. "What did you two get up to?"

"Oh nothing, I just showed him my kickass card collection," Maddy said nonchalantly.

Ally raised an eyebrow. "You don't have a card collection."

Maddy sighed and rolled her eyes before admitting, "All right, so we talked about us. Happy?"

Ally giggled. "Say no more. You can keep it between yourselves if you like."

Maddy raised an eyebrow this time. "Oh? No juicy details for you?"

Ally laughed. "Nope!" Then she winked at Maddy as if to say *I know you'll tell me anyways.* Maddy got the hint and laughed aloud. Bart and Derek exchanged looks and shrugged.

Maddy and Ally found the guys' reaction even more hilarious. They laughed and laughed until Maddy was doubled up on the floor clutching her sides and Ally was rocking back and forth. Then, Ally rocked too far forward and slipped off the couch, ending up in the fetal position at the foot of the loveseat, still laughing. This got Bart and Derek started, and soon all four of them were fighting tears from laughing so hard. Every time they would start to regain their composure, one of them would start in again, and soon all four would start right back into fits of laughter.

When the merriment finally died down, it was nearly 10 p.m. All four of them were splayed out on the floor, gasping for breath after laughing so hard for so long. Ally sat up and said, "Guys...we can do this."

One by one, the others sat up too. Bart nodded. Derek said, "Yes, we can."

Maddy yelled, "Fuck yeah we can!"

Ally stood up and brushed herself off. She looked at them all as they got to their feet and said, "Let's go find that journal, and when we get back, let's have a fucking party."

Maddy punched the air and whooped. Bart grinned, and Derek laughed. A party for four was enough. Each of them was all the others needed. With more enthusiasm than any of them had expected, they grabbed their jackets, the asylum keys, and Bart's backpack, and then they got into Derek's black sedan. Derek turned on some music, and it happened to be a song they all knew. They all sang along as they took off into the night, even Bart. The mood could not have been more different than what they had all felt that morning.

However, as they reached the outskirts of town and the road that eventually led to the asylum driveway, the bright mood began to fade. Derek turned the music down as houses gave way to thick groves of trees on either side of the road. Ally sat in the passenger seat beside him, their hands clasped over the center console. Her grip tightened as they reached a stone pillar with a faded bronze plaque reading *Corbant Sanitarium* at the mouth of the driveway. As Derek turned onto the cobblestone road, she felt her heart leap into her throat. The fear of what lay ahead was suddenly very real.

The cobblestone driveway eventually brought them to a tall wrought-iron gate with the name Corbant written in the arch overhead. On either side of the gate were brick pillars topped with statues of angels, their hands outstretched as if in welcome. *They look sad.* The thought reminded Ally of all the tragedy that had befallen both her family and the asylum. *I'd be sad, too, if all I could do was watch it all happen.*

A brick wall extended from the angel pillars into the surrounding woods, topped with wrought-iron bars to match the gate. Derek put the car in park and said, "It's on foot from here."

No one said anything else. Ally looked at them all. Their expressions betrayed the same trepidation she was now feeling. Bart reached into his bag, pulled out the flashlights, and passed them around. Once everyone had a flashlight, they all got out. With the car shut off, the oppressive quiet struck Ally as ominous. The weeds rustled in a gentle breeze, and crickets chirped, but no other sound could be heard. It was as though they had been cut off from the rest of the world entirely.

Ally stepped up to the gate and examined its enormous, padlocked chain. She tried the largest key on the ring first, and the locked clicked open. Derek pushed the gate open, and all four of them stepped onto the asylum grounds.

The lawn was heavily overgrown, with weeds up well past Ally's knees. As they approached the enormous west wing, they passed a large fountain with a statue of a dancing cherub in the middle. Like the angels, its expression seemed forlorn. Ally paused and panned her flashlight up at the structure before them. As her friends followed suit, what they saw drew from them a collective gasp of awe.

The west wing looked like a cross between a cathedral, a school, and a prison all wrapped up into one massive building. It spread out several yards in both directions, with numerous broken windows and a towering structure in the center looming high into the night sky. The architecture seemed to Ally almost as if the tower were about to lurch forward like some great beast. Stone steps led from the ruined driveway up to a massive arched porch and the front doors of the asylum. They were carved with what appeared to be angels. Bart whispered, "The s-s-saints. P-p-patrons of the af-f-flicted within."

Ally didn't have to ask what he meant. Swallowing, she led the way up the steps to the doors. Again, the images of the saints on the doors seemed to echo the miserable state of the asylum. Ally grabbed one of the door handles, but it was locked. *No surprise there.* With trembling hands, Ally tried the next key on the ring. It turned, and the door creaked open ominously. She pulled the key free and, after a deep breath, led her friends into Corbant Asylum.

14. Abandoned

The moment she crossed the threshold, Ally was overwhelmed by a feeling of sheer wrongness. Even with the front door hanging open, the sounds of the night outside were quashed utterly, plunging them into deathly silence. Ally's chest tightened, and her breath caught in her lungs. The air was heavy with mildew, but it was all overshadowed by a feeling of something wholly unnatural. Ally couldn't describe the feeling very well, but it made the hair on the back of her neck stand straight up and her skin crawl. She tried to shake the feeling and panned her flashlight around the room.

The entryway was enormous, with a great stairway at the far end that led up to a painted mural of men reaching up to heaven, and above, a gathering of angels reached down. After the mural landing, the staircase split off in both directions to head to the upper floors. On both sides of the room was a set of three large, arched doorways, with a reception desk extending out from the nearest doorway. Set back under the arch was a door with a faded plaque reading "Staff Only."

Ally walked up to the desk and then turned to her friends. "Now we need that map." Her voice seemed almost painfully loud in the oppressive silence of the entryway.

Bart pulled the map from his bag and held it out. Ally took it and laid it out on the desk before looking it over with her flashlight. Bart asked, "Any idea wh-wh-where the j-j-journal might be?"

"Not specifically, but if I had to guess..." She pointed to a small square on the third floor, directly overhead from where they were now. "I'd say it would be in Aros's office."

Bart stepped up and traced a path from the entryway to the office. "We'll t-t-take the stairs h-h-here, then it'll b-b-be a couple hallways, f-f-followed by another f-f-flight of stairs. O-o-one more h-h-hallway, and we're th-th-there."

Ally looked at him. He made it sound so simple, but God only knew what they might find on their way there. Still, she hadn't come this far for nothing.

She took a deep breath, turned away from the desk, and made her way towards the stairwell. Derek, Bart, and Maddy hurried to her side. Derek said, "Careful, Ally. The last thing we should do is split up."

Ally reluctantly slowed her pace. "Sorry...I just really want to get this over with and get out. This place feels so..."

"Wrong," Maddy finished for her, her eyes darting around nervously.

"You feel it, too?" Ally asked as they began climbing the staircase. Maddy nodded. Ally looked to Derek and Bart. "What about you guys?" Without hesitation, they both nodded grimly. A part of Ally was glad it wasn't just her who felt it, but that did little to ease her apprehension.

They reached the landing in front of the mural and took the left staircase, which led into a long, empty hallway. Simple wooden doors with peepholes lined the walls on both sides. Ally was surprised; she had expected heavy doors leading to padded rooms.

"It almost looks like a poorly decorated hotel," Maddy said.

Bart explained, "The r-r-regular p-p-patient rooms aren't what y-y-you'd expect in an asylum. There are t-t-two b-b-beds per room and a w-w-wardrobe each for p-p-personal belongings."

Ally asked without looking back at him, "How do you know so much about this place?"

Bart's reply was quieter, as if he were embarrassed. "I s-s-spent all w-w-week researching it."

Maddy whispered, "Where would we be without you?"

Glad we don't have to find out.

Suddenly, there was a heavy but muffled grating sound, followed by what sounded like an engine starting up. Puzzled and a little frightened, the four of them exchanged bewildered looks. As Ally opened her mouth to ask what the sound might be, the fluorescent lights overhead sprang into life one by one. Ally gasped. "That...that's not right."

"What do you mean?" Maddy asked nervously.

Ally breathed a slow, trembling sigh before responding, "Dad doesn't pay for power here. Since there's nothing going on here, he says it'd be a waste of money. There's no way this place has power."

Derek looked up at the lights. "Looks like there is one way."

"Don't even say it," Maddy said, her wide eyes dissuading Derek from further comment.

Ally bit her lip and continued down the hallway. "The sooner we get out, the better." The others followed suit, and they followed the hallway until it turned a corner and continued to a metal door with a silver handle and a thin window on the latch side. Ally pulled it open and they found a stairwell that led upwards, with a similar door immediately to their right. Ally snuck a glance through the other door's window. It led down the same style hallway they had just come out of.

The stairwell lights flickered eerily. She hated the way the shadows seemed to shift beneath them. Nervously, the four of them made their way up the stairs. They climbed to a landing and then U-turned to continue up another set of stairs to a pair of doors just like the ones below. "Which door?" Ally asked.

Bart answered, "S-s-straight ahead."

Ally pushed the door opened and entered the third-floor hallway. It was a perfect reflection of the one below.

"Definitely not creative with the décor," Derek observed.

"It feels like we're in the exact same hallway," Maddy said quietly.

Ally shuddered. The repetition alone could become maddening. Cautiously, she led the way down the hall, her eyes alert for any sign of trouble. They reached the corner and turned to find that the hallway continued the full length of the building. For the first time, Ally was glad the lights had come on. In the dark, the hallway would have seemed utterly endless.

"S-s-staff offices are n-n-near the c-c-center," Bart informed them.

Ally took a deep breath. "All right, let's go," she said, as much to herself as to her companions, as she set off down the hallway. Unlike the floor below, some of the doors were ajar. Ally didn't want to peek into the rooms, but a combination of curiosity and a need to ensure that they were empty made her sneak an occasional glance despite herself.

In one room, a bed was overturned, and the sheets strewn about the floor. In another, the door was wide open, held fast by one of the wardrobes lying face down. In a third, the door was ripped entirely off its hinges and propped against an overturned gurney. Finally, they came to a set of doors on the right with brass plaques declaring to whom the offices belonged. Ally looked for Aros's name, but instead they found an unlabeled set of oak double doors.

Bart said, "Th-th-this is it."

Ally nodded grimly. "I thought so." She pushed the doors open, and they groaned as if in protest. Inside was a massive wooden desk that looked like it would take at least four men to move. An office chair was smashed in the corner, and wardrobes were on either side of the door.

Ally walked up to the desk without hesitation, but there was nothing on it. She immediately went behind it, stepped over a crumbled and moldy corkboard, and started pulling out drawers. Moldy papers were strewn inside, their writing illegible. Ally opened drawer after drawer without pause, but there was no journal.

"Dammit!" she said, standing up behind the desk, "It's not here. Where else could it be?" Nobody answered her. *Odd.* "Guys?" she asked nervously as she looked around the empty office. *Oh no.* She peeked out into the hallway, looking both ways, but there was no sign of Maddy, Derek, or Bart. *No, no, no!* Her heart pounding in her chest, she called, "Guys, this really isn't funny."

The only answer Ally got was silence. She stepped back into the office, her breathing accelerating. *This cannot be happening.* There was no way her friends would have ditched her. They all knew and understood what was at stake, and they seemed to believe the stories she'd told of what she'd experienced at home. Why, then, did they abandon her?

Trembling in fear, she was forced to accept the only logical conclusion. Somehow, the asylum itself had separated them.

With no foreseeable alternative, Ally walked out into the hallway. She had to find her friends, both for their sake and hers. She scanned down the hallway they had come from, but there was nothing. Then she turned around to see someone standing just around the corner at the far end of the hall. It looked like a man with canvas pants and no shirt, but Ally couldn't make out a face. Then, it suddenly rushed around the corner and extended its arms towards her. Its feet hovered inches off the floor as it glided along, spidery fingers outstretched. The entirety of the thing's face was engulfed by a slavering maw with a long, serpentine tongue that lashed the air as it came at her.

Ally screamed and took off in the opposite direction. As she ran, the doors behind her opened and slammed repeatedly. She glanced over her shoulder to find the thing still chasing her, though thankfully it was gaining no ground. Drool dripped from its horrible tongue, and its gnashing maw was a madman's nightmare of teeth jutting in all directions.

She turned the corner at the end of the hall and ran towards the stairway, not stopping to see if the thing turned after her. She entered the stairwell and pressed her back against the door. *Wait...wasn't it a pull door?* Just as it started to open, Ally bolted down the stairs, taking them three at a time before rushing through the door at the ground floor and pressing her back against it. She sank to the floor, whimpering, "Guys...where are you?"

Suddenly, something thumped against the door, and Ally screamed again. She looked up at the window and saw the face of a man. Three rings of barbed wire encircled his face at the mouth, eyes, and forehead. Some black substance oozed from beneath his tightly shut eyelids, and his tongue slid out of his mouth, cutting itself along the barbed wire as he lapped dog-like at the window.

Ally turned away with a shudder, but the man's lapping squeaked against the window, reminding her that he was still there. She ran her trembling hands through her hair and pressed her back against the door harder until, at last, the squeaking stopped.

Not wanting to see if the man was still there, Ally got up and started heading down the hall back to the entryway. From what she had seen of Bart's map, the treatment rooms were on the ground floor. If the asylum itself had taken them away, then she had no doubt that that was where they would be.

She managed to make it to the stairwell landing in the entryway without any other unexpected company. As she was taking a moment to catch her breath, something shining on the mural caught her eye. She turned and screamed. Written in what appeared to be blood across the mural were the words *WELCOME HOME ALLY*.

Ally backed away slowly, tears dripping down her face. *This...this is too much.* She wished none of them had even come to the asylum in the first place. She turned around to face the entryway. *Get a grip, dammit!* Her friends' lives could be in danger. She couldn't afford to have a mental break-down while they depended on her.

Ally descended the stairs, considering where she would go next. On the left side of the entrance hall behind two of the arched doorways was a large salon with overturned and broken furniture strewn about and a single closed door in the far corner. On the right, each arch led to a single unmarked door.

Ally decided to start with the salon door. She jogged up to it and pulled it open to reveal another long hallway, though it was twice as wide as the ones above. At the end, she found three sets of double-doors, one on each wall. Unsure of where to go next, Ally took the doors directly ahead.

Inside, there was a heavy iron door with a square glass window that looked as though it might have pressurized locks. To Ally's left was a caged-in desk with several strait jackets and other restraints on the wall behind it. *Maximum security. It has to be.* As if in confirmation, there was a grunt from behind the iron door. Ally glanced to find a massive man flailing about on the other side of the iron door. He banged his head against the glass, cracking it, then as quickly as he had appeared, he was gone, and the cracks in the glass with him.

Ally immediately backed through the double doors and turned to face the hallway. That left the pair of doors on either side. Ally chose the left and pushed through them without breaking stride. Inside was a long room filled with steel tables, wash basins, and surgical tools beyond counting. *Great. Surgery.* Trying not to think of what the tools on the tables had been used for, she continued down the room, looking for any indication of where her friends might be. In the middle of the room on either side of her she found a single swinging door with a round window.

If I'm not careful, I'm gonna get lost. Deciding on the left once again, Ally went in and found several beds with curtains hanging around them in disar-ray. The wallpaper looked like it might have been a bright color at one time but was now heavily faded and peeling. *Recovery or something?* Gulping, Ally looked around and pulled curtains aside to see if one of the beds contained one of her friends. However, as she pulled at one of the curtains, it came loose from the ceiling and fell.

Ally's heart nearly stopped. As the curtain fell onto the bed it encircled, it formed the shape of a human sitting upright. Ally backed away in horror, and the thing coughed and then vomited blood all over the sheet. Then, the sheet collapsed to the bed as if nothing had been under it in the first place, but the thick, shining stains of blood remained. Ally screamed as a bed flew across the room, smashing against the wall with a thud. Seconds later, the other beds began to rattle. Another bed launched across the room, followed swiftly by a third.

Ally turned from the room and ran back through surgery to the other swinging door. Inside she found a vast, disheveled locker room. For the moment, all was quiet. Steadying her panicked breathing, Ally took a look around. She walked down each row of lockers, ready to turn and run at the slightest sign of strangeness. Sure enough, as she turned the corner of another row of lockers, a single locker near the end started opening and closing repeatedly.

Against her better judgment, Ally went down to it and peeked inside. There was a disembodied hand inside the locker opening and closing the door. Before her eyes, the hand reached out, revealing an arm attached to it. Ally backed away in horror as the torso of a man without a face pulled itself out of the locker. Then, another locker slammed further down the way. She turned towards the sound to find another man standing at the end of the row, clad in a lab coat and surgeon's cap, face mask, and rubber gloves. What little Ally could see of his flesh appeared withered and leathery, and his eyes were two black orbs that reflected the light from the fluorescents overhead.

Suddenly, a hand closed around Ally's ankle and yanked her feet out from under her. She fell to her hands and knees with a scream. She glanced at her captor and screamed again. It was the needle-toothed creature from the floors above, reaching out of a locker from underneath the faceless man. She tried kicking its hand off, but its grip was like iron. It dragged her towards its locker as Ally frantically grabbed for something to pull herself from its grasp. As she searched, the doctor began walking towards her. His legs distorted beneath him, causing him to seemingly spring forward in bursts. Desperate to escape, Ally kicked at the thing holding her, but its slimy tongue wrapped around her free ankle.

It was the most loathsome sensation Ally had ever known. Screaming frantically, she clawed at the floor as both the tongue and hand dragged her towards the locker. The doctor stood over her now, watching in absolute silence. She shrieked and grabbed for his legs, but she had to have misjudged the distance. Her swipes met only empty air, with him seemingly an inch out of reach. When she looked up at him, however, he seemed to be right next to her. Tears in her eyes, she grabbed for him again, kicking both her legs with all her might. She fought desperately to free herself from it, but to no avail, as the thing continued dragging her into the locker.

As Ally screamed and clawed at the floor, she heard a deep voice in her head whisper, "Welcome home, Ally." With a final scream, she slipped into the locker, and all went black.

15. Therapy

When Ally came to, she couldn't move. She was strapped securely to a gurney, her head locked in place by a freakish clamp as she was wheeled down a hallway with fluorescent lights overhead. Her head pounded and her vision swam, but slowly everything started to come into focus. Her eyes darted around, but she couldn't see anyone pushing the gurney. It turned and banged through a swinging door, the high ceiling giving way to a low one. There was a closeness to the room that Ally didn't like at all.

The gurney turned and parked in the center of the room with a lamp directly overhead shining into Ally's eyes. She closed her eyes until she felt its brightness turn away, then opened them and screamed, though the plate over her mouth left it muffled. Three different people were looming over her, one of which was the black-eyed doctor. The second was a nurse with blackened and split lips, jagged needle-teeth, and two wide, stark-white orbs for eyes that Ally could see her reflection in. The third was another nurse with a surgical mask on, but her eyes were sewn shut.

The doctor said in a strangely calm voice. "Hello, Ally. How are we feeling today?" Ally didn't respond, too horrified to form words with or without the mouth plate. The doctor sighed and shook his head. "That's unfortunate. We had hoped that after therapy your behavior might have improved, but it seems you still cling to the notion that you don't belong here."

The doctor turned and walked out of view with that same distorted movement from the locker room that made Ally's skin crawl. The white-eyed nurse looked Ally up and down and then leaned down so that they were face to face. Ally tried to turn away, but the head clamp prevented any movement. She was terrified to keep her eyes open, but somehow shutting them felt as though it would be even worse. The nurse said in a soft, dainty voice that seemed echoed by at least three other voices at various pitches, "You belong here with us, Ally. They all do." As she spoke, her head contorted strangely, her jaw shifting to the left while her forehead shifted to the right, then back again in the blink of an eye. She stood up and asked, "Ready for surgery, doctor?"

"I believe so, yes. We shall proceed with the recommended procedure," the doctor said matter-of-factly. Ally's heart skipped a beat. *Surgery?* He came back into view holding a small surgical hammer and a long, needle-like instrument with a curved grip at the end. He held it up so that Ally could see it clearly. "Do you know what this is, Ally?"

Ally replied with a muffled, "No." Her wide eyes were locked on the bizarre instrument. Her chest rose and fell rapidly as sweat beaded on her brow.

The doctor explained, "This is an orbitoclast. We insert it into your forebrain through your tear duct using this surgical hammer." He held up the hammer like he was demonstrating before a class. "Once inside, we can perform a transorbital lobotomy. This is a state-of-the-art surgical technique, mind you. You should feel fortunate that your case qualifies you for such treatment."

Ally's chest contracted as she began to hyperventilate. She had thought she'd known terror before, but this brought her to a whole new level of panic.

"With the appropriate motions, we can effectively liquefy your forebrain, which should render you more receptive to further therapy sessions and less likely to attempt to escape."

"What are the chances of success in this procedure, doctor?" the white-eyed nurse asked with her many voices. Before the doctor replied, Ally thought she heard something that sounded like a projector running. The doctor thought for a moment, then replied, "Chances of survival are optimal. I would say a thirty-seven percent chance of her ending up comatose, however, along with a twenty percent chance of developing a form of epilepsy, but a one hundred percent chance that she will belong with us forever and ever."

Ally barely listened to the doctor's assessment. *This is it. It's over. I am about to die.* The words echoed in her mind, draining the strength from her limbs. If this was what awaited her, then it was already too late for her friends. Maddy, Bart, and Derek were most likely already dead, and she was about to join them. Tears spilled from her eyes. *All because of me. They're dead because of me.* Ally fell limp on the gurney, the last of her strength spent. She had led her friends to their deaths. *All for nothing.*

"That is good, Ally," the doctor said encouragingly. "Do not fight. Everything is so much easier when you do not resist."

Ally blinked more tears from her eyes. What was the point of fighting anymore? They weren't ready for the asylum. After everything she had dealt with at the mansion, nothing could have prepared her for this place. They were up against forces they couldn't hope to understand, and in the end, those forces had won. Ally's chest ached with despair. *I'm so sorry, guys. I'm so, so sorry.* Unable to bear the pain of her failure, Ally mumbled, "Just...just do it."

"Pardon?" the doctor asked as he distorted back into view.

"JUST KILL ME!" Ally screamed through the device. *Just let it end. Let it all end.*

The doctor's brow furrowed. "There is no need for that. We can do so much more with a living mind than a corpse."

Ally groaned miserably. So, she would be kept alive instead? Who knew what horrible things they would do to...?

Wait. Ally's brow furrowed as realization struck her like a bolt of lightning. *They don't want us dead.* Her heart leapt. *They could still be alive!* Feeling surged through her body as her despair was quelled with excitement. *There's still hope! We can still do this!* First, Ally needed to get out of her situation.

"Shall we proceed, doctor?" the multi-voiced nurse asked.

"Yes. It is time," he replied as he stepped into view, the point of the orbitoclast aimed at Ally's eye. *Now or never.*

Ally jerked her body violently to the left and the gurney tipped. The white-eyed nurse screamed, and all her voices screamed with her. A work tray flipped, spilling surgical instruments all over the floor. Something metal snapped as the gurney hit the floor and suddenly Ally's hands were free. Working frantically, she undid the clamps around her head and threw the hellish apparatus across the room. As she undid the straps around her ankles, she paused. *Where are the doctor and nurses?*

Ally looked around the room. It was a small chamber with a single swinging door. The projector sound had come from an antique mounted video camera, its lever spinning of its own accord. The lamp stood in the middle of the room with an attached tray that had upended when she fell. Other than that, the room was empty. Out of curiosity, she looked around for the orbito-clast, but neither it nor the surgical hammer were anywhere in sight. *Where did they go? Were they even there to begin with?* Ally slid her feet out of the straps and stood up, brushing herself off. *Best to not think about that.*

Unfortunately, Ally had no idea where in the asylum she could be. Still, at least for now she was free to continue looking for her friends. Hopefully, their situations were far less harrowing than her own.

She walked through the swinging door and found herself in an unfamil-iar hallway. Heavy, windowless doors lined both sides, and at the end was an arched doorway that led into a chamber containing a massive, brass sarcoph-agus-like apparatus hooked up to several pipes. As Ally walked towards it, a door burst open on her right, and out spilled a much-disheveled Derek. He slammed the door shut and pressed his back to it, his brown eyes wide and his chest rising and falling rapidly as he gasped for breath.

Thank God! "Derek!" Ally exclaimed and ran up to him.

Derek spotted her and blinked in surprise. "Ally! Oh my God, you're all right!" He opened his arms for her and she let herself fall into them, hugging him tighter than she had ever hugged anyone.

Ally started crying as she said, "It was so horrible! I was strapped to a gur-ney, and there were two nurses and a doctor, and they were talking about lo-botomizing me..."

"Shh," Derek said, stroking her hair soothingly. "It's all right now."

Ally pulled back and looked up at him. "What about you?"

"I...I'd rather not talk about it," Derek said with a shudder.

Ally decided not to press the issue, but instead asked, "Where are the others?"

Derek shook his head dejectedly. "You're the first one I've found."

Ally groaned and slipped out of his arms, pacing back and forth while staring at the ceiling. "Where could they have been taken?"

"I don't know," Derek said softly, "but I've got something I want to show you."

Ally frowned at him, puzzled. "What do you mean?"

Derek pointed towards one of the heavy doors directly opposite from where he had come through and said, "I found it before...things...happened, and I think it might help us."

"Oh?" Ally asked, still confused. "What is it?"

"You'll see," Derek said cryptically, then took Ally by the hand and led her to the door. Once they reached it, he let go of her and pulled it open before turning to her expectantly. Still not understanding, Ally frowned. Derek sighed. "You have to go inside. Come on, I'll show you." He then walked into the room, motioning for her to follow. Ally hesitated, something not feeling right about the situation. Still, Derek's smile offered reassurance, so she followed him.

Whatever Ally had expected on the other side of the door, it wasn't what she found. The room reminded her of the cargo hold of a ship. The walls were made of massive iron plates with huge rivets, and a fan rotated slowly overhead. A bed was chained to the wall in the corner, and a wooden table and a chair were against the wall with an overturned cup of pencils. Ally asked, bewildered, "What is this?"

Derek closed the door behind them and explained, "It's solid iron. Ghosts can't pass through iron."

Ally blinked in disbelief. "So, this is a safe room basically?"

Derek nodded. "Here we can be completely alone."

Ally stopped her gawking at the bizarre chamber to look at Derek curiously. "What do you mean by that?"

Derek walked up to Ally and slid his arms around her. She let herself melt into his comforting embrace as he said, "It's just been...terrifying. The things I've seen around here...I've needed you."

Ally blushed but whispered as she rested her head against his chest, "I've needed you too..."

Derek whispered, "I love you, Ally."

Ally looked up at him, tears in her eyes. Her heart melted, and for a moment she completely forgot where they were or why they had come there in the first place. She fumbled for the words for a moment but eventually whispered back, "I...I love you too."

Then Derek kissed her, and it was as though they were back on Maddy's couch. His lips pressed against hers, moving with an instinctive rhythm that left Ally breathless. Before she knew it, the backs of her knees were on the edge of the bed. She fell back onto it as Derek climbed on top of her, still kissing her. She ran her hands up and down his back, losing herself in his kiss with complete abandon. Then, he started to undo her pants.

Ally froze and pushed Derek's hands away. "What are you doing?"

Derek looked taken aback. "I said I needed you..."

Ally was stung by the hurt look in his eyes, but said, "Don't you remember where we are?"

Derek nodded reassuringly. "The only safe place in the asylum. Here it's just us."

Ally had to admit she did like the sound of that, but something about this situation felt horribly wrong. "No, Derek. Not now."

Derek hesitated but then began kissing her again. Though Ally was taken by surprise at first, she couldn't resist his lips. Once again, she began to lose herself to him, sliding her arms around him as they continued kissing. Before too long, however, she felt him fumbling with her pants again. She batted his hands away. "I said no!"

Derek sighed, his eyes both angry and hurt. "But you want it, don't you?"

"I..." Ally began, but if she had to be honest with herself, it was true. She did want him, but now was not the time. Her stomach was doing cartwheels, and she couldn't shake the feeling that there was something horribly wrong. She admitted, "Yes, I want you, but Maddy and Bart..."

"They'll be all right. The asylum won't harm them," Derek cooed as he reached for her pants again.

Ally's eyes widened, and she pushed him off of her with all of her strength and sat up, staring at him with a mix of shock and anger. "What the hell does that mean?"

Derek stumbled but stood up and walked back towards her. "Don't you think if it wanted to hurt us, it would have done so already?"

"It sure as hell tried!" Ally snapped, not liking the look in Derek's eyes. It didn't suit him to look at her so...hungrily.

"Are you sure? Did it *actually* try to hurt you, or did it just seem that way?" Derek countered as he leaned over her, resting his hands on her shoulders.

"I..." Ally began again but was forced to reconsider. In truth, would she have been lobotomized if she hadn't done anything? Maybe it wouldn't have happened after all. As she was thinking, Derek tried to kiss her again. She turned away, but then he seized her by the shoulders and forced her down onto the ramshackle bed. "Derek, no!" Ally gasped.

Derek climbed on top of her and smiled darkly. "You're mine now." Ally shuddered as one of his hands traced the swell of her breast, though whether out of fear or desire, she couldn't tell. His touch simultaneously excited and repulsed her. She could almost imagine him taking her then and there, but then she looked into his eyes again. She didn't see love or passion in those brown eyes. Instead, all she saw was a voraciousness that reminded her of a rabid animal.

As his hand slid down her stomach and undid the button of her pants, Ally made up her mind. She swatted his hand away. "Not now, Derek!"

Derek narrowed his eyes, his lips almost curling into a snarl as he pinned her to the bed by her throat. Ally was in shock. *What the hell had happened to him?* He pressed down on her hard enough to keep her from rising but not hard enough to cut off her air. This time his free hand slowly slid her shirt up, his fingers slithering under her bra. As they slid slowly along her breast, Ally began to panic. Out of desperation, she kicked him in the crotch. "I said no, dammit!"

Derek gasped in pain and rolled off of her. Ally sat up, fixing her shirt and buttoning her pants, then turned to look at him. He had slid off the bed to huddle on the floor, coughing and clutching at his groin. Then he looked up at her. Ally's blood turned to ice. Derek's warm brown eyes had turned to a reptilian orange and yellow with slits for pupils. He snarled, "Why can't you give yourself to me?"

Ally pushed herself against the wall, horrified. "D-Derek..." she whimpered.

Derek pounded his fists into the floor, his luminous eyes bulging in their sockets as he coughed and spat. Then he shrieked in an inhuman voice, "You BITCH!" His head split open to reveal row after row of needle-like teeth and a serpentine tongue. His fingers elongated with a stomach-churning popping sound, and his eyes melted into the flesh of what had once been his forehead. Ally pressed herself against the wall, wishing she could slip through it. To her surprise, however, it didn't feel like iron. She glanced up at the ceiling to see the iron plates rusting away to reveal canvas padding behind them. *It's not real. None of it was real.*

With a lump in her throat, Ally turned her eyes back towards the Derek-thing, its monstrous transformation complete. Its torso was still dressed in the rags of what had been Derek's clothes, but its feet had turned to shapeless clubs with two claws on one and three on the other. Its arms had extended, its fingers as long as Ally's forearm. Its flesh had yellowed, with purple veins extending across its arms and up its neck to its horrible face. The head bore a striking resemblance to a Venus flytrap, but with teeth and a serpentine tongue. It lifted its head towards the ceiling, revealing the vague image of Derek's face under its gnashing maw where its chin should be. Ally felt like she might vomit.

The Derek-thing scurried spider-like towards her as it hissed, "Take you! Ourssss!" Ally kicked at it as it scrambled onto the bed, and it fell onto its back with a loud exclamation that was part scream and part hiss. She leapt over the Derek-thing and ran for the door. It rolled over and snarled, "Come back! No escape! Oursssssssss!" but Ally was already through the door and closing it behind her. The Derek-thing shrieked and threw itself against the door, but Ally held fast with her back against it, tears in her eyes once again.

The asylum had somehow pulled her deepest desires from her own mind and manifest them before her eyes. First was the room where there were no ghosts. Ally had dealt with ghosts at her house for so long that she forgot what it was like to know they weren't around, and then Derek himself...finding him...kissing him...making love to him...

Ally sobbed quietly. *If I don't get out of here soon, I'm gonna lose my mind.* She buried her face in her hands and tried to collect her thoughts. *It's trying to break me.* Ally's tears turned to anger. How many times was she going to be toyed with by these things? First Sam, then the One That Dwells Below, and now the asylum—they were all treating her like a plaything. *This has to stop.* With a cry of frustration, Ally turned and punched the wall.

To her surprise, the drywall crumbled beneath her fist. Blood gushed out of the wall like an open wound. She stumbled back in horror. The chunks of drywall fell into a sopping, crimson heap at the base of the wall, but Ally's gaze was locked on the hole she had made. Inside, a single green eye peeked out at her, wide in horror. *Maddy?* A sharp gust suddenly whipped through the hallway, joined by a bizarrely distorted high-pitched sound. *Screaming?*

Ally shook her head, closing her eyes momentarily. When she opened them, the hole was gone, along with any evidence of what she had seen. Ally ran her hands through her hair. *Enough! Get a grip and go find them!*

She took a deep breath and reassessed the hallway. Maybe the Derek-thing had meant to keep her from finding someone? *Worth a shot.*

Ally went to the door the Derek-thing had come through and opened it. Inside, she found another unfamiliar hallway. Heavy doors lined the walls once again, but further down on one side was a caged window with a glass counterpart on the opposite wall.

Ally walked up, examining the caged window. On the other side was a selection of strait jackets and restraints chained to the walls. A set of archaic-looking manacles were attached to the far-left side of the wall, and on the wall to the right was a heavy iron door like one going to the maximum-security ward. *I don't even want to know what this is for.* She then turned to look through the glass window and gasped. Strapped to an upright gurney more thoroughly than even Ally had been was Bart. His eyes were wide and darting back and forth, and his hands were locked in an open position by individual straps for each finger. The room itself was padded.

Ally examined the room for the door in and found it on the wall to Bart's right. She ran further down the hallway where it split into a T, then turned to the right, finding the door to Bart's room. Ally opened it and ran up to him, calling, "Bart, it's me! Snap out of it!"

Bart blinked a few times before he seemed to get a sense of where he was. He looked at her in disbelief. "Ally...?" he said, his voice broken and weak.

Ally nodded. "It's me. It's all right, I'm gonna get you out." She began fumbling with the elaborately woven leather straps but paused, looking Bart in the eyes. "Is it really you, though?" she asked skeptically, her eyes narrowed.

Bart bit his lip. "I...i-i-it's me."

"Because I met Derek not too long ago, and he tried to rape me before turning into some kind of monster," Ally said coldly.

Bart shuddered. "D-D-Derek wouldn't d-d-do that..."

"I know he wouldn't, but it wasn't him, which is why I'm asking if this is really you."

"H-h-how can I p-p-prove it t-t-to you?"

Ally thought for a moment, and then asked, "What happened outside the doctor's office? Why did you all leave me?"

"I...w-w-we d-d-didn't. I...I j-j-just b-b-blacked out all of a s-s-sudden...and when I w-w-w-woke up, I w-w-was h-h-here..." His voice trailed off as he shuddered in horror. His eyes had grown distant.

Just like what happened to me. "All right, I believe you." At first, he didn't stir. He simply stared blankly at nothing, but then Ally gave him a shake. "Bart! Come back!"

Bart shook his head and blinked again before focusing his eyes on Ally. "Ally...I...I c-c-can't st-t-tay here."

"I know, and I'm sorry I doubted you, but..." All the coldness in her voice had left, and now Ally felt horrible. Still, how could she not suspect that Bart was another doppelganger? Instead, she focused on undoing his straps while trying to comfort him. "I'll have you out soon. Then we have to find the others."

"A-a-any idea where they are?" Bart asked as he finally slipped off the gurney.

"I figure they're in one of the therapy rooms, probably separated," Ally replied.

Bart shuddered but nodded in agreement. "M-m-most likely. H-h-have you ch-ch-checked any of them?"

"No," Ally admitted, "but I have been a little preoccupied. At least I found you though."

"Th-th-this is a s-s-suicide w-w-watch room," Bart observed. He looked out the glass window. "W-w-we're r-r-right in the m-m-middle of the therapy r-r-rooms."

"I did see a big brass coffin-like thing."

"The h-h-hydrotherapy t-t-tank?"

"The what?" Ally asked bemusedly.

"It's a t-t-tank of c-c-cold water that they d-d-dunk you in," Bart explained.

Ally's eyes widened. *Sounds about as therapeutic as a lobotomy.* As the thought crossed her mind, her eyes widened further. If she had faced lobotomy, then there was little doubt that the others would face something just as bad. Panic threatened to overwhelm her as her imagination conjured a myriad of torturous "treatments," but she took a deep breath. *Get a grip, dammit.* Her friends needed her, and she had little doubt that one of them was in that tank. She grabbed Bart's hand. "Come on!"

Together, they raced back the way Ally had come and up to the brass apparatus beyond the arch. There was a wrought iron platform on the far side. Ally ran up the platform and looked down into the tank. Around where the face would be was a small glass window. She could just make out Derek pounding his fists against the lid frantically in the dim lighting, his face barely breaking the surface of the water. "It's him! He's in there!" Ally exclaimed.

Bart came around to the platform, explaining as he came, "G-g-get the t-t-top off!"

Ally immediately began looking for the latches, but all that held the lid in place were winged nuts and bolts. *Shit.* Ally set to unscrewing the bolts, joined quickly by Bart as he reached the top platform. Once the last bolt was loosened, they heaved and pushed the heavy lid from the tank. "Ally!" Derek exclaimed as he pushed himself out of the water and reached for her, his torso bare.

"Come on, we'll get you out of there!" Ally said as she took his forearm.

The moment they had ahold of each other, something tried to pull Derek back into the water. "Something's got me!"

Ally grabbed his other arm and pulled. "Don't let go!"

Bart stepped in and took one of his arms while Ally took the other in both of her hands. Derek's head bobbed in and out of the water a few times before whatever had a hold on him finally let go, and the three of them fell back against the railing of the platform.

Derek coughed and sputtered, shivering and naked. "Thank God you found me."

"How did you get like that? Where are your clothes?" Ally asked breathlessly.

"It...it's all kinda hazy. First, I was outside the doctor's office, but then I just blacked out. Next thing I knew, I was lying naked in this tank."

Ally pulled off her jacket and draped it around his shoulders. "Yeah, we all blacked out, too..."

"Ally..." Derek whispered as he pulled the jacket around himself, "after the tank filled up, I could hear whispers from under the water. They were saying...some pretty fucked up shit..."

Ally caressed his cheek soothingly, though his skin was ice cold. "Shh. Just forget about it. This place is trying to fuck with us. We just need to find your clothes and then find Maddy."

"Here th-th-they are!" Bart called as he kneeled beside them, Derek's clothes folded neatly in his arms.

Derek frowned. "Did you need to fold them first?"

"Th-th-that's how I f-f-found them," Bart replied with a shrug.

Derek took his clothes back. "Sorry, I'm just a little shaken is all."

"We all are," Ally added. She and Bart turned away to let him get dressed.

Bart asked, "Wh-wh-where all have y-y-you been?"

"Well..." Ally began, but she was paused as the lights overhead began to flicker. There was a high-pitched ringing accompanied by a low, pulsing hum that made Ally's ears hurt. *A power surge?*

All color drained from Bart's face as he gasped, "My God..." He then sprinted off the platform and out into the hallway.

"Come on, we can't lose him again!" Ally cried as Derek hastily finished dressing, then the two of them took off after Bart. As they ran, the humming grew louder. "What is that?" Ally called to Bart, but he didn't answer. Instead, his pace quickened as he opened a door and ran in, followed closely by Ally and Derek. He ran past two doorways on the right and one on the left before turning into the second doorway on the left. Ally held her hands over her ears as they followed him. The pulse was deafening. Inside, Maddy was strapped to a bed with wires tied into leather straps on her head. A machine nearby sparked and pulsed as she flailed wildly in her restraints.

Ally looked around frantically for a way to shut the thing off, but Bart got there first. He opened a box and threw the switch inside, and the machine shut off immediately. The humming stopped, and Maddy fell limp on the bed, her chest rising and falling rapidly. All three of them rushed to her side and removed her straps. Once she was freed, they helped her gingerly to sit up. She was trembling violently.

Bart asked, "Are y-y-you okay?"

Maddy looked as if she would answer, but then pitched forward and vomited. Ally instinctively reached forward and held her hair back as Maddy coughed and a fresh wave of vomiting overcame her. She coughed again, then leaned against Ally, sobbing. Ally wrapped her arms around her and rocked her gently. Maddy clung to her, still shaking violently. Ally looked from Bart to Derek, then said gravely, "We need to find that journal and get the hell out of here. None of us can take much more of this."

Derek draped Ally's jacket over them both as Bart said, "If it w-w-wasn't in h-h-his office, then it m-m-must b-b-be in experimental th-th-therapy."

Ally looked at him with wide eyes. *That does* not *sound good.* "Where is that?"

Bart looked back at her with grave eyes. "M-m-maximum security."

16. The Experimental Ward

It took several minutes for the four of them to leave the shock therapy ward. Every time Maddy tried to stand up, her legs would buckle. Only once she was finally able to stand did they start to make their way out, and even then, she needed Bart's help to walk.

When at last they got moving, Bart and Maddy led, with Derek and Ally hand in hand only a few steps behind. She kept her eyes fixed on Bart and Maddy in front of them, refusing to look to the sides as they passed door after door, both closed and ajar. Still, she caught glimpses of movement out of the corner of her eye every now and again. Though she wanted both to look and to hide her eyes, she kept her gaze fixed on her friends. *Can't let any of them out of my sight again.*

It took several minutes, perhaps even an hour, but at last they found their way back to the entrance hall from the unlabeled door opposite from the waiting area just before the stairs. When they came out from under the arch, Maddy said, "All right, I think I can walk on my own now."

Bart paused. "Are y-y-you s-s-sure?" She nodded and slowly stepped away from him to prove it, but she held his hand tightly as she did so.

Ally pointed to the door opposite them. "Maximum security is a straight shot through there."

Bart nodded. "I h-h-hope the d-d-door is unlocked."

Ally bit her lip. "It seemed locked when I saw it."

"I hope you just didn't get a good look," Derek said softly, squeezing her hand. Though he appeared stoic and resolute, Ally could tell by his grip and his eyes that he was just as eager to get out as she was. He then looked up at the mural and gasped. "Ally..."

"I know." Ally groaned miserably, recalling the words. "It appeared right after I lost you guys."

"C-c-come on," Bart said, and all four of them started towards the door.

"Just straight ahead," Ally mumbled to herself as the memories of recovery and the locker room replayed in her mind. Strangely enough, they made it to the maximum-security entrance without incident. Bart and Derek set to examining the door. Ally and Maddy stood shoulder to shoulder, their eyes constantly in motion around the room. The menacing feeling that had plagued them ever since they had entered the asylum was growing stronger. Their eyes darted from one shadow to the next, expecting almost anything to appear.

Ally's imagination conjured horrors she'd never thought possible before tonight. Everything she had seen had combed the depths of her darkest nightmares, then went deeper still. Maddy whispered, "What do you think we'll find in this experimental therapy room?"

Ally shrugged. "Hopefully just the journal and some inanimate objects." *Like it'll be that easy.*

Bart heaved a sigh of exasperation. "Dammit, it's l-l-locked."

Derek stood up, looking the door up and down. "Shouldn't the pressure valve have given out by now?"

"The what?" Maddy asked.

"The valve keeping the air in to pneumatically lock the door," Derek explained.

"How do you even know what that is?" Ally asked with a frown.

"My dad and I like to tinker with pneumatics together."

Bart said, "There was p-p-probably a f-f-failsafe on the d-d-door itself to k-k-keep the p-p-pressure locked in."

"In case of some kind of power failure," Derek added with frustration, pounding a fist against the door with a muted thud. "Oddly prophetic for World War II era technology."

"No one said Aros was an idiot," Maddy interjected.

Ally looked at the caged desk, then thought aloud, "Maybe there's a release switch in there..."

Bart looked at the desk. "M-m-maybe."

Derek walked up to the door to the cage and pushed, but it didn't open. "Great, another—"

Suddenly there was a loud hissing noise, and something on the iron door clicked. Bart backed away slowly, stammering, "Th-th-that's n-n-not r-r-right."

Maddy moved up to Bart's side, her eyes locked on the door. "What is it?"

"The d-d-door..." Bart began, but his stutter seemed to have worsened with his increasing fear, rendering him speechless.

"It unlocked itself?" Derek asked.

Ally nodded fearfully. "I get the feeling that whatever did it wants us in maximum security."

"Or maybe just the experimental therapy room," Derek said quietly. *Did he have to say it?*

Bart grabbed hold of the door and pulled it open slowly. The heavy iron scraped deafeningly loud against the concrete floor of the small room. With the door open, Ally got a glimpse at where it led. It was a wide hallway with brick arches every few yards and hanging lamps overhead. She looked at Derek. "Any chance this thing will lock us in?"

Derek shrugged. "I'd like to say no, but..."

Maddy whispered, "Don't even fucking say it."

Ally sighed. All logic was out the window, but what choice did they have? "We have to go in, though. Where is experimental therapy?"

Bart answered, "D-d-door on the l-l-left once we r-r-reach the end of the h-h-hall. The d-d-door on the r-r-right leads to the c-c-cellar ward."

"What's down there?" Maddy asked nervously, as if she was half-afraid of the answer.

Bart replied, "M-m-more cells and s-s-solitary c-c-confinement."

Ally shuddered. "Sounds more like a prison than a hospital."

Derek nodded grimly. "Some people are the worst kind of crazy. They need places to put them."

Ally groaned. "Let's just get through this, please?" Her uneasiness was beginning to mount. Whatever they might find in here could be the most dangerous or disturbing of all the things in the asylum. Without another word, Bart and Maddy led the way, and Derek and Ally followed. On both sides of the hallway, the arches were separated by twenty-foot-wide cells with heavy iron bars across the front. Ally shuddered. Every cell door was wide open. As they walked, she caught glimpses of shadows moving around in the cells. She couldn't make out their shapes properly without giving them a full look, but she preferred not knowing.

After what felt like an eternity, they reached the end of the hall. As Bart had said, they found a door on their left and another on their right. He opened the door to the experimental ward, and his eyes widened. "This...th-th-this c-c-can't b-b-be..." he stammered, aghast.

Ally craned her neck to see around him only for her own eyes to go wide. It was not a room, but a decrepit passageway leading at least thirty feet straight ahead. The walls were made from simple lath and plaster, and the hallway was illuminated by more overhead lamps. She asked, "Was this on the map?"

"N-n-no," Bart murmured in response.

Derek asked, "Didn't the interview with Aros's wife say something about an expansion project?"

"But it must not have been mapped," Ally added fearfully.

"Only one way to go if we want to get what we came for," Maddy said, and at a nod from Bart, they set off into the passageway. Gulping, Ally and Derek followed.

The moment they crossed the threshold, Ally felt a nauseating sense of dread. It was like what she had felt when they had first entered the asylum but amplified. Judging by the look on Derek's face, he felt it, too. Ally couldn't shake the sense that they were nearing the root of the asylum's evil.

The first thing Ally noticed was the deathly silence. A low hum had been ever present in every room and hallway they'd been in throughout the asylum, but the experimental ward was as quiet as a tomb. The fluorescent lights were also absent, with the overhead lamps providing a drab, yellowish glow that made the shadows seem just a little deeper. Ally's grip tightened on Derek's hand as they wove around one corner followed swiftly by another in a different direction. Less than ten feet later, they reached yet another corner.

Derek's hand squeezed Ally's as he whispered, "What did they have in mind when they designed this?"

Ally shook her head. "Whoever did couldn't have been in their right mind in the first place." As she spoke, she noticed something oddly disquieting. Neither Derek's nor her voice echoed despite the emptiness and composition of the halls.

"What was this place even for?" Maddy wondered aloud as she looked around at the crumbling walls.

"Th-th-they said it w-w-was n-n-never clear what experimental th-th-therapy was there for w-w-when it was p-p-put in," Bart explained, but then stopped dead in his tracks. They had come to a T, and he was looking down the hallway to the left. "G-g-grandpa?" he gasped, his eyes unbelieving.

Maddy glanced around him as Ally and Derek came up behind them and peeked around the corner, but the hallway was empty. Maddy then looked at Bart with worried eyes. "Bart...there's no one there."

"B-b-but I s-s-see him!" Bart exclaimed, pointing with his free hand. "G-g-grandpa!" he cried as he let go of Maddy and raced into the hallway. "Grandpa, I th-th-thought you w-w-were..." Seconds later, Bart was screaming.

Maddy, Ally, and Derek ran up to his side as he backed against the wall. His eyes were bulging from their sockets and locked on the empty wall at the end of the hallway where it turned right. His hands trembled as they pressed against the wall and another scream tore from his lips. Maddy grabbed his arm and called, "Bart, there's nothing there!"

Bart looked at her, his eyes still bulging. For a moment, he looked as though he might start screaming again, but then he blinked and shook his head. "Wh-wh-what..." he stammered, his face ghostly white.

"There was no one...nothing there," Maddy replied earnestly, gripping his arm hard.

"I...I d-d-don't know wh-wh-what happened..." Bart gasped.

Without another word, Maddy pulled him into her arms. Seconds later, he was crying as he held her in return. Ally shuddered as the memory of the Derek-thing danced across her mind. She had little doubt that Bart had just seen something similar involving his grandfather. If her initial feeling about the experimental ward was correct, this was just the beginning.

"This place..." she whispered, "it messes with you. It gets in your head...makes you see things."

Maddy looked up at Ally, their eyes meeting for a moment before she said, "We need to find that damn book and get out. Now."

Ally nodded grimly. Whatever was here in the asylum was more than any of them had bargained for.

Reluctantly, Ally pulled Derek past Maddy and Bart, and the pair of them took the lead. The labyrinthine hallways continued in all directions, leaving Ally's head spinning. Occasionally in a corner they'd find a large, circular convex mirror granting a glimpse down both where they had come from and the hall ahead.

"Odd," Derek said with a frown.

"What's odd?" Ally asked, half afraid of the answer.

"No cobwebs," he answered, pointing along the ceiling. "For as long as this place has been empty, you'd think that all sorts of bugs and rodents would be everywhere."

Ally frowned. "You know, I didn't think about it until now, but the whole time we've been here, there's been no sign of anything like that. No rats, no spiders...nothing." She turned to look at Derek, and their eyes met.

"Maybe they can feel it, too," Derek whispered, his eyes fearful. "Whatever it is, no living thing wants to be near it."

Ally shuddered, but then Maddy screamed. Ally whirled around to find Maddy hiding her face in Bart's shoulder from one of the mirrors as he tried to console her. Despite herself, Ally asked, "What was it?"

Maddy choked, "I...I saw us...in the mirror...all looking back. Then we all yawned, but...it...it didn't stop...our mouths just got wider...and wider..."

Ally shivered, sneaking a glance down the hallway of the corner they were standing in. It seemed to extend much longer than most of the hallways they had wound through thus far, striking Ally as odd. Then suddenly, the hallway lurched to the side, slowly twisting before her eyes. Ally blinked in disbelief, but when she opened her eyes again, the hallway was back to normal. *My turn.* "Come on."

They continued into the hallway, Ally's sense of dread growing in her with every step. They had to be close now. As they approached yet another T, Ally thought she caught a glimpse of movement through one of the holes in the plaster wall. Despite her better judgment, she stopped to take another look. To her relief, there was nothing there. Derek's voice behind her called, "Come on, we can't stop."

Ally turned to look at him, and her blood froze. It was Derek, but his hair was slowly growing out and turning white. His skin began to wrinkle and sag, with liver spots popping up in odd blotches. Horrified, Ally glanced at Bart and Maddy, but they, too, seemed to be aging before her eyes. Maddy's black hair slithered down her shoulders and turned to shimmering silver as the flesh on her cheeks and neck seemed to sink. Bart's skin shrank, clinging tighter to his bones as though he were wasting away. Ally let go of Derek's wrinkled hand and backed away from them.

"Ally? What is it?" Maddy asked, but it wasn't the voice of Ally's best friend. Instead, it was the high-pitched croak of an old woman. Before Ally's horrified eyes, her friends continued to age, with even their clothes succumbing to the hands of time. The threads frayed and unraveled as they fell to the floor, unable to cling to their wearers any longer for the weight of unnumbered years.

Tears filled Ally's eyes, but she couldn't bring herself to look away from her friends as their flesh continued to droop and sag until, one by one, their eyes glazed over and their heads fell to the side with their mouths slack. Soon their flesh, too, began to peel away to the bone beneath, and Ally was finally able to let out a final scream of terror as she turned away to bury her face in the wall.

She huddled against the wall, her cheek resting in a hole in the plaster as she sobbed. She told herself that it wasn't real, that it was just a hallucination like the Derek-thing, but the image of her friends turning to dust before her eyes was burned into her mind.

Hoping that the hallucination was over, she opened her eyes to find a single yellow bloodshot eye peeking out of the hole in the wall at her. With a scream, she jumped back and was caught by Derek, now blissfully youthful again. "Ally! Are you okay?"

Ally sniffed and shook her head. "Just...just fuck this place, already," she sobbed.

"No shit," Maddy agreed, her green eyes wide and fearful.

"W-w-we have to b-b-be c-c-close," Bart observed.

Ally nodded. "We are." She had no idea how she knew, but there was no doubt in her mind. When at last she collected herself, they set off again.

Sure enough, as they wound their way through the nonsensical layout of the ward, Ally felt Derek's grip tighten on her hand. As she was about to ask what was wrong, Derek began murmuring, "It's not real. It's not real." Ally glanced up at his face. His eyes were wide and staring off to their left, a mere wall. He repeated it to himself as they walked, but his grip on Ally's hand continued to tighten. His entire body seemed to stiffen, and his muttering grew faster and faster. Ally reached up with her free hand and touched his cheek, whispering soothingly, "Whatever it is, it isn't real. Look at me?"

Derek turned to face her with his wide eyes. She looked back into them, ignoring the shiver that ran down her spine at the raw fear in them. "It's not real."

Derek closed his eyes and took a deep breath. "I know."

Ally stopped and leaned up to kiss his cheek. "Come on." Derek nodded, and they continued.

After several more twists and turns, they rounded a corner and came to the only part of this section of the asylum that resembled an actual room so far. Inside were tall glass boxes smeared all over with a dry, rust-colored substance. Maddy asked in a hushed whisper, "Is that...blood?"

Derek replied simply, "Yes." Ally shuddered. There was enough smeared on the boxes and throughout the room to account for at least a gallon. She then noticed the anatomical posters pinned to the walls. They were so nonsensically scattered that they nearly resembled a collage. However, if there was an image they were supposed to create, Ally couldn't make any sense of it.

Suddenly, there was a bang on one of the glass panes, and Maddy screamed. Ally turned in the direction of the sound. A girl with matted, dark hair, pounded her hands on the glass from inside one of the boxes. She then threw her hair back and screamed back at Maddy, revealing a gaping mouth with crooked teeth and eye sockets with flesh stretched seamlessly over them.

As the four of them watched, another person materialized in each of the other boxes, pounding their hands and fists on the glass frantically. One had only two fingers on each hand, with the stubs of its missing fingers crudely sewn shut and its lips held apart by what looked like fishhooks. Its wide, electric-blue eyes wept tears of blood that dripped into its opened mouth and outlined its teeth in glistening red.

A third apparition had a bulbous, swollen forehead and eyelids that hung uselessly over empty sockets. Its cracked and bleeding lips were turned up in a wide grin that exposed jagged, misshapen teeth.

A fourth beat its face against the glass instead of its hands. Its dark, ragged hair hung over its face with an opening just large enough to see an eye sewn shut. Its hands scratched and clawed at its own body frantically with dirty fingernails that were at least two inches long.

As the group watched in horrified silence, the girl with no eyes retched and vomited forth a great wave of blood. Gallons and gallons filled her glass container until she seemed to be drowning in it, her hands clawing frantically at the glass until they too disappeared in the frothing, gory bile.

The four-fingered man shriveled and withered, his flesh turning a somber grey until he disintegrated into a pile of silent ashes.

The big-headed thing pulsed and flailed, its head swelling further and further by the moment. Soon, its entire body pulsated like an oversized heart, swelling larger with each beat until it burst into a pink pile of gunk and ichor, splattering the interior of its box entirely.

The fourth apparition ripped his own flesh open and black insects spewed forth from the wounds. As the insects tumbled from his body, it shriveled until it dissolved into a teeming mass of bugs.

"Guys, are you seeing...?" Ally asked.

"Yes," Bart answered with an unusually high-pitched voice.

"It...it's just trying to mess with us," Derek stammered, his hand trembling in Ally's grip.

Maddy whimpered, "It's not trying, it's fucking succeeding." She looked as though she was about to vomit again.

Derek took a step closer to Ally. "Let's just move on. Real or not, this is disgusting." His eyes were fixed on the remnants of the big-headed thing, which appeared to still be pulsating. Bart's eyes were likewise fixed on the two-foot-high pile of insects in their own case.

Swallowing, Ally looked away from the macabre displays to a door on the other side from where they had entered. It was another iron door, heavily rusted, with a narrow sliding panel at eye level and a single handle. Although it didn't appear as heavy as the door into maximum security, something about it gave Ally an overwhelming sense of foreboding. *This is it.*

She trembled as she walked up to it, one hand outstretched and the other gripping Derek's tightly. Her fingers wrapped around the handle slowly and pulled. There was a sharp screech as the door shifted forward several inches, but no more. Ally pulled, but it wouldn't budge. She let go of Derek's hand and wrenched with both hands as hard as she could.

"Ally, watch out!" Maddy yelled as the door came free of its rusted hinges entirely and started to fall.

Derek lunged forward and pulled Ally aside as the door came crashing down with a thunderous clang. Ally stood against the wall with Derek's arms around her and her wide eyes fixed on the door. It had happened so fast that she hadn't even had time to register it. In all likelihood, Derek's quick action had saved her life. She looked at him and whispered shakily, "Th-thank you."

Derek looked her up and down. "Are you all right?"

She nodded earnestly. "I'm fine, thanks to you."

"Guys..." Bart said quietly.

Derek and Ally looked at him to find his gaze transfixed by the room ahead. Ally slid away from Derek and stood in the doorway to see what she had uncovered. The room was small and square, the lath and plaster motif that had carried throughout the experimental ward continuing within. However, the floor inside was wooden and severely rotted. The only object in the room was a heavily decayed corpse reposed against the wall opposite the door. Its tattered and heavily stained clothes consisted of a lab coat and scrubs, and similarly stained spectacles sat crookedly on its withered face. There was barely any flesh left to speak of, with empty sockets for eyes and no lips to hide blackened teeth. Its arms hung limp at its sides with a rusted scalpel on the floor next to its right hand and a little leather book next to its left. Somehow, Ally knew that she hadn't merely found Aros's journal. She had found Aros Corbant himself.

Maddy gasped. "Is that...?"

Ally nodded. "I think it is."

"H-h-how is h-h-he still h-h-here?" Bart stammered quietly.

Derek whispered, "Maybe something kept them away."

"What are you saying?" Ally asked, unable to look away from the desiccated corpse.

"I'm not sure how to explain, but I bet the answers are in there," Derek said, gesturing towards the journal.

Ally said, "I'll go first," then stepped over the threshold, planting her foot tenderly. As she began to shift her weight onto the foot in the room, the floor creaked loudly, and Ally swore it sagged slightly beneath her weight. She pulled back and looked at them all with wide eyes. "My God..."

"Don't tell me..." Maddy whined.

"I have to go in alone. It...it's just not stable enough," Ally said nervously.

Derek shook his head. "No way. I'll go in instead."

Ally looked at him resolutely. "I'm the lightest of the four of us. Besides, that's my great uncle in there. It has to be me."

Maddy stepped up to her. "Ally..."

Ally looked away from her, unable to bear the fear in her eyes. "I've made up my mind. Either I do this, or all of this has been for nothing."

Maddy bit her lip, then threw her arms around Ally. "Please come back safely."

Ally sighed but hugged her best friend back. "I won't be any more than ten feet away. In and out in no time." *I hope.*

Maddy hugged her tighter for a moment and whispered in her ear, "I couldn't live without you, girl. Please don't make me."

Ally tightened her own arms around Maddy and assured her, "I won't. I promise."

Maddy then released her and took a step back. Tears were in her eyes, but she nodded encouragingly. "You got this, girl."

Ally closed her eyes and sighed before turning to face the room once more. She made to take another experimental step into the room but thought better of it. Instead, she got down on her hands and knees and crawled in. The floor groaned beneath her, but not as loudly as when she had tried to walk in. She moved slowly, keeping her weight as centered between all four limbs as she could.

Inch by inch, she crawled closer to Aros's corpse. At the edge of her vision, she swore there were little yellow eyes peeking out at her from inside the lath in the walls. Whatever was watching was whispering to itself, though Ally couldn't make out any words. Trying her best to ignore them, she kept going until at least she was within arm's reach of the journal.

Nervous and trembling, Ally reached out slowly to grab it, her eyes fixed on the corpse now inches from her. From everything she had seen that night, she had little doubt that it might move to stop her. She never looked away from it even as her fingers closed around the leather binding of the journal. Slowly, she pulled it to her and backed away. The floor groaned again, and she paused, her wide eyes still rooted to Aros's corpse. *Don't move. Don't fucking move.* She had no idea how long she sat frozen there before she finally worked up the courage to turn around, but once she was facing the door and began to make her way towards it, the floor gave out beneath her.

Ally lunged for the door. Derek and Maddy both squeezed through the doorway to throw their arms out to catch her, but not quickly enough. Their outstretched fingers passed within inches of Ally's before she fell, screaming. She landed on her stomach, knocking the wind out of her. She couldn't have fallen more than twenty feet, but there had been no light in the room above. She coughed as she tried to catch her breath, but the smell of mildew and sod was overwhelming. She rolled over and sat up, trying to breathe shallowly.

Then she heard Derek's voice overhead, "Ally! Are you all right?" Three flashlight beams angled down towards her.

Ally shielded her eyes and called back, "A little bruised but alive. Can you toss my flashlight down?"

"On it!" Maddy replied, and then Ally's flashlight rolled down the side of the hole to her feet. She picked it up and turned it on as she climbed to her feet and brushed herself off. Ally took stock of where she had landed. The wall in front of her was thick with stones and roots and wasn't quite a nine-ty-degree angle to the top. Ally nodded to herself. She might very well be able to climb out. She looked around for the journal. It had fallen only a few feet away. She snatched it up and began planning her course up the dirt wall. However, a strange hissing sound behind her disrupted her train of thought. Slowly and fearfully, she turned around.

Aros's corpse lay in a crumbled heap nearby, but that was not what arrested Ally's attention. Instead, set into the wall of the hole opposite from her was a massive stone sarcophagus, wrapped with huge chains as thick as Ally's arm. It stood upright with the lid facing her. Her flashlight revealed hundreds of bizarre symbols engraved in the stone. The hissing sound issued forth again, but much louder and accompanied by a low growl. The sense of dread that had plagued her from the moment they had entered the asylum was now overwhelmingly intense, bringing with it outright panic. As she backed against the dirt wall behind her, Ally called "Guys...get me out of here!"

A voice from the sarcophagus answered, but not alone. As it spoke, other voices repeated its words but with slightly different inflections that seemed to change the meaning of what it said, "There is no *need* to run, Ally. You are home now. You are free. Like all of them. All of us."

"Who...what...are you?" The voices made her skin crawl. She had never heard such a loathsome, unearthly sound.

The hissing sound came again, and Ally swore she saw the roots around the sarcophagus writhe and twitch as it answered in a cascade of words, "I...we...I am...we are...we were...we will be...we are...freedom...instinct...I am...chaos...ruin...defilement...what we will...what I desire...we are...I am...Madness."

Ally couldn't bring herself to reply. The voices all repeated the words over and over again like a bizarre, discordant chant. Then to Ally's horror, numerous faces emerged from the dirt around the sarcophagus. Most of them she didn't recognize, but most horrifying of all were the ones she did: her father, her mother, Gladys, Chad, Carol, Matt, Gary, Bart, Maddy, Derek, and even Cassie. All their eyes opened, but they weren't the eyes she recognized. Instead, they were yellow and bloodshot, with slits for pupils. Some laughed at her mockingly, others said things such as, "You will be free here," "Now you can do as you please," and "Stay with us."

Ally could take no more. Of everything she had seen up until then, nothing could have prepared her for this. She turned and began the climb up the dirt, trying not to let panic overwhelm her despite her desperation to escape. The roots went deep and thick, allowing her easy purchase as she ascended, even with the journal clutched in hand, but the voices below grew louder. She quickened her pace, nearly at the top when something wrapped around her ankle. Instinctively, her free hand tightened its grip on a root, but she couldn't stop herself from looking down at what had grabbed her any more than she could have stopped the scream that erupted from her lungs when she saw it.

Inches below Ally was a seething mass of blackness, dotted with glowing yellow eyes of various sizes. Wrapped around her ankle was a long, pink tentacle-like appendage that extended from a torso that rose out of the blackness like a grotesque flower. Its flesh was pink and scarred as if burned, but as Ally looked down at it, she saw the pink flesh at the bottom of the torso turn a dull grey where it met the writhing shadows. The head of the torso had no face, but only the vague shape of humanoid features, and its free arm extended down into the darkness just like its lower half.

Ally kicked, but the grip of the torso-thing was unshakable. Even as she struggled, it tried to dislodge her and drag her down into God knew what.

A hand closed around hers. She looked up and saw Maddy yelling, "Grab ahold!" Ally grabbed her hand, struggling to keep her grip on both Maddy and the journal, and then Maddy shouted, "Now!"

With a groan of exertion, Maddy hauled Ally up over the edge of the hole. At last, Ally managed to kick the tentacle thing off as she scrambled into the display room, the journal clutched to her chest. Derek had an arm around Maddy's midsection, and Bart had ahold of Derek's other hand by the forearm. As Ally got to her feet, they let go of each other. However, before they could even ask if she was all right, she said, "We need to run. Now!"

"Why..." Derek began, but then his eyes widened. They all turned to see the torso-thing climbing up over the edge of the hole, pulling the writhing darkness with a thousand eyes with it. As the shadows crested the hole's edge, they turned to a dull orange, almost brown. Tiny little mouths opened up within the bizarre cloud filled with razor sharp teeth and gnashing tongues. *Madness. Pure, uncontrolled madness.*

With no explanation needed, the four of them broke into a run as the grotesque thing slithered after them. Although the navigation of the experimental ward had seemed to take forever in getting there, getting back to maximum security took no time at all. Ally dared a glance back and saw that the torso had been replaced by a single, massive yellow eye with a slit for a pupil. The little mouths swirled around it, their writhing tongues lapping at its edges like grotesque eyelashes.

Ally turned around and burst through the door into the maximum-security ward. Derek, Maddy, and Bart quickly followed, slamming the door shut behind them. Without pausing to take a breath, they made for the entrance door as the experimental ward door blasted wide open on its hinges and the room filled with hundreds of voices laughing mockingly. As the grotesque mass of smoke, flesh, eyes, and teeth slid into the room like a tidal wave, Ally swore she felt the asylum itself shudder at its touch. The doors on the cells slammed open and shut frantically as the thing's laughter was joined by agonized screams from invisible throats.

The four of them rushed through the iron door. Derek slid to a stop in the maximum-security entryway. He glanced back at the door. "We could close it..."

Ally grabbed his hand and pulled him forward. "No time! Move!" Even as they spoke, the great eye appeared in the window of the heavy iron door. Without further hesitation, the four of them broke into a run once more, bursting through the swinging doors into the hallway. Ally's lungs burned and her legs ached, but the end was near. Together, they fled the hallway and rushed out into the entrance hall.

The entire building seemed to be alive with screaming and laughing. It echoed maddeningly throughout the entrance hall as decayed papers flew about and doors slammed again and again. Ally only had eyes for the front door, however. Squeezing Derek's hand, she pulled him back into a run towards the exit.

The moment they reached the door, however, it slammed shut. "No!" Ally screamed, pounding her fists against the door.

"Fuck!" Maddy yelled and joined Ally pounding the door.

Derek shouted, "Move aside!"

As the girls turned, they saw the horrific mass slide into the entrance hall. At first, it seemed to flow in like rushing water, but then it rose and engulfed the entirety of the stairwell behind it. It spread itself across the room, a horrific wall of writhing flesh, snarling maws with razor teeth, and innumerable eyes. In the center of it all was the single enormous slit-pupil eye, its gaze fixed on them. As Ally watched in utter horror, the eye split open horizontally across the center to reveal an enormous mouth with long, needle-like teeth and a writhing, serpentine tongue.

Suddenly, there was a splintering crack, and cool air hit their backs. Ally whirled around. Derek was standing across the threshold, his hand outstretched for them. "Come on, guys!" Without hesitation, Ally took his hand, but Maddy let out a blood-curdling shriek. Ally turned to see Maddy holding onto Bart. The thing's tongue had wrapped around his midsection and was trying to drag him into its gaping maw. Maddy held both his hands in her own, but as they watched, her feet slid slowly towards the thing.

Ally let go of Derek's hand and rushed to Maddy's side, grabbed Bart's arm, and pulled with all of her might. Derek did the same on her other side. The shrieking and laughing from the entryway grew louder as the three of them struggled to pull Bart free. Bart himself was expressionless, his eyes wide and vacant.

Maddy grunted with exertion, "You...can't...have...him!"

The thousand voices answered as one, "He is already ours."

"Not...yet!" Maddy snarled as she wrenched. At last, Bart slid out of the grasp of the thing's tongue, and together the four of them spilled over the threshold and out of the asylum. They rolled down the steps as the screams of the thing pierced the night. With a thunderous crash, all the windows in the asylum shattered, and a brilliant light flashed from within. Before the glass of the top floors even reached the ground, the light was gone, and the asylum had turned dark and silent once more.

The four friends lay scattered in the driveway. Ally felt bruises all over but sat up and turned to look at the building. It looked almost exactly as it had when they had first entered, but she swore she saw a slight glow outlining the images of the saints on the front doors. Then, Maddy's sobs drew her attention. Ally whirled around to see Derek kneeling next to a hysterical Maddy. She was cradling a seemingly catatonic Bart. His wide eyes stared blankly upwards at the sky while Maddy frantically shook him and called his name.

Ally's heart was in her throat. She couldn't bring herself to consider the possibility. Her stomach churned and her legs shook. *Surely not. Bart couldn't be...*

Maddy kissed him. She kissed him fully and forcefully with a desperation that Ally found difficult to watch. Tears streamed down Maddy's cheeks, but she held her lips to his for several seconds. When at last she broke away, she cradled his head and sobbed. Then, he began to stir. Maddy gasped. "Bart?"

He looked up at her, his eyes slowly gaining focus. "M-M-Maddy?"

Maddy pulled him into her arms and sobbed, "I thought...my God...Bart..."

Bart stammered, "I...I'm okay...Maddy."

She pulled his face to hers and kissed him again.

Ally's heart leapt. *He's okay!* She looked at Derek, who looked back at her with his half-smile. "We did it," he said.

Ally looked down at the leatherbound book clutched to her chest, then back at Derek with a triumphant smile. "Yeah. Yeah, we did."

17. Truth and Tragedy

Relieved but still shaken, the four friends hastily made their way back to Derek's car, eager to get as far away from the asylum as possible. The things Ally had seen inside would surely haunt her for many nights to come.

As she slid into the passenger seat, she rested the old journal on her knees. *Will this thing be enough?* Her finger traced the edge of the front cover as she contemplated opening it and seeing for herself. The engine roaring to life startled her out of her thoughts. *Later.*

Maddy asked from the backseat, "So...party at my place?"

Ally groaned. "God, yes!"

Derek shifted the car into drive. "Fine by me."

Bart added, "J-j-just g-g-get us out of h-h-here."

Maddy threw her arms around him and held Bart tight to her chest. "Amen! Punch it!"

"With pleasure," Derek said with a slight grin, and with a sharp turn in the old driveway and a satisfying burnout, the asylum faded in the rearview mirror.

Ally had never been so relieved to leave a place behind. She leaned back in the seat and closed her eyes, only to find a hand sliding gently into hers. She didn't need to open her eyes to know who the owner was. Ally smiled. Already the night seemed a little brighter.

As they drove along, Ally snuck a glance into the backseat. Maddy was cradling Bart with his head on her chest. She stroked his hair like a mother soothing a frightened child. The sight both warmed Ally's heart and saddened her at the thought of all they had been through. Of the four of them, Bart seemed to have taken things the hardest. Whatever the place had done to him, he was clearly haunted by it. *He'll be all right, though. Maddy will take care of him.*

The four of them rode in silence. Ally held Derek's hand as she watched the scenery roll by. Little by little, however, the sense of triumph over the asylum began to fade as exhaustion crept in on them. Ally stifled a yawn and tried to rub the sleep from her eyes, but every blink grew steadily longer and longer until, at last, they were at Maddy's house. All four of them sluggishly got out of the car and made their way inside. Once the door was closed behind them, Maddy yawned. "How long were we gone?"

Derek checked his watch, "It's 5 a.m. now."

Ally yawned as well. "Maybe the party can wait until tomorrow."

Maddy agreed. "I think so. You two can have the couch again. Bart and I are sharing my bed."

Bart looked at her nervously. "I..." he began.

Maddy pressed a finger to his lips. "No way in hell am I letting you sleep alone tonight, and I sure as hell don't want to, either. I need someone to cuddle with, and since Ally has Derek, I get you, okay? Good, now come on, or I'll consider stripping."

Ally giggled as Bart blushed furiously. As Maddy dragged him back to her bedroom, Bart looked back at Ally and Derek with nervous eyes. Ally nodded encouragingly, so Bart allowed Maddy to pull him into her room and close the door behind them.

Derek asked, "Think they'll be all right?"

"Yeah," Ally answered, "so long as Maddy doesn't decide to change in front of him. He's been through enough." At first, she had meant it to be a joke, but the truth of her words brought the memories of the asylum back to life in her mind, and she shuddered.

Derek pulled her into his arms and held her tight. "We all have."

Ally leaned against him, laying her head against his chest. She didn't want to think about the horrors of the asylum, but the images wouldn't leave her mind. She could still see the faceless man coming out of the locker, the morbidities in the display room, and the great eye that was actually a mouth with its serpentine tongue. She shuddered again in revulsion and whispered, "Let's lie down."

Without question, Derek went over to the couch, slipping off his shoes as he went. He then stretched out and pulled the blanket off the back down to cover himself. Ally laid down beside him and slid her arms around him, and he kissed her forehead. She whispered, "If I tell you no, you'll listen, right?"

Derek looked at her in surprise. "What brought that up?"

Ally blushed a little, but explained, "In the asylum...I ran into a you that wasn't you...and it practically tried to rape me..."

Derek's eyes widened. "I would never, ever do that to you."

"I know," Ally tried to reassure him, "but it looked and acted just like you...until it was climbing on top of me...and until then...I honestly wanted to...with you...but now...I don't know...if I can..." Her voice broke as tears filled her eyes. The memory of the Derek-thing made her feel violated, but she was also ashamed of how she had let it taint her feelings towards Derek himself.

Derek kissed her forehead and whispered, "There's no rush. Don't do anything you're uncomfortable with."

Ally looked up into his eyes, nervous for the answer to the question that burned in her mind. Swallowing her fear, she asked, "Even if it takes quite a while...years maybe...for me to be okay with it?"

Derek smiled warmly as he ran a finger across her cheek. "I plan to stick around either way if that's okay with you."

Ally smiled, fresh tears filling her eyes. She buried her face in his chest. "Thank you...thank you so much."

Derek stroked her hair gently. "Whatever you need, Ally."

Ally lay with her face in his chest for several minutes before she looked up at him again. Once again, she found those warm brown eyes looking back at her. This time, there was no hunger or malevolence, only concern and affection. *Never stop looking at me that way.* She reached up to caress his cheek and whispered, "I love you."

Derek smiled as the ghost of a blush played across his cheeks. "I love you, too." Then she leaned up and kissed him softly. Though the passion she had become accustomed to was absent, the soft warmth of the kiss was comforting to her. She held onto his lips for as long as she could before finally breaking away and laying her head back on his chest. Within moments, exhaustion claimed her.

Unfortunately, even Ally's exhaustion couldn't keep her nightmares at bay. Once again, she was in the entrance hall of the asylum, moments before their escape from the monstrous eye. However, before any of them could grab him, the slimy tongue pulled Bart into its mouth, ripping him apart as it dragged him across its misshapen teeth. Even as Ally watched, screaming, chunks of Bart's flesh flew in all directions, while he neither struggled nor screamed. He merely stared at them all with a wide-eyed, blank expression.

Before Bart was entirely obliterated by the gnashing maw, the tongue shot out again and wrapped around Maddy's waist. Maddy shrieked and scratched at it but to no avail as it lifted her up into the air and pulled her towards the mouth that still held pieces of Bart between its teeth. Ally wanted to run to her best friend's aid, but her legs felt as though they were weighted to the ground. Try as she might, she couldn't make more than baby steps towards Maddy. With one last desperate scream, Maddy disappeared entirely into the thing's mouth. Seconds later, a geyser of blood and gore spewed forth. Ally looked on in horror as Maddy's severed head bobbed in the visceral tide, her eyes wide and mouth frozen in a permanent scream of agony.

Ally wanted to turn away to find Derek, hoping against hope that somehow, he had escaped this horrible nightmare, but then the wave of gore hit her, drenching her from head to toe in her best friend's blood. Disgustingly soft objects bumped against her in the crimson tide until she felt the tongue wrap around her midsection and lift her high above the sea of blood. Try as she might, Ally couldn't look away from the great maw. Its jagged teeth glistened with blood, and its throat was a slimy tunnel riddled with eyes and writhing tongues. The thing's thousand-voices boomed, "I...we...are...desecration...and...defilement!"

Ally screamed for help, for Derek, and for her friends, but the only answer that came was the mocking laughter of the thing's chorus. Then, the tip of the serpentine tongue slid into her mouth. Ally gagged and retched as it forced its way down her throat. She could feel it snaking its way through her, its loathsome sliminess filling her with a disgusting feeling that would have had her begging for death if only she could speak...

Ally sat bolt upright, breathing heavily and bathed in sweat. She looked around to find herself still at Maddy's house. Derek was fast asleep beside her, completely oblivious to what she had just endured. Ally's stomach rolled with the memory of the thing's tongue running through it.

She slid off the couch and ran to the bathroom, barely getting the toilet seat up before she vomited. She heaved three times before finally slumping to the bathroom floor, trembling. She had never felt such a disgusting sensation, whether awake or asleep. How her imagination could have conjured such a horrific feeling was entirely beyond her.

After sitting on the floor in the bathroom for several minutes, Ally eventually got to her feet and went back to the living room. Sleep was well out of the question now. In fact, Ally wasn't sure if she'd ever be able to sleep again.

She ran a hand across her throat, trying to let its soft feeling remind her that it had only been a dream. Her eyes fell onto the journal on the floor next to the loveseat. For a moment, Ally considered getting rid of it, as though it would drive all remnant of the asylum's memory from her mind, but then she remembered why she had needed it in the first place. Still, a question remained unanswered. *How will this journal stop Sam?*

Curiosity replacing her revulsion, Ally grabbed the journal and went to the kitchen. She turned the light on and sat down at the table, flipping to the first entry and reading. At first, it seemed like a perfectly ordinary journal. Aros remarked upon his daily struggles with caring for the mentally ill, as well as with the staff and board of directors. Ally was shocked to learn that Aros was a staunch opponent of most modern (at the time) treatments for mental illness. He condemned both lobotomy and shock treatment as unnecessarily barbaric. He wrote:

In this era of modern science and medicine, is it not possible to innovate and develop treatments that result in far less physical damage to the patients? The results of these treatments may be unquestionable, but are the side effects and potential for error truly worth what progress they offer? We must strive to synthesize treatments that are far less invasive so that patients will not fear their doctors and will welcome our help with open arms.

Ally felt her heart sink. Aros was a humanitarian just like his wife and Bart's grandfather had said. He sympathized deeply with his patients and went out of his way to give them comfort. In a later entry, he even rejected the advances of his personal nurse, whose last name was Dowry, on the grounds of his happy marriage to Arabella. He considered petitioning the board of directors to have Nurse Dowry relocated following a second incident but refrained since she seemed to be one of the few who shared his sentiments about finding better treatment for their patients. In the end, the only petition he made to the board was to have the ECT facility uninstalled as a gesture of goodwill to the patients, but it was denied.

Then Aros wrote about being forced to expand the asylum due to over-crowding. With World War II in full swing, there were simply too many cases, both mental and physical, for the asylum to accommodate as it was. He seemed stretched thin and fearful for the well-being of those in his care, insisting that he would still make it a personal goal to say hello and offer personal comfort to every patient in the asylum. The last part of that entry stated:

We break ground on the expansion tomorrow. God, give me strength that I do not fail those who depend on me.

Then, Ally turned the page and gasped. Instead of another entry, she found nonsensical scribblings of both images and words saying things like *Too many eyes!* Or *Fingers in mouths makes the ugly come out!* Page after page was covered in these frighteningly childish scribblings, some of the pages even sporting splatters of a brown substance Ally was certain was old blood. At last, she reached a page where Aros's old, tidy handwriting returned. It read:

This is my final entry. I have barricaded myself in what has become known as the "Whispering Room." A riot broke out among the maximum-security inmates mere minutes ago. I dare not think of what has become of my staff, but perhaps it is all that can be expected.

What has become of us all? We used to care about our patients, but over the last few weeks we have taken to outright torturing them! The horrors we have committed...how can we possibly be absolved of these atrocities? It was as though I could see it all through my own eyes but was powerless to control my own actions or words. I ORDERED these terrible things! My own lips issued these horrific commands, and my staff readily carried them out! Why?

It has to be that which lies beneath me at this very moment. When they were digging the foundation for the expansion, the construction crew uncovered a stone sarcophagus carved with ancient symbols. One by one over the next week, the construction workers were admitted to the asylum as they began developing extreme psychoses. It wasn't long until the fog came over us all and the construction of the maze-like "experimental ward" began. It all made so much sense at the time, but thinking of it now, I realize that only a true madman could have designed such a structure. Whatever was in that sarcophagus put us all under its spell. God, what have I done?

Now I unburden my soul. Now I confess my participation in heinous muti-
lation, torture, and even adultery. Within the fog, I gave in to Dowry's advances
more times than I wish to remember. Oh Arabella, my love, I was and never
will be worthy of you for as long as I live! I have failed my wife, my daughter
Constance, my nephew Wayne...I have stained our family name with gallons of
blood, and whatever foul thing infected the asylum, in its infinite cruelty, saw fit
to grant me clarity as it all finally collapses around me.

My only solace is knowing that I shall die in full control of my faculties. I
will not allow myself to be influenced by this thing any longer. Never again will
I let my will be subsumed, and now these hands will spill no more blood but my
own. For the crimes I have committed, there can be only one sentence. May God
forgive those I misled, and may He have mercy on my stained and twisted soul.

With a shudder, Ally closed the book. *That's what the scalpel had been*
there for. In the end, he had taken his own life. Ally pitied her great uncle now
that she knew the truth about him. He *had* been a good man, but whatever
that thing was that had been in the sarcophagus had influenced him and his
staff into committing their crimes.

As much as Ally hated to admit it, the stories about what Aros had done
were far from exaggerated. Still, she couldn't hate him for the legacy he had
left them all with. Just like what Sam had done to Lamuel, he had been dri-
ven to these acts by something he couldn't understand.

Ally sighed with a heavy heart. This last revelation about her family history was the most difficult yet. All along, the Corbant family had been at
the mercy of forces beyond their understanding. The One That Dwells Below, Sam, and the thing in the asylum all had influenced them, using them
for their own ends. Still, Ally couldn't figure out what the journal contained
that the One Below would want.

She opened it back up and leafed through it again, this time examining
what she had dubbed the "fog pages" more closely. Extraordinarily little was
consistent about the scribblings and drawings that Aros had made. However, the more Ally looked, the more she noticed that one sketch repeated itself
with almost perfect clarity on every page.

Though eyes were a common motif in the "fog pages," one stylized eye
kept appearing. It was a very basic concept of an eye—an almond shape with
a single dot in the center, but then Aros added five eyelashes along the top

that were oddly positioned and angled to look like four fingers and a thumb coming out of the top of the eye. Adding to the illusion were two eyelashes on the bottom lid, but in the corners of the eye and angled inward. If Ally placed her finger over the pupil of the eye, the illusion was complete: instead of an eye on the page, there was a hand with spidery fingers. *Maybe it's some kind of symbol? Maybe that's what the One Below wants?*

Ally's thoughts recalled the similarities between the thing in the asylum's sarcophagus and the One's own sarcophagus. She hadn't been able to tell if the symbols were the same, but she was almost certain that somewhere on either sarcophagus she would find the eye symbol.

Ally considered getting up and leaving Maddy's at that moment. The desire to give the journal to the One Below and hopefully put an end to all of this was almost overwhelming. However, she wasn't sure she was ready to face another supernatural force after having survived such a close brush with one so recently. *No, best wait until my parents' call.*

She could have concocted several excuses, but the ultimate reason was simply that she wanted to be around her friends for a bit longer and maybe get some sleep. Maybe having fun with them would help to drive the memory of the asylum from her mind, and maybe she could rest before facing the One Below and Sam for what would hopefully be the final time.

Ally looked out the window. It had still been dark when she had first woken up, but now the sun was fully up. *The others will probably be asleep for a while yet.* She laid back down with Derek. She managed to slide up next to him without waking him and lay her head on his chest, closing her eyes. With exhaustion weighing on her yet again as the sun rose, she was able to relax lying next to him. She inhaled his scent and exhaled with a soft sigh. *Soon, there won't be any more nightmares. Soon.*

Ally wasn't sure if she fell asleep or not, but next she knew, Maddy came in and said, "Rise and shine, lovebirds! It's party time!"

Ally blinked and looked at her sleepily. "What time is it?"

"Nearly one o'clock, so up and at 'em!"

Ally sat up and stretched, then turned to see Derek slowly blinking his eyes. He looked at her and smiled. "Good morning, beautiful."

Ally blushed. "Do you always sleep so soundly?"

"Only when I'm thoroughly exhausted."

"And last night was thoroughly exhausting, so that's why we're having fun today!" Maddy declared as a still sleepy looking Bart shuffled into the room. Maddy then slipped past him and disappeared back into her bedroom. Ally rolled her eyes as Maddy emerged toting an armful of board games. "Time to get our game on!"

Derek laughed. "So, this is your idea of a party?"

Maddy winked slyly. "Only because Ally's too shy to strip." Ally frowned, grabbed a throw pillow off the loveseat, and threw it at Maddy. She ducked under it and set the games down on the floor before crawling up to Ally and laying her head in her lap. "It's okay, girl. We all know that your hotness is too great for our eyes."

Ally shoved her away playfully. "Speak for yourself. If you stripped, it might give all the guys nosebleeds."

"More like have them paying me to put my clothes back on."

Ally rolled her eyes. "Only because they can't handle you."

Maddy giggled again and started setting up a game board. "Handle this then!" she challenged.

The next few hours were passed eating chips and losing spectacularly to Maddy game after game. They joked and teased each other as though nothing horrible had happened last night, and Ally almost forgot about the reason they had gotten together in the first place. Then around five o'clock, Bart got up. "It's t-t-time for m-m-me to head h-h-home."

Derek, Ally, and Maddy all looked up at him. Maddy whined, "Aww...really?"

Bart nodded with downcast eyes. "S-s-sorry."

Maddy hopped up and threw her arms around him. "Don't apologize, sweetie. I'll see you at school, okay?"

Bart mumbled, "Of c-c-course." Ally's heart leapt as she watched Bart's arms tighten around Maddy. Then she kissed him. At first, he didn't seem to know what to do, but Ally grinned as she saw him start to kiss her back. When they broke apart, both were breathless.

Derek got up and offered his hand to Bart. "Thanks for everything."

Bart nodded and shook Derek's hand. "N-n-no p-p-problem."

Ally stood up and hugged him, whispering in his ear, "Thank you...so much."

Bart simply nodded as he hugged her back, and without another word, he was out the door.

The three of them sat back down, and Maddy asked Ally, "When do you need to be home?"

Ally shrugged. "Dad said he'd call when they start to miss me."

"Huh. Okay," Maddy observed with a frown before turning to Derek. "What about you?"

He looked at his watch. "I've got another hour."

Maddy grinned. "Then why don't I kick your ass some more?"

Without further delay, they launched into another game from Maddy's collection. Ally was relieved to see Maddy back to her old self, perhaps even a little happier than usual. Her smile lit up her eyes in a way that Ally enjoyed. Best yet, Maddy's happiness was infectious. Even as she thoroughly destroyed them once more, Ally couldn't stop grinning. Before long, however, the hour was up, and Derek stood up to say his goodbyes.

Maddy hugged him and said, "See you at school!"

Derek nodded. "Sure thing." He turned to Ally.

Without hesitation, Ally threw herself into Derek's arms and kissed him fully. Using it as her way to say thank you, Ally put every ounce of passion she could into the kiss. To her delight, he answered her in kind. She pressed a hand to the back of his neck and kissed him more, never wanting to let him go. All too soon, he pulled away and said breathlessly, "I'll see you at school."

Ally nodded and leaned her forehead against his. "Thank you."

Derek kissed her again briefly. "Anytime." Then he, too, was gone.

Ally turned to see Maddy grinning from ear to ear. Her cheeks flushing, Ally asked, "What are you doing?"

Maddy grinned slyly, "Oh don't mind me."

"You watched it all, didn't you?" Ally asked, mortified.

Maddy shrugged, her grin broadening. "You guys made me feel dirty."

Ally sat down beside her. "You don't need our help for that."

Maddy shrugged. "I guess not, but I'll have you know that Bart's innocence remains intact."

Ally chuckled, but then Maddy's phrasing reminded her of home. She furrowed her brow, saying more to herself than to Maddy, "Why hasn't Dad called yet?"

Maddy's grin died on her face and her eyes became fearful. "That is weird. Usually don't they just give you a time to be home?"

Ally nodded and bit her lip, thinking for a moment before standing up. "Maybe Derek's still here," she said before running to the front door to find Derek just putting his car into drive. She waved her arms at him, and he shifted back into park. She ran up to his window and tapped on it. He rolled it down and asked, "What's up?"

"Could you give me a ride home? I'm starting to get a little worried," Ally confessed.

"Of course. You'll just need to direct me."

"No problem. Just let me say goodbye to Maddy," Ally said as she turned to head back inside.

Maddy was still sitting on the floor. She looked up at Ally expectantly. "Well?"

Ally replied, "Derek's gonna give me a ride home."

Maddy got up and threw her arms around Ally. She was taken somewhat aback by Maddy's reaction but embraced her, nonetheless. Maddy whispered, "Be careful, girl. I meant what I said last night. Don't make me live without you."

"I know, and I don't plan to make you. Everything will be fine, I promise."

Maddy hugged her a little tighter. "You're the best friend I could have ever asked for."

Ally sighed softly, tearing up a little. "That title belongs to you, not me."

"Please be careful," Maddy said as she looked Ally in the eyes.

Ally nodded reassuringly. "I will. Promise."

Maddy smiled, but Ally could still see the fear in her green eyes. "Then go get 'em, girl."

Ally gave Maddy one last hug before grabbing her things and heading out to Derek's car. She slid into the passenger seat, set her book bag between her legs, and slid the journal inside before telling Derek how to get to her house.

The trip was short with little conversation until they reached the entrance to Ally's driveway. Derek asked, "Do you think something's happened?"

"I don't know," Ally admitted, "but I want to be sure."

"Want me to come with you?"

Ally thought for a moment, then shook her head. "Best if you don't. If everything's fine, they might ask too many questions if you show up with me."

Derek nodded. "All right then. See you at school."

Ally leaned across the center console and kissed him quickly before getting out of the car. "Of course." She then began the trek up the cobblestone driveway to her house.

Once Derek pulled away, the silence crept in and set Ally's nerves on edge. It was the first time she had been alone since they got separated at the asylum, and with that realization, all of her fears came surging back with a vengeance. *It's okay. Everything will be fine once I get home.* Still, her stomach tied itself in ever-tighter knots with every step.

At last, Ally crested the hill, and the mansion loomed into view. She sighed. Everything seemed to be as it should be. She opened the front gate and walked up to the porch, but she froze once she got a good look at the front door. It was slightly ajar. Suddenly her heart was hammering in her chest. It was such a simple thing for the front door to be left partially open, but with Matt, Carol, and Chad's cars all parked in the driveway alongside the family vehicles, and the air turning chilly with autumn, the oddness of it struck her as painfully ominous.

Ally walked slowly up to the door and pushed it open. The entrance hall was deserted. Swallowing, Ally stepped inside, calling, "Mom? Dad? I'm home!" No sound answered her. *Not good.*

Disturbed, Ally nervously made her way upstairs. She looked into her dad's office, but no one was about. She called again down the hall, "Hello?" Still, there was no answer. She then checked her sister's room, but it, too, was deserted. *Really not good.*

Finally, Ally came to the master bedroom. She knocked, calling once more, "Mom? Dad? Are you in there?" No answer. Breathing steadily to try and slow her racing heart, Ally opened the door. Just inside, her mother was sitting in front of a vanity mirror similar to the one in Ally's room. Ally sighed with relief. "Oh, thank God! Why didn't you answer me?"

Ally's mother didn't turn to look at her. In fact, she didn't even seem to acknowledge Ally's presence at all. "Mom?" Ally asked, giving her a gentle shake. Without warning, her mother's head fell off her shoulders and rolled to the foot of the bed. Ally screamed and jumped back against the door. "Mom!" Her mother's eyes were empty and staring. Ally leaned on the door handle for support as sobs overtook her. Her mind was numb with shock and grief. "Mommy..." she whimpered, tears spilling from her eyes. *Why? Why did this happen?*

A familiar voice called mockingly from the hallway outside the bedroom, "Ally, home at last? Good, Daddy needs to speak with you."

18. Desperation

Ally's breath caught in her chest as her book bag hit the floor. That had been her father's voice, but it sounded nothing like him. She struggled to control her sobs as she slid back through the door and away from her mother's headless body. Once in the hall, the voice spoke again, coming from the top of the stairway to the third floor. "I'm so glad you decided to join us, Ally. I've been dying to speak to you!"

Ally called back, "You're not my father!"

The voice laughed, chilling Ally's blood. "Oh, but I am...in a way." The speaker started down the stairs, each step slow and deliberate just like in the foyer so many nights ago. "Once dear old Dad saw what he did to Mommy, he killed himself, leaving his empty shell behind. Things could not have worked out better for me!"

Understanding hit Ally like a lightning bolt. "Sam?"

The voice laughed again. "The one and only. At last, the Corbant family dies tonight!"

"What have you done with Cassie?" Ally asked, panic welling in her chest.

Sam paused in his descent, heaved an exasperated sigh and spat, "The little bitch is hiding from me, but once she hears your screams, and I tell her that her entire family is gone, her cries will lead me straight to her!"

Ally's heart leapt. There was a chance after all. *I'm coming, Cassie.* She summoned up all her remaining nerve and called back, "Well, then come and get me, you FUCKING ASSHOLE!"

With a snarl of rage, Sam charged down the stairs. Her mind now astonishingly clear, Ally dashed for the foyer. Taking the stairs three at a time, she ran to the ground floor hallway with Sam's footfalls racing by in the hallway overhead. Ally ran to the kitchen, hoping to find something to defend herself with. Once inside, she screamed. Chad's head sat on the stove, the flesh sizzling as the gas burner flared beneath it. Sam's laugh answered her scream. "Careful where you look, Allison! You never know who you'll find!"

Cursing herself for screaming, Ally went to look for a kitchen knife, but they were all gone. "Looking for this?" came Sam's voice from the door on the other side of the island counter in the middle of the room. He held up a butcher knife, grinning maliciously. It was her father's face, but the eyes were crazed and murderous. Any trace of the good man her father had been was gone, and Sam's hatred filled the void left behind. She turned her back to the counter as Sam slowly stalked her from across the room. Ally kept the island between them as she asked tearfully, "What did you make him do?"

Sam grinned his wicked grin. "It wasn't hard to break him. He was so torn up about little Crysania's death that all it took was a little prodding in the right direction. I told him repeatedly that *she* was the one who started the fire. At first, he didn't believe me, but I left clues. By this morning, he was so blinded by rage that he strangled her in bed!" Sam laughed as if it was all a joke to him. Ally's stomach turned, but she held her grip and watched Sam carefully as they moved a slow circle around the island.

"Unfortunately, he came to his senses after she was already dead. Pity about that, so he got a bottle of whiskey and downed the entire house's stock of sleeping pills. Poor boy never had a chance of waking up from that one!" Sam laughed again, delighting in the pain that Ally couldn't keep from showing on her face.

Ally hissed, "You're a monster!"

Sam cackled again. "Of course I am! I've been hiding in your closet ever since you were nothing more than a scared little brat in diapers! I've been under your bed since before you were more than a lustful twinkle in your dad's eye! I am not just a monster, darling. I'm *the* monster!"

Ally saw her chance. "No, you're not."

Sam laughed sarcastically. "Oh, is that so?"

She glared at him for a moment before turning her lips upward in a cruel smile. "The real monster is the One That Dwells Below."

Sam froze, his eyes wide, but then his face contorted in rage, "YOU FUCKING LITTLE BITCH!" He threw himself over the counter at her. Ally ducked under him and darted for the door as he screamed, "I'LL CARVE MY NAME INTO YOUR FILTHY FUCKING GUTS!"

Ignoring him, Ally dashed back to the foyer. *Why was Sam up on the third floor?* Hesitantly, Ally glanced at the front door. If she left now, she could beat Sam to Maddy's and get help. *But Cassie would be here alone with him.* Ally's heart contracted. Leaving Cassie behind wasn't an option. *Maybe he was looking for her up there?*

Ally ran up the stairs as silently as she could while Sam called from the hallway below, "If you run away, it'll only give me more time to make a nice big mess out of your sister!"

Ally's stomach did a backflip, but she shook her head. *Don't let him get to you!* With renewed focus, she made her way as quickly and quietly as she could up the stairs to the third floor. She crept down the third-floor hallway. On Ally's left were three doors which led into the servants' quarters, small rooms with little furnishing. *She can't be in any of those. He'd have found her already.* Instead, Ally took the lone door on the right that led into the mansion's massive attic. Inside were numerous boxes and various furniture pieces covered in cloth. A few old toys from past generations sat on top of the boxes. Ally whispered as loudly as she could after closing the door, "Cassie? Are you in here?"

A little voice answered her, and Ally's heart leapt with relief. "Ally? That you?"

Ally slowly walked towards the source of the voice, and after lifting one of the dusty cloths over a desk, she found Cassie curled up underneath it with tearstains on her cheeks. Ally said, "Yes, it's me. Come on, we have to get out of here."

"Ally..." Cassie sobbed, "It...it's Daddy...he..."

Ally scooped Cassie into her arms and said, "No, it's not Dad anymore. It's Sam now."

Cassie looked at her, her blue eyes wide with fear. "Sam took over Daddy?"

Ally nodded. "Now we need to get away."

"And just where do you think you are going to go?" Sam's voice thundered through the room as the attic door burst open. He glared at them both from across the room, his eyes wild with malice. "Did you honestly think you could sneak up here and I wouldn't notice? You led me right to her, you stupid little whore! Now I'm gonna gut you while she watches and begs for me to stop, but I won't stop until there's nothing left of you but little, tiny pieces!"

Ally held Cassie tight against her chest. "You're gonna have to catch us first, you sick bastard."

Sam grinned wickedly. "This is *my* house! The game is over, and you LOSE!" He rushed towards them, but Ally immediately ducked to the left and pulled a chair down on top of him. With a crash and a scream of rage and pain, he fell to the floor, dropping the knife. Ally kicked it under a nearby dresser, then leapt over him and raced to the door. As she ran, she heard Sam scream, "The house is mine! It won't let you escape from me! Every soul that has met its end in this miserable mansion will rise to stop you at my command!"

Ally's blood chilled as she entered the hallway to find the doors opening and closing of their own volition repeatedly. The house seemed to shudder as it came to life at Sam's call. Not daring to stick around to see what would happen, Ally raced for the stairs. As she ran, she told Cassie, "Remember, no matter what you see, it can't hurt you, got it? This is all just like a bad dream, and it'll be over once we get out. Okay?"

Cassie nodded and buried her face in Ally's chest. Satisfied, Ally raced down the stairs to the second-floor hallway. Once she rounded the corner she found the hanged woman, Marie, blocking her path. With her arms outstretched and her mouth distended, Marie rushed at them, but Ally ducked her head and shouldered through her. Expecting to collide with her, Ally instead passed through empty air. Not stopping to ponder what had just happened, she continued to race towards the end of the hallway, narrowly avoiding the slamming doors on the way. At last, she reached the foyer, only to find the entourage that had surrounded her in the shower crowded in the middle of the room, their dead eyes fixed on Ally.

"Don't look, Cassie," Ally said as she raced down the stairs towards the door. As with Marie, the people in the entryway dispersed as she passed through them. Her fear of them considerably lessened, Ally grabbed the front door handle triumphantly, only to find it unmoving. "No!" Ally growled as she threw her shoulder against the door, but it was as though it had become a solid wall. The handle wouldn't give even a little.

Ally groaned and turned her back to the door as the ghostly gathering began to form around her once more, their arms at their sides and their stares cold and lifeless. She cradled Cassie's head. *I didn't make it through that fucking asylum for it to end like this.* Suddenly, an idea struck her. Why had she gone to the asylum in the first place?

"The book!" Ally exclaimed.

Cassie looked up at her, asking, "What book?"

Ally buried Cassie's face back in her chest. "Don't worry about it. I know someone who can help us." Without further explanation, she shouldered her way through the apparitions again and began her ascent back up the stairs. The book was in her backpack that she had left in her parents' bedroom. With any luck, she would retrieve it with no trouble and get down to the cellar to entreat the One That Dwells Below. Then, a cold hand closed on her shoulder. Ally turned her head and found herself eye-to-eye with Lamuel. The gaunt apparition shook his head grimly as he tugged her back down the stairs, nearly throwing her off balance.

"Let go, dammit!" Ally grunted and wrenched her shoulder free. She had thought the spirits couldn't touch her, but apparently, she had been mistaken. Lamuel made another grab for her, but she deftly stepped out of his reach and continued up the stairs. However, Crysania blocked the doorway to the hallway. Crying tears of blood that seemed to peel the ashen flesh from her face, she held out her arms as if beckoning Ally to pick her up. Ally slid past her, but Crysania turned and opened her blackened mouth to emit a blood-curdling shriek.

Ally felt as though her head might split open. Cassie groaned, "Ally! It hurts!"

Ally kicked at Crysania, and she exploded into a pile of ashes, taking her unearthly scream with her. Ally whispered to Cassie, "It's okay, she's gone now." Then, the white-haired Gwendolyn reached the top of the stairs. Shivering at the sight of her, Ally turned to head down the hallway, but her way was blocked by the little boy and the black-eyed man. Ally hugged Cassie tight as she turned her head from Gwendolyn to the pair of specters closing in from the hallway. Her back was against the door of her bedroom, but she doubted there would be any escape from this nightmare there.

Suddenly, the house shuddered as if from an immense thunderclap. The spirits all recoiled in terror, cowering and shielding their heads as though whatever had caused the tremor would harm them. Ally stood in shock despite herself, but Sam's terrified scream of "No! You will not interfere!" from somewhere in the house brought her to her senses. The spirits faded, and Ally bolted for the master bedroom, sending a silent thank you to the One Below for saving her once again.

Ally whispered, "Whatever you do, don't look, Cassie." When Cassie nodded, she opened the master bedroom door. The sight of her mother's corpse brought fresh tears to her eyes, but Ally fought through them to reach her backpack. Opening it with one hand, she pulled out the leather-bound book and her flashlight, then turned her back on the grisly scene to make her way back downstairs. There were no spirits in sight. Not pausing to consider where they went, Ally rushed as quietly as possible down the foyer stairs and hallway to the storage room door. Once again, however, she found it locked. Throwing caution to the wind, she stepped back and launched a kick at the handle, cracking the frame and slamming the door open.

Suddenly, the kitchen door behind Ally burst open and Sam erupted out of it, swinging a fresh knife wildly. "SURPRISE, BITCH!" Ally screamed as the blade caught her deep across her shoulder. She slid into the storage room, dropped Cassie, and slammed the door into Sam's face as he pursued them. Roaring with rage, he slammed against the door. "You can't escape this time, Allison!"

Cassie looked around. "Should we push something...?"

"Yes!" Ally exclaimed. *I fucking love you, Cassie!* Her shoulder stung as she pressed it against the door, but adrenaline lent her strength to hold back Sam's furious onslaught. Meanwhile, Cassie tried to roll a sizable box over towards the door, but it was too heavy for her. Ally held against Sam's pounding for a few moments until he finally paused, hopefully to catch his breath. She seized her chance and, with a grunt of exertion, rolled the box on its side to block the door.

Sam's next bombardment against the door was held fast by the box as he roared, "YOU CAN'T KEEP ME OUT FOREVER! YOU ARE MINE! THE HOUSE AND EVERYTHING IN IT IS MINE! MIIIIIIIINE!"

Ally gritted her teeth and hissed, "This ends here." She grabbed Cassie by the hand. "Come on, Cassie."

Sam roared and threw himself at the door furiously, but Ally didn't even pause as they descended the cellar stairs. The jar room had been thoroughly cleared out, leaving nothing but empty space. *Thanks, Dad.* Fresh grief washed over Ally, but she took a deep breath. *Not now. Mourn later.* Instead, Ally led Cassie across the jar room to the wine cellar.

Cassie gripped her hand tighter. "It's scary down here."

"It's okay, Cassie. We'll be safe soon." Ally couldn't stop her right arm from trembling as blood ran down from her wound to stain the book in her hands. *Hold on just a little longer.* Hoping that her strength would hold out, she told Cassie to stand back as she pulled the wine shelf down with a tremendous crash. After helping Cassie climb over it, Ally could feel her head swimming. She turned to her little sister and handed her the now blood-stained journal. "Take this and go on ahead. I need a minute to catch my breath."

Cassie took the book but looked at her nervously. "But it's so dark..."

Ally clicked her flashlight on and handed it to her. "Take this. It'll be okay, I already know the way. Just follow it to the end and once you're there, all you have to do is touch the statue and you'll be safe. I'll be right behind you."

Cassie hesitated for a moment but said, "Don't wait too long, Ally."

Ally smiled and nodded. "I won't be long." Seemingly satisfied, Cassie headed off down the tunnel. Ally leaned against the wall for support, breathing slowly and deeply. With all the pushing and running she had done, it was no surprise that blood loss was getting to her. *It's okay, though. Just a breather. Two minutes at the most.* She took a moment to think of her family. *I'm sorry, Mom...and Dad. I'm sorry I wasn't here.* Her thoughts then turned to Chad, Carol, and Matt. Maybe one of them got lucky? Chad's had been the only remains she had found, so maybe there was hope for them still, but she may never know.

At last, Ally's friends swam through her mind. *Maddy...Derek...Bart...Cassie...you guys are all I have left.* She wiped away fresh tears with her clean hand and took a deep breath. *We can do it. I can do this. We'll survive together. All five of us.*

With her strength renewed, Ally climbed back to her feet and turned to face the tunnel. Her head still swam, but she closed her eyes for a moment and breathed slowly. Finally, she said, "All right, here I come," and stepped into the tunnel.

Suddenly, there was a sharp pain in Ally's lower back that pierced all the way to her stomach. Ally let out a gasp of surprise and pain as her limbs begin to tingle. A loathsome voice whispered in her ear, "I told you—the house and everything in it are mine."

Sam pulled the knife out of her back and Ally fell to her knees, the feeling quickly leaving her legs. Her eyes fell to the floor, where a dark pool was spreading around her. *Cold...I feel...cold.* Ally sat back on her feet, all feeling in her legs completely gone as Sam stepped around to face her and dropped to a knee. He grinned with malicious triumph. "At last, I win. You brought this on yourself, of course. I had no intention of eliminating the entire family, but your interference forced my hand."

Ally's vision was blurring. Somehow though, she had to keep Sam talking. *For Cassie.* "You...fucked up," she gasped.

Sam chuckled sarcastically. "Not this time, child. Once I'm finished with you and your little sister, I'll use this vessel to chase down that charming little friend of yours, and no one will be able to stop me. I have won!"

Ally coughed, and blood splattered Sam's shirt. *Keep talking, dammit!* She grabbed Sam's sleeve and gasped, "Leave...Maddy alone!" She coughed again. *Can't even tell if it hurts anymore. Just...so cold.* She could barely make out the fresh blood her cough had splattered on Sam. Her grip slacked as her hand went numb. She then fell forward, unable to hold herself up any longer.

Sam laughed again, "Even at the end, you plea for the lives of others. Pathetic. Still, after the trouble you caused, I would almost prefer you to witness your failure firsthand as I slaughter those you tried to protect..." Sam's voice suddenly trailed off. Ally couldn't see it, but she imagined with grim satisfaction the horror on his face as he realized what Cassie was about to do. With a roar of fury, he raced down the tunnel after her.

Ally lay there at the entrance of the tunnel, her vision fading in and out. *Let him out, Cassie. Let him out.* So long as Cassie managed to release the One Below, Sam was doomed. It was her last hope, but it was enough. *So...tired...*

Her thoughts began to lose cohesion, and her cheek felt damp. *Please...let him out...Cassie...* Ally felt as though she were seeing the cellar floor from down a dark tunnel. Still, her lips parted for a moment to gasp, "Please...keep her...safe." Was that a tear Ally felt trickle down her cheek, or just more blood? Everything felt so far away, but maybe that was best. Maybe it was time to rest.

Ally closed her eyes and breathed a final sigh as darkness claimed her.

19. The Beginning

How long Cassie ran, she had no way of knowing. Still, Ally had told her to keep going, so she did. The tunnel's darkness yawned out in front of her, but with Ally's assurance, Cassie's courage held. Then, someone yelled from behind her. *Sam.*

Cassie quickened her pace, her tiny heart racing in her chest as she ran. At last, she passed through a doorway into an underground chamber. In the center was a stone slab sticking out of the ground with a statue of a skeleton man lying on it. *That must be the statue Ally told me about.* A dry voice whispered, "Do not be afraid, Cassandra. I will not allow you to come to harm."

Cassie didn't know where the voice came from, but she asked, "Are you the one Ally said would help?"

"I am," the voice replied, "but first there is something you must do."

"What?" Cassie asked, her flashlight beam darting around the room. The dark was still very, very scary.

"You must place your hands upon the sarcophagus in front of you. Do this, and I will help you."

Cassie looked at the sarcophagus. "That's it, just like Ally said?"

"That is all I require," the voice said simply.

Cassie walked up to the edge of the sarcophagus and set the book down on the floor. She then reached out with her bloodstained hand for the lid.

Suddenly, Sam yelled, "Cassie, no!"

Cassie turned and pointed the flashlight at the doorway to see Sam standing there, his pants splattered with fresh blood. She looked up at him and frowned, asking, "Why not?"

"Because I'm your friend, and friends don't do bad things to each other," Sam said cajolingly.

Cassie glared at him. "You did bad things to Mommy and Daddy, and you scared Ally. You talked about hurting me!"

"I was just angry, Cassie! People say and do things they don't mean when they're angry! I thought Ally wanted to get rid of me, so I got angry!"

Cassie narrowed her brilliant blue eyes at him. He still held the bloodied knife. "You hurt Ally," she accused.

"It was an accident, I swear! Believe me, Cassie! Please!" Sam pleaded with terror in his eyes.

Cassie bared her teeth at him. "You called her names! You're a bad man, and you should be punished!"

"CASSIE, DON'T!" Sam shrieked, but she dropped the flashlight and pressed both hands to the side of the sarcophagus. "NO!" Sam roared and lunged at Cassie with the knife.

AT LAST.

The lid of the sarcophagus exploded, blasting both Samuel and Cassandra off their feet.

At long, long last.

The shadows around the chamber came alive and wrapped themselves around Samuel as they had over two hundred years ago. Cassandra's flashlight lay abandoned at the chamber's threshold, its beam pointing towards its petrified owner.

I am free.

Though he had no physical form to speak of, Asmodeous felt his spirit rise from the withered bones within the sarcophagus. How long had he been held within that accursed prison? It mattered little, for at last he had been released. Sensation that had been denied for centuries flooded back, and Asmodeous could feel the presence not only of Samuel and Cassandra, but of every soul trapped within the confines of the mansion. However, he now turned his attention to himself.

Though he had no physical eyes, Asmodeous could see that he was little more than a shadow standing beside the ruined sarcophagus. *A shadow...nothing more.* That would be dealt with soon enough. First, Samuel needed to answer for his foolishness.

"Samuel Corbant," Asmodeous said, his once weakened voice now thundering with power. "For too long you have tormented the Corbant family. Too long your presence has been a blight upon this house and all within it. The time of reckoning is at hand."

"I...I..." Samuel stammered, his eyes bulging from their sockets.

"Enough!" Asmodeous commanded, and with a gesture of his immaterial hand, the shadows wrested Samuel from Elliot Corbant's body. The vassal crumbled to a heap on the floor, silent and unmoving. The shadows held Samuel's spirit aloft as he once again writhed in vain against their grip. He looked exactly as he had the night he had died. Asmodeous held up his hand once more to seal Samuel's fate once and for all, but before he willed the shadows to finish the job, Asmodeous paused to reflect on all that had transpired since Samuel's dark deed.

True, Asmodeous had been angry with Samuel for failing to properly interpret the key to his freedom, but the death of both his wife and daughter had left Asmodeous with enough strength to punish him. Though Samuel's vengeful soul had done all in its power to prevent Asmodeous from being freed, every death that Samuel had orchestrated had only made Asmodeous stronger. If not for Samuel's schemes, Genevieve would not still be alive (as it were). If not for Samuel's dark dabbling, Asmodeous would never have had the strength to call out to him in the first place. Even Samuel's panicked murder spree that very night had worked in Asmodeous's favor, leaving Allison as Cassandra's protector, and allowing him to be released.

Asmodeous's thoughts then turned to Allison. She had performed her part perfectly. If not for her meddling, Samuel would have never felt threatened enough to react so drastically. Asmodeous had given her just enough guidance to allow her to come to her own conclusions, and Samuel had reacted accordingly. *In truth, Samuel, I should be grateful for everything you have done. However, now that I am free once more, your hatred for me is a liability.* "Goodbye, Samuel," Asmodeous declared.

Samuel screamed, and Asmodeous savored his terror, a sweet nectar that he had not sampled for centuries. Still, the work needed completing. Asmodeous closed his ethereal fist, and the shadows enwrapping Samuel's soul tore it into incandescent pieces. The shreds of his spirit fell to the floor as shimmering particles of dust. *Thus, to those who defy me.*

Epilogue: Those Left Behind

Despite Samuel's consignment to oblivion, Asmodeous still sensed fear within the chamber. *The girl.* Asmodeous turned to face the cowering Cassandra. She hugged her knees against the wall, her eyes fixed on Asmodeous's shadowy form. To her, he must have appeared blacker than even the surrounding darkness. Still, he needed her. If he were to leave the mansion, he needed a willing host. "Fear not, my child. It is over."

Cassandra bit her lip. "Is he...gone?"

"Yes."

Cassandra reached out a trembling hand to retrieve her flashlight. "What will happen now?"

Asmodeous had anticipated the question. "People will come to take you away from here."

"What about you?"

Asmodeous was puzzled. *Was that...concern...in her eyes?* "I shall remain here, unless..."

"Unless what?" she asked.

"Unless you agree to allow me to live within your shadow."

Cassandra frowned. "Does that mean you'll be with me all the time?"

"Yes, at all times."

Cassandra bit her lip. "I...I don't wanna be alone."

"You will never be alone again. Ever," Asmodeous assured her.

Cassandra pondered for a moment, then asked, "What's your name?"

"You may call me Asmodeous."

"As...Asmodeous?"

"Yes." *Impressive pronunciation...for a child.*

Cassandra nodded slowly. "Okay, Asmodeous, you can live in my shadow then."

Asmodeous was triumphant. Though he would need a more permanent vassal as a body, this arrangement would suffice for now. "Let us leave this chamber then. We must prepare for what is to come." *This chamber must be hidden, lest the unwitting complicate matters with their curiosity.*

Cassandra stood up and turned to leave, but then turned back around. "What about the book?"

"It is of no consequence. We will return for it in due time." The book would be seized the moment Cassandra was found with it, and its contents were too vital to Asmodeous's plan. *No, best if it is safe here until the time is right.*

"Oh. Okay. Let's get outta here then," Cassandra said and started back up the tunnel.

If Asmodeous had had a face, he would have smiled at that. "Yes. Let's."

MADDY'S HEART WAS IN her throat. Ally hadn't been at her locker that Monday morning. Maddy had tried calling both Saturday night and throughout the day Sunday, but the line was dead. She would have made the trip to the mansion herself if her dad hadn't come home early. Maddy had managed to soothe herself to sleep with the assurance that she'd see Ally that morning, but when Maddy arrived at her locker to find Ally missing, her fear returned in full force.

Maddy sat in her first class of the day. She ignored the teacher completely as she formulated a plan. *After school, I'm going to the mansion. Dad can't stop me if I don't go home first.* She'd deal with the consequences after she confirmed that her best friend was safe and unharmed. Nothing else mattered.

Then, the school-wide PA system beeped for the morning announcements. However, instead of the usual student council member reading off the daily school news, Principal Marr said, "Students, there is no easy way to say this. Many of you have undoubtedly heard on the news already, but for those who haven't..." Mr. Marr took a deep breath.

Maddy gripped the edges of her desk with white knuckles. *No. Don't say it. No. No. No. Don't say it. Please don't say it.*

"This past weekend a terrible tragedy occurred, a tragedy which claimed the life of one of our students, Allison Corbant."

Mr. Marr might have continued speaking, but Maddy didn't hear. Chills shot through her body, and her lungs suddenly seemed incapable of functioning. *I...I heard him wrong. It wasn't her. It was someone else,* anyone *else.*

All eyes in the classroom were turned on her, but Maddy didn't care. *It's not true. It just...it can't be.* Then, Mr. Marr said Ally's name again, and tears filled Maddy's eyes. She remembered laughing at Gladys's expense on the walk home.

No.

Ally's laugh echoed in her mind as they hit each other with pillows.

No!

Tears welled in her eyes as Maddy remembered hugging Ally that Saturday evening, not knowing that it was for the last time.

NO!

Maddy's mind went entirely blank. The rest of the morning passed in a haze. She felt nothing. She completely ignored the students silently staring at her as she passed. She barely heard the teachers going about their lessons as though the world hadn't just collapsed. Maddy was completely numb. Then lunch time came.

Maddy didn't even grab a food tray. She instead made for the usual lunch table, hoping against hope to find Ally, Derek, and Bart all waiting there for her. There was only Derek, and when he saw her, he stood up with red-rimmed eyes. Maddy could deny it no longer. "No," she whimpered as tears filled her eyes. "No..." she whispered before her voice broke into anguished sobs, and Derek rushed over to keep her from collapsing. She buried her face in his chest and bawled freely. Her chest felt hollowed out, leaving only pain.

Maddy looked up at Derek, and their tear-filled eyes met. She whispered, "Why...why didn't you go with her...?"

Derek's lips trembled. "She...she said it wasn't...a good idea."

"You should have anyways." Rage ignited inside Maddy and she screamed, "YOU SHOULD HAVE GONE WITH HER, YOU FUCK-ING IDIOT!" She pounded her fists against his chest until her screams turned to anguished sobs, and he held her once again. The lunchroom was silent as all eyes turned to them, but Maddy could not have cared less. She clung to Derek like a lifeline, but it wasn't the same as...

Bart. I need Bart. "Wh-where's Bart?" Maddy choked.

Derek's face paled. "He...he had a bad seizure when the news broke this morning. They took him to the hospital."

Maddy's body suddenly felt far too heavy. She collapsed into a cafeteria chair. *This can't be happening. First Ally and now Bart?*

Derek pulled a chair over to face her, sat down, and started talking, but Maddy had no idea what he was saying. Her mind rapidly relived all the time spent with both Ally and Bart, tearing her heart to shreds with the knowledge that she would never see either of them again. Derek might have said something about finding out what really happened to Ally, but Maddy didn't hear him. Instead, she was making a plan of her own.

Sam's curse meant that Ally would still be at the mansion. She wouldn't be alive, but it would still be her. That night after school, Maddy would sneak over to the mansion and kill herself. Then, she could at least spend eternity with her best friend. Even though they'd both be trapped, at least they'd be together.

I told you not to make me live without you, so I'm not gonna. The tension in Maddy's body eased. It would all be over soon.

"M-Maddy?" Derek's fearful voice cut across her thoughts.

"Huh?"

"What are you planning?"

Maddy blinked and shook her head. "Nothing."

Derek was unconvinced. "Seconds ago, you were a mess. Now you're just...calm? Maddy, tell me what you're thinking."

Shit. Maddy shook her head again. "It's nothing. Forget it."

Derek wouldn't forget it, though, and he pressed and pressed until Maddy finally broke down and told him her plan. "Maddy, don't. Just don't. Ally wouldn't want this."

"How the fuck do you know?" Maddy snapped. "You didn't know her like I did! She needs me!"

"She needs you to not give up! How do you think she'll feel when she sees you there? She'll be watching you do it! Do you think that'll make things any easier on her?"

Maddy's lip quivered, "B-but..."

"And what about Bart?" Derek continued. "What if he pulls out of this and finds out you died? How is he gonna feel knowing that he will never see you again?"

Maddy buried her face in her hands. "What do you want from me?"

"Promise me you won't do it."

Maddy looked up at him. "I..."

Derek placed a hand on her shoulder and looked her in the eyes. "Promise me."

Maddy couldn't speak. Derek was trying to appear stoic, but behind his eyes she could see the same pain that was eating away at her. As fresh tears filled her eyes, Maddy nodded before falling into his arms once again. She choked, "I just...I miss her...so *fucking* much."

Derek heaved a miserable sigh. "I know. So do I."

MADDY SAT ON HER BED that night after crying for hours. True to her word, she hadn't followed through with her plan, but the pain was unbearable. She and Ally had been inseparable ever since they had met, and without her, the world felt hollow. Maddy had never imagined a time that she'd have to go on without her, but now she faced that very situation, and it was pure agony.

There was pounding on her bedroom door. "Maddy? Why is this fucking door locked?" Her father's voice cut through her thoughts with an unusually exaggerated drunken slur. *Great, just what I fucking need.* However, before she could even think of a reply, her dad broke the door open and stumbled into the room. He was a thin, prematurely wrinkled man with long hair and a short, dark beard flecked with grey. His jeans had holes in the knees, the steel was showing through the toes of his boots, and his navy blue button-down shirt was hanging open over a white wifebeater. He looked around and then narrowed his reddened eyes at her. "What the fuck is your problem?"

For years, Maddy had held her tongue to keep from goading him into something, but this time she snapped. She bared her teeth. "I don't know, maybe MY BEST FUCKING FRIEND IS DEAD!?"

Her dad blinked in reply, his eyes wide for a moment before he sneered. "So what? Who the fuck cares?"

His apathy hit Maddy harder than any blow he had ever thrown in her direction. She gasped, "Who...the fuck...*cares*?!"

Her dad was completely oblivious that Maddy trembled with rage. "Yeah, who the fuck cares? That don't mean shit compared to the fact that I got fired today."

Maddy's eyes bulged from their sockets. "About fucking time!"

"The fuck you just say, you little cunt?" he slurred as he tried in vain to focus his gaze on her.

Maddy stood up from the bed and squared her shoulders to him. "I said it's about fucking time they realized how fucking worthless you are!"

Her dad slapped her across the face, nearly knocking her back onto the bed, but Maddy didn't feel that pain. The only pain she felt was the hole in her chest Ally had left behind. Nothing else mattered. She spat, "I FUCK-ING HATE YOU!"

"Oh yeah? We'll see about that!" her dad grunted as he dove for her. Maddy punched him in the jaw, sending him sprawling into her dresser before she made a break for the kitchen. He grabbed at her ankle, but his grip was weak. She kicked his hands away and ran to the knife drawer. *Defend first, call cops second.*

"What the fuck do you think you're doing?"

Maddy grabbed the largest knife in the drawer before whirling around to see her dad massaging his jaw. "You are not gonna touch me again! I put up with your fucking ass for too fucking long!"

Her dad's red-rimmed eyes flashed. "Who the fuck do you think you are?" Before Maddy could answer, he grabbed the saltshaker from the kitchen table and hurled it at her. Maddy ducked, but in the next second, he was on her, trying to wrest the knife from her grip. He pinned her by the throat against the kitchen cabinets as he tried to pry the blade from her. "My life would be so much easier without you, you know!" he spat through grit-ted teeth.

Maddy held onto the knife with all of her might. *If he gets it, he's gonna kill me.*

As if in response to her thoughts, his hand tightened around her throat. "Oh well, say hello to your cunt of a friend for me!"

Ally. Her name was fucking *Ally!*

Rage unlike any Maddy had ever known surged through her. With her free hand, she grabbed her dad's thumb on her throat and wrenched as hard as she could, snapping it backward. He wailed in pain and released her to huddle on the floor, cradling his broken thumb. Maddy coughed and slowly rose to her feet, holding the knife point towards him shakily.

Her dad looked up at her as tears rolled down his face. "Look what you've done! Look what you've done, you FUCKING WHORE!" He lunged for her. With instinct taking over, Maddy thrust the knife forward in response, burying it hilt deep in his throat. He fell against her hips before sliding to the floor. Blood sprayed in all directions as he thrashed about with bulging eyes, his hands clawing at the base of his neck as though to stop the arterial fountain.

Maddy stared with wide eyes, her entire body trembling violently as her head swam. *I killed him. My God, I killed him.* She felt as though she were about to faint. His blood covered her from the waist down. *No, don't pass out now!* She held herself up against the counter with bloodless hands as she stepped away from her dad's writhing body. *Away. I have to get away.* However, her trembling legs carried her only as far as the living room before giving out beneath her, and she fell against the wall with a blank stare.

Maddy had no idea how long she lay there, but slowly feeling crept back into her legs. She sat up and turned to look at her dad's body. He had fallen silent and still, his wide, shocked eyes staring emptily up at the ceiling. *I have to call the cops.* She had only defended herself, but it hardly mattered. Whether she went to jail or an orphanage, anywhere was better than here. She grabbed the phone off of its receiver on the wall and dialed 911.

"911. What's your emergency?" a woman's voice asked.

"I-I just killed my dad."

"Excuse me?"

"He...he was gonna kill me, so I swung...a knife...I-I killed him," Maddy stammered, suddenly trembling again as the scene replayed in her mind.

"Calm down, honey! Where are you?" Maddy took a deep breath and gave her address. The woman paused to write it down. "The cops are on their way now. Are you sure your dad is dead?"

Maddy nodded, "I-I...the knife..."

"It's okay, we'll make sure you're taken care of. Everything will be okay."

It's over. It's all over. The woman on the phone was still talking, but Maddy wasn't listening. Too much had happened that day, and she had gone far beyond the limit of what she could handle. Still, there was one thing that had gone well.

As police sirens closed in on the house, Maddy buried her face in her hand and cried once more. *Well, I kept my promise. I'm alive.*

CPSIA information can be obtained
at www.ICGtesting.com
Printed in the USA
LVHW011344311021
702036LV00010B/20/J